P9-CFE-024

DARKER
Than
NIGHT

A NOVEL OF
THE SHADOW GUARD

KIM LENOX

A SIGNET ECLIPSE BOOK

SIGNET ECLIPSE
Published by New American Library, a division of
Penguin Group (USA) Inc., 375 Hudson Street,
New York, New York 10014, USA
Penguin Group (Canada), 90 Eglinton Avenue East, Suite 700, Toronto,
Ontario M4P 2Y3, Canada (a division of Pearson Penguin Canada Inc.)
Penguin Books Ltd., 80 Strand, London WC2R 0RL, England
Penguin Ireland, 25 St. Stephen's Green, Dublin 2,
Ireland (a division of Penguin Books Ltd.)
Penguin Group (Australia), 250 Camberwell Road, Camberwell, Victoria 3124,
Australia (a division of Pearson Australia Group Pty. Ltd.)
Penguin Books India Pvt. Ltd., 11 Community Centre, Panchsheel Park,
New Delhi - 110 017, India
Penguin Group (NZ), 67 Apollo Drive, Rosedale, North Shore 0632,
New Zealand (a division of Pearson New Zealand Ltd.)
Penguin Books (South Africa) (Pty.) Ltd., 24 Sturdee Avenue,
Rosebank, Johannesburg 2196, South Africa

Penguin Books Ltd., Registered Offices:
80 Strand, London WC2R 0RL, England

First published by Signet Eclipse, an imprint of New American Library,
a division of Penguin Group (USA) Inc.

First Printing, April 2010
Excerpt from *Night Falls Darkly* copyright © Kim Lenox, 2008
10 9 8 7 6 5 4 3 2 1

For my "little" brother.
I write adventures. You live them!

ACKNOWLEDGMENTS

In every book a writer publishes, he or she has the opportunity to acknowledge those individuals who have inspired them or in some way helped them maneuver from PAGE 1, through the following span of months to "THE END." While it's an honor and a thrill to be able to share one's stories with the world, the process by which that occurs is at times a real challenge. Writing and storytelling are not always easy—or at least it's not for this author. I couldn't call a book complete without saying a very big and sincere "thank you" to the following people:

To Eric, who I am convinced is the best husband on earth, for supporting me in all things. I love you!

To my kids and my parents and the rest of my family for always—*always*—encouraging my dreams.

To Cindy Miles, my angel of a friend, for all the talks and texts and brainstorming. Sometimes I think we share a brain.

To Kelley Thomas, Julia Templeton, Kim Frost, Sharie Kohler, Kerry Sparks, Tera Lynn Childs, Colleen Thompson, Jami Bevans, Christie Craig, TJ Bennett, Jessa Slade, Annette McCleave, Sharon Ashwood and all the members of Romancing History, WHRWA, NWHRWA and RWA for your friendship, inspiration, encouragement and camaraderie.

To my agent, Kim Lionetti, for her expertise, unwavering support and enthusiasm.

To my editor, Laura Cifelli, for allowing the Shadow Guards to come to life and save the world from evil!

Many thanks also to Jesse Feldman and everyone else at NAL for giving me and my book such attention and care.

Prologue

He awoke to darkness, his limbs twisted in linen sheets, his hands seizing at nothing. Perspiration bathed his skin.

Her taste lingered on his tongue. The scent of lotus flowers clouded his nostrils, a seductive tease. He ached—oh, God, how he ached, the intensity of his unsatisfied need leaving him almost sickened.

Groaning, he rolled to his side and curled inward upon himself, alone in his room save for the blinking raven perched on a brass stand beside the window. A gust of wind rattled the shutters and Big Ben tolled three o'clock. Male voices, drunken sailors from St. Katharine Docks, volleyed curses at one another. Bells rang softly on barges that were anchored on the nearby Thames.

The bird shifted and rustled its wings.

Torn between agony and shame, he threw off the linens and abandoned his bed. Wrenching the door open he took to the dark hallway, his hands skimming over ancient stone. The stairs. One flight. Two. Fevered blood pulsed inside his head. Closing his eyes, he drew upon his inner power to change, to become a shadow. A different sort of heat consumed him, one that seared his bone, muscle and flesh from the center of his solar plexus out. Unnoticed, he slipped past the two brothers who had been assigned to night duty.

A large brass cage hung from above, higher even than the large circular candelabrum that provided the room with a comfortable light. The cage contained six of the Tower's seven resident ravens—all but his, which remained in his room below.

Tres, silent and serious, sat at a long desk, his pale head bent in concentration, transcribing the day's surveillances and communications into a leather-bound tome. His younger brother, Shrew, mumbled the words to a tune and crouched beside the fire. With a curl of his muscles, he wrenched a length of chain and, from inside the flames, out clattered a narrow brass cage onto the stone floor. Inside would be a stack of sealed envelopes, unmarred by the incinerating heat—the night's communiqués from the Primordial Council and others within the immortals' protected Inner Realm, the pure-aired paradise that existed as an alternate plane over the same land and space as the mortal world.

As part of their nightly duties, the two Raven warriors also guarded over . . .

Wood-plank doors bound by studded metal bands hung open on massive hinges, granting him entry to the shadowy chamber.

Over *her*.

Wind rushed through the shutters to awaken his skin and incite the purple curtains into a rippling dance. A gilt statue of Hecate hung over the bed, carved to appear as if the goddess were bursting through the wall. Beautiful, bare breasted and arms outspread, she wielded in each hand a lantern in the shape of a blazing torch.

But he was a Shadow Guard, gifted with the ability to see through the most fathomless dark. He didn't need her light to see the woman below.

This night, as in each night past, her dark hair spilled in a glossy river across the pale linens. Raven's-wing lashes lay against her cheekbones, concealing the dark eyes that tormented his dreams. Her skin, golden rather than alabaster, shone with the inner light of vivacity and health. With each breath, her breasts rose and fell, the intricate lace of her undergarments faintly visible beneath the fine lawn gown she wore. A garnet the size of an Egyptian scarab glimmered on her finger. A narrow gold band in the shape of a serpent encircled her wrist.

Careful not to touch her skin, not a single strand of her hair, he pressed his fists to the mattress at either side of her face. He leaned down until his nose was aligned just beside hers so that their lips nearly touched.

A moment later, transformed into shadow, he escaped the White Tower through the window and descended the cool surface of Caen stone. Once on Postern Road he traveled quickly—in a rage of speed and power. He skimmed and turned against brick, wood and cobblestone, leaving behind the Tower of London, the wharfside warehouses and the tenements. Everything—the dead-fish stench of Ratcliffe Highway and the granite arches of the Bridge of Sighs—dissolved into a blur as he hurtled past.

At last there were the green parks, high stone walls and rows of palatial white town houses. The shadowy figures of well-dressed gentlemen hovered on horseback and doorstep as they returned home, discreetly and quietly, from private clubs, gambling houses or from within the arms of their mistresses.

He found the numbers imprinted onto a bronze plaque and hissed under the black-lacquered door and past the slack-faced doorman asleep on a bench. Cool marble. Blue silk. Rich gilt. He mounted the stairs and entered her room by way of the crack beneath the door. The power of his arrival snuffed the candle in the lamp and sent the crystal teardrops of the unlit chandelier jangling. He materialized at the foot of her bed, his chest heaving, still barefoot and wearing only his loose linen trousers.

She pushed up, white satin hugging every curve.

"I knew you'd come," she whispered.

She beckoned, arms outstretched. He didn't look at her face—only at her hair, which was the precise shade of blond to make him remember.

To make him forget.

Chapter One

Rourke, Lord Avenage, had faced history's most blood-thirsty warriors on the field of battle and had stood knee-deep in shocking carnage, the memories of which would turn any other man insane.

Yet now, assessing the scene before him, England's guardian Ravenmaster realized that in eight centuries as an Amaranthine immortal he had never experienced true apprehension until now.

He narrowed his eyes and whispered a prayer.

God, let him survive *this*—the queen's garden party.

Behind him, the most staid and brooding of monarchial residences arose: Buckingham Palace. All around the remaining circumference of the lawn and gardens coursed a high stone wall, penning inside what had to be five thousand invited guests. The decorous lilt and refined laughter of too many voices cluttered the summer air. There was also the fragrance of cut grass and of sweet alyssum. He grasped on to those scents, and in doing so, reminded himself there was still something natural and real to be found in all of this human madness.

The lord chamberlain's card had specified that the garden party would be held between the hours of five and seven. Rourke had presented precisely at six for the express purpose of avoiding the queen's grand entrance and what would certainly prove a torturously slow processional through the assemblage of adoring guests.

"You're not afraid of them, are you?" a man's voice taunted.

Rourke shot a dark glance to his right. Who had approached and joined him so stealthily that he had remained unaware?

There wasn't much that surprised him anymore, but to find Archer, Lord Black, the most ancient of the Shadow Guard's Reclaimers, standing beside him, was unexpected—and highly displeasing. The cropped hair on the back of Rourke's neck bristled at the intrusion into his territory.

Within the immortal Amaranthine society, there were the protectors and the protected. Rourke and the immortal beside him were of the warrior class. Though both were members of the Shadow Guard and governed by the same Primordial Council of Three, their positions within the organization were distinctly different.

Archer was a Reclaimer, a skilled hunter responsible for tracking and Reclaiming mortal souls who had grown so exceedingly evil in their mental deterioration that they attained a dangerous supernatural state known as Transcension, which, among other unpleasant traits, made it possible for them to elude discovery, justice—and even death.

Rourke's duty lay with the Ravens, a smaller order chartered in 1071 by the Primordials and their mortal ally, William the Conqueror. In 1066, just a few years before the Ravens' inception, mercenary immortal warriors had turned the tide at Hastings in William's favor. As a reward he had granted those mysterious men-at-arms lands and titles and, in doing so, had forever woven the destinies of England and the Inner Realm together.

Set forth as William's choice, Rourke was installed as Ravenmaster. With his acceptance of that honor, he had also accepted immortality.

The Ravens' responsibilities were twofold: First, to act as liaison between the Primordials and the present British monarch and higher-level government officials on matters of policy affecting the Amaranthines' interests in the mortal world. And second, to utilize surveillance, subterfuge and, when necessary, assassination to ensure England's perpetual survival. For that very reason, not all of the isle's monarchs boasted the support of the Ravens. Indeed, the order had been responsible for dethroning an unworthy few. However, Victoria had long ago proven herself to be an ally.

To Archer, Rourke growled, "If one of your blasted Transcended souls is here, drinking tea with the queen, then you must make an immediate and full disclosure—"

"I'm not here on business." Archer, never one to kowtow to the current century's fashions, wore his dark hair long and nearly to his shoulders, but today had drawn it back into a discreet queue. The glass of champagne in his hand indicated that his arrival at the garden party had preceded Rourke's.

In times past, it would be decades, sometimes centuries before Rourke crossed paths with another Shadow Guard outside the ranks of the tightly knit Ravens. Competitive by nature, Shadow Guards did not seek out one another's company unless specifically ordered by the Primordial Council into cooperative maneuvers.

However, recent events, namely the threatened escape of the Amaranthines' ancient foe, Tantalus, from his eternal underworld prison, had brought an unprecedented gathering of Reclaimers to London. Empowered by the concentration of misery and poverty in the city, namely that emanating from the Whitechapel district, the Dark Ancient sought to break free of Tartarus and make London his stronghold.

Tantalus was a Transcended soul, and thus the strict domain of the Reclaimers. Despite being a breath away from the action, Rourke and his Ravens had yet to be officially called upon to assist, something that chafed his soldiering sensibilities. In recent centuries, the business of king—or queen—making had become less of a physical event. He craved a good, *extended* bloody fight.

Which, in a roundabout way, had brought him to the queen's garden party.

Archer chuckled, low in his throat. "You must want something very badly to have come here in full visibility."

There were those among the Amaranthines who enjoyed the mortal balls, country house parties, horse races and scandal making.

"What about you, Black? You've never been a slave to this mortal society. Why are you here, playing the part of courtier?"

"Like you, I wouldn't be here unless I wanted something very, very badly." Archer deposited his still-full glass of champagne onto a nearby tray held by a bewigged, liveried servant. "That said, you and I had both better get on with it before someone approaches and wishes to discuss the weather or, worse, the queen's choice of party frock."

The very idea of being forced into such a conversation put Rourke into the dourest of moods. Long out of practice with pleasantry, he felt his blood and marrow warm with the instinct to change, to become what was natural to him in overpopulous situations as this: *aoratos*, a shadow.

Instead he stood in gray morning coat, necktie, trousers and top hat on the steps of a palace, fully visible to anyone who cared to look. Conspicuous. Exposed. Vulnerable. He thrust a finger between his collar and throat, and jerked a bit of additional space.

Only then did he notice the three young women standing to his left beneath a leafy green canopy of tree branches, eyeing him and Lord Black with pink-cheeked, carnivorous interest.

"No, not me," said Black. "I do believe they are looking at *you*."

The debutantes wore hats piled with gauzy netting and waxy flowers, and summer dresses constructed of layer upon layer of silk, lace and pleated ruffles. Black was right: Their not-so-innocent thoughts—which he could not help but perceive with perfect clarity—focused on his squared jaw, thick neck and masculine form—most *specifically* his thighs and his shoulders. Bloody hell, and his—

Archer leaned closer, his lips quirked into an amused smile. "Wherever do you suppose she learned *that* word?"

Rourke glanced pointedly toward the women. His displeasure at being so invasively noticed intensified, and a searing heat moved like a dark wave from inside his mind out through his eyes.

Their faces paled. The girl in blue dropped her parasol. Retrieving it, she hurried to join the others as they strolled, rather quickly, in the opposite direction toward the gardens. They would not have observed anything out of the ordinary in his countenance. No inhumanly glowing eyes or supernatural effect. Rather they would have experienced the unexplainable suspicion that their darkest, most private thoughts had been laid bare.

"A man after my own heart."

"Enough of this," said Rourke. "Where is she?"

His query fell upon empty air. He stood alone on the steps. He did not need to look around to judge the reactions of those about him to the mystifying disappearance of a man from their midst. No one would have observed the Ancient's shift to another location. Instead their minds would commit his disappearance to a momentary lapse in attention or a distracted blink of the eye.

He returned his gaze to the crowded lawn. Although it was he, as Ravenmaster, who had been ultimately responsible for Victoria's safety since the day of her coronation, it had been years since he and Britain's queen had looked each other in the eye. But that was the way of the Ravens. It was enough for the queen to know he and the others were there, always vigilant and prepared to act. There was no requirement that they should be seen, or that they should involve themselves in any sort of social relationship. All in all, it wasn't prudent to form personal attachments to the present monarch. One never knew when one might be given the order to depose him or her.

Rourke concentrated, filtering a singular, narrow thread from a tangle of thousands of others. Not scent, and not color, but something infinitely more complicated. A combined essence formed of physicality and soul. Within moments, he discerned her distinct imprint, her *trace*—the fragmented evidence of her existence that she left behind as she passed from *here* . . .

He tilted his face.

To *there*.

His gaze narrowed on a saffron-yellow tent, one of many that puffed and rippled in the wind like a fleet of lethargic Thames jellyfish. Rourke stepped off the stair and crunched across the gravel terrace onto the rolling lawn. He passed by the small lake, on which were floating a number of rowboats manned by servants in scarlet. Four foot guards from the queen's mortal security detail and eight sharply uniformed Indian troops, sword blades glittering, controlled the perimeter of the queen's temporary domain.

A young guard stepped briskly forward as if to question Rourke's approach, but an older fellow with gray hair and time-etched skin stayed the younger man with a lightning-fast hand and a quiet word.

Rourke nodded as he moved past. "Mr. McGregor."

A flinty spark of respect lit bright blue eyes, and the bowed shoulders straightened proudly. "Your lordship."

Mortal minds had difficulty grasping the concept of Amaranthines. Their frailer psyches were unable to retain memories of immortals for very long, a clouding of thought that made it convenient for Ancient Ones to move in and out of society from year to year and decade to decade without suspicions being raised as to their identity and lack of aging. Yet for administrative purposes, a select number of trusted mortals within key governmental offices were granted the ability of Recollection. McGregor was one such mortal. Rourke had first come to know McGregor as a fresh-faced youth of twenty-three, newly recruited to the foot guards. Now, at sixty-four, McGregor was their most senior member.

Heavy, tasseled cords held back the silk tent flaps, which offered only a tantalizing glimpse of the interior to passersby. Rourke removed his hat and bent to enter the pavilion. He immediately registered a number of things. First, that the space was crowded with all manner of recognizable English and European royalty—persons he did not know but made it his business to know everything *about* due to their ease of proximity to the monarch his Order of Ravens was sworn to protect. In the party were the king of Denmark, the king and queen of Belgium and the Grand Duchess Serge of Russia, to name a few. Second, he noticed that Erik and Flynn, the two steel-eyed Ravens he had assigned to the event, stood in shadow just behind and on either side of the queen.

And third, that the seventy-year-old English monarch, seated in a high-backed rattan chair, observed his arrival and spewed an arc of scarlet punch across the Aubusson carpet at her feet.

It was not the greeting he had hoped for.

An elegant blond woman—

Blond, yes—but not that particular shade of blond.

—in a green-striped gown rushed to offer assistance, followed by the queen's daughter, the Princess Beatrice. The Prince of Wales broke free from a circle of gentlemen to inquire after his mother's welfare. Everyone else stared from the far side of the tent, against a backdrop of a cluttered buffet of carved beef, champagne bottles and sweets, their questions over Rourke's arrival and the queen's dramatic reaction clouding the air.

"Well-done, Avenage," murmured a male voice beside him. "It seems your appearance has sent the queen into a fit of apoplexy."

Archer again.

Rourke nodded curtly, before demanding in silence, *Why. Are. You. Here?*

Dark brows slashed upward. *It pleased my wife to attend.*

Lord Black's silver gaze shifted possessively toward the blonde, who brought a fresh glass of punch to the queen. Rourke now took the time to truly examine her face and realized he had, indeed, seen her before. Just a few weeks before, in fact, in the Westminster Clock Tower along with lords Black and Alexander and the Countess Pavlenco—and a host of seething, twirly-eyed Transcended souls.

That had been a different sort of party altogether, the one that had resulted in the countess's sleeping in the Ravens' headquarters in the Tower of London.

Lady Black's multicolored eyes—one blue and one brown—lifted to her husband, and she smiled radiantly, a secret smile of intimacy. At once, Rourke knew what it was that Black wanted so badly. Badly enough to subdue his reclusive nature and attend the queen's annual garden party. At observing this, Rourke felt his heart harden just a bit more.

The monarch, still seated, accepted the glass and offered Lady Black a gracious but tempered smile. Unlike those around her, she wore a staid black, unembellished gown and a white lace cap. Still, she commanded the eyes of everyone present with her stately bearing and queenly hauteur.

With a sharp glance to Rourke, she muttered into the prince's ear. He nodded.

Straightening, Bertie offered Rourke a hard stare. "Avenage."

Neither Rourke nor the Primordials had settled on their opinion of him.

Still, Rourke lowered his head in acknowledgment. "Your Grace."

"Her Majesty wishes to speak with you."

Rourke approached. Victoria's dark eyes pierced him through, and instantly, he forgot everyone else in the room. Though he sensed the electrified excitement coursing through her, he purposefully did not examine her thoughts. He would give her that respect. Leave her that dignity.

"Your Highness, my apologies for startling you." He claimed her extended hand and pressed his lips to her faceted jet ring. "I did, however, receive an invitation."

Victoria sucked in her cheeks and chided, "I have sent you many invitations over the years, Avenage. I can say with a certainty that this is the first you've ever accepted. You and Black visible, under the same tent at my garden party? I suppose I can hand the crown and scepter over to Bertie and call life complete."

Rourke's brows went up. "Please, not on my account."

She rocked back in her chair, chuckling dryly. "You must want something very badly to have submitted yourself to this. You detest such follies."

Rourke glanced testily toward the cluster of riveted onlookers. What everyone at the event facetiously referred to as "tea" had once again begun to flow. Green bottles tilted, pouring golden spouts of champagne. The guests' mental jabbering and collective curiosity bored a hole through his skull.

. . . '74 vintage champagne! . . .

*. . . the count*ess has grown fat *. . .*

. . . who is that man with Her Majesty? . . .

. . . must find out and send him an invitation to my dinner party . . .

What's the matter, Avenage? Headache? said Archer in the silent language of the Amaranthines. He walked past with two glasses of champagne and extended one toward his pretty wife.

Rourke ignored the silent prod, and attempted to ignore Bertie, who stood protectively close.

To Victoria, he said, "You did not respond to my repeated requests for a private audience."

Her gaze did not waver, but a flush touched her aged cheeks. "There was a time when you did not respond to similar requests of *mine*."

Above the line of his neatly trimmed beard, Bertie's face purpled.

Rourke glanced at Erik and Flynn, who remained in place behind the queen, invisible to all but himself and the Blacks.

Leave us, he commanded.

A shimmer of light and shadow, one that only an immortal's attuned vision would perceive, indicated their shift in position to the opposite side of the tent.

"Let today be remembered as the day I drew you out of your self-imposed seclusion," she declared with subdued joviality. "I hereby declare myself the victor in our battle of wills. Let us consider the past all water under the London Bridge."

"Thank you, Your Highness," Rourke answered tightly, hating to be the brunt of any jest, no matter how well intended.

"What is it that forces you into my company, face-to-face, after all this time?" Her gaze moved over his features. Memories and thoughts of him spilled out of her mind, laid bare for his viewing, more fond and wistful than he cared to realize. Again, he shut his mind to hers, not wishing to know more.

"I come on the matter of a sleeping countess."

"Ah . . ." said the prince, his eyebrows climbing his forehead. He drifted closer, stroking his short-clipped beard. Two cigars jutted from his front pocket. "The Countess Pavlenco."

His eyes took on a distinct gleam.

"*Bertie*," his mother reprimanded.

"Yes?" He straightened to attention.

"Fetch me another glass of punch."

He frowned and glanced to her lap. "You've not touched the one in your hand."

She lifted the cup. The punch sloshed against the crystal. "This glass has grown tepid."

The prince scowled. Victoria's nostrils flared and her eyes widened, an expression that transformed her from an elderly woman into a dragon.

"Very *well*," he retorted, claiming the glass. He looked around as if searching for a servant, or at least his sister, to assume the task, but neither stood near. He grimaced and strode toward the punch bowl, holding the glass before him like a dirty stocking.

"The Countess Pavlenco, is she well?" demanded the queen.

Rourke nodded. "She sleeps."

"Is that not what was intended?" Victoria drew her shoulders up in question. "That she would sleep until such time as she could be safely reawakened and the dangerous madness present inside her mind completely eliminated?"

"Indeed . . . Your Highness." He struggled to maintain what he hoped was a pleasant, easy expression.

"Then tell me, my dear old friend Avenage, what dire circumstance has arisen so that you must in the meantime seek to curry favor with me?"

Rourke realized he had curled his fingers into the brim of his hat, thereby warping the expensive silk. Standing before Victoria, hat in hand, he felt more like a beggar than the elite immortal warrior he was.

He chose his words carefully. "The task of holding constant guard over the countess has stretched the Ravens' resources thin."

Victoria's eyelids lowered to half-mast. "Really, Avenage, how much trouble can one sleeping countess be?"

"Our first duty must be to preserve you and this country. That is why the order of the Ravens was created."

"But we—I and this country—owe the Countess Pavlenco our every gratitude." Victoria leaned forward in her chair. "The Dark Bride would have enslaved us all if not for her. Do you not believe she deserves our highest regard and protection from those who would do her harm whilst she is in so unconscious and vulnerable a state?"

Archer came to stand beside her chair. "I, for one, am in complete agreement, Your Highness." One dark brow curved devilishly. As if his tongue were a fireside poker, he quietly jabbed it into the flaming pile of logs that was Her Highness. "Clearly the Raven is not convinced."

Rourke countered, "I understand the need for her protection. I simply ask you to reconsider who should be responsible for the task. The Ravens are seven in number, and at any given time half may be assigned abroad to deal with international concerns. At present, Clive is in the Sudan, and Garrick in Madrid. In the time the countess has been in our care, two of the remaining five have been removed from the active service of protecting Your Highness and the welfare of the country and instead dedicated to the countess."

"What do you suggest as an alternative?" she asked.

"Perhaps her brother, Lord Alexander, could assume her care?"

"I'm afraid that's not possible," Black answered. "The Primordial Council has reassigned Lord and Lady Alexander. They are not in the country at the moment."

Rourke suggested, "Then she could be removed to Black House. It's a veritable fortress."

Archer straightened and cast a glance to his wife. "That's not possible either, for reasons I won't explain now."

"How convenient—for you," Rourke responded darkly.

Archer's jaw flexed. "Do not forget that despite our recent victories, Tantalus has not been stopped. The Reclaimers are also stretched to their limit, working to anticipate his next move. If you'll recall, the Eye of Pharos was lost. It must be recovered quickly so it cannot again be used against us. Although two of Tantalus's *brotoi* have been vanquished—"

Rourke nodded with an impatient jerk of his head, the other immortal's words striking on an already ragged nerve. "It is only a matter of time until another such monster arises to take their place. As they do, you, Black, the Primordial Council keeps me apprised of the present situation. I'm certain you have been privy to my written objections to the Ravens' exclusion from the ongoing maneuvers for the sole purpose of playing nursemaids to a sleeping countess."

"Nursemaids." The queen gasped. She shook her head vehemently, and her lips scrunched into a tight bow. "And to think I believed I bestowed a great honor on the Ravens by choosing them as her guardians."

His eyebrows raised into an expression of innocence, Lord Black murmured, "You must recall that, historically, women have never been allowed into the Ravens' quarters in the Tower of London—"

The queen's mouth slackened. "So that is the issue here."

Heat rose to Rourke's cheeks. "Your Highness, I said nothing about the countess being a wom—"

Eat glass, Black.

Archer chuckled. Victoria leaned forward, grasping

both hands around the lion's-head pommel of her cane. "The Countess Pavlenco is no tart being smuggled up the back stairs for the entertainment of one of your warriors. She is a *Reclaimer*, not to mention the daughter of a queen. If I must petition the Primordial Council myself, I will ensure that she is afforded the same respect as any other of her rank."

Rourke seethed. "My request has nothing to do with a lack of respect for the countess."

More somberly now, Archer said, "We cannot forget that the countess also has the potential to become a terrible danger to us all. So whilst we protect her we also must protect ourselves from the evil of which she is capable if she falls under Tantalus's control. There is no safer place for her than in the Tower."

Rourke closed his eyes. Archer had hammered the last nail in that coffin, a fact confirmed by the queen's next statement.

"Then there is nothing left to discuss." She planted her cane against the carpet and heaved up to glare at him like a bulldog. She was quite the intimidating woman—even if the top of her head came to only the middle of his chest. "She shall remain with the Ravens in the Tower until she awakens and can safely resume her duties with the Reclaimers."

"Your Highness—" he attempted once more.

"Bertie," she barked. Her gaze searched the tent and honed in on the prince, who approached with cup in hand. "Put that punch down. It is seven o'clock, and I have had quite enough entertainment for one afternoon."

After depositing the cup onto a service tray, the prince returned to her side to provide escort. Within moments the tent had emptied of everyone, including Erik and Flynn in shadow, leaving only one lone male palace servant and the three immortals. A gentle wind pushed at the sides of the tent, and the sounds of voices from those who accompanied the queen, both as attendants and security, grew distant.

"Might you give me that glass, good sir?" Archer inquired of the servant, who in turn lifted a crystal flute and handed it over. In doing so, Archer touched his wrist. The servant's face lost all expression, and woodenly he set about retrieving the glassware that had been left by the garden party's attendees all about the tent.

The privacy of their conversation ensured, Lord Black grasped the neck of a gilt-labeled, green-glass champagne bottle and approached Rourke.

Chapter Two

"Care for a cup of *tea*, Avenage?"

"No, thank you ever so much, I do not." Frustration heated his skin. He felt like dropping his silk top hat to the floor and grinding it to shreds under his heel, for all the good the silly piece of frippery had done him. He should have worded his request differently. Tried to regain some of the easy rapport he and Victoria had shared those years ago when she had been a young woman and he had been her fiercest protector.

Archer tipped the bottle and a stream of golden liquid splashed into the glass. With a pointed stare, he presented the glass to Rourke.

"Have one anyway," he suggested firmly. "My wife has something to tell you."

An odd thing to say, when Rourke and Lady Black had never spoken so much as two words to each other. Lady Black, for her part, appeared a bit anxious at her husband's announcement.

She hugged one arm around her slender waist, and with her other hand toyed with a gleaming curl. "Ah, yes. I suppose I do. Thank you, Archer, for putting the subject out there so suddenly, and without speaking to me first."

Mischief—and the burning passion of one fully smitten—glinted in Archer's eyes.

To Rourke, he said, "If you will recall, her ladyship, while not a Shadow Guard, is a fully trained Amaranthine Intervenor, with exceptional healing and laboratory skills."

In truth, Rourke had the Lady Black to blame for his present state of misery. It had been Lady Black who had put the Countess Pavlenco to sleep, sparing Selene from execution at the hands of her fellow Shadow Guards— the usual end judgment when one took on the dangerous and powerful state of Transcension, even if for all the right reasons, such as sparing civilization from the most dastardly of underworld villains.

"An Intervenor." Still gripping the glass, he nodded to Lady Black. "Yes, so you are."

Archer continued, "Lady Black has worked tirelessly to perfect a vaccine to reverse the state of Transcension." His lordship looked down on the pale crown of his wife's head, his expression a mixture of pride and concern.

Lady Black was an ethereal beauty, but weariness did, indeed, show in the shadows beneath her eyes. However was the vaccine Archer referred to possible? A vision of Selene, vibrant and laughing, flashed across the dark curtain of his mind.

"To *perfect* the vaccine . . ." Lady Black gnawed on her bottom lip. "Perhaps 'perfect' is not the word we should use when describing the current state of my research. I won't know the exact effects, of course, until I administer the serum."

"So the serum is imperfect? Should we not wait until you are certain?" The words were out of Rourke's lips before he could stop them.

Lord Black's gaze sharpened on him. The Reclaimer clearly made note of the contradiction: a man who demanded a woman be removed from his proximity, only to question the means by which she would make said departure.

Rourke added, "Whilst I desire the countess to be removed from the Tower, the fact remains that my men and I have been charged with her care. I will not share blame for any harm that comes to her through haste."

Archer, still staring with unnerving intensity, crossed his arms over his chest and leaned his shoulder against a tent column.

Lady Black approached Rourke. "Lord Avenage, I welcome your concern for the countess. Please be assured I hold Selene among the dearest of my friends and would never hurt her by intention." She looked between the two Shadow Guards. "Yet the development of every cure involves some experimentation. Some controlled testing. In Selene's case, we do not have that luxury. As you know, Transcension grows stronger with each passing moment, and the madness Selene took into herself was already exceedingly powerful. I fear we simply cannot wait any longer. We've got to move forward with the vaccine in its present formulation."

"Or what?"

"Or take the chance that she'll fully Transcend and awaken on her own."

"In a very foul and dangerous mood," Archer added. "It would be quite the challenge to defeat her once she reaches that strength."

Rourke nodded pensively. "How does your vaccine work?"

Elena moved closer to him, resting her hand on the queen's empty rattan chair. "That night in the Clock Tower, before the countess was taken into the Ravens' care, I took a sample of her blood. Analysis showed certain . . . abnormalities, caused by the influx of Transcension in her veins. By taking a sample of blood from Lord Alexander, who is not only her brother, but her twin, I was able to methodically compare the differences between the two and, in effect, create a counterserum, one that would repair and reverse the damage done to hers."

Archer joined his wife and topped off her half-empty glass. He bent to kiss the tip of her nose, after which he turned to Rourke.

"Such a possibility deserves a toast, don't you say, Avenage?"

Ancient gray eyes flashed as hot as ash-covered embers, challenging Rourke to disagree.

Four hours later, as Big Ben tolled eleven o'clock over the city of London, the Intervenor, Lady Black, arrived for her appointment.

The scrabble of carriage wheels turning against paving stones echoed up from the direction of the curtain wall entrance. Out from the fog burst four coal black horses, drawing a polished town coach. The vehicle slowed to a stop at the base of the southwesternmost tower. Its side lamps formed yellow half-moons of light on the cobblestones of the courtyard.

Black's footman leapt from his high perch and briskly opened the door. Two figures descended the carriage stairs, one taller than the other, each a swirl of dark cloak.

Lady Black would indeed be one of the first women allowed inside the Tower, second only to the sleeping Countess. For the ages-old organization, such traditions had become a matter of pride and were difficult to break. Despite glares and grumbles from the Ravens, Rourke had explained the absolute necessity of her visit.

Rourke withdrew from the window. "Tres, please go down and show Lord and Lady Black the way up."

The way up involved passage through a wooden door nestled into a nondescript arch formed of specially harvested Caen stones. Constructed eight centuries ago, the portal allowed the Ravens to coexist in the Tower, unseen by the mortals who also conducted their business there. More specifically, on the first floor of the White Tower, whereas any mortal opening the door would find only a nondescript storage room, an Amaranthine touch revealed an overlapping plane—three stories of living quarters and strategy rooms belonging to the Ravens. Such access was unattainable to mortals.

Even William the Bastard, or the Conqueror as he eventually became known, had been unable to pass through the portal to see the result of his treaty with the Primordials.

Lady Black's voice preceded her up the stairs. "I've always heard there are ghosts in the Tower. Is that true?"

Peering up at Tres, her face appeared small within the deeply cowled hood of her cloak, which, upon her arrival on the landing, she pushed to her shoulders. They paused side by side on the threshold, two fair-haired immortals—the golden Raven, Tres, towering, solid and powerful, over the delicate female Intervenor.

"The ghosts keep mostly to the chapel, ma'am," Tres answered. Like Rourke and the other Ravens, he kept his hair clipped short, like a soldier's.

Archer followed them, clearly uninterested in any talk of phantoms. He carried a brocade bag constructed of burgundy-and-green paisley velvet, the sort one might use for overnight travel. His silver gaze moved from floor to table to the cavernous vaulted ceiling, where his attention fixed with interest upon the circular metal frame that supported the brass cage.

Scratching, fluttering sounds came from within, the settling night sounds of seven unseen ravens.

"What of Anne Boleyn? Is she in residence?" the marchioness inquired, her cheeks bright with obvious excitement.

Tres nodded. "I encountered her just this morning. Her floating and screaming head, that is."

She unfastened the ornate silver clasp of her cloak, and drew it from her shoulders. "And what of Sir Thomas More?"

"He is not quite as venturesome as Anne, but yes, he is often seen. He has a rather disturbing fixation with self-flagellation, so we give him wide berth. There is also Simon Burley." He shrugged. "Dudley, Cromwell, Surrey and . . . Well, I could go on."

"Truly?" Lady Black's eyes widened. In a hopeful, hushed voice she queried, "Or are you just teasing me?"

"No, my lady," Shrew interjected from his place near the fire. "He wouldn't tease about the Tower's ghosts."

Elena looked to Rourke, as if for confirmation of the outlandish tales.

He nodded. Ghosts were a simple fact of the Tower, born of a bloody history they had all witnessed first-hand.

Lady Black's jaw fell open. She pressed a gloved hand to her breast as if to calm the beat of her heart. "Forgive my state of excitement, but my previous circumstances never allowed me an opportunity to visit the Tower. Eighteen acres, thirteen towers and a host of resident spirits. It is all much more impressive than I ever realized." Wide-eyed, she insisted to Tres, "You must take Lord Black and me to the chapel after we're finished here."

The Raven frowned. "Only if you like angry headless people. They're rather surly and apt to throw things if they think you take any pleasure whatsoever in their situation."

"I can certainly understand their point of view." Lady Black's brows furrowed. "What about the two young princes? The ones who disappeared here in the fifteenth century?"

Tres's expression grew even more solemn. "No, ma'am, I'm afraid the princes aren't amongst our resident ghosts."

Lady Black examined a faded tapestry hanging above the fireplace. "I am glad to hear that. They were children. Innocents. Perhaps they weren't murdered, as so many have supposed. Perhaps they were rescued by some honorable soul and went on to live out their lives in happiness."

"It's best, I think, to assume that they did," Shrew said from where he stood, arms folded and leaning against a wooden cabinet.

"Darling," said Lord Black. "Let's get this under way."

Elena nodded, pressing her lips together. "Yes, you're right, of course. Let us proceed."

She removed her gloves, tugging them off with a little pinch to each fingertip. Lifting her arm, she unsnapped the green satin reticule that hung from a gold chain on her elbow. She tucked the gloves inside, and rooted about for a moment before producing a small black leather pouch tied with scarlet cording.

To Rourke, she asked, "Where is she, please?"

At those softly spoken words, Rourke's heart stopped beating.

Lack of sleep did strange things to one's mind. Whatever fantasy his mind had created, whatever supernatural connection he felt with the women who lay in the next room . . . it was just that. A fantasy.

Yet like an opium addict, he was torn between the overwhelming hope that they would take away the source of his torment—and the snarling impulse to ensure they did not.

He subdued that impulse, as he knew he must, and lifted his hand toward the open doors.

"This way, please."

It was time for the fantasy to end. He led them through the open doors, into the countess's shadowy room.

Lady Black paused in the doorway. She sighed softly and tilted her head. "Just look at her, Archer. Isn't she lovely? I don't believe I've ever seen her at such peace."

Archer responded dryly, "She's asleep. Not harping or plotting or manipulating. How right you are. She's absolutely lovely."

"*Archer*," she reprimanded.

A mischievous smile turned his lips. "Tell me again why we can't leave her that way?"

Elena's eyes flashed, but he had coaxed her into smiling as well.

To the Ravens, she said reassuringly, "He does not really mean that. Any harping or plotting or manipulating Selene does only makes her a better Shadow Guard. When men do the same, they're called decisive and cunning."

Archer pressed his hand against the small of her back, just above her layered bustle. Elena leaned into the arc of his arm. They painted a striking picture, he so dark and she so ethereally pale. Like yin and yang, two opposite, yet perfectly matched pieces of a puzzle.

Rourke subdued the stab of . . .

"Envy" wasn't the right word to describe what he felt at seeing their obvious connection. "Restlessness" was more *en pointe*.

He had been very restless of late.

He allowed his gaze to settle on Selene. "My interaction with the countess was brief, but it was clear she had strong inclinations."

Archer chuckled. "Strong inclinations. How very diplomatic of you."

Elena approached the bed. The heavy silk of her skirts rustled with her movement. "Selene *is* strong. There is no one else in the world like her. She would do or give up anything for the few of us she holds dear." She smoothed Selene's dark hair. "As for you, Archer, I'm certain she heard every word you just said about her, so now I'm going to wake her up so she can make your life miserable for the next few decades."

Archer stared at his wife, looking like he wanted to devour her whole. Elena stared back, the brightness in her eyes saying she wouldn't mind that at all.

Rourke exhaled through his nose, signaling his impatience to begin.

"What's in there?" he asked the Blacks, indicating the velvet bag Archer carried.

"Books," said Archer. "She might be hungry when she awakens."

What the hell did that mean? The countess might be hungry for books? Or had he misheard?

"A gown and shoes and . . ." Lady Black smiled blithely. "And *everything else*."

Rourke felt quite certain she meant underthings. Images of Selene stretched out across the bed, purring like a kitten and clad in clocked stockings, ribbons, corset and lace shattered his mental reserve. That damn Hecate statue, a gift from the countess's brother for the furnishing of his sister's chamber, only added to the eroticism of Rourke's fantasy.

Oblivious to the torture she inflicted with her vague talk of *everything* feminine, the marchioness added, "The countess is very particular about her appearance. She's going to be horrified when she sees that dowdy sleeping gown I put her in."

Archer deposited the bag beside the stone wall.

From inside the pouch, Elena withdrew an oblong glass ampoule and held it aloft.

"Well . . . here it is," she announced in a husky voice.

The purple liquid shone with phosphorescent light, painting a lavender glow across Elena's face. Rourke approached the bed, remaining outside the circle of light cast down by Hecate's torches.

"How is the vaccine to be administered?"

"By mouth," Lady Black answered. "I shall require assistance in lifting her—"

"What are you sulking about?" demanded Shrew of his brother.

Just inside the door the two stood side by side, tall and golden. Rourke had been so focused on the matter at hand he hadn't noticed the brothers follow them into the room.

"I'm not sulking," Tres responded sullenly, his hands on his hips. His lips were taut and turned down at the corners.

"You don't want her to awaken, eh, brother?" Shrew teased, always the more playful of the two. "Because then she'll leave, and you'd rather the countess to stay forever—"

"Shut up."

"So you can ogle her whilst she sleeps."

"One doesn't ogle the daughter of Queen Cleopatra," Tres answered testily, his hair glinting in the lamplight. "One admires her beauty. Ogling and admiring are two completely different perspectives."

Eyes twinkling, Shrew whispered to Lady Black, "He ogles."

Lady Black smiled. Archer crossed his arms over his chest and leveled an impatient look upon them.

"Ladies," Rourke interrupted crossly. "Your presence is not required here."

"Of course, your lordship," said Tres. The brothers backed toward the door. "We'll be in the next room if you should require any assistance."

Wind whispered through the curtains, and the sound of a horse's hooves clip-clopping over cobblestones sounded in the distance.

Lady Black instructed Rourke, "Come closer. Here, on the other side of the bed, opposite me. Take her by the shoulders. Don't hurt her, of course, but be sure to hold her firmly."

Already, Rourke's hands, his fingertips throbbed in anticipation of touching her.

Elena added, "She's very strong and I can't predict exactly how she'll react to the awakening. And if the vaccine doesn't succeed in reversing her Transcension, things could get very ugly."

"How ugly?" he asked.

The marchioness's eyes gleamed, and she bit white teeth into her lower lip. He couldn't decide if she was afraid, or just very excited about the impending experiment. "She may grow tentacles and spew green bile for all I know. We have to be prepared for any possibility."

Meaning they might be forced to execute Selene. The evil within her could not be allowed to progress.

Archer paced the length of the floor beside them. His eyes had darkened, taking on a silvery, hematite sheen that indicated he prepared himself for whatever physical battle might be necessary.

He said, "Given her immortality and the strength she already possesses as a Shadow Guard, Transcension could make her even more vicious than Jack the Ripper or his Dark Bride."

A long sword flashed into being, grasped within his fist. Formed of Amaranthine silver, mined from inside the Inner Realm, the blade emanated an ethereal glow.

"Understood," Rourke said.

Elena broke off the narrow tip of the ampoule and nodded. *"Now."*

For the first time since Selene had come under his care at the Tower, Rourke touched her. With one arm he lifted her up from the pillow, so that she rested against the crook of his elbow. Her head lolled onto his shoulder, and her lush, floral scent rose to his nose. He forced himself not to look at her mouth, the column of her neck or her breasts—undeniably magnificent breasts that in his dreams he had—

The countess sighed and shifted, as if even in her deep sleep she was aware of their manhandling.

Lady Black reached, but without forethought to his actions Rourke cut her off, using his own hand to lift Selene's chin and coax open her mouth.

"If you could tilt her head back just a bit," Elena whispered. "Yes . . . perfect."

Elena held the ampoule against Selene's lower lip. The purple liquid emptied from the narrow glass tube. The countess's throat moved as she swallowed and her lips closed against Rourke's thumb. Her tongue, warm and wet, touched the sensitive pad.

Heat and blood surged through his groin.

"*Ah*," he rasped.

"What is it?" hissed Elena, wide-eyed.

"I'm just praying this works," he hissed back.

Archer chuckled. Rourke clenched his teeth.

Elena bit her lower lip and watched the countess's face expectantly.

An hour later, Rourke held vigil at the foot of Selene's bed. He rubbed a hand over his forehead and over his whisker-roughened jaw.

Damn.

Archer stood at the window, peering out between the narrow wooden slats of the shutter. Elena sat at the nearby escritoire, writing into a leather-bound book. With each passing moment, she grew more agitated in her scribbling.

At last, she woefully proclaimed, "She has not moved so much as an eyelash."

"Perhaps the vaccine just needs a bit more time to

take effect," suggested Rourke, repeating the fervent mantra that had already played a thousand times in his mind.

She offered him a grateful look, though her lips did not quite achieve a smile. "I don't understand. I felt so certain the formula would work."

Archer came to stand beside her. He rested his hands on her slender shoulders. "Let me take you home. You're exhausted." Bending to her ear, he murmured something more softly, something even Rourke, with his acute Raven hearing, could not make out.

Rourke said, "We'll send word of any change."

At the door to the stairs, Elena gripped Rourke's hand. The familiarity startled him. It was not often anyone touched him. Not out of friendship. Not in the light.

She said, "I can't begin to tell you how disappointed I am. I'll review my notes in the morning and see what adjustments can be made. Give me one more night, Lord Avenage. I'm close to unlocking the precise formula. I can feel it."

To Tres, she said, "We'll visit the chapel another time. I'm not at all in the mood for ghost hunting now."

Flynn, the youngest of the seven Ravens, appeared on the landing and passed the Blacks on their way out. He arrived on schedule to relieve Tres for the remainder of the night.

Rourke turned back to the open doorway of Selene's chamber and stabbed his fingers through his hair. Another night under the same roof with the countess. Perhaps longer?

God, he needed to get away from London—from *her*, for just a few short days. If he didn't, he would explode. He glanced at the map of England affixed to the wall and followed the eastern coastline north to Northumbria, almost to Scotland.

Swarthwick. His mind filled with the memory of purple skies, waving grass and high, jagged crags. A weighty darkness settled over his heart, deep inside his chest. What better place to return his mind to his priorities?

Just the week before, he had received an inquiry from

the local land office as to whether the property might be for sale. He supposed he had neglected the estate for too long. Perhaps he would, indeed, sell the place, or better yet, transfer its ownership to some local charity. To earn even a single shilling from its sale would be an abomination.

He drew a sheet of parchment from the desk and took the ink pen in hand. Moments later, he signed and sealed his request. Taking up the stamp, he pressed its triangular base into the cooling black wax and laid the envelope on top of the other documents to be transported by fire to the Inner Realm.

He was exhausted and wanted nothing more than to surrender to the oblivion of sleep. That wouldn't be possible. Not tonight. Not until she was gone.

To Flynn, he said, "I'm going out for a bit."

"Yes, sir." The Raven, a sturdy redheaded lad of Viking stock, looked up from the desk where he reviewed the night log. Like Rourke, all of the Ravens were Amaranthine recruits, born mortal, but inducted into immortality to serve a necessary purpose. Membership in the Order was not an eternal appointment, and from time to time, replacements were necessary. "Don't concern yourself with things here. We'll give a shout if we need you."

Rourke returned to the narrow cell that had served as his private quarters for eight centuries and changed into clothing more suitable for an evening out. He glanced at his reflection in the small round mirror above the water basin. He knew he was not handsome in the classical sense of the word. His features were a bit too angular, his nose too wide at the bridge, and pronounced. But women, nonetheless, had always seemed to find him attractive.

It couldn't be his personality. He knew full well that he wasn't all that pleasant a fellow to be around.

Leaving the Tower, he retrieved Assassin from the nearby stables and rode to Belgravia.

The London Season had officially drawn to a close, but there were still dinner parties and gatherings, just on a smaller, more intimate scale. While many of the great houses were dark and shuttered, others blazed with light and activity.

The address where he eventually dismounted reflected a life somewhere in between. Soft lamplight wavered through the polished windows. After a single knock, a liveried servant opened the door and within moments she was there, gliding out from a back room, dressed in azure satin, with jewels at her throat and a peacock feather in her hair.

The top of her head came just to his shoulder. She laughed softly, silkily, and said something about the theater and a wonderful performance. Though he didn't look directly at her face—no, not ever—he knew she had been drinking. The fragrance of wine wafted from between her lips. Male and female laughter sounded from deeper inside the house, accompanied by the tinkling of silver and crystal.

"You have guests," he murmured. He touched the tip of his hat and backed away. "Another time, then."

"Join us, Avenage. It's Mr. Irving and Miss Terry from the Lyceum, and a few others. There's a writer. Mr. Wilde. Terribly odd and uncouth, but charming." She gripped his hands. "Please. They would adore you, as I do."

"Not tonight."

Not ever. It wasn't like that between them. As politely as possible, he extricated himself and turned to the door.

"I'll send them home." Her heeled slippers sounded on the marble behind him. "Just stay."

He didn't like the strained tone of her voice. It signaled an unfortunate change in her feelings for him. He had been clear with her from the start. Pretending not to hear, he kept walking.

"Avenage!" She pushed through the doorframe and followed him outside, onto the stairs.

He stopped, only because he wished for her to stop as well. He could not bear the idea of her chasing after him into the street.

"Then let me come to you," she whispered. "Tonight. In the Tower."

"You know that's not possible."

"Because no one except for your precious Raven warriors is allowed?" she snapped, her words hurled like stones against his back and shoulders.

He would participate in no lover's spat. They were not lovers. "Lovers" implied an emotional attachment. There was none of that between them.

He answered, "It has always been so."

"But *she* is there," she prodded, her voice as sharp as a wasp's sting.

He could have responded in a number of ways: She *is a Shadow Guard.* She *is worthy of the Tower.* She *belongs there among us.*

Instead, without so much as a glance back, he took the steps to the street and thrust his boot into his saddle stirrup. The stableman's eyes widened, and, releasing the reins to Rourke, he skittered away. Something shattered behind Rourke. Out of the corner of his eye he saw dirt and flowers, and the shards of a small planter.

For the next hour he rode aimlessly through the city, only vaguely aware of its lights, smells and sounds. He considered stopping for a drink, but the idea of sitting shoulder-to-shoulder with a thick press of strangers held no appeal. For three nights he had not slept and yet he shunned his bed. He wanted nothing more than to sleep, but sleep took him to a sweet and terrible perdition.

Ravenmaster!

Shrew's silent shout struck him like a battering ram to the chest, so hard and urgent the breath vacated his lungs.

The tails of his greatcoat whipped out behind him as he twisted . . . warped into shadow, abandoning Assassin to the street. Within moments he arrived at the Tower and bounded up the stairs—only to be hurled back by an unseen force.

He impacted the earth *hard*, shoulder first. He rolled, recovering into a crouch, and shook his head clear. A bright flash commanded his gaze upward. Searing, white beams of light emitted from the uppermost windows of the White Tower. A crash sounded, metal against stone.

His vision blurred and his bones impacted against their surrounding muscles and flesh.

Weakened by whatever had just happened, he rasped for breath, crouching on all fours. His mind produced only one explanation: the ravens' cage. Had it fallen from the ceiling?

At the door he again confronted the invisible wall of resistance. He grabbed for the iron handle, but the force repeatedly deflected his hand, like two opposite sides of a magnet refusing to connect. With a bellow of rage, he pushed every muscle and ounce of his willpower to its limit, forcing himself, inch by torturous inch, *into* the barrier. Like boiled tar the force enveloped him, filling his eye sockets, nostrils and ears, so hot and thick he feared he would smother from it. At last he broke through.

Inside the tower was dark as pitch, even to his night-seeing eyes.

In all his existence as an Amaranthine, he had never known true darkness.

Not until now.

Shouted curses echoed down—Shrew's guttural, frantic voice—along with battering sounds. All but blind, and relying on memory, he lunged up the stairs three at a time, into the tower room.

Chapter Three

All lanterns and candles had been extinguished. The ever-burning hearth lay cold and black. The doors to the countess's chamber, always kept open, were shut. Searing, incandescent light speared out from between the cracks in the wood, so bright his eyes stung and watered.

Shrew hacked at the door with an ax.

The cage that had hung above the room lay at the center of the stone floor, upside down. As Shrew continued to batter the door, Rourke, his head pounding with disbelief and dread, curled his fingers into the vertical wires and righted the metal cage onto its base.

Seven ravens staggered and flapped their wings, stunned by the impact of falling to the floor. One bird lay motionless, its neck canted in an unnatural position, eyes open and unblinking.

"Where is Flynn?" Rourke demanded.

"In"—Shrew hacked again—"*there*."

Peering into the light, Rourke shielded his eyes.

What in the hell was in there? What in the *hell* had invaded his tower after eight centuries of absolute impenetrability?

Whatever it was, he was going to tear it to shreds and eat its heart. Rage corded his muscles with supernatural strength, and his eyes grew heated . . . glowed with the inner fire of his turning. With a guttural shout, he kicked the door with the flat of his boot. Backing away, he kicked again. Weakened by Shrew's assault with the ax, the door cleaved inward, splintering into shards. The light—

Disappeared.

In darkness, the Ravens entered the room. An unnatural wind, coming from all directions, tore at their clothes and tossed the shredded curtains. The windows yawed like shocked mouths, open to the night, their shutters scraping against the stone and hanging in fragments.

Though the countess was gone . . . the bed was not empty.

With a great, sucking sound, the wind vacated the room, leaving them alone in utter silence with the broken body of a dead Raven.

Even in the blackness of the alley the wide butcher's blade gleamed brightly, a jagged metal incisor, save for the dark stripe smeared along its sharpest edge.

Realizing it was *she* who held the knife, Selene felt her heartbeat quicken. Still cradling the handle between her thumb and index finger, she spread her fingers in a pale fan.

The same darkness painted her fingers, her wrist and the lace cuff of the sleeping gown she wore. Wet and glistening, the stuff gave off a distinctly metallic scent.

Repulsed . . . *confused*, she flung the knife. The blade clattered into some resting place hidden by the deeper shadows of the warehouse above her. Her palm stung and she lifted her hand. She had cut herself. The darkness hovered so thick and impermeable around her, she felt suspended in it. Seeking a physical anchor, she glanced over her shoulder.

The dingy orb of a streetlamp glowed in the distance, a bleary cataract. Selene backed toward the lamp, her bare feet touching upon cold pavement, and bumped into the wooden slat of a wagon.

She remembered being in the belfry of the Westminster Clock Tower, and knowing the Dark Bride had been vanquished and that her twin, Mark, was safe. Everything else remained hidden by the persistent spottiness of her mind. How much time had passed since then, an hour or a century?

High walls surrounded her. The darkness was so deep she could barely see through—

Impossible. She was a Shadow Guard. The dark hid nothing from her eyes. Something was wrong.

Run. Escape. Now.

She scooted back, feet skimming over damp, grainy paving stones. Her heels bumped onto—*ach!*—something both hard and soft. She fell with a jarring impact onto her bottom. Moisture dampened her buttocks, thighs and flat-pressed palms. Her legs lay over the thing that had tripped her, something formed of cloth and skin. Again, there was the smell. The smell of blood.

Selene recoiled, scrambling free of the woman's loose limbs and damp skirts. She pushed herself onto her feet, and whirled—

A score of shadows receded like slithering, smoky serpents in all different directions.

Bloody hell, her heart beat so fast it hurt. What had she just glimpsed? A host of curious wraiths gathered at the end of the alley to observe whatever had happened—*whatever* it was that she could not remember.

In the distance, a woman cackled and a police bobby's whistle sounded in a high-pitched stream. Common noises for a dark London night, and yet she felt trapped here, and a thousand miles away from anything civilized.

She twisted back again, peering down the alley, praying she had been mistaken about the dead woman, but no—the crumpled figure lay there between two parked wagons, sprawled as awkwardly as a child's discarded doll.

She harnessed all the emotion inside her. Using it as impetus she urged her body to transform into shadow. Invisible, she would grow more powerful and find the clarity she needed. A shimmer of heat twisted within her bones, but . . . nothing happened. Shock thundered inside her head and numbed her lips.

Her night rail twisted between her legs. The sound of her breath echoed off the high brick walls that had become so familiar. This was London's Whitechapel district, and this street—Castle Alley. The blackened windows of the Whitechapel Bath and Washhouses watched, dispassionate and unblinking, as she ran past.

The night air chilled her skin into gooseflesh. Something sharp and small, a pebble or bit of glass, pierced her heel. She cried out, drawing her leg upward in reaction, and nearly fell again.

The confounding darkness. The discomfort of cold. Herself, nearly crippled by such an insignificant wound. *No, no, no.* Not her, the Shadow Guard's only female warrior. It had been centuries since she had suffered such human failings.

Something *was* horribly and terribly wrong. She had to find Mark, her twin. He would help her know what to do.

Whoosh.

She looked up toward the sound. A shadow hurtled toward her, blotting out the light of the gas lamp. The shadow took shape, materializing into a muscular, broad-shouldered silhouette with burning red-ember eyes and outstretched black wings. Leather boots touched down upon the paving stones.

He advanced toward her.

"*Avenage*," she said, recognizing him at once.

The Ravenmaster—the Shadow Guard warrior she had persuaded to help her in the days leading up to her confrontation with the Dark Bride. Despite their brief liaison, he remained a complete mystery to her.

He moved with power and grace, the muscles rippling along his shoulders and neck. Long legs carried him closer. For a moment, admiration for his terrifying beauty held her frozen in place.

"Countess," he growled, reaching for her arm.

Thick silver claws curled out from his fingers, the enviable weapon of the Ravens. Instinctively she hissed and feinted away.

"Under whose orders do you come at me with your weapons drawn?" she demanded, half circling him. Again, he lunged, cutting her off, denying her any path of escape.

"My orders." The words, spoken in a low rasp, conveyed fury and scorn.

"Surrender," he demanded.

The clouds in her mind cleared further, and she remembered the madness—the Transcension—she had taken inside herself to spare her twin brother from death. Elena had put her to sleep to protect her.

But she was awake now, here on the street. A dead woman lay in the alleyway behind her.

What had she done?

One part of her conscience knew she must do as the Raven demanded and surrender herself, even if it meant her execution—her immortal *death*. The other part of her insisted she preserve herself at any cost.

Whoosh. Whoosh. The air shifted beneath the powerful sweep of more wings.

Along the periphery of Selene's vision, three Raven warriors lit, one by one, to crouch upon the roofs and cling against the walls, their wings dark slashes against the deep blue sky, like something out of a Gustave Doré illustration of hell.

Selene lifted her gaze to the Ravenmaster's. Whatever glimmer of emotion she hoped to see within him . . . whatever evidence of understanding she needed from him was not there. The hellish glow of his red-ember eyes did not waver.

Slowly he reached out his hand, palm upturned.

The claws were gone. There was only the dull sheen of leather.

"Surrender . . . yourself . . . to me," he repeated, more softly this time.

Tentatively . . . haltingly . . . she lowered her palm against his. The cool leather closed, as rigid as a snare, around her hand.

"Why am I so cold?" she asked. "I have never been so cold."

Though she resisted, digging in her heels, he effortlessly pulled her closer.

Heat radiated through his leather breastplate, through the thin layer of her gown, yet they did not touch, save where his hand clenched hers.

She felt helpless against him. She had not been *helpless* in centuries.

Deep inside, anger flared.

"What has happened to me?" she demanded.

Curling her free hand into a fist, she struck him in the chest. He did not so much as flinch, but merely closed his larger one over hers, preventing her from striking him again.

She *did* want to strike him again, this time harder. She wanted someone else to hurt as badly as she did, to experience her isolation and fear, but a deep surge of exhaustion came over her, so consuming she could not even curl her fist again.

"What has happened to me?" she repeated in a whisper.

Her vision wavered, and her consciousness dimmed. Her final memory was of the firmness of his chest against her cheek and strong arms preventing her fall.

"But aren't vaccines supposed to heal?" Selene demanded groggily from her bed. She was so sleepy. She could barely lift her head from the pillow. But Elena did not answer. She simply continued to transfer Selene's folded garments from the bag into a large wooden chest of drawers.

Selene had awakened to find herself at Black House, Lord and Lady Black's palatial Mayfair estate, in the same room she had occupied before their marriage— but not afterward. Then, her presence in the house hadn't seemed right.

The wallpaper and upholstery were still the same green-and-gold stripe, but there were no stacks of old books or baskets of beloved snakes. It didn't feel like her room at all anymore.

It was just a room for a guest—or more accurately, a prison cell, judging by the two towering, fair-haired Ravens posted at the door, their arms crossed over their broad chests, their faces devoid of expression. She had overheard Elena refer to them as Tres and Shrew. Her gaze narrowed upon them. If she were at her full strength, it would take at least twice their number to keep her here, if she did not wish to remain. She sighed and closed her eyes. However, in her present state, the mere thought of engaging them in a tussle wearied her.

A brass lamp on the table beside her emitted soft light. The curtains remained drawn, and she did not know whether it was night or day. Elena poured water from a pitcher into a basin. Registering a dull throb of pain across her palm, she glanced down to the gauze binding that wrapped around her hand.

Fragmented memories flashed like shards of broken glass across the blank canvas of her mind. The dead woman. The knife in her hand.

Avenage.

She pried the gauze from her skin, untwisting several rounds until she saw a faint scarlet stain on the cotton. Her blood. An uncomfortable sensation, much like cold water, sluiced down her spine. Another tug and twist, and she revealed the terrible truth: a neat row of stitches traversing her palm.

While serving in the ranks of the Shadow Guard she had suffered countless injuries: cuts, deeper wounds and even gunshots inflicted by the vicious, empty mortal souls she hunted. Yes, she had experienced pain and injury, and yes, she had bled, at times profusely, but she had never required a single stitch. Like all Guards, her Amaranthine body healed with astounding speed, leaving her without even the slightest of scars. The only scars on her body were those she had earned in childhood.

Though she had been made an Amaranthine immortal when she was twelve years of age, she'd had to wait for her extraordinary abilities until her body matured to its most perfect state before fully transforming.

Her back bore the scars of narrow lash marks, her wrists and ankles the scars left by Octavian's golden chains.

Now she stared at her offensive palm. With the wound naked to the air, the throbbing, which had been barely perceivable before, increased tenfold and stung as if a fissure opened wide . . . wide . . . wider. Though weak, Selene slammed her palm against the mattress, as if the blow would stamp out what she saw and felt.

"Am I mortal now?" she whispered.

"No." Elena fluttered along the edge of the bed, finally seating herself in the nearby chair. Her cheeks were pink and her eyes wide, as if this tragedy were her own. The two Ravens watched, hard-eyed, from their post at the door.

Elena explained, "You *are* healing faster than any mortal would, just not as quickly as before. Your body seems to be in some sort of transitional state."

Selene voiced the foremost questions on her mind. "Is the Transcension still here, somewhere inside my head? Will my mind deteriorate? Will I go mad? I don't *feel* mad, and I don't hear any voices such as those my brother described. . . ."

Elena shook her head. "I don't believe so . . . I . . ."

"Tell me the truth," blurted Selene.

"I can't say for certain."

Selene pushed up from the mattress. "You must tell me. Is it possible that I killed that poor woman?"

"You wouldn't have," Elena assured her. "Couldn't have."

And yet Selene saw the doubt in her friend's eyes.

"Who was she?"

"A prostitute."

"Just like Jack the Ripper and the Dark Bride preyed upon."

"Yes," her friend acknowledged with a whisper.

Where was Avenage? Against all reason, her thoughts returned to him, as if he would provide some anchor amid the confusion and terror of these moments. She imagined his arms around her. His calming voice in her ear—but she had never known him in such a way.

Her pulse spiked at the memory of him towering above her, a mystery of shadowy wings and leather, his eyes glowing like red coals. When he was not transformed, his eyes were green. An uncommon, pale green.

Given the date on the newspaper beside her bed, it had been three weeks since he had helped her and her fellow Reclaimers defeat the Dark Bride. Yet it made no sense whatsoever that she should crave his comfort. Their time together had been measured in mere minutes rather than hours, and of a professional nature, without any intimacy whatsoever. He was nothing to her, and she was nothing to him.

She had requested a meeting with him, and he had consented.

She had talked, and he had listened.

She had asked for his help, and after some thought, he had agreed. The rest had happened shockingly fast, in a flash of flight and swordplay. He had been an attractive and exciting mystery, one she had hoped to explore further. But that night in the Clock Tower had changed everything.

Elena perched on a chair beside the bed, her hands clasped tightly in her lap.

"I wish I could predict the course of your recovery, or how long it might take for you to return to normal." She blinked away tears. "I can't tell you how sorry I am, Selene. I feel so responsible. I know the Shadow Guard is everything to you."

Fury sparked deep in Selene's heart, but she swallowed the sharp words that leapt to her tongue. She had always been hot tempered and imperious, so much like her mother, Cleopatra. She wanted to rage, to rail against her dearest friend—her only female friend—for committing her to this unfamiliar and vulnerable state. Instead, she forced her attention to the black lotus flower floating in a crystal bowl of water beside the bed.

Elena, always so thoughtful. Of course she would

know that the lotus flower was Selene's favorite. The bloom in the bowl was extra special because, as mortal invention and ingenuity had dirtied the Outer Realm's atmosphere, the flower had eventually gone extinct. Now, black lotus grew only in the purer air of the Inner Realm. Despite the name, the petals weren't really black, but a deep purple, edged in vibrant green.

Although their friendship had been brief, Elena seemed to understand her better than anyone and realize what neither of them would say: Without her powers and status within the Shadow Guard, Selene would be left with nothing. The houses, the jewels and riches she had accumulated through her existence would offer her no comfort. None of that was Elena's fault.

And so Selene acted against her sharper nature and tempered her words by saying what she knew she *ought* to say. "You did not intend this. Whatever happens tomorrow or the next day remains to be seen."

Elena squeezed her hand and whispered, "Your abilities may never return. I pray that they will, but—"

"I'm not dead, Elena."

But even as she spoke the words, Selene wondered if perhaps she *was* dead. She felt dead inside, ripped empty of anything she had been before. She would change nothing about that night in the Clock Tower, when she and the others fought to defeat the Dark Bride. In a heartbeat, she would sacrifice herself again—even her life—to save her twin brother from the madness of Transcension that had threatened to forever claim him, and what would most assuredly have followed: his death. But wouldn't it have been better if her fellow Reclaimers had executed her, rather than throwing her into this state of powerlessness?

Archer appeared at the door. "We're ready for her now."

"Is it Mark?" Selene asked Elena. More than anything, she wanted to see her twin. Why had he not come to visit her already? Certainly, in the happiness of his new marriage to Willomina Limpett, he had not forgotten her. She could not believe that, not when ancient tragedy had bound their lives together so completely.

"No, dear," whispered Elena. "I'll explain about that later."

Selene curled her fingers into the counterpane. "Then I do not wish to have visitors."

Unless it was Avenage. But even then, she should like to dress and have her hair put up. She hated being seen in a dressing gown, as if she were an invalid. The weakness in her limbs and her persistent drowsiness reminded her she was just that.

Elena glanced at Archer and frowned sharply. "She is still very weak and can barely walk. Can this not wait?"

Tellingly, he avoided Selene's gaze. "One doesn't tell these visitors to wait."

"Perhaps I can be of assistance," said a male voice from the hallway.

A familiar face, one defined by a black eye patch, appeared. It was Leeson, Archer's immortal secretary, and he pushed a wheelchair. Instantly, her hackles rose.

She and Leeson had never gotten on well at all, and she had scored the last point in their clash of personalities by devouring every last one of his extensive collection of penny dreadfuls.

Ever since the burning of the Library of Alexandria, a highly traumatic event in her past, she had suffered a bizarre and very literal appetite for the written word. Quite simply put, she sometimes suffered a craving to eat books.

If Leeson chose to exact his revenge, her present vulnerable state would put her at an enormous disadvantage.

"Now, don't you look at me like that, my dear," he murmured softly, peering at her out of his one good eye. Always the dapper dresser, he wore gray trousers, a white shirt and a gold-and-blue-striped brocade vest. "We'll go right back to despising each other when all this is over, but for now, let us observe a truce."

With everyone reaching for her elbows and helping

her from the bed, what else could she do? Elena brushed her hair, smoothed the collar of her copper satin robe and, with a wide velvet sash, bound her to the chair before allowing Leeson to push her down the hallway toward the grand center staircase.

A large glass skylight, centered above the landing, revealed a clouded night sky. Two burly male servants waited. They lifted and carried her in the wheelchair to the first-floor landing and, after pausing for a moment's recovery, proceeded to the ground floor, where Archer took over pushing the handles of her chair. Elena walked beside them.

Several royal attendants and foot guards stood beneath the rotunda, indicating the presence of the queen. They politely averted their eyes as Archer rolled her past. Selene's pulse skipped. Why would the queen be here?

They entered Archer's study. Indeed, the queen leaned on a cane beside the desk, a striking portrait in black. She wore a white lace cap and pearls at her throat. Gray haired and stern, she met eyes with Selene and nodded a curt welcome.

"Your Majesty," whispered Selene, her throat constricted almost too tightly to speak.

She attempted to stand, but Victoria lifted a staying hand.

Behind the queen, ancient terra-cotta tiles painted with black and red lotus flowers framed an enormous fireplace large enough for a man to stand inside. Wood crackled and flames leapt high. Heat radiated outward to bathe her skin with an almost uncomfortable intensity.

Victoria seated herself and peered expectantly into the flames.

Selene's blood quickened in realization. Archer wheeled her closer, but positioned her wheelchair a substantial distance from the queen. The two Ravens, Tres and Shrew, took places immediately behind her. Archer left her to stand behind the queen.

She did not need anyone to explain that they were providing protection to the queen from her.

"I'll blindfold you now, Your Highness," said Elena.

"Yes, of course."

From behind, the marchioness tied a length of black silk around the regent's head, covering her eyes, a necessary precaution, as the light would be too unfamiliar and damaging to mortal eyes.

Selene's powers were gone. What if the light shriveled her eyes in their sockets?

Archer spoke the ancient words to unlock the portal.

The flames darkened from yellow and orange into indigo and then, finally, purple. Selene stared rigidly into the light, her hands curling around the armrests of the wheelchair. A low hum filled the room. A face appeared, one that transformed moment to moment from one set of features into another—those of Aitha, Hydros and the female Primordial, Khaos.

The light from the Inner Realm did not scorch Selene's eyes, a small relief and one she welcomed, given the magnitude of everything else that had taken place.

"Greetings," announced an otherworldly voice, formed of three distinct yet harmonious tones. "We come together to decide the fate of the Reclaimer."

Selene closed her eyes. That would be her.

Archer responded, "We do not know for a certainty that she killed the woman."

The Primordials countered, "The Raven observed her from the sky. She was standing over the dead woman, holding the knife."

Avenage had offered testimony against her, then. Though he had spoken the truth, the knowledge stung.

The Ancients continued, "There were bloodstains on her clothing and on her hands. What other conclusion can be drawn?"

Their expressions and voices reflected no anger or accusation. They merely stated facts.

Archer said, "I would like a chance to examine the victim's body at the mortuary. Perhaps there is some discoverable clue to what happened in Whitechapel last night. Of a certain, Tantalus is somehow involved in everything that occurred last night, the murder of Alice McKenzie and—"

"What are you suggesting, Ancient, that Tantalus or one of his *brotoi* are responsible for the murder and the countess is not? What if Tantalus guided her hand? Guides her even now?"

Archer answered, "Anything is possible. However, I believe Tantalus would take considerable pleasure in our executing one of our own—especially Selene, who played such a pivotal role in slaying his most recent champion. Perhaps she was simply maneuvered into place to take the blame."

Archer's words only strengthened her heartfelt and deeply intuitive belief that she had not, indeed, murdered an innocent woman. *Brotoi* and Tantalus she could fight. But if it were proven that her powers had been twisted into something evil, if even for a moment, and had resulted in an innocent's death, that knowledge would destroy her. She could never forgive herself for being so weak as to be manipulated in such a way.

"What about Flynn?" demanded a deep voice from the back of the study.

Selene twisted around. Avenage stood in the shadows, the tense line of his jaw and his frowning lips revealed by the firelight.

"Flynn?" she whispered. "Who is Flynn?"

His gaze lowered to her, cold and passionless.

"I'm sorry you don't recognize the name, Countess." He stepped closer, until the purple light revealed his stark, unsmiling face and brilliant green eyes that accused. "He's the Raven you murdered last night."

Chapter Four

"*Murdered*?" The Countess Pavlenco's shoulders went rigid and her face blanched.

A rush of self-hatred washed over Rourke, because his first instinct was to go down on one knee before Selene and assure her she couldn't be guilty of the murder he had just accused her of committing. But then he reminded himself who she was—the daughter of history's most infamous seductress—and that he suffered from the effects of her skillful bewitchment.

"*No.*" With visible effort, she stood from the chair, a statuesque beauty in copper satin. A round, crystalline tear formed on the lower lashes of one eye. At the same time, her expression went fierce. Turning back to the others, she addressed the Primordials directly. "I couldn't have done that. I did not kill that woman—and I most certainly did not kill the Raven."

The tear fell over her cheek.

Archer crossed his arms over his chest. "With all respect, Ravenmaster, there is not sufficient evidence to condemn her of Flynn's murder. Neither you nor your Raven, Shrew, were in the tower room with Selene prior to her disappearance. None of us can say what happened behind those doors, not without further investigation. These are uncommon times. Just consider all the evidence and commonalities involved. Whitechapel. The knife murder of a prostitute. Unexplained paranormal activity. Tantalus's involvement must be an assumed element in all of this. It is only to what degree that remains to be seen."

The queen nodded sagely, her lips tightly pursed beneath the dark slash of her blindfold.

"We owe her that. A full investigation," she agreed.

Lady Black added, "And as all of you know better than I, the making of a Reclaimer takes centuries of training. Candidates are rare. You could not easily replace the countess."

Rourke steeled himself against the united barrage of their arguments. Selene bent her head and closed her eyes, as if in thanks to them for speaking on her behalf. Her dark hair shone thick and rich over her shoulders, a lovely complement to her vibrant skin. Rourke tore his gaze from her, hating himself for the attraction he felt for someone who might very well have killed one of his men.

Archer continued, "Until Tantalus is stopped, there will be more Transcended souls and more powerful *brotoi* that must be swiftly Reclaimed." He approached the fire. "If she can be proven innocent of these allegations, and if she regains her powers, we need her, just as we need all of the Reclaimers to provide the necessary defenses to London and the Inner Realm."

Selene swayed and reached for the armrest of the wheelchair. Lady Black moved to her side and, with a supporting hand to her elbow, urged her to sit.

The room filled with the sound of unintelligible murmurings as the Primordials debated the matter among themselves.

At last, they announced, "We are in agreement. We will stay our judgment until a full investigation is completed, at which time we shall reconvene."

The countess exhaled and her regal shoulders sagged with visible relief against the back of the wheelchair.

The Council continued with their edict. "The countess will be held under a protective watch until such time

as she can either be fully exonerated of these crimes—
or convicted."

Archer nodded. Elena gave Selene's shoulder a reassuring squeeze.

"Where am I to be taken?" whispered Selene.

"I'm afraid she can't remain here any longer," announced Lord Black.

"*Archer*," implored Elena, her cheeks darkening.

Resolutely, he shook his head. "I won't allow it."

Perplexed by their exchange, Selene sought out Elena's gaze, but Elena's remained fixed on her husband.

"We have . . . news," he announced. "Lady Black is expecting."

Selene's heart leapt at this revelation—but also fractured just a little bit. Her emotions on the subject were tangled. Complicated. She had once loved Archer, and now he and Elena, her dearest friend, would experience the joy of a child with one another.

The queen clasped her hands together. "Delightful."

The Primordials' light brightened into violet. "The Inner Realm will celebrate this news. An impending birth! We are pleased beyond measure."

Elena knelt beside her, taking Selene's hands into her own. "Selene . . ."

"I am very happy for you," Selene said, wondering whether it was possible to lie and to tell the truth at the same time.

Archer nodded, his eyes smoldering with pride. "As we all well know, in recent centuries, Amaranthine births have become rarer and rarer. Not only that, but this is my child. Mine and Elena's." He turned to Selene. "I hope you understand, Countess, that I won't allow my wife or our unborn child's welfare to be endangered. I don't believe you're guilty of murder. Indeed, I hold out all hope that Elena's serum has worked. But until we know for sure whether you have escaped the effects of Transcension and are in control of your actions—"

"Of course," she responded, doing her best to hold

her emotions steady. "Might I instead stay with Mark and Willomina?"

Archer shook his head, his expression apologetic. "While I'm certain your brother would like nothing better, Lord and Lady Alexander have been tasked with recruiting members for the Atheatos."

"Atheatos?" asked Selene.

"Much has happened whilst you have slept in the Tower," Elena answered. "The Primordials seek to assemble a phalanx of intellectual mortals with knowledge in ancient languages, texts and artifacts. By gathering this knowledge they hope to anticipate Tantalus's next move. Your brother and Mina are presently in Egypt to initiate contact with a potential candidate—"

Avenage interrupted, "Must we truly work with mortals?"

In his role as Ravenmaster, it had been necessary for Rourke to liaise with a number of mortals within the queen's household, as well as Parliament and the House of Commons. Aside from hearty souls like McGregor, it seemed that at the most critical moments, they would plead sick or resign their positions due to scandals or the nebulous "personal matters"—or worse, unexpectedly die. Mortals were undependable in that way.

The Primordials responded, "Times have changed. Over the centuries, our numbers have lessened. We are left with no choice but to strengthen our ranks with those mortals who might be able to unlock the answers to our preservation."

"What are you saying?" Rourke demanded. "That the Amaranthines are in danger of extinction?"

Archer said, "Again, Avenage, when was the last time you heard of an Amaranthine birth?"

"Immortal births have always been rare," Rourke countered.

"When was the last time, Avenage?"

He shook his head. He could not even remember, but then, he did not concern himself with such matters.

Archer's lips thinned. "We're back to the original question. Where will Selene be taken? Out of the city, preferably, because as we learned with Mark, Tantalus's power is stronger in London, which he seeks to claim for his throne. His influence is lessened with distance."

"*Swarthwick*," the Primordials announced.

The pronouncement echoed inside Rourke's head. He moved past Selene . . . Archer . . . Victoria until the heat of the flames scorched his skin. To the Primordials he said, "Swarthwick is isolated and unstaffed. There's no means of communication there."

Archer joined him at the hearth. "Not only that, but Avenage believes she's murdered one of his men. Is he the best choice to be her keeper?"

Rourke glanced sharply at the immortal beside him.

The flames leapt and intensified to an ethereal brightness. The faces of the Primordials grew clearer, and their ageless beauty was revealed.

"It is decided."

Rourke stormed toward the massive front doors of Black House. Two doormen grasped the metal handles and heaved them open for his passage.

"Avenage," called a voice.

Pivoting on his heel, he faced Archer. He bit his tongue, holding in a barrage of angry words and thank-you-very-much sarcasm. Somewhere in the depths of the house, Leeson was showing the queen the collection of Black House silver and porcelain. He would not take the chance that she would overhear his tirade. Secretly he feared that if he spoke so much as a word, they would all see him for what he was—a smitten fool, in danger of losing his mind over an unobtainable seductress who had also likely murdered Flynn.

Over the Reclaimer's shoulder, he observed the servants conveying Selene up the stairs. Her bronze-colored dressing gown shimmered darkly, a rich foil to her dark hair and lustrous skin. Her stormy, questioning eyes met his. It was clear to him that she despised her present helplessness.

"I can see you're angry," Archer said.

Silence.

"But I think it's necessary to warn you . . ."

"Of what?" Rourke growled.

Archer glanced over his shoulder. "Of *Selene*. Until we know for certain that she can be trusted, you must remain always on guard. Remember whom you're dealing with. This is Cleopatra's daughter, and let me assure you the progeny has inherited the best . . . or some might say the worst of her mother's traits. She can be mercenary with her charms, something that works well against her enemies, but at present, her loyalties may be confused. She's persuasive, and—"

"Beautiful and seductive," Elena added, suddenly present at her husband's elbow. She whispered, "She'll eat you alive if given the chance, and I suspect you'd rather like it until it was too late. Please know we say all of this with complete admiration for her, and the sincere underlying belief that she has committed none of the crimes of which she's been accused."

Rourke stared at the empty marble staircase. Selene didn't seem dangerous. She seemed bewildered. Wounded.

God, when had he become such a damned fool?

"Whatever the case, consider yourself warned," said Archer.

Elena sighed. "I wish she could stay here with us."

"Well, she can't," Archer said.

"I just *know* she didn't kill Flynn or that woman."

"But we *don't* know."

Lady Black gnawed on her lower lip. "She's going to prove us all wrong, and we'll feel horrible for sending her away."

"I hope she does."

Rourke abandoned them to their stomach-turning couplehood and aimed for the door.

"Avenage."

He turned again.

Archer nodded. "We'll have her ready for the morning train to York."

*   *   *

"I wanted to tell you about the baby, but the time didn't seem right." Elena spoke softly and beneath the hearing of the two Ravens and Archer, who talked quietly among themselves just a short distance away in the small sitting room area of Selene's room.

While the Shadow Guards would be able to overhear the whisperings of mortals, the skill did not apply so invasively to those of their own kind.

Selene stood from the wheelchair and gripped the bedpost, carefully stepping out of her slippers. "You will be a wonderful mother."

"You would be a wonderful mother as well."

The words, though intended as a compliment, stung.

"I don't see that ever being a part of my future. Maternal instincts aren't part of my makeup. It's a familial weakness, I suppose."

"I don't for one moment believe that." Elena lifted the coverlet and the white sheet beneath.

Selene crawled beneath them, robe and all. It offended her dignity that her keepers remained in her room, but the previous hour had exhausted her so greatly she could not summon the energy to challenge the arrangement.

"I'm so tired," she whispered.

"I suspect you'll be easily fatigued for days. You don't just wake up out of such a deep state of sleep without some residual effect."

"Maybe when I wake up," Selene said softly, "my powers will have returned and I'll have been proven innocent."

"Wouldn't that be wonderful?" Elena smiled. "And certainly it could happen."

Elena drew the blanket over her shoulders and sat on the edge of the bed. "So . . . Avenage. What do you think of him?"

Selene grew pensive. Avenage had clearly been displeased—no, *furious*—at the announcement of his new duty as her keeper. He truly believed her capable of murder.

"You have seen his reaction to me. My days at Swarthwick will be torture. A prison."

"He isn't the warmest or most conversant of men."
Elena leaned down and whispered near her ear, "But
then, Archer wasn't either. Not at first. Things changed
over time. Perhaps, given a few days, the Ravenmaster
will not be so terrible a companion as you await the return of your abilities."

Selene hoped what Elena suggested might be true.
Few men had the ability to strike Selene silent. To arrest
her attention. And yet even in the midst of the miserable exchange downstairs, whenever Avenage's green-
eyed glance had shifted over her it was like the ball of
thatch at the center of her chest—the messy, dead thing
her heart had become over the centuries, by necessity, to
protect herself from hurt—stirred into flames.

Some visceral part of her reacted to him in a way she
did not understand. Despite the admittedly overwhelming evidence against her, the idea that he hated her so
thoroughly and believed her capable of such unforgivable crimes left her mired in misery.

"Just think of all the reading you can catch up on."
Elena smiled hopefully. "Look what I brought for you."

From the bedside table, she produced a gleaming
leather-bound book. *Tales of the Amazon.*

"Looks very meaty," Selene responded with a yawn.

She enjoyed books and other publications in the
same way she enjoyed sweets: in moderation. She wasn't
a glutton. It took a fine edition or subject to truly trig-
ger her desire. But then again, in times of anxiety, she
might eat an entire ten-volume collection and feel terribly guilty afterward.

Given her present state of agitation it was strange
that she did not feel at all hungry. But perhaps the first
step to returning to normal would be to return to her
customary habits.

Without lifting her head from the pillow, Selene took
the book in hand. She ran her finger over the smooth
gilt-edged pages and flipped the weighty volume open
against the mattress. With a little sigh, she perused the
table of contents.

"Very interesting."

Tearing a long vertical strip from the first page, she twisted the paper around her finger and placed the curl into her mouth.

Tasteless. Disappointing.

"That's right," encouraged Elena.

Selene nodded in response, and swallowed.

The paper stuck midway down her throat.

She coughed, and pressed up from the mattress. She *choked*.

"Selene?"

When she attempted to respond that she was all right, her throat closed even tighter. Archer strode to the dresser, where he poured a glass of water from a crystal carafe. As Selene gasped for breath, Elena pounded her between the shoulder blades. Archer urged the glass into her hands.

She coughed, and gulped, and the paper went down.

Elena said, "Perhaps you should hold off on eating books for the time being."

"Yes, Doctor," rasped Selene, collapsing to the mattress again.

To her horror, tears welled in her eyes. *Tears*. How her mother had despised tears. Even in the end, when Cleopatra had gone mad with grief over Mark Antony's death, the queen had shed no tears.

To hide her emotion from Elena, Selene turned away, embracing her pillow. She stared at the floating lotus flower on the far bedside table. The petals were the same color as the sky above the Nile at twilight.

"I'd think I'd like to go back to sleep now."

Selene sat alone inside her private first-class railway compartment, staring out the window. The train, though still at the station, vibrated beneath her, ready at any moment to make its departure. Archer and Elena stood on a raised portion of the platform, above a bobbing field of black hat tops.

Though narrow and exceedingly limited in space, her temporary quarters were comfortable enough. The bench she presently sat upon had padded armrests and brocade cushions. Just across from her was a narrow bed. Crisp white linens peeked out from beneath a gold coverlet, patterned with scarlet fleur-de-lis. A washbasin, towels and soap sat atop an upright cylindrical storage chest. There hadn't been time to send for all her things from the Metropole, the hotel where she had resided while hunting the Dark Bride. She traveled with only a valise and the promise that more of her belongings would be delivered to Swarthwick. Elena had warned her that her stamina and healing abilities might remain sluggish and that even traits she had come to take for granted, such as balance, agility and warm-bloodedness, would likely be affected.

Even with Elena's assistance, it had taken all her energy to dress for the journey and walk the distance from her room at Black House to the carriage, and again from the carriage to the train. Archer had lent her the support of his arm until he and Elena could follow no farther. Then Avenage had stepped forward.

Silently he had guided her through the dense crowd on the station platform, deftly protecting her from being unduly jostled, and assisted her up the stairs and along the center aisle into her private compartment. And then he had left her.

She had always loved mysteries, and Avenage was certainly that. Would she learn any of his secrets during her confinement at his estate, or would she depart there days or weeks from now, knowing as little about him as she did now?

He had been nothing less than gentlemanly in his behavior, but his unspoken mistrust scorched her like an invisible flame. Not so long ago, in the few brief hours they'd spent together tracking the Dark Bride, she had possessed his respect. Call her a glutton for any challenge, but she wanted his respect again.

She ought to have been relieved when he left her alone in the compartment, but his departure left her inexplicably agitated. Distracted. To confess the truth, she did not want to be alone. Just that morning she'd received a telegraph from her twin, Mark, who had been informed of her awakening. He offered words of encouragement and promised to return to England soon. While the message had comforted her, it had also ripped open a wound that might never fully heal. When she'd sacrificed herself to save Mark's life that night in the Clock Tower, they'd both been left forever changed. Though they would always be family, bonded by blood, nothing would ever be the same. Her brother's message had been brief, but his carefully chosen words had conveyed a powerful message. Elena had offered gentle confirmation, helping Selene to understand what she had not before: Mark was no longer a member of the Shadow Guard. Her brother had embarked on a new adventure with his wife, Willomina, with the formation of the mortal Atheatos Society.

However, thinking back on the painful past they had shared, and the way they had forged through time together, she grieved his loss. Not to death, but to a different sort of future. To happiness, and a life with Willomina and the children and grandchildren that would follow. She could not be happier for him, and yet, she had never felt more alone.

Too weary to remove her gloves or even her hat, she rested back against the cushions and closed her eyes. . . .

Where was Swarthwick? To the north or the south of London? She had been so thickly escorted she hadn't been able to see any destination signs.

At last, just as she had begun to doze, the train gave a little lurch. Sleepily, Selene straightened and peered through the glass. Elena waved a gloved hand. Selene did the same. Within moments, the only thing she saw outside her window was a blur of gray sky, dark buildings and advertisement murals.

A bizarre image flashed across her mind, that of an empty train where she was the only passenger, ramping up in speed—fantastically so—until the locomotive took flight and hurtled straight off Dover's cliffs into the sea below.

Before she had become a suspect in multiple murders, the dark fantasy would have made her chuckle. After all, if such a thing really occurred, the "old" Selene would have simply kicked out the windows and swum to the surface, woolen skirts, two petticoats and all. But in the present, given the vaccine's numbing effects on her powers, would she even survive?

"I thought you might wish to know more about our destination."

Startled awake, she opened her eyes just in time to observe Rourke materializing into place. Unsmiling, he stood against the far wall.

"My apologies." Holding her gaze, he removed his top hat. "I did not intend to alarm you."

She didn't like being caught unaware. Not by anyone, but especially him.

"You could have knocked," Selene responded, more snappishly than she intended.

His nostrils flared, and the green of his eyes seemed to intensify in their frostiness. He tilted his head toward the door. "We're on a public train and you are an unmarried woman. It would be disconcerting to the other first-class passengers to see three different men going in and out of your cabin."

His cool demeanor and curt way of speaking reminded her that she was no longer his peer, but his prisoner. The superfine wool fabric of his coat could not hide the breadth of his shoulders or the muscled strength of his upper arms. His coat gaped open to reveal the crisp expanse of a white linen shirt and a narrow black necktie. Perfectly tailored trousers emphasized his athleticism and height. The perfect combination of physicality and civilized polish.

That she could be so admiring of a man who held her in such low regard vexed her completely.

"So I shall be subject to intrusions without warning?" she argued—just for the sake of arguing. "What if I had taken my clothes off and gone to bed?"

The light of her small lamp revealed the tight flex of his jaw. "We've barely pulled away from the station. Even so, what if you had disrobed?" he answered. "You're a

Shadow Guard Reclaimer. You don't get to play the 'I'm a woman' card on me just because it's convenient."

She stiffened at his allegation, which was, of course, completely justified. She *had* tried to play the woman card.

Usually, the strategy worked.

"Make yourself comfortable," he advised. "Take your clothes off if it pleases you. We'll be traveling north to York, where we'll disembark and travel the rest of the way to Swarthwick by private carriage."

Selene avoided his intense regard and instead stared sullenly at her valise. She hated being spoken to in such a manner. As if she were an unruly, uncooperative and unwanted complication. Her eyes stung. Tears, stupid tears.

"Are you unwell?" he inquired gruffly.

She rubbed her eyes and lowered her chin, tilting the brim of her hat to obscure his view of her face. "It is just that something in the room irritates my senses. Perfume or smoke from a previous occupant, perhaps."

"I shall leave you to your privacy."

"Please do," she said firmly.

He left in the same manner that he had come.

Selene swore that if she did not return to her normal faculties soon, she would steal her own train and drive it off the cliffs at Dover, just to end her misery.

But Rourke didn't leave Selene's compartment. Unseen . . . in secret . . . he allowed his eyes to take his fill of her. Asleep in the Tower, she had been an intriguing mystery.

Her mother, long dead by the time he was recruited into immortality, was reputed to have been an uncommonly alluring woman, and arresting in appearance—but no great beauty. But Cleopatra's ill-fated love affair with the Roman triumvir Mark Antony had resulted in something spectacular. Awake and animated, Selene was, quite simply put, ravishing.

She wore her hair pulled back at the temples and pinned into shining dark curls at her nape. The style set off the dark-lashed, catlike shape of her eyes and the fine curve of her cheekbones. Like all Amaranthines, immortality had captured her when she was in her most perfect state, at the height of her beauty, and that was how she remained. In appearance, she was a young woman of perhaps twenty-three or twenty-four.

She was no pale English beauty. If he were commissioned to paint her with words . . . Exotic. Lush. Warm. Striking. Vivacious. Those were the sorts of descriptors that sprang into his mind. Not to mention the undercurrent of mischief that always simmered in her eyes and on her lips.

In her heeled leather shoes she was nearly as tall as he. She could never be described as delicate or fragile. And yet she was all elegance and grace—with a daring edge of flamboyance.

At present she sat on the seat opposite him, her cheeks flushed and her eyes bright with tears, something he found morbidly intriguing. Vulnerability had heretofore been a facet of personality he had never observed in her.

Apparently *he* had caused her present state of agitation, although he could think of nothing specific he had done to antagonize her. Perhaps the thought of being under his guard for the coming days was simply too atrocious for her to bear.

Just weeks before, she had sought him out and requested his assistance in ending the Dark Bride's bloody rampage against London. She hadn't explained her motives for seeking him out over one of her fellow Reclaimers, but he, already disgruntled at having been excluded from the ongoing fray, he had been all too eager to comply with her request.

Only . . . he had been aware of Selene's existence long before then.

She just wouldn't know it.

Chapter Five

His first glimpse of Selene came on a battlefield in Cravant, France.

Recruited into his own immortality only a few short centuries before, he had never laid eyes on anything like her.

With her dark hair bound tightly by gold bands and her arms and legs sleek beneath their fitted leather and armor, she had fought and hacked and slashed her way through walls of men to advance her position on the field.

How many warriors had lost their lives that day, distracted for one fatal moment by the same terrible vision of beauty?

In the dense, bloody fray he had soon lost sight of her . . . but he had never forgotten.

Centuries later he had been guarding an English prince in Venice during Carnival. The young noble had wished to see the street festivities for himself, but from behind the protection of a mask.

As they'd meandered through the thick press of revelers, Rourke had spied Selene across a narrow canal, vibrant and laughing in a jeweled gown, in the company of an Italian nobleman. A gilt mask had hidden half of her face, a coy tease that had only enhanced the beauty of her dark eyes and painted red lips.

He had remembered her instantly from Cravant, she his wicked fantasy come to life. As they had passed each other on an arched stone bridge, he had satisfied himself with one illicit touch to her hand.

Her glance had fallen on him sharply. Their eyes had met and he had allowed the full measure of his desire to burn through the eyeholes of his own mask. The crowd had thronged about them, and again, as he believed it was intended to be, he had lost sight of her.

Imagine his shock when a carriage had sidled up beside him on a London street just three weeks ago, and her unforgettable face had appeared in the polished wood frame of the window. She had asked him to join her inside. That moment had been the answer to his prayers—and a nightmare come true.

Fantasies were fantasies. They ought to never cross over into reality, for they would certainly be shattered and destroyed.

At the time, before all the accusations of murder against the countess had come about, Rourke had been certain that the devil had created Selene to tempt him, to torture him and cause him to abandon the eternal vow he had made.

He tensed as Selene leaned forward and scooted to the far end of the bench. The movement filled the small space with her lotus-flower scent. She unpinned her hat, removed her gloves, and laid both on the narrow side table. With a quick swipe of her fingertips across her eyes, she appeared to calm herself. Exhaling, she again rested against the pillows and closed her eyes. Within moments, she had fallen asleep.

Rourke had no such possibilities for escaping, even temporarily, that which troubled him.

Eight hours and an excruciating additional five-hour delay later, due to repairs on a bridge, and Selene feared she truly would go out of her mind. The countryside landscape outside her window had long ago been obscured by darkness.

She had dozed off and on for the entire journey, alternately escaping her troubles through sleep—only to awaken to their reality again. She had tried, unsuccessfully, to prevent her mind from revisiting the murders and her nonexistent powers, desperate to not sink into despair. Though she had brought a few books in her valise, she had had no appetite to read or consume them. The words twisted and rearranged themselves on the page, leaving her nauseous and miserable. Her compartment, which had been more than comfortable at the onset of her journey, had become stuffy and smothering.

She hammered her palm against the window fastening, but the panel refused to open. She had to get out of her tiny room, if only for a short while. The voices and intermittent laughter of the other passengers could be heard through her door.

At the water basin, she washed her face, smoothed her hair, and pinned her hat in place. The mirror on the wall reflected a pensive young woman with shadows of weariness under her eyes. She opened the door.

Shrew and Tres, seated in chairs on either side, immediately set aside their newspapers and stood to block her path.

The passengers in the adjacent compartment watched with rapt interest.

"Can I get something for you, Countess?" inquired Shrew, in all politeness. "A newspaper? Fresh water?"

Tres murmured, "Perhaps a plate of broken glass from the dining car?"

Shrew cast him a sharp look, but the elder brother's hatred washed over her. Apparently this Shadow Guard would give her no benefit of the doubt where the death of his comrade-in-arms was concerned. She did not see Rourke anywhere.

"My window does not open and the compartment has grown stuffy. I would like to go out to the vestibule for a few moments of fresh air."

Tres responded curtly, "Our orders are that you remain in your room."

"I won't be long." Grasping up her skirt, she sidestepped him.

Again, Tres blocked her path, tall and broad of shoulder. His eyes, simmering with heat, issued a challenge.

Selene wasn't accustomed to having her freedoms limited or being told what to do by anyone except the Primordials.

"Please be assured I have no intention of escaping or of wreaking any sort of havoc," she said, unable to keep an edge of sarcasm from her voice.

"Of course you won't," he retorted. "Because you'll remain inside your quarters. My brother and I won't be played for simpletons. You won't distract us with your hair and your silk and your . . ." His gaze dipped to her throat, breasts and waist.

Selene growled like a displeased cat.

Shrew interrupted. "What my brother is trying to say is that your legend precedes you, Countess. You take an almost unnatural pleasure in tracking and Reclaiming the Transcended souls to which you are assigned, and have made an art of precision assassination. Rumor tells that you married the Count Pavlenco and then—"

"Bloody bombazine!" Selene gritted. "I can barely keep my eyes open for more than a quarter hour at a time. What sort of trouble do you expect me to cause?"

She stepped toward Tres, but he straightened and squared his shoulders.

Selene lowered her voice to a hiss. "Accompany me if you wish, but if you do not let me pass I shall scream bloody murder—and believe me, I know precisely what that sounds like—and leave you to answer whatever questions the conductor and other passengers may have."

Without waiting for Tres to grant or deny her passage, she shouldered past him and moved along the center aisle. She smiled pleasantly at her curious fellow passengers.

"My brothers," she said. "How they do, at times, try my patience with their overprotective ways."

At last she came to the end of the car. She reached for the handle. Another hand reached out and grasped it first.

Her unfortunate bookends stood on either side of her.

Tres said, "We'll all go out together, then. I'll go first, and then you. Shrew will come out behind."

The look she leveled on both of the Ravens would have withered weaker men to dust. They stared back at her, two handsome, powerful creatures, clearly determined to remain in control of the situation.

Her eyes narrowed. *"Little boys."*

The door swung outward, as if of its own volition.

"I'm here," said Avenage.

At hearing his voice, Selene felt an inexplicable rush of satisfaction.

Passing through, she found him standing against the corner rail of the platform, his face half illuminated by the light from inside the next railcar. A small red circle burned in the area of his fingertips. Behind his shoulders, jagged forks of lightning tore across the distant sky. The chuff of the train's engine and the roll of the wheels on the tracks drowned out any resultant thunder.

Tres and Shrew peered out through the door.

Rourke said, "You are both relieved to take your evening meal in the dining car. I'll return the countess to her compartment."

The brothers hesitated, and Selene suspected a brief conversation took place in the silent language she could no longer hear.

"As you wish, your lordship," answered Tres, throwing her a parting glare.

At last they pulled the door closed and disappeared into the car.

Moving to stand opposite Rourke, Selene gave him her back and leaned slightly forward and over the rail so that the wind struck her full in the face. The vibration of the gridded metal platform moved up through her shoes, inciting an almost ticklish sensation in her belly. Her hat lifted, and she clasped a hand against the top to keep it from flying away. She inhaled deeply. The air smelled of rain and earth and all things simple.

Railroad ties flashed beneath her feet. The night moved past, a blur of shadows.

Clearer of mind now, she turned to face her silent companion. She leaned back against the rail, her gloved hands encircling the cool metal on either side.

Avenage lifted a slender cigar to his lips, all the while his green eyes—startlingly light, even here in the darkness—perused her from hat to hem. He wore his dark hair cropped short, like a soldier. His features were pleasant enough, but not at all beautiful. He did have a rather perfect nose, not too large and not too small, with an attractive, masculine arch to the bridge. Within the stiff boning of her corset, her chest tightened with awareness, yet suspecting he sought only to intimidate her, she boldly let him look his fill.

After a moment, he exhaled. Gray smoke issued forth from his nose and lips to dissipate on the wind.

"Care for one?" he offered.

From his chest pocket, he withdrew a slender silver case and, with his thumb, flicked open the lid. Leaning forward, he offered the contents to her.

Surprise lightened her mood. "Thank you."

She selected one. She enjoyed a good cigar on occasion.

"It's a nasty habit," he said. "One I've only recently resumed."

Despite his comment about smoking being a nasty habit, all Amaranthines could indulge in mortal vices such as liquor and tobacco and suffer none of the unfortunate results. Their superior bodies rejected all contamination or disease. Except, perhaps, for hers, in its present weakened state. One puff and she would likely die of black lung on the spot. The uncertainty wasn't enough to make her abandon the cigar—or the prospect of sharing the moment with England's intriguing and mysterious Ravenmaster.

He fished in his hip pocket and a moment later cupped his hand around a lit match. Their gazes locked as she inhaled the smoky sweetness in a succession of breaths until the cigar took light. The tension in her shoulders eased, while a different sort of tension settled low in her belly.

They stared at each other in silence. It wasn't often that Selene found herself speechless, without anything to say, but somehow silence with Avenage seemed natural. Electrified, but natural.

Wind, formed by the travel and speed of the train, rushed beneath the covered platform and loosened her chignon. With their travel north and the onset of night, the temperature had grown cooler. Given her new sensitivity to the cold, she was glad for her fitted woolen jacket. At the same time, she welcomed the awakening brace of air against her cheeks.

She broke the quiet at last, believing it best to say her peace without the brothers in close audience. "I want you to know, Lord Avenage, I truly don't have any memory of anything before waking up in Whitechapel with the knife in my hand and an already dead woman at my feet. I have no memory whatsoever of being in the Tower with you and your Ravens."

She fully expected him to shun her with continued silence. But he shifted his stance and met her eyes directly. His gaze, as cool and dangerous as absinthe, seemed to probe her mind. Amaranthines had the ability to do that, to look inside a person's thoughts—but not another immortal's. Given her weakened defenses, she wondered what, if anything, he saw inside hers.

"I believe you," he said.

"But you believe I killed that woman and Flynn." Just speaking the fallen Shadow Guard's name—a man she had never known—sucked the air from her lungs, and her voice faltered.

She closed her eyes and tightened the grip of her gloved hands upon the metal rail.

"I don't know if you killed them," he responded, lifting the cigar again.

"But you despise me still. I can see it in your eyes."

He exhaled from the side of his mouth. "What does it matter what I think?"

"I am still a Shadow Guard, at least for now," she answered. "It is important for me to know I have not been condemned by my peers."

He looked out into the darkness. "I have been given the responsibility of guarding you until the investigation is complete. Until a determination as to your innocence or guilt is made you shall be treated with all the respect due your rank. But don't expect to be trusted, Countess. You know as well as I that Transcension can lie dormant for weeks, even months, before consuming the rational mind of its host. I don't know what you're capable of. You don't either."

"I understand," she whispered, knowing the truth of his words. After a long moment of silence passed, she whispered, "I can't help but wonder how this will all end."

Lightning forked across the sky behind him, illuminating a rolling, empty meadow.

He answered, "If it's proven that you killed Flynn, you won't have to wonder. I will kill you myself."

She nodded. His words cut her deeply, although she would never expect any different response from a Shadow Guard. Indeed, if her guilt were proven or if her mind descended into rapid deterioration, she could expect to be executed by any one of her peers. It was simply the way of things.

"How much longer until we arrive in York?"

"Perhaps another two hours."

She nodded, and with the movement of her head the darkness around her appeared to encircle her completely. To tumble and turn. Her head, arms and chest grew heavy, as if weighted by lead. Unsteady on her feet, she pivoted away from him and grasped the railing for support. Blinking into the wind, she whispered a curse. She despised being so weak, and hated that he saw her this way.

"Countess?"

"I'm all right," she answered, her voice brittle.

"I'll see you back to your cabin."

She nodded but, not trusting the support of her legs, did not release her grip on the railing. There came a sudden heat against her . . . his chest almost, but not quite touching her back, his legs brushing into her skirts. Reaching around, he deftly removed the cigar from between her fingers and, placing it alongside his own, smashed out their glowing ends on the rail before dropping them to the tracks below.

"Come." With his hands beneath her elbows, he pried her away, and led her toward the door.

From beneath her hat brim, she wearily, almost drunkenly considered his profile. He had a tendency to purse his lips, which only enhanced the fullness of his lower lip.

Why had she thought he wasn't beautiful? And why was she always drawn to the brooding, difficult types? How would she ever survive being alone with him for another week or two or twelve?

Her vision hazed and her legs weakened. Despite her best effort to regain her strength, she slumped against his side. He caught her with a firm arm around her waist. Her fingers curled into the superfine wool of his coat. Her nose filled with his scent, that of soap and tobacco. Fortunately, in the time that had passed since she had gone onto the train's outer vestibule, the compartment lights had been turned down by the railcar attendant and most of the passengers had drawn the curtains on their semiprivate compartments and now turned their efforts toward sleep.

"I'm sorry," she whispered.

He did not respond. He merely tightened his hold and conveyed her along the center aisle until they reached her compartment. Leaving the door open, he guided her inside and lowered her to the narrow bed. The pillow against her cheek was cool and smooth and smelled of lavender soap.

When he fumbled for her hat pin and worked to ease the velvet-and-net creation from her hair, she could not help but smile. The gesture—one that could only be intended for her comfort—conflicted with his dispassionate exterior. He set her hat aside. The metallic wince of the springs sounded as he lowered onto the bench across from her.

In the dim half-light and through slitted, heavy eye-lids she perceived only the barest outline of his face. His appearance was that of a young man, of perhaps thirty-two. Only his eyes were old. She wondered, faintly, what it would be like to see him smile.

As her breathing slowed and she drifted toward oblivion, he whispered, "Damn it."

The train idled at the platform. Though it was midmorn-ing, the skies above were gray with thick, unbroken clouds.

"She has not awakened?" Rourke inquired, sidling down the center aisle of the empty car.

Tres glanced through the crack in the door and shook his head. "I'm afraid not."

Rourke pushed inside the narrow space.

Selene lay half reclined on the bed, her head tilted against a round, tufted pillow. At some point in the night she had awakened long enough to remove her fitted jacket. A rosy flush stained her cheeks, and she looked even younger than usual. Desire stabbed through him. He had never seen anything as alluring as the countess last night, when she had stood across from him on the train's exterior platform and lifted one of his cigars to her lips. Thank God for Shrew and Tres. Their company provided a necessary buffer to blunt the temptation.

"Countess." He gripped her shoulders and shook her gently, but firmly. "Wake up."

She did not awaken.

Carrying an unconscious woman from the train, in full view of scores of onlookers, simply wasn't an option. They'd garner too much interest and likely find them-selves questioned by local authorities.

From the door, Tres announced, "The conductor is nearly through with the adjacent car. They'll be board-ing this one next."

"You'll have to cloak me."

Shrew said, "I don't mind carrying her. If you don't want to, that is."

Tres smirked at his brother.

Shrew retorted, "Well, I don't mind. Because I don't think she's guilty."

"Cease your bickering," Rourke growled. "And do as I've instructed."

He bent over her and lifted her into his arms. Her skirts hung over his elbow and a white froth of lace-edged petticoats peeked out from beneath, along with two slender ankles and pointed-toe black boots. Her head lolled against his shoulder and she exhaled.

Shrew and Tres faded from view. Though no longer visible, they remained close, spreading themselves in shadow form about him and the sleeping countess. They absorbed *and* refracted the array of light and color about them, and in doing so, formed a cloak of invisibility.

Rourke carried her to the stairs and onto the wooden platform. The large sign above proclaimed their present location as York. He delved through the thick press of passengers awaiting embarkation, and those who had come to see them off. Because of the brothers' protection, no one could see them, but more than one person along their path twisted and twirled about, perplexed at being brushed aside by nothing but empty air.

Men in top hats and women dressed in demure black waved at welcoming relatives and dragged trunks to waiting wagons. A large town carriage waited at the curb, its size, highly polished dark green paint and matched foursome of geldings setting it apart from the other dusty vehicles waiting there.

"I hope it meets with your liking, sir," said Shrew, as proudly as if the equipage belonged to him.

"Well-done," Rourke responded.

Though the Ravens had a number of vehicles at their disposal in London, Rourke hadn't personally owned one in centuries. There simply hadn't been a need. He had Assassin, and the organization provided for any means of travel beyond that. But the necessity for privacy with regard to the countess had compelled him to dispatch Shrew immediately upon their arrival in York to purchase a carriage and horses for the remaining trip to Swarthwick. Two additional horses were tied to the back.

The stairs gleamed, silver and new. He climbed them and bent, entering through the door sideways, and lowered her to the bench. The smell of leather and . . . something else filled the cabin. Lotus flower, as if Selene had already been there. On the opposite bench sat a small trunk, and atop it, a round, lidded basket.

"What's all this?" he inquired over his shoulder.

"They are for the countess. There's more to be loaded up top. Two trunks. They were delivered just moments ago, though the boy I paid a coin to watch the vehicle didn't get so much as a glimpse of the deliverer." He gestured at the basket. "I checked everything out, and . . . triple warning, sir. I wouldn't look in there if I were you."

"Why not?"

"Because there's an asp in there, that's why."

"An asp? As in a snake?"

"Yes, sir, the deadly kind."

"What for?"

"Apparently the countess keeps them as pets. That one there is supposedly"—Shrew glanced down to the note in his hand—"a Mrs. Hazelgreaves."

"Who sent these things?"

Shrew held up the thick parchment, which bore a heavily scrolled B. The brief note was not signed.

"That's Black House stationery," Rourke concluded. He ensured that the basket's clasp was fastened tight. "Whatever. Let's get started."

Tres stood beside his brother. "The horses have been watered. Shrew and I can take turns driving if you like."

Rourke nodded. "I'll ride with the countess, starting off."

He took his seat across from her, beside the snake basket. Moments later, at the first forward lurch of the carriage, both the basket—and Selene—slid off the polished leather seats. He reacted, reaching for and catching both.

Poised between a half-seated, half-kneeling position,

he felt his heart thundering. Something rustled heavily inside the basket; he felt the movement against his arm through the reeds. But more thrilling was the crush of Selene's high, corseted breasts into his chest. The highly structured nature of the garment could not conceal their splendid shape and size.

Her eyes opened dazedly.

Frowning, she asked thickly, "Where are we?"

"In York," he answered plainly.

She nodded slowly. "I'm feeling much better."

"That's good to kno—"

Her mouth pressed against his.

His every muscle flared to life, but he held himself in position, too stunned, too cursedly curious to move. Still kissing him, Selene tilted her face . . . moaned softly . . . and sucked his bottom lip. Sinking her teeth in lightly . . . she pulled away.

He exhaled a tight, controlled breath.

Through slitted eyelids, she peered at him and chuckled low in her throat. "Don't . . . look . . . so shocked." She stroked his cheek with her fingertips. "It's just a dream."

"It is?"

She nodded and whispered. "I dream about you . . . all the time."

Rourke's lips parted. Her words stunned. He dreamed about her too. Nearly every time he slept.

Her shoulders relaxed and she lowered her head against his shoulder. "I'm just going to sleep . . . a bit longer."

Carefully he lowered the basket to the floor and gently lifted her onto the bench beside him. Like a silky serpent she slid out of his grasp, and *down* until her head rested in his lap.

Bewildered, Rourke stared at her lovely profile and disheveled hair. He felt paralyzed, as if jolted through with electricity, because unfortunately—*unfortunately?*— her temple pressed against the underside of his swiftly growing erection, pinning his length against his upper thigh.

The carriage bumped. The movement jostled her head.

He gripped her shoulder and exhaled harshly. Yet he didn't ease out from underneath her or lift her away. Instead, he closed his eyes and rested his head back, hoping, like the bastard that he was, for a long and bumpy road to Swarthwick.

Chapter Six

A knock on the window beside her head roused Selene from slumber. She opened her eyes to shadows broken by jagged shards of moonlight. She lay on a bench and faced an identical one. She had known she was in a carriage for some time now, aware of the scrabble of the wheels on stone and every little bump of the road. She just hadn't been able to break free from the deep bonds of sleep.

The wheels weren't turning now.

She pushed up from the velvet bag upon which her head had been resting. A man's coat slid from her shoulders. Dazed, she lifted it up and inhaled against its satin lining. Nose-tickling soap and tobacco. The garment belonged to Rourke.

The dream she had just awakened from collided with reality. She was here, with him. For a fleeting moment, the prospect thrilled her. Yet almost instantly, the dream faded, and a different reality took control of her thoughts. The reality in which she was a suspected murderess and an outcast from the Shadow Guard. Fog and darkness pressed against the windows, obscuring any view of the landscape beyond. The sudden appearance of a face startled her—Shrew's, pale and handsome.

He opened the door and leaned inside. "We've arrived, my lady."

"At Swarthwick?"

He nodded. "I'm sorry, but you've got to walk the last bit. Are you able?"

"Yes, I feel very rested, thank you. I'll be out in a moment."

Once he had retreated and closed the door again, Selene quickly ran her fingers through her hair, removing the loosened pins from her tangled curls. Rubbing her hands over her sleep-numbed cheeks, she forced the haze from her mind. Thank God she was immortal and did not have to concern herself with foul breath. On second thought, she cupped her hand over her lips and puffed a breath. Reassured, she drew on her jacket, and fastened the buttons.

It was then that she saw the basket. With a smile, she opened the lid and peered inside.

"Mrs. Hazelgreaves," she breathed. "Elena must have sent you."

A moment later, after returning the snake to her basket, she climbed down the carriage steps. She had expected a walkway and a grand door, flanked on either side by blazing lanterns, but there was only fog and a muddy road lined by black, lichen-covered tree trunks. Heavy branches arched overhead, wet and dripping from a recent rain.

Shrew swung the lantern northward, and there Selene perceived another lantern that appeared to hover, suspended by darkness. She drew Rourke's coat over her shoulders and moved in that direction. Tres held the second lantern.

"He's waiting for you," he instructed tonelessly.

The mist shifted enough to reveal a tall figure ahead. Rourke, more easily seen because of the white shirt he wore. Behind him a stone tower arose out of the mist, as jagged and stark as an ancient crag.

"It's beautiful," she whispered, joining him. She had always admired a good, solid fortification. She shared her mother's affinity for military strategizing and sometimes wished for an army of her own to order about. Did she misread his expression or did she see pride in the firm set of his jaw and the green heat of his eyes?

"We've got to cross by foot," he said. "The bridge is old and I don't trust it to support the weight of the carriage."

In that moment, his face distorted and multiplied into not one, but four Rourkes.

She blinked hard and shook her head.

"Countess?"

Her windpipe seemed to constrict. She cleared her throat. "Please, I want to see more. . . ."

If only her strength would last until they arrived inside the keep, and then she could sit and rest and decide what to do next.

Side by side they walked across. A natural moat of stone and dirt surrounded the structure.

All at once, her mind no longer controlled her feet or her legs. She stumbled, grasping his arm. He lifted her, holding her steady.

"Countess . . . ?"

"I'll be fine." Yet her thoughts dimmed. "Let's just go on. . . ."

"Why are you so pale?"

"I don't even . . . want to tell you," she muttered. The night grew even darker and turned upside down.

"Tell me exactly what you mean by that," he demanded.

He touched her face, as if gauging her temperature.

Vexed by the whole tiresome situation, she swatted him away, but he seized her hand, and by the thundercloud of curses that filled the air she knew he had seen the two puncture marks on her palm.

His face illuminated by moonlight, Rourke glowered down at her.

She managed to say, "This weak female experience . . . is beginning . . . to wear upon me."

Her vision and her mind went black.

Something held her hand motionless. Something *else* pressed against her palm. Something nice. A man's lips. She could tell by the brush of whiskers against her fingertips.

The lips kissed—no, *sucked* her skin.

Pleasure streaked down her arm to culminate at the bottom of her stomach, a sensation that almost numbed the deep sting of Mrs. Hazelgreaves's bite. But had it reversed the flow of poison into her blood?

Did it matter? Pleasure like this might be worth dying for. She sighed.

"Damn it," Avenage muttered.

She had no time to react before he grasped the collar of her blouse and tore the edges apart, baring her neck and the upper edge of her corset. Her eyes flew open, but still, she saw nothing but a maddening blackness. Again—warm skin and the stiff brush of whiskers, but this time pressed against her breasts, over her heart. Fingertips sought the pulse in her throat.

"Countess?" he demanded, his voice a rasp.

She felt his breath on her cheek, so his face had to be right in front of hers. She lifted her hand and found his cheek and his lips.

"Either the poison . . . has blinded me . . ." she croaked through parched lips. "Or we need candles."

A slight whoosh of air signaled that he stood. Eventually, a small hiss preceded a flare of light. Rourke carried a thickly sooted glass lantern close, and set it on a table beside her.

Selene reclined on a sofa, still covered in its dust cloth. Due to the shadows, she could not see much of the room about her, but a vaulted ceiling soared high overhead, and faded tapestries covered the walls. There were a few chairs and tables, all covered by the same linen cloth, and an enormous blacked-out fireplace. The air smelled musty and old and . . . something else. Something gray and furry jumped down from the mantel. A myriad of gold, blinking eyes glimmered from the shadows.

"Are those rats?" Selene asked, squinting.

"No, cats." He scowled, stomping his foot. The nearest of the felines streaked away. "There are at least twelve of them in residence, from what I've counted so far."

She wrinkled her nose. "That accounts for the smell."

"Ah, but at least we know there are none of the afore-mentioned rats or mice." He frowned, seating himself in the closest chair. A puff of dust sprang out into the air. He closed his eyes and his jaw tightened as if he prayed for patience with their present situation. "I did warn the Primordials that the place had not been kept up."

"As you can imagine, I've certainly passed the night in worse. Freezing moors. Steaming mud bogs. Jungles swarming with insects." Selene added softly, "Swarthwick is a paradise compared to such places, so don't concern yourself over my comfort."

His gaze moved over her face, scrutinizing her. "How do you feel?" He spoke the question brusquely, without any inflection that would reveal true concern.

She considered the fang marks on her palm. The puncture wounds stood out quite distinctly from the cut left by the Whitechapel blade, and Elena's neat stitches. The skin around them was still damp and pink where he had sucked the poison. She laughed wryly. "Would it surprise you if I answered that I feel overwhelmingly fatigued?"

"It would surprise me if you said you weren't."

She unfastened the buttons at her cuff and examined her wrist and forearm. "My hand and arm are a bit tender, but there is no paralysis or necrosis of tissue." She lowered both hands to her lap. "Thank you for what you did."

He shrugged.

"I apologize for tearing your ..."—he gestured toward his own neck, but stared hard at hers—"your clothing, but I thought you were dying."

Selene gathered the destroyed remains of her bodice together.

He glanced around the room, avoiding her, it seemed. "Given your weakened state, and your compromised powers, I didn't know how the venom would affect you. All I could think of was how I would explain to your brother that you had died from the bite of an asp."

Selene's heartbeat stumbled. Obliquely he referred

to her mother's death, and how her demise by similar means would bring pain to Mark.

She cleared her throat. "How long did you say it's been since you visited Swarthwick?"

He peered up into the rafters, which were encased in dust and spiderwebs. "Longer than I thought, apparently. I've always employed a caretaker, but after the last one passed on, I neglected to hire another."

Just then, Selene spied a large raven perched on an overhead beam, blinking down at them. Legend told of ravens who resided in the Tower of London. Legend also told that England would fall if anything ever happened to them. Without asking, she knew the bird belonged to Rourke.

Footsteps sounded from the hall. Shrew emerged, carrying an earthenware jug in one hand and a cord of wood in the other. Rourke claimed the jug. Removing the cork, he handed it to Selene. She sniffed and found the contents had no scent.

"It's water," he confirmed.

Lifting the opening to her lips, she drank in long, deep gulps. Finally, when she had taken her fill, she returned the jug to him and collapsed back on the bench. "You need a Leeson."

"A what?" His brows raised in question.

"A Leeson. There's only one Leeson, of course, and he is attaché to Lord Black. He's a personal secretary. He fixes problems like this"—she glanced pointedly around the room—"and with astounding speed." She mumbled beneath her breath, "When he's not tormenting me, that is."

Shrew stacked the wood into the hearth. Over his shoulder, he grinned. "Let's see if we can get that contraption the Primordials provided in working order and ask if we can have our own Leeson. That's what I suggest we do."

"Contraption?" asked Selene. She was always interested in new contraptions, especially those provided by the Primordials.

After throwing Shrew a sharp look, Rourke deftly ignored her question. "I'm afraid we have only ourselves to rely upon, at least for now. In any case, we'll stay here tonight and see what condition the rest of the place is in, in the morning."

"I'll go help Tres secure the horse and carriage," said Shrew, leaving them again.

Selene scanned the room. Though she spied her velvet travel bag, she didn't see her basket anywhere. "Where is Mrs. Hazelgreaves?"

"Who? Oh. The snake. Considering how she sank her fangs into you, I had Tres leave the basket outside."

"Outside?" Selene sat up. His gaze shot to her blouse, which, with her sudden movement, again gaped open. She grasped the edges together, not out of modesty, but because she had the distinct impression her sex, and present weakness, worked against her in this situation. "Please, you must bring her inside. I've spoiled her. She's not at all accustomed to the elements."

He leaned forward in the chair. "I'll retrieve her. But her basket stays closed."

"Of course," she agreed. "Until the cats are gone."

His eyes widened. "Yes, at least until then."

"What are you smiling at?" she demanded. He *had* smiled, his lips taking on the barest tilt of humor.

After a long moment, he said, "At you, I suppose."

Something inside her crumbled. She suspected it was the half-constructed emotional wall she had been desperately attempting to build against him so he couldn't hurt her with his persistently cool stares and distant manner.

She frowned. "And yet you believe me to be a killer, in the same classification as Jack the Ripper and the Dark Bride."

He rubbed his eyes and leaned back in the chair. The movement stretched the linen of his shirt over his shoulders and arms, inadvertently putting the powerful flex of his muscles on display.

"I don't know what to believe," he said softly, his green eyes flickering over her face. "If you didn't kill Flynn or that woman, then who did?"

He seemed to earnestly be asking her thoughts on the matter. She wished she had an answer.

"I don't know. But I've observed a lot of strange events in the last several months. Enough to know that things aren't always what they seem." She blinked, and her scowl deepened. "Did I really just say that? I'm so exhausted I've resorted to clichés."

"Yes, you have." Suddenly, something intense and raw arose in his stare. "So why don't you go to sleep again so we don't have to talk anymore."

The words stung, like a slap in her face. They'd been getting along rather well, and now this.

She closed her mouth and blinked. "Pardon me?"

"I don't want to like you, Selene."

Rourke struggled to keep his gaze on her forehead, rather than on her full lips . . . or the shadowy dart between her breasts. The rigidity of her shoulders relaxed, indicating she understood, at least on some level, what he had just confessed. He prayed that her perception of his thoughts and emotions went no farther than that. He was here now, at Swarthwick. Memories of his past clustered around him like clawing, greedy ghosts, hissing in his ear that he *couldn't*. He *wouldn't*. He'd *promised*. He belonged to them now and forever.

He could never, ever allow himself to feel with any true depth of emotion, or to love again.

"I don't want to like you either," she retorted softly, her eyes reflecting a restrained spark of flirtation. She yanked his coat from her shoulders and tossed it to the floor. "Do you see? I don't even like your damned coat."

They stared at each other. Despite the heightened, frenzied whispers of his ghosts—or perhaps simply his guilt-ridden mind—something stirred in his chest, something hot and searing and achingly painful. God, he had to get away from her. All he could think about was her kiss that afternoon in the carriage, a kiss of which she clearly had no recollection. Her mouth on his and her body in his arms had awakened memories of all-too-real dreams he had exhausted himself trying to end.

He stood. "I'll go get Mrs. Hazelgreaves."

"Thank you." She studied the banner hanging over the mantel, the one displaying his crest, a simple white cross on a verdant green background.

He left her. Outside, a steady rain fell. He allowed the cool water to bathe his face and clear his mind. All he had to do was survive a week with the countess. Perhaps two. There was nothing wrong with showing her a restrained bit of professional respect and regard while her guilt or innocence in the murders was decided, but that was all. Why was he overthinking the whole situation, anyway? She was just a woman, like all the others in the world.

Once he truly set his mind to it, he could make her faceless too.

Whatever he'd built her up in his mind to be had been mere fantasy. As a man, he was certainly entitled to a few of those, was he not?

He spied the snake basket perched on the stone wall where he'd left it. Tres and Shrew would return shortly, after securing the carriage and horses in the forest, across the bridge, and he wouldn't have to be alone with her again. As Ravenmaster, it certainly wasn't his responsibility to entertain her.

When he returned inside the keep with the empty basket and the unfortunate news that Mrs. Hazelgreaves had apparently escaped and gone for a slither, he found Selene already asleep and even snoring softly. She looked vulnerable and young, and although he knew neither instance to be true, he instinctively took up his coat from the floor and returned it to her shoulders.

Only to swipe the garment off again.

He shouldn't be in the habit of offering her that sort of kindness. She was a Shadow Guard, more than accustomed to whatever discomforts an assignment required. If it were Shrew or Tres in the same situation, accused of murder, would he be draping his coat over their shoulders? He snarled inwardly. Of course not.

She sighed and shifted in her sleep.

With a groan, he laid the garment across her again.

To keep himself occupied, he carried in more wood and started a fire. To his relief, nothing wild seemed to be nesting in the chimney. Shrew and Tres soon joined them and made beds on the floor, using their own bags as headrests and a few green wool blankets they'd discovered stowed beneath the carriage bench. Rourke threw himself into a chair and sprawled in as close to a reclining position as possible for the passing of the night.

Still denying himself sleep, he stared into the rafters, remembering what Swarthwick had looked like all those centuries before, gleaming, clean and new. As a mortal man he had had so many hopes and dreams for the future.

They had all died here.

His gaze fell again on Selene. They'd gotten along far too well tonight for his comfort.

He would have to be an ass to her tomorrow.

Selene awoke on the same sofa she had fallen asleep on the night before—only now she wasn't alone. Three felines, all gray-and-orange-striped tabbies, dozed on her hip, stomach and legs.

She shifted position and they sprang off. She shivered in the absence of their warmth.

A fire burned on the stone hearth and early morning light pushed through the shutters. Aside from stiff limbs and an aching neck—bothersome afflictions she hadn't suffered for centuries—she felt more rested than in the days before.

For a while longer, she huddled beneath the warm layers of Rourke's coat and a carriage blanket that had somehow found their way to cover her in the night. She congratulated herself on her rather pleasant exchange with the Ravenmaster the night before, relieved to know that despite everything, it appeared they would all be able to pass the coming days with a certain degree of civility.

Especially Avenage. She did not need to be coddled or comforted. Indeed, despite her misery over her situation, she understood why the Primordials had ordered her into isolation. But for whatever reason, Rourke's opinion mattered to her.

In the night she had dreamed of him again, although, just as before, she couldn't remember any details other than that he had remained frustratingly out of reach. She hadn't minded so much. Even though she knew the dreams were only that—dreams, and productions of her unconscious mind—the simple fact that Dream Rourke had been there had given her comfort, just as his words had last night. She was content enough to know that the Ravenmaster would not condemn her for the recent murders in London outright. Given the enormity of evidence against her, she could not demand more.

At last, with a kick of the blankets, she pressed her still-booted feet to the frigid stone floor and broke free of the warm sofa. At the window, in the wan blue light, she examined her injured hand and saw no evidence of Mrs. Hazelgreaves's bite. She experienced not even a hint of tenderness. More amazing still, with a brush of her fingertips, the thread that formed her stitches fell away, a fact that pleased her enormously.

Closing her eyes, she attempted to force a transformation—to will her body into shadow—but her limbs and her blood experienced not the slightest burn nor shimmer. Although she'd been fully prepared for such a result, the sting of disappointment burned deep inside her chest.

With a little growl she opened her trunk. Inside she found a carefully folded stack of dresses and shawls and undergarments, separated by tissue, and a note from Elena assuring her this would all be over very soon and to please keep her apprised, through Avenage, of any changes in her physical condition or abilities. Just off the great hall she found a small closet with a heavy curtain for a door. Shadowed by one of the braver cats, she shuttled her valise, her garments and one of the jugs of water to the tiny room and shortly thereafter emerged freshly scrubbed, clothed and perfumed. After stowing her things away, folding the blankets and carefully draping Rourke's coat over the back of a chair, she pulled a wool shawl over her shoulders and went in search of breakfast. She couldn't remember the last time she had eaten and was suddenly ravenous—though not for books, of which she still had plenty in her valise, if she ever wished to eat a chapter for breakfast.

She found Tres and Shrew in the kitchen, a cavernous room that appeared a bit newer than the primary structure, and added onto the keep at a later time in history. The brothers stood on either side of a rustic wooden block table, their shirts plastered damply against their muscular frames, and their hair wet and disheveled. At the center of the table was a metal pot. Behind them, a fire burned on the raised brick hearth. At the center of the interior wall, a doorway hung open, revealing shelves lined with a few dusty pots, pieces of earthenware, crocks and bottles. She even perceived a set of crystal glasses.

Shrew sawed at something with—of all things—an Amaranthine short sword, while Tres chopped with his.

"Good morning," she said.

Tres pretended, rather obviously, not to hear her. *Chop*. Shrew glared at his brother before offering a terse smile.

"Good morning," he responded. "We shall have breakfast prepared shortly."

Again, she was starving. So starving she was prepared, even, to assist in cooking, an activity that she detested. "Would you like some assistance? I can't claim any talent in the kitchen, but I am very good at chopping and hacking things."

"Which is why we're all here, isn't it?" Tres muttered.

"I asked for that, didn't I?" Selene responded with a rueful smile. "I suppose it's just that I haven't gotten used to being accused of two murders I'm positive I didn't commit."

Tres scowled. "While I'd be more than happy to relinquish my duties to you, we've been instructed that you're not allowed to handle any weapons until future notice. So just sit down on the stool over there. Or better yet, take up the broom by the door and sweep."

Didn't he realize that with just a few quick alterations, a broom would make a fine weapon? Selene kept her mouth shut on that revelation.

"Less talk, more chop, brother," ordered Shrew.

Tres chuckled caustically. "Easy to say, but not so easy to do."

Another narrow table stood against the wall. Atop it lay an overturned bucket and a jumbled array of wooden spoons in all different lengths and sizes.

Selene asked, "There are no kitchen knives?"

"Not a one, it seems." Shrew chuckled testily. "We are, instead, awash in wooden spoons."

Tres glanced to Selene, his eyes flashing. "Do you know, Countess, that we have discovered that Amaranthine silver, which beheads, disembowels and severs the limbs of the wicked with ease, does not do such an efficient job with—"

He paused to lift from the table a gnarled segment of vegetation, which, though earthy in color, appeared to have been scoured free of dirt.

He demanded of his brother, "What did you say these were called again?"

Shrew lowered his sword. His nostrils flared. "I've told you three times already. They are root vegetables. They are just like a potato or a radish or a carrot, but ... different."

Tres smiled at her again. "We have resorted to vague generalities in identifying the genus and species of that which we intend to consume for breakfast. *Root vegetables*, Countess, harvested from the soil just outside the door behind us. Have you ever cooked with root vegetables?"

Selene replied, "I cannot say that I have."

"Neither have we." He waggled the point of his blade at her. "I think there must be a reason for that."

She crossed to the window and peered out. Rain drizzled down the panes, warping her view of the landscape around the keep. She perceived only green and indistinct rolling hills. Just beyond a simple courtyard there were stables and, she assumed, uninhabited servants' quarters. Coldness seeped into the room through the windows. With a shiver, she moved to stand within the warm, mellow glow of the fire.

"I take it the road to the village is impassable?"

"Indeed, the road has become a bog overnight."

While the Ravens were fully capable of traversing a hopelessly muddy road or a swollen river, either in shadow or in flight, such travel would not be an effective way to transport sacks of potatoes or the like. If the road would endanger the horses or destroy the carriage, then they must make do and stay put.

"What is the name of the village?"

"Thorn-on-the-Moor," answered Shrew.

"More like Tedium-on-the-Moor," Tres grumbled, poking the tip of his sword into a chunk of vegetable. "Did you see the village last night when we passed through? I think two people live there. Two old people who eat nothing but root vegetables."

"It matters not. We've got food here." Shrew sawed. Bits and pieces of vegetable flew into the air. "I've gathered some wild onions that should enliven the flavor quite nicely."

Tres rolled his eyes. "What he has deemed wild onions—"

"Brother."

"—I prefer to call *grass*."

Shrew slammed his blade against the table. "I've had quite enough of your heckling."

Tres wedged his blade into his belt strap. "I've had quite enough of your root vegetables." He stormed toward the door.

"Where are you going?" Shrew strode after him.

"To see what else can be foraged from this godforsaken place to eat," Tres growled. "Perhaps one of those cats."

When he was gone, Selene asked Shrew, "Is it the root vegetables that offend him or is it me?"

He shrugged and offered a reluctant grin. "He has always preferred the city and all its conveniences. As for you, he's actually quite smitten, and determined, under the circumstances, not to let it show."

"Truly?" Selene took up the broom. Who knew if his theory was true, but many men did find her attractive. It would be a lie, after nineteen centuries, to say she didn't realize that. She began to sweep the old straw and other clutter from the floor.

"When your innocence is proven"—he waved the blade—"I guarantee you, suddenly, he'll be Prince Charming."

Exactly the opening she had been waiting for. "Speaking of Prince Charming, where is Avenage this morning?"

"Upstairs, I think. He said something about unlocking another storage room. We may actually all be able to sleep on beds tonight."

A cat sauntered in from the hallway to press against Selene's skirts and meow loudly. "Swarthwick certainly isn't what I expected."

Shrew lifted one shoulder in a shrug. "Avenage rarely takes leave from his duties as Ravenmaster. It's no surprise the place has fallen into neglect."

"He's very mysterious. You all are, for that matter. I can't say I know much about him or the rest of you Ravens. There are so many things I'm curious about."

Shrew gathered up the cubes he had chopped into one great pile. "What do you want to know?"

"Well, for instance, is the legend of the ravens true, that if anything happens to them—the actual birds, I mean—the country of England will fall?"

"Mmm." He lifted a handful and dropped them into the pot. Water plunked and splashed. His gaze grew hooded and the next words he spoke were more subdued than before. "I can't say I know for sure. Fortunately, we haven't had to find out. We've never lost the ravens. Not all of them at once, anyway."

She wondered, but did not ask, whether Flynn's raven had perished that night in the tower.

"How do members of the Order get their wings?"

"Oh." Shrew frowned. "Now, *that's* a secret."

"Says who?"

"Says we." He chuckled. "The Ravens."

"Is there a secret ceremony where you took a vow of silence never to tell, or is there a special Raven book with secret rules?"

He leaned forward, resting his elbows on the table. "That's a secret too."

"Pah!" she muttered. "Secrets!"

"You're a curious one, aren't you? But certainly you have some secrets of your own."

She shrugged. "I suppose I do."

Transporting the pot toward the hearth, he hung it on a hook over the fire. "For example . . . do you know where your mother and Mark Antony are entombed?"

Her mood altered instantly. Darkened. "Some secrets were never meant to be revealed."

"In the same way, it is important that we never share the secrets of the Order of the Ravens."

"Even with your wives?"

He barked out a laugh. "*Wives?* There are no wives."

"So you aren't allowed to marry."

"Marriage isn't forbidden." He shook his head. "There's just never been a question of it—our first devotion is to the Order."

"So you're like monks, wed by choice to your cause."

His lips curved into a wicked smile. "We're not celibates, Countess, if that's what you imply."

"Not even Avenage?" she prodded lightly, doing her best to conceal the true level of her interest.

"Especially Avenage."

"*Especially* Avenage?" Her stomach clenched. "What does *that* mean? He's so fierce. So unapproachable. How would he even meet a woman?"

Did she truly want to hear the answer? Yes, she did.

Shrew shrugged. "For the most part, they seem to find ways to meet him."

Selene's emotions twisted into an unexpected jumble at that response. She propped the broom against the door. "Tell me more."

Chapter Seven

Shrew leaned closer. His uncommon male beauty, like that of a fine-featured elfin warrior, sent a thrill through her. However his presence did not affect her as Rourke's did, not in the least.

"I suppose it's no great secret, not the way things get around amongst Amaranthine society."

He was right. Amaranthines were a gossipy bunch.

Still, he glanced over his shoulder toward the doorway as if to confirm they had no audience. Turning back to her, he crouched over the table and whispered, "He has a woman in London."

"Oh, yes?" Selene smiled . . . although she felt more like kicking the cat.

Morbidly interested, she *had* to hear more. She sidled around the corner of the table, drawing closer to him, and forced a light tone to her voice. "Who is it? Someone he . . . pays?"

"A courtesan?" Shrew chuckled, taking up his sword again, and the "onions." "That depends on whom you ask."

Visions of a thousand different beautiful women played in rapid succession through her mind. Brunette. Blond. Redheaded. Svelte. Buxom.

"What do you mean by that?"

"It's Helen," he whispered. "She'll make him pay, all right. Helen makes every man pay. Dearly."

Shock sucked the air from Selene's lungs. There was only one *Helen*, and that was the immortal temptress who had once been known as Helen of Troy.

Her temper flared. "Oh, please. Not her."

Shortly after the fall of Troy, Helen had cast off the handsome yet feckless Paris. She had moved from powerful man to powerful man ever since.

Shrew shrugged. "She comes to London for the Season."

"The Season is over."

"Not man-hunting season, apparently. And by all accounts, she came hunting for Rourke." He gestured with his sword. "She's been making inquiries about him for decades."

Selene closed her eyes and gritted her teeth.

Shrew looked up from chopping the onions or the grass or whatever it was he intended to add to the root vegetables. "You seem upset."

"Not at all," she snapped. When something jabbed at her temper, the truth always came pouring out. "It's just that Helen's a . . . a . . . stupid hippopotamus and we don't get along well at all."

Not a surprise. Selene didn't get along with most women. But *Helen*.

She fisted her hands. "She's a conceited, self-serving wretch."

"As many immortals are, myself proudly included." Shrew paused halfway between the table and the pot, his hands full of the chopped mystery foliage. His brow furrowed quizzically. "You're certain you're not upset?"

Selene crossed her arms over her breasts and turned to glare out the open window. "Why would I be?"

Because you're infatuated with Rourke.

Because you dream about him every time you sleep.

Because there's something different about him. He makes your heart hurt.

"I'm just surprised, that's all. Perplexed. Their personalities are so different. Whatever would they find to talk about?"

At the fire, he lifted the lid and tossed the stuff in. "I don't think they talk very much, if you understand my meaning. Personality would have very little to do with it."

Selene closed her eyes against the twist of nausea she experienced at imagining Rourke romping in bed with the beautiful, fair Helen—a woman whose doe-eyed, delicate beauty could turn the fiercest of allies into sniping, murderous competitors.

"Say, I almost forgot," said Shrew. "Could you hand me that bag hanging on the door hook?"

Selene retrieved the linen sack. "What's in there?"

"A few mushrooms I found growing on the hillside. I'll just chop these up and add them to the stew."

"No, don't," said a voice behind them.

Rourke stood at the doorway, filling the opening with his broad shoulders. Shrew paled visibly. Had Rourke overheard their whisperings about Helen? Truth be told, she didn't feel guilty at all. Not about the whispering. She had a shamelessly curious nature about all things, a trait that had enabled her to amass a staggering amount of useful knowledge throughout her lifetime.

However, Shrew looked entirely abashed. For a moment, she feared he would blurt out a confession and thereby condemn them both to what would certainly be a reversal of civilities in the keep.

"Why not?" asked Shrew in a hushed voice.

Rourke walked toward the table. His green gaze touched upon her, and her legs weakened.

Was it possible he had grown more handsome in the night? He wore an old, rough-hewn coat, and beneath that a coarse linen shirt open at the throat. His thick-soled boots, already edged in mud, sounded dully against the stone. He stood close beside her, so close his heat touched her skin. He bore the scent of rain and burning wood.

Stupid Helen. She despised Helen, but never more than now.

"They could be poisonous," he said.

Jealousy could also be poisonous. Selene's fingers curled into her palms, and she winced as her nails gouged her palms.

Shrew stared into the bag as if the mushrooms inside were the most fascinating fungi he had ever seen. "We've never worried about that before."

"The serum has weakened the countess's physical defenses. Just as with the asp bite, we don't know how any poison would affect her. I'd rather we not resort to trial and error."

"It's all right," said Selene. "Use them. I'm really not hungry anymore."

"Of course we won't use them," said Shrew, tossing the bag toward the door that led to the courtyard. He pointed at her with the tip of the blade. "And you will have some of my stew. You haven't eaten in two days. I know that for a fact."

"If it pleases you," she answered. "I'll be in the great room, sweeping there."

If it pleases you. Her words echoed in Rourke's mind as he followed Selene to the great hall, where he found her, empty snake basket in hand. From the moment he'd entered the kitchen, he'd felt like an intruder. Shrew had always had a way with women. They were drawn to him like flowers to the sun. Rourke had never felt the slightest jealousy toward the younger Guard before, but something inside him had hardened at finding him and Selene alone together, so clearly at ease with each other.

"Have you seen Mrs. Hazelgreaves?" she asked, her brow furrowed with visible worry. She seemed to avoid his gaze.

"She wasn't in her basket last night."

"Oh, dear." She bit into her lower lip.

"But I've found her. Would you like to see?"

"Yes."

"She's outside, and it's raining, so . . ."

The countess grabbed up her shawl, which she had dropped onto the sofa, and again pulled it around her shoulders. "Take me, please."

He guided her out of the front entrance, which was formed of a deep stone arch. For a long moment they walked in silence, side by side through quiet darkness, before breaking out into the gravel yard. Rain pattered down, dampening the shoulders of his coat. Selene pulled the shawl over her hair. The air had grown chillier since last night.

They continued up an earthen incline that wrapped around the southeastern corner of the keep. There, time had hewn a narrow fissure in the gray stone wall. His raven perched atop the wall, silent and watchful.

Rourke crouched and peered into the darkness. From deep inside, Mrs. Hazelgreaves's flat, triangular head and tiny black-bead eyes peered out at him.

"She has nested in the crevice," he said.

Selene bent, clasping the shawl to her breast. "Indeed she has."

She straightened and met his gaze. "I don't think there's any way to remove her until she decides to come out. Perhaps she's frightened of him." She glanced to the raven, who, as if acknowledging her accusation, spread his wings and let out a low *kraaaak*.

"Perhaps." Rourke studied her face. The rain fell more heavily.

"Swarthwick is a beautiful place. I don't understand why you don't spend more time here. As Shadow Guards, we all work very diligently, but at the same time, we are allowed to partake in life's personal pleasures and holidays."

Rouke rested his hands on his hips and shifted his stance. "Since you like it so much, I'll sell it to you."

"You're jesting," Selene retorted.

"Yes." He smiled, but reservedly. "I have considered selling the place. I find myself staying away longer and longer each time. Perhaps next time I return there will be nothing here but a pile of stones."

"That would be a shame."

He lifted a guiding hand toward the keep. "I'll walk you back."

Inside, he followed her to the great room.

"A few other things arrived with your trunks and Mrs. Hazelgreaves," he told her. "There's a box of books."

The night in the Tower of London, when Lady Black had arrived, she'd brought with her an assortment of books and stated that Selene might be hungry. And just yesterday, Tres had mentioned hearing a rumor that the countess *ate* books. Could that possibly be true?

Selene nodded. Raindrops sparkled on her dark hair like diamonds. "I suppose I'll get some . . . reading in while I'm here."

"I asked Tres to convey them to your room."

"My room?"

He nodded, glancing in the direction of the stone staircase. "Upstairs and to the left. It's nothing like what I'm sure you're accustomed to in London. There were blankets and pillows in the storage room. It's yours while we're here."

"Avenage," echoed a voice from somewhere in the keep.

Rourke nodded to her before striding down the hall. She followed at a distance, curious to see the rest of the place. She walked through three massive, Romanesque stone archways that made her feel like Jonah within the ribs of a Gothic-styled whale. Farther along the way her feet passed over a mosaic floor of ancient vintage—very likely the remnants of Roman ruins upon which the present structure was eventually constructed. The tiles depicted a large tree, with various birds alighted on its branches, including a large raven. Twined about the base of the trunk, peering up at the birds, was a serpent.

She arrived at the oversize doorway of what appeared to be a study. Empty wooden shelves lined the walls, begging to be filled with books. The stone floor lay bare as well, without a single carpet. No fire burned on the hearth.

Near the large window, over which spread a similar pointed arch, Tres sat at a large desk. Before him sat a contraption fashioned of bronze bars, cylinders and wheels.

"So that's the contraption," said Selene.

Both men glanced at her sharply.

"Must I leave?"

Rourke said to her, "You must go if I ask you to."

Tres turned one of the knobs. "I think we're almost there. Your lordship, if you would hand me that roll of paper."

Rourke did so and watched as Tres fastened the paper onto a thin brass bar. With another turn of the same knob the contraption whirred to life and the needles scratched. The roll of paper turned.

Tres's smile lit up the room. "It appears we've successfully received our first message from London."

"Without the necessity of a wire, or cable? Astounding," marveled Shrew, who entered with a tray bearing four steaming earthenware mugs. Selene accepted hers and peeked inside. She had certainly eaten worse. With the spoon, she sampled a small bite and winced. Perhaps not. Maybe it was time to give the books another try.

Shrew lowered a mug before Tres. "If you're not already full of cat."

His brother ignored the jibe and scooped up a mouthful. His face reddened and he coughed. A smile turned Rourke's lips.

When the scratching stopped, Tres ripped off the resultant rectangle of paper and handed the message to Avenage.

"What does it say?" his brother asked.

His eyes skimmed the words. "That Lord and Lady Black visited the Pavilion Yard mortuary in Whitechapel and examined the dead woman's wounds."

Selene tensed. Setting down her stew, she asked again, "Should I leave?"

"No." His gaze held hers. "Though she suffered a number of cuts on her body, Miss McKenzie died from two knife wounds to the throat. However, the size and depth of wounds . . ."

He paused.

"*Yes?*" demanded Selene, frantic to hear the evidence.

"Do not match the butcher's blade you were holding. This woman was killed with a much smaller, abbreviated knife."

"The countess is innocent," exclaimed Shrew, grinning at her, his blue eyes glowing bright. "I knew it."

Rourke frowned. "They stop short of making such a conclusion."

"Hell," muttered Shrew.

"Is that all?" asked Tres, glancing to Selene.

In a quieter voice, Rourke revealed, "The report also states that they scoured the tower room where Flynn was killed."

The brothers' expressions grew more solemn at the speaking of Flynn's name.

"And?"

"And they discovered that the walls, the ceiling and the floor were covered with a thin layer of residue."

"What sort of residue?" whispered Selene, moving closer.

Rourke looked up. "Volcanic sand."

"That's Tantalus's calling card," she exclaimed.

"They discovered faint impressions in the dust."

"Footprints?" Selene clenched her hands together.

He nodded. "Shoe prints, actually. Several sets, in various sizes. You were barefoot and there was not a single barefooted print among them."

Selene held her breath, too afraid to exhale, too afraid to believe.

"So what does all that mean?" queried Tres, his gaze on Selene. "Officially."

Rourke set the paper onto the desk. Selene strode forward and picked it up. The page appeared all but blank to her, other than some faint indentations. Communications from the Inner Realm were visible only to Amaranthine eyes. That she could not read the message stung. Despite her relief at hearing herself absolved of the charges against her, she remained trapped in between, still in possession of her immortality, but with few of the associated powers.

"They aren't certain yet, but they feel it is safe to conclude that the countess did not kill Flynn. Not directly, at least."

Selene understood what he implied. The Dark Bride had never dirtied her own hands with the blood of her victims—she had influenced others to do her killing. Certainly no one believed her capable of the same. Did they?

His voice lowered. "They examined Flynn's body. Every bone was crushed and yet there was not a single outward marking. Whatever happened to him . . . well, Selene didn't do it."

"How terrible," she whispered. Not only the shocking manner of Flynn's death, but that apparently she had been unconscious and unaware in the room where he had been killed and, to whatever extent, under the control of those doing Tantalus's bidding.

And yet what a relief to be cleared of Flynn's murder. She felt light-headed with it. She had known, deep in her soul, that she hadn't killed anyone, and yet the inability to remember anything about that night had worked to create doubt even in her own mind.

"We are to await further instructions."

"Ladies and gentlemen, I suspect we may soon be on our way back to London." Tres rubbed his hands together. He flashed a warmish glance toward Selene.

She left them, marveling over the workings of the contraption. Returning through the three archways, she climbed the stairs. Already a cursed lethargy took over her arms and legs, making each upward step an exhaustive trial. Yet she had remained awake hours longer than ever before since awakening from her deep sleep. That knowledge, along with the announcement of her innocence in the Raven's death, buoyed her spirits and the hopes that soon she would be returned to her normal faculties.

On the narrow stone landing, two doors awaited her, one on the right and one on the left. Rourke had told her the door on the left would be the room belonging to her. Inside, she found a large but simple bed, without headboard or footboard. A plump feather mattress had been loosely made up with linens, as well as a heavy coverlet. Of uncertain vintage, the textile—intricately woven of once-colorful threads—remained in good condition and gave off only the faintest musty scent, having apparently been stored with fragrant herbs. Indeed, the room smelled of lemon oil, basil and thyme. A few simple, yet sturdy pieces of furniture finished the room.

It had been some time since she had lived in such rustic quarters, but the room and its contents pleased her. Shutters covered a large window. Unlatching them, she found no glass panes, as in the rooms below, only an unimpeded view of grounds she hadn't had the opportunity to truly see until now.

Green grass, its color vividly intensified by the storm-dark skies above, rolled down a steep incline to meet the wide, stony banks of a swollen river. There she saw the bridge from the night before, and on the far side, a dense swath of sycamores and ash trees where the horses and carriage would be secured. From behind those trees, a stone ridge rose up from amidst a swath of heather, appearing to wrap around behind the keep.

Selene crossed the hall. The door opposite hers was closed, but she turned the knob and peered inside. Faded green velvet curtains dressed a poster bed. There were no personal items, no bag or shaving items. A window, narrower than hers, had been cut into the far wall. Curious, but at the same time feeling like an uninvited intruder, she crossed the room. Again she unlatched the shutters. As she had suspected, the ridge carried all the way around, culminating in a wide, flat plateau edged by blackthorn shrubs. Jagged white rocks stabbed upward into the sky, like enormous upside-down stalactites. Just beyond lay a narrow strip of gray-blue scored by rolling white—the ocean.

A sturdy breeze chilled her cheeks and carried the complex tang of sea spray, a smell of deterioration and renewal.

"Is your room to your liking?" a voice asked from behind, one she instantly recognized.

Rourke stood in the doorway, stooping slightly to see inside. Her heart jumped at the mere sight of him.

The shadows of the windowless hallway painted hollows along the sides of his mouth and beneath his cheeks.

She nodded. "And this room is yours?"

Solemnly, he nodded and leaned a shoulder against the frame.

She continued, "I wanted to see the view. It's lovely, in a rugged and forbidding way, as all good military fortifications should be."

He didn't come any nearer. Somehow he did not need to. Even across the room, he held her interest and awakened her blood.

He said, "You must be . . . relieved to hear of the evidence supporting your innocence."

Selene closed the shutter and latched the brass hook. Turning back to him, she adjusted her shawl over her shoulders. "I'll be more relieved when I am completely absolved, and there are no more questions about the stability of my mind. I truly believe Lady Black's serum has reversed the claim of Transcension. Now if only my abilities will return to their full strength. I am sure you and your Ravens are eager to return to London and join the efforts there. I am as well."

He nodded, his wolflike green eyes considering her through dark lashes. How he unnerved her with his watchful intensity.

"Well . . . is there anything else I can get for you?" he asked almost gruffly, his dark eyebrows lifting in question.

Selene's cheeks grew warm. Clearly she had misunderstood the intensity of the moment. He wasn't flirting with her, or even attempting to make polite conversation. He simply wanted her out of his room. "Not at all. I'm tired, and think I shall lie down."

He nodded.

She neared the door.

He shifted his stance, but did not draw aside to make way.

Selene hesitated, as passing through the narrow opening would bring her close to him. Too close. Her pulse jumped.

Ridiculous. She was an immortal woman of years and experience, not a frightened, skittish ingenue. So why did she feel like one?

"Good afternoon, then." She sidled past. Her skirts brushed against his legs, hissing softly. A tremor moved through her shoulders and her spine, one inspired by simple nearness to him.

She avoided his eyes and bent her head so that he would not see her burning cheeks. She would move past quickly and—

His hand on her waist stopped her.

She did not look up into his face. Instead she stared down, where his hand spread possessively against the blue silk of her bodice. Her pulse thundered in her ears, and her lips parted on a breath.

Slowly . . . purposefully . . . his hand ascended her side, the flat of his palm sending heat and pressure through her bodice and corset.

Still wary of trusting him, she closed her eyes and tilted her head back until she felt the wooden frame of the door at the back of her head, her hands clasped behind her back above her bustle. . . .

She ought to tell him to stop.

By allowing his touch, she gave him the upper hand and revealed a dangerous weakness that could be used against her.

He touched her face, smoothing his fingertips over her cheek and her jaw.

Instinct overruled her caution. Unable to resist, she turned her cheek into his palm. His thumb dragged over her bottom lip, as if he sought to memorize her features by touch. Desire moved like mercury through her veins, out through her arms and along her spine—a primal sensation that left her light-headed and hot all at once. Her clothes felt heavy, fashioned of stone and utterly ridiculous.

"Selene." The whisper became a growl. His shadow fell over her—

His hand fisted in the lapel of her bodice. He pulled her against him and his mouth pressed onto hers. The hallway appeared to spiral as she pitched onto her toes, kissing him back. She grasped him just above his elbows and savored the steely flex of his arm underneath his loose linen shirt. His legs pressed into her whispering skirts, and they struggled, each trying to get closer.

He crushed her lips, while just as fervently her mouth sought more, demanded more from his. His back struck the far wall, halting their movement, but neither the kiss nor their passionate grappling came to an end. He groaned and, with the pressure of his hand and thumb, widened her mouth. With his tongue he plumbed its depths, filling her lungs and mouth with his urgent breath.

His hands squeezed her waist, skimming over her corseted rib cage to her shoulders, where he dragged his thumbs along the bare skin of her collarbone. His touch tantalized and teased in a way that made her shiver and hold absolutely still all at once.

Don't stop. Please don't stop.

His palms arose with near-crushing strength to frame her face.

Selene pulled him closer until at last her arms seized under his and her hands gripped his muscled shoulders. *Perfect.* She *fit* him, and he her.

But then, with a tilt of his shoulders, he shrugged free, binding her wrists with his hands.

The movement, though not angry, was firm and decided.

The breath rasped from his lips. "I was depending on you . . . to say no."

Green eyes fierce and burning, he turned and descended the stairs, running his hand through his hair. His boots sounded on the stones. A door opened, closed.

She pushed through her room to the window. Rourke strode across the courtyard, dragging his overcoat onto his arms. The long, dark tails whipped on the wind behind him. With definite purpose he took a stone path, one that led in the direction of the cliff she had viewed from his room. Something about the straight line of his shoulders and his arms held at his sides made him look as if he faced an unpleasant but necessary task. Swarthwick was a beautiful place, but she could not shake the feeling that it had once witnessed a terrible tragedy. Soon he had disappeared from view.

She crawled, fully clothed, onto the bed and flopped down onto the coverlet. When he had touched her just now in the hallway her heart had twisted in such a troubling combination of pleasure . . . and pain.

Love hurt, which was why she didn't like it so much. Not that she loved Rourke. Of course she didn't.

Early in her childhood she had learned to starve, sever and cauterize her emotions until her heart no longer felt with any depth of happiness or pain. Born into a royal court where betrayal and assassination were more common than affection or love, she'd been kept alive by mistrust.

The intensity of her feelings, of her need for Rourke, frightened her. Terrified her.

But in the most strange and wonderful way.

Rourke's boots crunched into the mixture of mud, damp earth and stone. He followed the wending trail nearly grown over from decades of disuse.

He had kissed Selene. Here, in this of all places.

He prayed his instincts were not wrong about her. That she was not truly a vicious murderer, slyly seducing her way toward freedom. He had not expected to feel such a soul-deep relief at hearing evidence of her innocence in the prostitute's and Flynn's deaths. He could not help but feel certain she would soon be cleared of all of the accusations against her. It had taken everything within him to hide his satisfaction from Shrew and Tres. In the aftermath, he had allowed his mind to confuse fantasy with reality. The feverish pleasure that had come with touching her—in indulging in the forbidden—still scorched his blood and tangled with sweet visions from his dreams.

Certainly the countess had been thrown into his life's path to ensure his eternal damnation, a punishment he had delayed for centuries by forsaking his mortal blood and becoming England's Ravenmaster. He wasn't ready to go to hell just yet. He wasn't finished punishing himself.

He arrived at the ancient steps cut into the wall of stone. He grasped handfuls of earth and grass and hoisted himself up. The salty air filled his lungs, and memories crowded his mind. The steps crumbled a bit under his weight, but higher and higher he climbed until at last, with the wind tearing at his clothes, he stood on the flat plateau overlooking the ocean.

Waves crashed, and white spray flew. Gulls soared overhead. Dread and nearly a thousand years of regret weighted his chest. Breathing deeply, he clasped his hands at his hips and turned to look out over the vale. Swarthwick's tower rose up from the earth, proud and fierce. Selene was there, a thousand miles away, it seemed, and likely cursing the day he had been appointed her keeper.

Turning his back to the keep, he drew a hand over his perspiration-dappled lip. Just as he had stayed away from Swarthwick for so long, he avoided the distant ledge, the one that overlooked the broad vista of the ocean. Regardless, his rebellious mind threw out memories of the jagged stones below, threaded between with the outgoing tide, and once—long ago, on a cold winter day—with pale blond hair and blood.

A stone marker stood at the center of the plateau, a monument to his sin. He had brought the slab of stone here, struggled with hoisting its weight and size up the endless climb of vertical steps. Time and weather had smoothed the edges of the letters he had carved himself with hammer and chisel.

He looked up into the dense gray clouds. His penance was not done. Would never be done.

He had only to return to this place to remind himself of that.

Chapter Eight

Selene awakened to the sounds of carriage wheels, male voices and hammering.

She gathered a blanket over her shoulders and, walking to the window, unlatched the shutters. The past three days had passed in a monotonous blur of clouds, root stew and books that she had already read a thousand times. She had explored the keep as much as she could, but had found many of the rooms, including the stairway to the tower itself, locked. Her sleep patterns had grown more normal, and it had become her custom to nap once in early afternoon, and then sleep again very solidly through the night. Though she felt stronger, none of her powers had returned despite the hours she had spent attempting to prod them to life.

With the diminishment of the rain the river had receded, apparently enough for the men Avenage had hired from the village to do their work on the bridge. There were at least eight of them, in addition to Shrew and Tres and, yes, Rourke.

Since their kiss he had avoided her, but not unkindly. He still inquired daily as to her health, and shared brief periods of time in her company, but mostly in reticent, withdrawn silence. He spent much of his time in his study, sending orders to the remaining Ravens in London and in other parts of the world and, in turn, receiving their reports. Clearly he had put a stop to whatever feelings he had allowed to develop for her. Either that or their kiss had not affected him in the same powerful way as it had affected her.

She had found it best for her bruised confidence to avoid him in a similar manner, and assured herself that the intensity of feelings she *seemed* to feel for him weren't authentic, but rather a result of isolation and boredom. Surely they would fade as soon as her powers returned, and they all traveled back to London to resume their duties.

She stood over her open trunks, the ones she hadn't yet bothered to fully unpack. There wasn't a thing inside them that could be considered serviceable or provincial. She liked a certain style. Rich, vivid hues, and expensive but tasteful trims and fabrics. Her intentions, when dressing, were never ostentatious—but like her mother, she believed in the importance of appearance. One could never underestimate the power of impression.

Selecting a blue-green gown fashioned of brushed silk, she dressed and took the time to pin up her hair. Lastly, she dug to the bottom of the first trunk and found a familiar leather case. *Thank you, Lady Black*. Opening the latch, she selected a thick gold ring studded all around with sapphires and slipped it onto her finger. Next she chose a pair of gold chandelier earrings she had acquired decades before in India. Stopping there, she closed the lid. Nothing overly bold for Tedious-on-the-Moor.

She avoided the kitchen and another breakfast of Shrew's dreadful root stew, which he proudly kept simmering and replenished at all times. Perhaps with the improvement in weather, they could all travel into the village and purchase additional supplies. At present, a plate of scrambled eggs sounded like nothing less than heaven.

Leaving the keep, she checked on Mrs. Hazelgreaves, who remained snugly nested in her stone crevice. She then crossed the courtyard and descended the drive down the incline to the bridge. She observed the men working for a short bit, but from their continuous smiles and glances—and Rourke's sharp frown—realized she created a distraction. She walked the bridge and, just on the other side, located the horses and carriage beneath a sheltering arch of sycamores. She rubbed the animals' noses and made small horse chitchat.

A wagon rattled past. Curious to see who had arrived, Selene returned to the road.

A small, gray-haired man with a sweeping mustache and wearing a dark suit and hat climbed down from a curricle. A slender woman remained seated on the narrow bench, beneath the shade of a painted Japanese silk umbrella.

As Selene drew closer, she saw the woman was very young, with alabaster skin, a delicate, upturned nose and blue eyes. A gleaming curl of blond hair rested fetchingly on her shoulder. She wore a muted pink skirt and matching fitted jacket fastened with black velvet frogs and finished with a prim collar. A wide straw hat, decorated with only a black ribbon, framed her face and was tied just below her chin in a large bow.

Rourke, Tres and Shrew approached the man, rubbing their dirtied hands on their trousers or on rags from their pockets.

"Lord Avenage?" the man called, striding forward.

Rourke nodded. "Yes, sir."

Rourke's hair, though short as a soldier's, had become slightly disheveled with the strenuous activity and spiked off in different directions, giving him a rugged and altogether appealing look. Daylight streamed through the tree boughs, making his green eyes appear even paler than usual. He did not even look at her, and still, Selene got goose bumps. Their spectacular kiss of days before now seemed to be only a distant fantasy, formed of her own secret desires.

"So very, very pleased to make your acquaintance. I am Edwin Gower, the parish parson."

"How do you do." Rourke nodded.

The parson raised his arm toward the curricle. "And this is Mrs. Thrall, whose brother has leased the Astley estate. Now that we have been blessed with a break in the weather, I have been showing her about the community."

"Mrs. Thrall, pleased to meet you," Rourke said, directing his gaze into the curricle.

Mrs. Thrall's eyes brightened visibly. She appeared transfixed and captivated—all the things Selene experienced when Rourke looked at *her*. "And I you, Lord Avenage."

She spoke in soft, delicate tones. Selene could not help but draw comparisons between Helen and Mrs. Thrall. Both were petite, the same shade of blond and exquisitely lovely. Only Mrs. Thrall seemed to dress more plainly, perhaps in simple consideration of her country surroundings.

Despite Selene's customarily healthy confidence when it came to the opposite sex, both women made her feel like a big, swarthy Amazon girl whose kisses were easily forgotten.

Growl.

Rourke stepped back, raising an introductory hand toward Tres and Shrew. "These are my . . . ah . . . *brothers*."

Tres caught sight of Selene and added, "And this, of course, is our lovely sister, the Countess Pavlenco."

So that was how they would play it! *Amusing.* She was always up for acting a dramatic part.

"Sister." Shrew chuckled as she drew nearer into their midst. Mirth gleamed in his blue eyes. "Dear, *dear* sister."

The parson's gaze moved from one of them to the next, clearly making note of the apparent differences in their appearances. There was Rourke, tall, muscular and bearing regal, Norman features. Then the two brothers, as platinum and lithe as elfin royalty. And then, of course, herself, with her dark, cat-shaped eyes, mahogany hair and Hellenistic features.

Selene supplied with a smile, "We are stepsiblings, of course. Our father, bless his dear soul, outlived three different wives."

"A life of tragedy." The parson nodded, apparently

satisfied with her explanation. "So well-known to the Avenage name."

Selene glanced to Rourke. He, in turn, looked in the direction of the bridge and the men still working there.

"Lady Pavlenco," called Mrs. Thrall, extending a shy but warm smile to Selene. "The parson has enlisted my help in gathering items to be sold at the annual church bazaar next Saturday. If there is anything at Swarthwick that you might wish to donate, we would be exceedingly grateful for your generosity."

Again . . . *growl*.

Still, Selene walked closer, leaving the men to talk among themselves. Though she wasn't one to seek out the company of lady friends, especially society ladies who undertook activities like church bazaars, she chafed under the prior week's seclusion.

She welcomed any distraction. "I am certain I can find a few items. Should I bring them to the church?"

"My brother and I could call upon you in a few days? He's due to arrive today or tomorrow. I'm not certain. We've been abroad for years and are only now returning to England. I traveled ahead to put the house in order."

"The parson mentioned the Astley estate?" Selene crossed her arms over her chest. "I'm sorry, I don't know where that is."

Mrs. Thrall laughed and turned on the bench to point toward the narrow ridge that ran along the river. "Why, it's the property adjacent to yours. Mr. Silverwest—my brother, that is—has always admired the stark beauty of this area and has arranged to lease the place through next December."

Selene shrugged. "I must admit to being shamefully unfamiliar with the area. You see, although Swarthwick has been in my family for ages, I've never visited the property myself until now."

Mrs. Thrall nodded. "I could not help but notice the keep's state of disrepair, but it is a lovely old place. I actually had my brother's barristers inquire as to its ownership just a few weeks ago, to see if it might be available for purchase. I'm certain Mr. Silverwest would be interested. He is an ardent student of history and architecture and would find this property ever so much more interesting than the Astley house."

"Would he?" Selene asked politely, resting a hand on the bench rail. "I did overhear Avenage mention the possibility of selling Swarthwick, but don't know how serious he was."

Now that she had said the words, she wished she hadn't. Swarthwick wasn't hers, but the keep and the land represented Rourke's past, a mystery she had yet to solve. She didn't like the idea of the property changing ownership.

Mrs. Thrall pressed her gloved hand atop Selene's in friendly familiarity. "Ask him, if you will. I shall tell my brother."

Selene glanced over her shoulder and saw Rourke, Tres and Shrew all looking over the parson's head, in her and Mrs. Thrall's direction. Undoubtedly the men were distracted by the blond beauty's presence.

Turning back to the curricle, Selene asked, "Is your husband here, in residence with you?"

Mrs. Thrall shook her head and offered a slight smile. "Sadly, I am a widow. Without much else to do, I busy myself with the administration of my brother's households."

Disappointment feathered through Selene. She had hoped Mrs. Thrall had a strong, dashing husband with whom she was madly in love.

"What of you, Countess?" Mrs. Thrall inquired.

"I share your widowhood."

Mrs. Thrall's blue eyes darkened in sympathy. "I regret to hear that. We are both too young for such tragic beginnings. I do hope you and I can be not only neighbors, but friends."

The parson approached from behind, peering down at a silver watch. "I'm afraid it is time for me to return Mrs. Thrall home." He reached the curricle and grasped the bench handle, but just before hoisting himself up, he turned back to them. "Before I forget, there is one more thing I wanted to ask."

"Yes?" asked Rourke.

"There's a girl from the village, Hannah Grose. She, like her mother and father before her, and her grand-parents before them, is a tinker."

"For a small fee she sharpens scissors and blades that have gone dull, and sells things. Household items and charming local linens." Mrs. Thrall nodded. "I bought a number of lovely wooden spoons from her just last week."

Tres grinned. "Heaven knows we could all use more wooden spoons."

Selene said, "Yes, send her to the keep. Of course we'd be pleased to consider purchasing some of her wares."

"That's just the thing," said the parson. "She told Mrs. Hounslow she was coming to Swarthwick, bad roads or no. Knowing how long the place has been closed up, she felt certain you'd wish to freshen the place up with some new . . . er . . . I don't know—"

"Spoons?" Tres supplied.

"Or soap or blankets." Mrs. Thrall smiled.

The parson climbed up onto the bench and untied the reins. "That was the day before yesterday. No one has seen her since then."

No one else would have felt the ripple of unease that moved through the four Shadow Guards, but Selene did. A missing girl.

The parson tilted his head. "I can tell, however, by your response, that she never made it this far." He chuckled softly. "Certainly we're all making much ado about nothing. She's a vagabond, that girl, and has just as likely gone over to the next village, or perhaps the next, in search of new customers."

Selene backed away from the curricle to join her "brothers" in bidding adieu to their visitors. Yet a feeling of dread had settled into the pit of her stomach. She'd spent the past two months hunting Jack the Ripper and the Dark Bride, both of whom had nasty habits of mak-ing girls go missing. She had also seen the quick glances thrown to her by the other Guards. Guards who were not yet convinced of her innocence.

She assured herself that the parson was right. The girl, who was clearly a known wanderer, would turn up in a day or two, her wagon full of wares lighter, and her purse heavier. The parson expertly turned the small vehicle on the road, and he and Mrs. Thrall waved as they rattled off in the direction from whence they had come.

"Damn, she's lovely," muttered Shrew.

"There is hope for you both in her heart," she teased, though it hurt her to do so. "Mrs. Thrall is a widow."

Until now she hadn't realized just how much she preferred being the only woman in the Ravens' midst. She didn't particularly care for Mrs. Thrall's intrusion, but in all honesty, the woman had been nothing less than earnest in her desire for friendship.

Hours later, Selene stood at the window of the great room sipping a cup of tea. Shrew and Tres drove the horses and carriage across the bridge to the stable. Their work complete, the workmen packed their tools and supplies into their wagons and trundled off down the road. Rourke, however, set off in the same direction as he had every afternoon.

Curiosity ate at her. Where did he go? She felt stronger now, and believed she possessed the stamina for a longer walk.

She took up her shawl and passed Shrew on her way out.

"Where are you going?" he asked.

"To make sure Mrs. Hazelgreaves is still nested in the wall. I don't wish to lose her."

"Don't go far, you," he called from the door. "It's already late in the afternoon, so there's no time to travel into the village for supplies." He grinned. "Thankfully I've plenty of stew prepared for supper."

When she was certain he had gone inside and no longer watched, she grabbed up her skirts and rushed in the direction of the path. Soon enough, she caught sight of Rourke in the distance. Shoulders straight and face forward, he walked with clear purpose. Unfortunately, around the next bend in the path she lost him. Her foot wobbled sideways, and a jolt of pain moved up her leg.

"Bloody—" Foolish high-heeled shoes.

In the past, she had always worn the most stylish of footwear and never suffered such discomfort, even when bounding from rooftop to rooftop in chase of some foul soul. Elena had warned her that in addition to decreased physical stamina, she might not be as dexterous as before.

Yet she was determined to find out where Rourke went each day on his mysterious pilgrimage. She had always suffered from excessive curiosity and a dislike for the unknown. She righted herself and shook the discomfort from her ankle. At this point, the path forked, forcing her to choose either a trail down a narrow incline, toward a ravine below, or a narrower path that would take her higher.

Even when in full possession of her powers, she would have had difficulty tracking another of her own kind. Her skills were in tracking mortals and, more important, dangerously Transcending souls. So in that way, she had only her instincts to follow, and in this case instinct told her to take the higher path. Perhaps she was wrong, but Rourke seemed to be headed toward the plateau she had spied from his window.

As she climbed higher, the wind loosened her hair until at last her earlier handiwork was destroyed and her long tresses snapped and whipped in the wind. With one hooked finger, she pulled a heavy strand from where it dragged across her eyes. Her skirts billowed and crushed against her legs. It was almost as if the wind protested her pursuit, and with physical admonitions, pushing her back, sideways, forward—anywhere but in a straight line to Rourke.

In the past, she'd have stood squarely on two solid feet, unaffected by nature's display of strength, but true to Elena's warning, it was clear the vaccine had left her more frail. More susceptible and more human.

Ahead, the hill grew steeper, and frustratingly her path came to an end against a wall of uneven stone.

At the same moment, she glimpsed Rourke on the path below. Apparently her instincts weren't to be trusted any longer.

The plateau arose high above his head, cut into the side of the hill. From here, one could hear the muted crash of the ocean, and taste its saltiness on the air. She inched out onto the edge, trying to gain a better view. Just ahead of him, there appeared to be steps cut into the stone. A hard shove pushed her between the shoulder blades.

A gust of wind . . . ?

She pitched forward, but circled her arms at her sides. Digging in her heels, she scrambled backward. For a scant moment she regained her bearings, but the ledge dissolved, and the resulting incline proved too steep.

She skidded.

Her skirts pitched, a green froth about her head. She stumbled and rolled.

Her back and shoulders struck earth.

Ouch. Pain.

Half stupefied by the fall, she pushed onto one elbow. Her eyes narrowed on a man's boots crunching toward her.

Her gaze drifted up. She expected to see Rourke's displeased face, but instead she found the unfamiliar expanse of a man's body . . . clothing . . . blond hair . . . and handsome face.

Not Rourke.

"Are you hurt?" The man's tempered smile and gathered brows conveyed both humor at what he had just witnessed, and concern.

Despite her having her brain half knocked from her head, a memory lingered . . . had someone pushed her? Peering upward, she saw nothing but dirt and stone and waving patches of grass.

On the narrow pathway above, there'd been no place where someone could lie in wait. And why would anyone have wanted to hurt her? Of course no one had pushed her. Still, it was as if the skin and muscles at the center of her back recalled the imprint of a hand.

It galled her to have lost her balance so easily, but more so to doubt her mind.

He crouched and, with a hand to her elbow, helped her sit. Behind him a white horse dappled in gray stamped a hoof and foraged in the brush.

"I don't believe I've ever seen anything quite so astounding. A beautiful woman falling from the sky."

But it was he who was beautiful, with an aquiline nose, wide cheekbones and longish, tousled hair—like something out of a Michelangelo painting. When she still did not respond, the smile fell from his lips. "Truly, are you all right?"

"I think so," she murmured, though her every limb felt thoroughly jostled. Really, how did mortals manage to survive even a day?

He was strapping, tall and golden; it was as if she had been discovered by Achilles brought back to life. Achilles, though, had been an arrogant ass, and one who assumed too much. The gentleman crouching over her emanated a genuine likability.

"I suppose I ought to introduce myself. I am Donovan Silverwest. I believe you and I are neighbors. You are the Countess Pavlenco, I would venture to guess?"

Selene nodded. "I am."

"My sister described you in the most flattering of terms, and I see she did not exaggerate." He chuckled deep in his throat, a charming rather than wolfish sound. "Although she did neglect to mention all the leaves you would wear in your hair."

He reached and pulled one free.

Selene smiled and brushed the dirt from her shoulder. She was thankful her gown had not been torn.

He continued, "I felt a bit guilty about crossing over into your property without asking permission first. Call me a trespasser if you will, but I'm not sorry now. What if no one had found you? I'd offer to go for a physician, but I don't believe the village has one. Are you able to stand, do you think?"

"Yes." She nodded, and allowed him to ease her up by the elbow—

She gasped as a searing pain tore up the inside of her foot and ankle, quite in excess of that which she had experienced moments before, after the turn of her shoe. She clenched both hands into his arm.

"Oh, back down." He lowered her again, so that she sat in the puddle of her skirts.

Once more he crouched beside her. "Which one?"

"That one," she whispered, more mortified by her clumsiness and the appearance of fragility than he would ever understand. She pointed to her left ankle.

"May I?" His hands hovered over her leather shoe.

"You may."

Gently he pushed her skirt up so the hem lay just above her ankles, which were covered in green-on-green striped stockings.

"Just look, and compare one to the other. I'm afraid there's already considerable swelling." Glancing up, as if to gauge her continued permission, he untied the glossy green ribbon at the upper arch of her foot and slid—

She bit her lip at the pain.

—the shoe from her foot. Holding it between them, he grinned at the high, narrow heel. "Here is part of the problem. What were you doing wandering about on this terrain in town shoes?"

Her eyebrows went up. "They, and more like them, are all I have."

"They *are* lovely." He smiled, setting the shoe down on the grass beside them. "Lovely and altogether impractical. Just as women's clothing should be."

"I wholeheartedly agree."

He glanced to her stockinged foot. "A very lovely foot too, if I may say."

Bold. But she liked him.

This close he was even more handsome, the sort of handsome that made women lose their minds and make reckless judgments.

"Pardon my interruption," said a voice above them, the words clipped and weighted with dour judgment. Rourke stood at the center of the path, his lips turned into a scowl.

"One of your brothers?" Mr. Silverwest inquired softly. Privately. Just between the two of them.

She nodded. "It is Avenage."

Mr. Silverwest stood. Selene's heartbeat increased in pace just from the experience of watching one exceptional male specimen examine and greet the other.

"Lord Avenage, I am Mr. Silverwest, your new neighbor on the Astley estate. Your sister, I'm afraid, has taken a fall and injured her ankle."

"Is that so?" Rourke asked her, his eyes cool and piercing. His attention dropped to Mr. Silverwest's hand, which still had possession of her shoe. From the look of displeasure on Rourke's handsome face, Silverwest might as well have been holding her garters.

"Yes," she answered.

"Then I suppose I must convey you home." Rourke stepped in her direction, but as he began to kneel Mr. Silverfish halted him with a manly grab of the shoulder. Rourke froze and glanced aside, his lips drawing into a flat, thin line.

"No need to carry her when I've a horse right here." To Selene, he asked, "You ride, Countess, do you not?"

"I do." His mount was fine boned and lovely. She knew horses, and this one was obviously expensive. The horse did not make the gentleman, but when the gentleman was already quite impressive, such exceptional horseflesh certainly enhanced.

A warm smile lit his handsome face. "And so we have the perfect solution."

At a cluck of Mr. Silverwest's tongue, the horse raised its head and its ears stood straight. The animal even took a few steps closer.

"I'll just . . ." Mr. Silverwest strode toward Selene, as if he intended to lift her up. His beast followed.

"*I* will put her in the saddle," Rourke gritted testily, brushing past Mr. Silverwest to lift Selene from the ground.

For a moment, as Rourke held her in his arms, pressed firmly against his chest, they peered at each other, nose-to-nose. A dark surge of pleasure rushed through her.

His scowl deepened. Her smile widened. Mr. Silver-west's attentions. Rourke's foul mood. Something about the whole exchange made her giddy.

"What were you doing here?" Rourke muttered be-side her ear.

His breath tickled her ear. The deep timbre of his voice thrilled, making her forget the pain in her ankle and leg.

With as much indifference as she could muster, she said, "Shrew asked me to tell you that supper was ready."

Chapter Nine

Once she was in the saddle, Mr. Silverwest led the horse by the reins and Rourke followed. It did not take long until the wending path returned them to Swarthwick. To her surprise, Shrew and Tres descended the steps and met them in the courtyard.

"We were just about to start searching," said Shrew, striding past Silverwest without a glance.

However, Tres's eyes narrowed on their neighbor.

The brothers followed them to the front steps, where terse introductions were made.

Rourke reached for her waist and pulled her sideways against him. Her petticoats and skirts formed a luxurious froth over his arms. Turning toward the house, he climbed the first few steps.

"Wait . . . *brother*," said Selene. "It is only polite that I offer Mr. Silverwest my thanks."

Rourke froze midstep and exhaled through his nose. Nostrils flaring, he turned back, returning her to closer proximity to Silverwest.

"Thank you, Mr. Silverwest. Would you like to come inside, perhaps for some tea?"

Shrew's and Tres's faces snapped toward her. Rourke's arms tightened on her.

"Another time, perhaps." He winked at her. Mischief glinted in his eyes.

"Yes. Another time," agreed Selene. "Good-bye, then."

The two brothers followed as Rourke carried her inside, where he practically tossed her to the sofa.

"My shoe," she exclaimed. She would not mind its loss so much, but she had bought them from her favorite cobbler in France, and they were the precise shade of green leather to complement her gown.

"Where is it?" demanded Tres.

To Rourke, who prodded the fire with the poker, she asked, "Avenage, might you have retrieved it?"

"I did not," he answered without turning.

She said, "Mr. Silverwest must have it."

Shrew raced out the door. Through the window she observed him running across the front courtyard and shouting to Silverwest, who cantered toward the bridge on his horse. At the same moment, another rider appeared, this one riding over the bridge and toward the keep. He wore the simple clothes of a country man, and a wide straw hat. Reining his animal to a halt, Mr. Silverwest waited for Shrew and the other rider. There was conversation and the nodding of heads. After patting his coat pockets, Silverwest produced her shoe. With a tip of his hat, he rode toward the bridge with the stranger.

Moments later, having returned inside, the Raven handed it to Selene, glowering.

"What's wrong, Shrew?" asked Selene.

"It's that girl, Hannah. The tinker. They found her wagon downstream, upside down and in the river."

Selene lowered her shoe to her lap. "What about Hannah?"

He shook his head. "No sign of her or her horse."

The discordant moans, formed of a host of voices, grew louder until they transformed into a thin, unified scream. Selene shuddered. The tiny hairs along the back of her neck stood on end.

"In all my life, I don't believe I've ever heard wind like that before," she murmured low in her throat. "It's almost disturbing."

Reclined on the sofa, with her bruised and swollen ankle bandaged and propped on a large, square cushion, she stared out the stone-framed window. Intermittent flashes illuminated a roiling purple sky and the distant crags. She shuddered again.

She didn't like to think of the girl, Hannah, out there alone, alive or dead.

"You're cold."

"I suppose I am."

Rourke rose from his place beside the fire, a leonine tower of leather knee boots, trousers and white linen shirt. In one elegant movement he claimed the folded blanket from the high back of his chair. The fire blazed behind him. Other than the sharp angle of his jaw, his face was blacked out by shadow.

She welcomed the weighty drape of wool around her chilled shoulders—and the pleasant wave of spicy male scent that accompanied his movement. Inside its slipper, the toes of her unsprained foot curled with girlish pleasure, a reaction she had not experienced in ages. The only thing better than a blanket would be if he sat beside her. She already knew from their embrace of a week before that his lean warrior's body would be hard all over and deliciously warm. The perfect cure for a bone-deep chill and an unsteady heart.

He backed away as quickly as he had come. His green gaze flickered over her, bringing to mind the eyes of an enormous wolf she had once observed skirting along the edges of a desert encampment. Eyes that had conveyed both interest and feral mistrust. The last she had seen Shrew and Tres, they'd been playing cards and telling lies in the kitchen.

"More whiskey?" Rourke lifted the dust-hazed bottle from the table.

Anything to draw him close again. "Yes, please."

A moment later, still woefully alone on the sofa, she swirled the amber liquid in her cut-crystal glass. The wind groaned and the windows rattled. She drank the whiskey in a single gulp. The alcohol burned her throat, and she gave a small cough.

"I suppose this will go on all night?"

She meant the wind, but also the tense air of discomfort between two people who had shared a passionate kiss days before and now avoided the subject completely.

A wary grin turned Rourke's lips. "The villagers used to tell stories of those driven mad by the sound of it."

In the firelight he appeared as nothing more than a normal mortal man. A very handsome mortal man, but a man no less. So different from the black-winged warrior with brimstone eyes who had captured her so easily that night in Whitechapel, two weeks before.

Selene circled her palms around her empty glass. "What did the parson refer to this afternoon when he made mention of the unhappy history of the Avenage name?"

The smile slipped from his lips. "We all have tragedies in our past, do we not?"

She eased herself deeper into the cushions. "Of course we do. It's not fair, though, that mine fill the history books, while yours remain shrouded in mystery."

The dark line of his brow rose. "If you're that curious, I'm sure you could ask around in the village. I'm certain the passage of time has added all sorts of interesting details."

She shrugged and set the glass onto a circular side table. "I'd rather hear your history from you."

Shadows painted the hollows beneath his cheekbones and the taut flex of his jaw. "There is not so much to tell to someone like you, who has seen centuries come and go."

"Tell me."

He shrugged. "I was an orphan, raised in the house of an uncle. I served him and learned to fight. Eventually, I came to England with William."

"As a mortal, then?"

"Yes."

"Then you must have fought at Hastings."

"I did." He stared down into his glass. "And afterward, William awarded me Swarthwick."

"So when, exactly, did you become immortal and a Raven?"

He stared into the fire. "Let's talk about something else, shall we?"

"All right." She pulled the blanket tighter around her shoulders. "Let's talk about that place. The place where—"

"Where you followed me," he interjected sharply.

"To tell you that supper was ready."

He leaned forward in the chair. A fierce stiffening rippled through his shoulders. Even his neck and face.

Selene prodded softly, "The stone plateau. Tell me about it."

Curse the shadows—shadows that used to hide nothing from her Amaranthine vision. They obscured his expression. But just as telling was the way he sat taller, more imperiously in his thronelike chair, leveling his shoulders against the seat back. "There are no stories or legends to be told. It's just a dangerous place."

"But—"

"Don't go there again, Countess."

She bristled at his tone. It riled her to be told what she could and could not do. If only her strength and powers would return, she would remind him she could stand side by side with him in any battle, and slay as many opponents as he. Ah, but she had no powers. She had nothing but a sprained ankle, a bruised ego and no hope of ever being allowed inside his high protective walls again.

"I think I'd like to retire," she whispered.

"Very well." He stood, looking both tense and relieved. "I bid you good night."

Silence hovered between them as he, she supposed, waited for her to stand. At last, he glanced to her ankle on the cushion.

"Oh, yes," he muttered. "I see."

"You don't have to carry me up. If you'll just get me a blanket, I'll sleep here tonight."

"Don't be ridiculous."

With strong arms he lifted her off the sofa. Selene bit her lip at the sharp stab of pain through her ankle.

"I'm sorry." He shifted her in his arms, gently canting her toward him.

"Don't be," she murmured, staring at his ear, which was encircled by a mahogany swath of his hair. He had small ears. But not too small. Delicious ears. Perfect for kissing.

By necessity, she looped her arms around his neck. Her corseted breasts crushed against the solid plane of his chest. The feel of him ... the scent of him ... sent her thoughts into what had become a familiar, light-headed blur.

He conveyed her from the room and down a narrow hallway lit by flickering caged lanterns on either side. She was no delicate flower. She stood taller than most mortal men, and yet she—who had never wanted nor needed a protector—felt safe and softly feminine in his arms. The muscles of his neck and shoulders flexed under her palms as he proceeded in the same manner up the stone stairs. All too quickly, he had twisted the handle of her door and pushed inside. Neither his touch nor his glance lingered as he deposited her onto the bed.

"I'll tinder a fire."

"Thank you."

He knelt at the hearth. It seemed only a moment later that flames leapt above the brass firedogs and he repeated his good night. With a curt tip of his head, he moved toward the door. Realizing her predicament, she called out after him.

"Avenage."

"Yes?" He turned, one dark brow lifting higher than the other.

"I'm afraid I require further assistance." She touched the buttons at the back of her neck. They ran all the way down her spine.

His gaze swept over her bodice and skirts. Perhaps the dimness of the light played tricks on her mind, but a flush appeared to ruddy his cheeks.

She offered a woeful smile. "I might as well be wearing a suit of armor. If I can't bear weight on both feet while I try to remove it all, I'll surely topple over."

He swallowed visibly. "All right."

Selene almost laughed aloud. Avenage was so handsome . . . so powerful and desirable. After hearing of his relationship with Helen, she rather suspected he had vast experience with women. And yet he stared at her and her garments as if they were on fire. In that moment, he became even more attractive in her eyes, although she felt rather certain after the last few days that the infatuation was one-sided. Regardless, she did need help getting out of her blasted garments.

"There's no need for either of us to feel awkward," she assured him. "We're peers, both Shadow Guards. You wouldn't hesitate to offer the same assistance to one of your fellow Ravens, would you?"

"Of course not," he answered, his response registering somewhere between a growl and a hiss.

"So why should it be unsettling for you to assist me?"

She wished he was unsettled because of the kiss they'd shared. She hoped its memory burned as brightly in his mind as it did in hers. She suspected all he felt was regret that he had dallied with her, for even a moment, and couldn't wait to return to London and Helen.

"It isn't unsettling," he retorted tightly. He stared at the space just above her head.

"Then help me."

"Tomorrow I will have hired a woman from the village to assist you."

"But tonight, Avenage—"

"Yes, of course." His lips compressed into a thin line.

Selene shifted, giving him her back, careful not to jar her leg. "If you can undo the buttons, to start with. I believe that once everything is unfastened, I can manage on my own."

His boots sounded quietly on the carpet. She tilted her head and waited.

A low, rough sound issued from his throat.

"What is it?" she inquired.

"Your hair."

The rich timbre of his voice reverberated through the room. Through *her*. She reached behind her neck and twisted the length of her hair so that the weighty mass draped over one shoulder and down between her breasts.

He plucked at the first few buttons. To Selene's surprise, she heard him chuckle. The sound inspired a shocking wave of pleasure that rolled from the top of her head down through her toes. An effect of her quickly downed whiskey, no doubt.

"They're so damn small," he said.

He worked his way from her neck, down her spine, to her lower back. Bit by bit, the heavy wool sagged open and cool air touched the bare skin of her neck and shoulders. A gentle tug came as he untied her overskirt.

"And this?" he murmured, touching her corset fastenings lightly.

"If you please." Selene closed her eyes and bit into her lower lip.

He moved even closer. She knew that to be true by the sound of his trousers brushing against the counterpane . . . but more so from the sensation of his heat against her back. Tiny pricks of awareness rose upon her skin. She resisted the urge to rub them away. Instead, her breath hovered in her throat, captured there by an anticipation so strong she feared she might actually scream at the first brush of his fingertips against her skin. His fingers dragged, ever so softly, across the center of her back.

"Are you in pain?" he asked.

"Why would you ask?" she whispered.

"You gasped."

"Don't be silly," she retorted. "I'm not a gasping sort of woman."

"Are you?"

"Am I what?"

"In *pain*."

"I . . . well . . ."

His hands slid into her gaping bodice to firmly press purposefully against her corseted torso. Even through the stiff layer of silk and boning, she felt the imprint of his hand like a searing brand.

Selene clasped her eyes shut, and braced her palms against the mattress. "Perhaps a little pain."

It was *true*. Being this close to him ... having his hands on her was pure, wicked torture. No ... pleasure.

Pleasure-torture.

He said, "Perhaps in the fall you broke a rib, and due to the tight stricture of your undergarments you simply did not realize ..."

Cursed, passion-inspiring hands. They skimmed over her rib cage, just beneath her breasts.

She inhaled sharply.

"That, my lady, was a *gasp*."

"It's not my rib."

"Then what is it?" he demanded gruffly.

She gripped his splayed, long-fingered hands with both of hers, halting their movement, and stared down at the swirling pattern on the counterpane.

"If I must explain that to you, my dear Lord Avenage, then you have kept to your raven's perch inside the Tower of London for far too long."

He pulled his hands away. She closed her eyes, disappointed that he had.

"Whatever the case, I'm certain my reaction is not at all what you intended. It's clear you regret our kiss and that it's made things awkward between us, so consider it forgotten. Erased from memory as if it never occurred. I see no reason why we can't move on and continue to be pleasant to each other."

Silence.

"These past few days have been pleasant, haven't they?"

He still didn't answer, but she knew he remained immediately behind her. She felt his nearness all along her back, although they no longer touched.

Suddenly, one hand pressed into her shoulder, and another pulled on her hip. He flipped her onto her back, flat on the mattress. She gasped at the wince of pain that jounced through her ankle, but forgot her blasted injury as he crouched over her so that they stared into each other's eyes, nose-to-nose.

"I can't be pleasant to you. Pleasant always leads us to this."

She couldn't tell if the heat in his eyes was lust or hatred—or perhaps both.

"What is so wrong with *this*?" she whispered.

"Everything."

He pushed away and backed toward the door.

"What does that mean?" she called after him.

"Bloody hell, it means go to sleep."

Hours later, Rourke lay on his bed, staring up at the rafters. Outside the wind continued to rampage and moan, setting everything in the castle to creaking and rattling. He glanced in the direction of Selene's chamber. The upstairs floor at one time had been one large, open room. Smaller, more private sleeping quarters were a relatively recent idea in history. He had added the dividing wall a century before—the last time he had considered selling the estate. One section did not rise all the way to the ceiling, leaving instead an open space at the rafters. An open space through which he swore he could smell the scent of lotus flowers.

Weariness left him irritable. How the hell much longer would he have to stay here and suffer this? If only she weren't so close, he could forget her.

Not that he had been able to forget her before. After that first time he had glimpsed her on the battlefield, she had always been the woman of his waking fantasies. The one whose face he had imagined when he made love to others.

But his *dreams* ... his dreams had always been claimed by a Saxon beauty with blond hair—the jealous, possessive ghost of his past. The one who still demanded his complete and unwavering fidelity.

When they'd brought Selene into the Tower of London, his dreams had become confused. The long, luxurious hair that had swirled about him in his dreams, filling his hands and teasing his skin, had gone from pale to mink brown.

Too weary to fight the delicious lure of sleep any longer, he dozed. At some point, though, he grew aware of intermittent flashes of light. A ripple of thunder followed.

In the quiet afterward, he heard a sound.

He honed in on the thrashing of sheets and the intake of sharp, labored breaths.

Fully aware now, he pushed up onto his elbow.

Selene screamed.

Rage and the instinct to protect her blurred his thoughts. He leapt from the bed and crossed the hall to throw open her door.

In the center of the bed, Selene huddled with her arms wrapped around her knees. Her luminous skin gleamed, a vivid foil to her black night rail. Her face was stark and her eyes wide.

The window hung open, the shutters rattling against the stone wall.

He smelled no blood. Sensed no intruder.

At seeing him she screamed again, and scrambled back over the mattress. He realized then that he had *transformed*. Not into shadow, but into the warrior he became when prepared to kill, his skin glowing, radiant with Amaranthine power, and his physical size increased so that his neck and shoulders were powerful and bull-like and his arms and legs corded with muscle. A searing, white-hot pain rippled through his shoulder blades, but with a groan he tamped down the instinct to unfurl his wings. To her vaccine-weakened eyes, the room would be dark and she would see only his glowing eyes and hulking stature—something that under normal circumstances would never frighten her.

So what had happened here?

His eyes returned to normal, and he strode forward to seize her shoulders. "Selene, it's me."

She tried to twist away. She struck his jaw. Kicked his thigh.

"Stop. Selene. Stop *screaming*. It's Rourke."

She froze. "Rourke?"

Her fingertips spidered over his face.

"Rourke!"

She sprang off the bed into his arms, entangling him in her hair, arms and legs. Her night rail rode up her thighs, exposing her smooth, golden skin. For a brief moment, he embraced her in a fierce rush of desire and concern, and then he lowered her to the bed. Yet still she refused to release him.

"What is it? What has happened?" he demanded.

"I don't know," she whispered, glancing down at the linens. "I think there was something here in my bed with me."

"Something? What kind of something?"

She closed her eyes. "Oh . . . it was disgusting, Rourke. Like a big . . . *worm*." Tremors racked her body. "White and cold and slimy. I can still smell it, *ugh*, like death. Worse than death." She pressed a hand to her nose and her mouth, as if she would be ill. "Don't you smell it too?"

He didn't. He just smelled her, and she smelled so damn good he wanted to press her down onto the mattress and drag his face and mouth along her neck and breasts and—

"Selene . . ." He pried her off him long enough to search her skin and the sheets for anything out of place, but saw nothing. No bruises. No slime. "I don't see anything, but I'm going to light the lamp so we can look together."

"Yes." She nodded, her face appearing small and almost delicate amid the mass of her disheveled hair.

He found the matchbox and lit the lamp. He again searched the sheets and, without touching her, examined her skin. Nothing.

Though she reached for him, he strode to the open window. She leapt off the bed and hissed, *"Ouch,"* as she apparently landed her full weight on her ankle, then collided against his back. He clenched his teeth and prayed for mercy. Her breasts, covered only in black silk, felt like lush, ripe heaven against his naked back.

"Was the window unlatched when you went to sleep?"

"I don't know," she whispered beside his ear. "I've never worried about such a thing before." Her fingertips traced the outline of his tattoo, the dark ink wings that spread out across his back and shoulders. His skin burned pleasurably where she touched him, and he shivered. Suddenly, she pointed into the darkness. "What's that light?"

He had seen it too. "Something is on fire in the village."

At that very moment a visible wall of rain moved across the valley, enveloping the keep. Heavy drops splattered against the window frame. A frigid chill accompanied the deluge. The orange light in the village flickered out.

He closed the shutters and latched the hook. Even then, the wind sighed heavily against the wood, rattling it in the frame. She released him, limped to the bed, and crawled to kneel at the center of the mattress clearly oblivious to the picture of sensuality she presented. Rourke's breath caught in his throat, and he forced his feet to remain fixed where they were. But his eyes rebelled and looked their fill.

"I don't understand," she whispered ruefully. "How could I have imagined everything? That smell."

One strap slipped off her shoulder. The bodice cradled her breasts, displaying their ripe shape and uptilted nipples awakened by the chill. Slits at either side revealed her long, lithe legs.

"You must have had a nightmare," he said.

Chapter Ten

"I *must* have." She nodded her head vehemently.

"You've had a very distressing few weeks."

"In the extreme." Her fingers curled into the sheets.

"Certainly your subconscious mind is simply reacting to the strain."

"I see no other explanation."

"Then that's settled. I'll just leave you...." He drifted toward the door.

"No, don't." She crawled, on all fours, to the edge of the bed.

His head buzzed at the sight, at her bright eyes, long hair and jutting breasts. She reached, grasping his wrists, and pulled him with her back onto the sheets, something he had, *yes*, imagined in his illicit fantasies of her.

She whispered, "Please just lie here, on that side of the bed. I'm so tired, but I won't be able to sleep unless I know you're here with me."

"Sleep," he repeated. "In the bed with you?"

"I know it's awkward after that silly kiss. But I won't touch you. I *promise*. I'll even write a letter of apology to Helen—"

He flinched at hearing Helen's name. What did she know of Helen?

"—whatever you want, but please don't leave me."

Her eyes were wide and pleading. He knew his were

dark and burning, and he prayed she didn't look at his crotch. He allowed her to shove him down by his shoulders. "You can even have the good pillow."

The moment they were both horizontal, she plastered herself against him and nuzzled her face to his neck.

"What in the hell are you doing?" he uttered hoarsely through clenched teeth, forcing his arms to remain at his sides.

"I'm sorry. I'm so sorry," she whispered fervently, moving her lips against his skin. "I just need to smell something else, so I can forget."

Abruptly, she twisted away, pressing her back against his chest. Grasping his wrist, she brought his arm around her. "Thank you, Avenage. This goes above and beyond the call of duty. Once I am declared free of any susceptibility to madness and we are called to return to London, I shall submit a request for your commendation."

"That's not necessary," he rasped into her hair.

Hours later, the pale light of early morning filtering through the shutters jolted Rourke awake. Selene lay half across him, her arms draped loosely around his neck and her thigh hooked high across his hips.

Once he had fallen asleep, he had slept like the dead and dreamed even harder.

His dream had been so vivid that for a moment he wondered if they'd actually made love. It would be so easy to stay in her bed, to let the attraction between them run its course. Easy now, but hell to pay later. Literally, on the "hell" part. Not because he thought she was evil. Quite the opposite. His emotions awakened for her. His heart came back to life. He couldn't allow himself to feel for a woman in such a manner.

Carefully, he removed himself from beneath her. She sighed, twisted and embraced her pillow. He stood, relieved to find his trousers still firmly tied at his waist—and an erection the size of Big Ben tenting the flannel. Fortunately he still had a chance to put a stop to this before things went too far. If there were any more nightmares or sprained ankles or dreamy kisses, it would be Shrew or Tres who dealt with them.

Glancing at her once more, he let himself out of her room. Across the hall, behind his locked door, he eased his erection, cursing Selene with every terse stroke. Afterward, he washed at the basin and shaved before dressing. Downstairs, he found Tres and Shrew in his study, bent over the contraption. The wheels turned and rattled.

"Is there a message?"

All at once he realized this could be it. Perhaps they would all be returning to London posthaste, and there would be no more torturous nights spent in the countess's company.

"It's coming through now." He nodded. "There's coffee."

At the sideboard, Rourke poured a mug full. Lifting the cup to his lips, he sipped, but tasted nothing.

"That was some storm that moved through last night," said Tres. "I awoke a number of times certain I heard a woman screaming, only to realize it was the wind."

Shrew replied, "Yes, but thankfully more wind than rain, so we should be able to travel into the village today, as we had planned." He chuckled to himself. "Even I grow weary of my root stew."

When the contraption had grown silent, Shrew ripped the sheet off and handed the message to his Ravenmaster.

Rourke read the contents, his mind spinning with a perplexing mix of thoughts. He lowered the paper to the desk and walked to the window. "The two of you have been ordered back to London. The Primordial Council wants all Shadow Guards there to actively search the city for any evidence of Tantalus's arrival."

Tres inquired, "What of you and the countess?"

"We're to remain here for the time being."

There was a long moment of silence.

"Why?" Tres asked coolly. "Why, when none of us— including the Primordial Council—truly believes she had anything to do with that prostitute's death?"

Rourke lifted his gaze to meet that of the eldest of the two brothers. He knew he did not imagine Tres's displeasure. He held Tres's stare until the subordinate Raven looked away.

"Less than a week has passed since two suspicious deaths occurred in her proximity. Until they are absolutely certain Transcension does not lie dormant in her mind, and that she cannot be controlled or manipulated by Tantalus, they don't want her near the city, where his influence would most certainly be more powerful, as it was proven in the case of her brother, Lord Alexander."

"Which makes complete sense to me," said Shrew. "Although I think we can all agree she's no more in danger of Transcending than you or I."

"Well, I guess that's that," announced Tres, standing from his chair. "I'll pack my things."

Selene lay on her back staring at the ceiling, her hands so tightly fisted her nails cut into her palms.

Rourke was her peer and, although of a separate order, her superior. Last night she had humiliated herself by begging the Ravenmaster to stay. She had singlehandedly undermined the centuries she had spent proving herself worthy of the Order of the Shadow Guard.

Now, with the daylight streaming across the foot of the bed, it made absolutely no sense that she had been so terrified by her dream. Likely Rourke was downstairs at this very moment dictating a message to the Primordials as Tres and Shrew chuckled over her humiliation.

She, frightened? She, who had shifted through the darkest darkness of the world and, sword in hand welcomed each new face of evil as a welcome and thrilling challenge? She pushed up from the bed, scowling.

She wasn't afraid of anything. She didn't *need* anyone. She was through with vulnerability, full-strength powers or no. She refused to be undone by a nightmare about a stinking, monstrous worm.

Her mind cringed at the memory. *Ugh.* She had never seen or touched anything so repulsive. And the smell. Like the flesh of a thousand rotting corpses.

Perhaps she had, indeed, lost her sanity. Since arriving at Swarthwick she hadn't been at all herself. She suspected the source of at least a fraction of her humiliating loss of faculties had nothing to do with Transcension—and everything to do with a tall, brooding Raven.

He wouldn't be her first love affair. There had been others. She was nineteen centuries old. What normal, flesh-and-blood immortal would not have fallen in and out of love numerous times during that space of eternity?

Why did her heart whisper that he was different? That he would not hurt her? That he would not leave?

Something smacked on her window. As daylight glimmered through the window, she felt safe in assuming it wasn't the Death Worm from her nightmare.

Smack.

Pulling the blanket over her shoulders, she tested her ankle and, finding it still tender, gingerly stood and crossed to the window. She opened the shutters—only to be pegged in the forehead by a pebble.

"Ow," she shouted.

"Shrew!" Tres accused, slyly dropping a handful of stones behind his leg. He held the reins to a horse.

His brother peered up from where he stood on the steps. Another horse wandered a few feet away. "Forgive us. We wanted to say good-bye, but Rourke thought pebbles on the window would be more acceptable than Tres and I pouncing on you in bed."

Rourke stood just behind Shrew, arms crossed over his chest. Unlike the two brothers, he did not look up toward her window.

"For the record, we disagreed." Tres grinned. "Vehemently."

"Good-bye?" Selene repeated. "Wait."

Barefoot and hair streaming, she limped out of her room and down the stairs.

A moment later, bursting out from beneath the shadowed arch, she called, "Where are you going?"

"Back to London. We're being called up in the battle against Tantalus."

"Is that true?" she asked Rourke.

"I'm afraid it is."

With his cool expression and downturned lips, he didn't look at all pleased. She did not have to ask why she and Rourke weren't leaving Swarthwick with them. Poor Ravenmaster—he had been leg-shackled to her.

"Countess," called Tres, leading his mount to the base of the steps.

She descended to meet him. "Yes?"

His gaze raked over her appreciatively. "Now that it has been determined that you had no part in Flynn's death, and I've been reassigned from your personal guard . . ."

"Mmm-hmm?"

She had a feeling where this would lead.

"Well . . ." He leaned closer. "When you return to London, I should like very much to call on you."

After the way he had behaved toward her, all but judging her guilty, Selene's first reaction was to laugh outright. Not cruelly, but did he believe her to be so superficial in her choice of men?

Instead, she lowered her voice, coquettishly soft, and said, "You flatter me, but I must decline."

Surprise lit his eyes. "Why?"

"If I were going to have a love affair with one of you, it would have to be Shrew."

Tres's face went blank. His cheeks flushed. Over his shoulder, Selene winked at his openmouthed brother. Shrew laughed.

Climbing into his saddle, Tres said, "I suppose I deserve your scorn."

"No, not scorn." She smiled. "It's called revenge, but all in good fun."

His lips twisted into a wry smile. "The game of revenge. I know something of that." He touched the tip of his hat. "I bid you adieu. For now."

As she again climbed the steps, the sound of hooves on stone grew distant.

Rourke stood with his arms folded across his chest. "You know you just declined the man who would have been—"

"I know who he is. Who they are. They are the two

young princes who disappeared from the Tower of London in the fifteenth century. Tres certainly has the temperament for kinghood. The only question I have is why he goes by that name. He was to be Edward the Fifth, not the Third."

After a long moment's pause, Rourke murmured, "There were three conspirators in the plot to murder Edward and his younger brother, Richard of Shrewsbury."

Selene's eyes widened. "And he had his revenge against them! His name is a trophy memorializing their deaths." She nodded. "I like it. But the princes weren't murdered. They are very much alive, not to mention immortal."

Rourke's green eyes darkened.

In realization, she touched the cuff of his shirt. The blanket slid from her shoulder. "They *were* murdered, but you didn't let them die. You intervened in their penultimate breath."

It was forbidden for immortals to intervene in the deaths of mortals, but sometimes it was done. Anyone who dared challenge the rule faced severe punishment, although the Primordial Council was known to forgive.

Rourke didn't confirm or deny her theory.

His gaze moved over her lips, to settle rather accusingly on her bare shoulder. She tugged the blanket higher.

"Go get dressed. Get your hat and bag."

"Why, where are we going?"

"Into the village. We need supplies—and some servants."

He strode off across the courtyard toward the stable. Selene smiled, certain that instead of servants, he meant *chaperones*.

Whitewashed cottages with thatched roofs lined the one and only road that ran through the center of the village of Thorn-on-the-Moor. There were also a few single- and double-story shops, though they were Lilliputian in scale when compared to those in London. What an odd picture she and Rourke must paint to any onlooker.

Anyone else would have driven a simple wagon or curricle into town. She and Rourke made their first visit to the village sitting side by side on the lofty driver's bench of the Avenage town coach.

Residents came out onto their stoops and porches to stare. Selene nodded and smiled and waved a gloved hand.

"There's your fire," said Rourke, nodding toward the tiny church, which was surrounded by a neatly kept square of green grass and a low cast-iron fence.

But shockingly a jagged black hole marred the roof of the simple white structure. The steeple lay in the yard, scorched at its base.

"Whoa," she whispered.

Several long-faced men stood around the fallen monument, hats in hand, clearly pondering the necessary repairs.

"Looks like a lightning strike," said Rourke.

He drew in the reins and stopped the carriage in front of a narrow shop distinguished from the others by being painted a shocking shade of periwinkle blue. Neatly painted on the window in gold Garamond lettering was the word "grocer." Hopping down from the bench, Rourke came around and, for what she assumed was appearance' sake, assisted her down. He held the door for her and followed her inside.

Inside the narrow structure, baskets hung from above. Bolts of fabric, wooden boxes and barrels of all sizes lined the walls, in some places stacked as high as the ceiling. A man sprang up from behind the wooden counter, round wire spectacles perched on his balding head.

"Good afternoon, sir," said Rourke. "I am—"

"Lord Avenage?" the shopkeeper queried.

"Yes."

"The parson told us you had returned. Some feared that you had decided to sell the place. It would be a shame to lose the Avenage name, after all these centuries." The man's eager gaze shifted to Selene. "And you there, most lovely of ladies, must be—"

Selene extended her gloved hand, which he kissed.

"My widowed sister," Rourke supplied. "The Countess Pavlenco."

"Widowed?" The shopkeeper peered up, his eyes crinkled in sympathy. "At so young an age? How very, very tragic."

"Thank you, sir."

"I am Mr. Harbottle. You must be here for supplies."

"Indeed we are." Selene drew a narrow slip of paper from her embroidered velvet bag. "Also, I wished to inquire about Hannah the tinker. We have heard her wagon was found. What about Hannah?"

Mr. Harbottle frowned and shook his head. "She's not been found. I must tell you, though, against my better judgment I filled half of her wagon with items from my store, because she convinced me she could sell them in her travels and provide me with a tidy profit. I'm not certain whether I should be fearful for the girl, or fearful that she has absconded with my goods. Whether they washed away in the river's current, or *otherwise*, I may never know.

"But now to the business at hand." He accepted and admired Selene's list as if it were a medal bestowed, but as he read, he *tsk*ed and shook his head. "I'm afraid we don't have any of that. Or that. We do have a smidgen of that."

Rourke nodded, barely hearing what the man said. Selene sauntered the length of the shop, perusing items in the glass cases. The movement of her stiff taffeta bustle drew his gaze. He had always thought bustles a ridiculous invention. He simply hadn't ever understood their purpose.

He did now.

He swallowed hard, and returned his attention to Mr. Harbottle. "I'm also in need of a cook and a housekeeper. Two to three maids and a houseboy, as well. Better yet if they are available to take residence at Swarthwick. Tonight."

If necessary, he would put all their beds in the hallway, between his and Selene's rooms.

Selene asked, "Do you know where we might be able to find out which villagers are available for such work?"

Mr. Harbottle shook his head. "We're a small village of farmers and herdsmen. Most keep their women close to home."

Over the shopkeeper's shoulder, Selene rolled her eyes and mimicked him beneath her breath: *Keep our women close to home.*

As if he sensed something, the shopkeeper turned to her. "Might I help you with something there in the case, your ladyship?"

"No, sir." She smiled dazzlingly, drawing her gloved hand along the polished wood frame. "I'm just admiring your selection of domestic wares."

The shopkeeper chuckled. "I'm certain you run a fine household."

"Oh, but I can't do it alone." She came closer. "The keep has been neglected for so long. Our parents never took an interest in it. We were surprised to find everything still there in the storage rooms, and not carried off by thieves."

His eyebrows rose on his forehead. "That's because any thieves from hereabouts believe the keep to be haunted." He chuckled. "But, of course, you'd know all about your ancestors' tragedies, more so than I."

Rourke scowled.

Selene smiled. "There is much to be done to improve the premises. Cleaning, refurbishment and sewing. The ghosts, you see, have made it clear they are not at all willing to assist."

Mr. Harbottle's cheeks pinked and he chortled at her jest.

She tapped her fingertip against the wood. "Are you certain you don't have any villagers to recommend? We anticipate being in residence for just a few weeks. A month, perhaps. So it wouldn't be a permanent commitment."

"I'll tell you what I can." Mr. Harbottle scratched his head. "Do you know of the Astley estate?"

"Astley." Rourke nodded. "Yes."

The shopkeeper drummed his fingers on the glass. "It's been acquired by some rich fellow. Silverfish? Silverdown?"

"Silverwest," Selene provided.

"That's it!" Mr. Harbottle agreed, placing sacks of flour and cornmeal into a crate. "An unfortunate bit of timing on your part, I'd say."

"Why's that?" asked Rourke.

"His lovely sister and her steward came into town just yesterday morning, asking the same sorts of questions you are now. Who's available for hire. I know they snapped up Mrs. Shaw, the Taylor girl, and old Jon Bruce to work in their stable. Still, I'd be happy to put the word out."

"We'd be very appreciative," Selene said before inquiring, "What is that delicious smell coming from the back of the shop?"

"Capons, pasties, shepherd's pie and stewed cabbage, all available for purchase. My wife prepares everything herself. Can I wrap some for you to take back to Swarthwick?"

"Yes, please," Selene urged.

Mr. Harbottle disappeared into the back. Rourke followed him, prepared to carry any packages. Behind him, the bell above the door jingled. Two elderly, white-haired women entered. Selene greeted them with a smile and, within moments, had been invited to peer into their baskets. She exclaimed something about eggs and, after opening her purse, retrieved some coins.

A few moments later she called to him, a basket in each hand, "I'm taking our eggs to the carriage."

He nodded, taking the opportunity to admire her bustle again.

Selene closed the carriage door and turned back to re-enter the grocer's shop.

"Lady Pavlenco," a voice called from the road.

A familiar white horse and broad-shouldered rider approached. She waited for Mr. Silverwest and within moments he skillfully dismounted onto the walkway and crossed to stand before her. He removed his hat and smiled broadly. His golden hair curled attractively at his nape.

"You're moving about quite well. Your ankle—"

"—must not have been as badly injured as first believed. I'm much improved, thank you."

He smiled at her. She smiled back. His cheeks flushed ruddily and he laughed. "I'm very sorry if I caused you any trouble with your brothers."

"Not at all. They have always been very protective of me."

"Do you think they'd shoot me if I . . ." He hesitated, the dimple in his cheek deepening.

"If you what?"

"If I came to call upon you?"

Selene flushed. "Why don't you and Mrs. Thrall come for tea tomorrow?"

He responded with warmth. "Invitation accepted."

A bell jingled as the door beside them opened. Rourke emerged bearing a large crate. Seeing them, he halted.

"Avenage," she announced. "Mr. Silverwest and Mrs. Thrall are coming for tea tomorrow."

"*Lovely*," he answered.

A brisk, cool wind bathed Selene's face, one that smelled of grass and earth and the approaching autumn. She heard every creak and rattle of the joists. Felt every jolt of the wheels as they traveled over the stones—likely because the man beside her had not spoken a single word in the half hour since they had left the village.

"You shouldn't have invited them," he said at last.

"Why not?"

"Because we're Amaranthines. Mrs. Thrall and Mr. Silverwest are mortal. What is the purpose of inviting them for *tea*?"

She straightened the seams of her gloves. "You mentioned wanting to sell Swarthwick. Mr. Silverwest is interested."

"How do you know that?"

"His sister told me. She said she inquired weeks ago as to the availability of the property."

The inquiry he had received from the land office, when still in London.

He pressed his lips together tightly. "You should have asked me first. If you had, you would know I've changed my mind."

"I am your dear widowed sister. Regardless of whether you wish to sell the place, I have as much right to invite visitors to Swarthwick as you do."

"That's not amusing," he retorted. "I am weary of playing brother and sister."

"You started the farce."

"No, I did not. One of the men I hired to work on the bridge was on the train up from London. He overheard you refer to Tres and Shrew as your brothers. *You* started the farce, and we simply were forced to continue with the story."

Selene chuckled. "Well, that is amusing. What alternative relationship would you suggest?"

"Why must we claim any relationship?"

"Don't act as if you don't know. Because this is Tedious-on-the-Moor, and anything else simply would not do. Not for a . . . What exactly is your title?"

"Officially I am an earl."

Selene laughed. "*Oh, yes.* A widowed countess and an unwed earl spending a few weeks in the country together. I can only imagine the scandal. No, brother dear, I do believe we suit as siblings. At least for the present. Besides, within a few days of our departure, we will disappear from their memories. Until then, this will keep them from waving torches and pitchforks on your front doorstep."

Silence again reigned on the carriage bench.

"Why are you still frowning?" she demanded.

"Are you attracted to that Silverwest fellow?"

Chapter Eleven

"I'm attracted to not being bored," she replied, though secretly, his agitation over her rapport with Silverwest tickled her twenty shades of pink. Unfairly perhaps, she prodded him with more words aimed to elicit a revealing response. "You have made it clear you would prefer to maintain a distance between us. And I understand you are already involved with someone else in London, and I must certainly respect that as a boundary."

He shot her a glare and snapped the reins. The horses jolted forward, rocking Selene backward on the bench. She grabbed the rail beside her hip for security.

She continued, "And so, in the absence of Shrew and Tres and the servants we cannot seem to hire, we shall instead invite neighbors for tea. In fact, I invited those two elderly women from the grocer's to come for supper the day after tomorrow."

His eyes widened. "You *didn't*."

She laughed, feeling boisterous. "Of course I didn't. I'm just teasing you. Do you know what teasing is?"

His nostrils flared, and he snapped the reins.

In the distant field, two farmers hacked at the earth with long hoes. One man was taller and bulkier. The other stood a head shorter and was as thin as a reed. A man and his son. The day's golden light filtered over the valley, transforming the scene into a perfect picture of provincial loveliness. Just like a painting she had once seen in a Paris museum.

The boy lowered his hoe to the ground and moved to hoist a burlap bag from the back of the wagon. In the next moment, the bottom seam of the bag gave way. Within seconds, the seeds slipped out, forming a pale heap over his boots, leaving him with only an empty bag clasped in his arms. His mouth fell open in apparent bewilderment. Selene could not help but smile.

A dark figure barged into her line of vision. The older man. His arm swung up, high above the boy. He held a horsewhip.

"No," shouted Selene, grasping hold of the narrow bench rail beside her hip.

She flinched as the whip caught the boy across the face.

Something slapped her palm—the reins. Beside her the bench was empty. Pulling hard, she slowed the horses. Turning on the bench, she peered back in the direction of the boy.

A narrow path of grass hissed, crushed—laid flat against the earth, revealing Rourke's path of travel.

Unseen by either the boy or the man, Rourke took shape and seized the man's arm as he lifted the whip again. Wrenching him around, he planted a fist at the center of his face. The boy stumbled away, blood streaming over his lip and chin, and fell to his knees—which was why he did not see Rourke's sword streak out in a searing flash of light.

"*Rourke.*" Selene leapt to the road and ran across the field as fast as her skirts allowed, praying he wouldn't use the weapon. Not here. Not like that. He stalked the man, who crawled away, scrabbling through the pile of seeds that had incited him to violence, in the opposite direction of the boy.

"Rourke, stop." She grabbed the back of his coat and pulled.

He whirled on her. Anger contorted his handsome face. His green eyes shimmered with flecks of red light, indicating just how close he was to changing from man into feral predator.

"You *must* stop," she shouted, trying to break through the haze of his rage.

He blinked and his eyes cleared.

"You must make him forget," she urged, gesturing at the man. Shadow Guards had the ability to use *lethe* to clear memories from the minds of mortals, but only if they acted quickly. Without her powers, it would be useless for her to even try.

"Let him remember," he growled, before turning toward the road.

Selene glanced at the man, who moaned and collapsed face-first against the earth. Pressing her fingertips to his throat, she found his pulse to be strong enough. He would live. Rourke walked the boy toward the vehicle, one guiding hand resting on his narrow shoulder. Heart pounding, Selene rushed ahead and opened the door. The boy clambered inside.

"Was that man your father?" she asked, sliding onto the bench beside him.

"No, ma'am," he mumbled past bloodstained hands, which he held pressed to his nose. "M'stepfather."

Rourke stood at the door. He had lost his hat somewhere out in the field and, in exacting his justice, ripped a seam in the shoulder of his coat.

Selene told him, "We're fine here. You drive and calm yourself."

He nodded and secured the door.

She unsnapped her bag and handed the boy a handkerchief. All too quickly she realized the square of linen wouldn't be enough, so she tore a wide strip from one of her petticoats and leaned across to examine and tend to his nose.

"This isn't the first time he's broken it, is it?"

He shook his head.

Blood and bones didn't bother her in the slightest. She had seen enough of that in her years as a Reclaimer, and in the various mortal battles in which she had chosen to participate. But this was just a boy of perhaps twelve years. She saw the hurt in his eyes. Not just the physical hurt, but the soul hurt.

"Your mother allows him to do this to you?"

He shook his head vehemently. "She died, ma'am. Last winter." His eyes filled with tears and a stream of angry words spilled out. "After one of 'is beatin's. Said 'e would kill us if we told anyone. 'E told everyone she left us for another man, but she's at the bo'om of the well."

She was struck by the sudden impulse to embrace the boy, but they were strangers. She settled for patting his arm. She and her brother had been about the same age when their mother had died, leaving them behind to answer Octavian's bitter fury. At least Cleopatra had made the decision to leave this life. She had not been murdered.

"You don't have to go back there."

"My . . ." His voice failed, and he cleared his throat. "My sisters are there. I couldn't leave them."

"Sisters? How many?"

"Two."

"We'll talk to his lordship about them."

"*He* is a *lor'ship*?" His eyes grew wide. "I ain't never seen anything like 'at before. Came out o' nowhere." He laughed—and winced. "Laughing 'urts."

"I'm sure it does."

Softly, the boy marveled, "Why would a lor'ship do somethin' like 'at for me?"

She wondered the same thing. Shadow Guards weren't incapable of kindness, but they tended to be jaded from century after century of being exposed to the worst mortal civilization had to offer. It wasn't that Rourke's intervention had stunned her. Rather, it was the intensity of his reaction to the boy's being harmed.

Today, like the parson before him, the grocer had made mention of Avenage's tragic history. Certainly the answer to today's mystery might lie hidden somewhere in his past.

Selene entered the kitchen from the back courtyard.

"You're certain he won't stay in the keep?" Rourke asked.

He unhooked the pot in which the shepherd's pie had been warming over the fire, and carried it to the block table, placing it on a large iron trivet. They'd already portioned out a heaping plateful for the boy, who'd told them his name was Nathan Birch. Nathan had seemed so in awe of Rourke, and even a bit frightened, that he had allowed Selene to see to the boy's settling in.

She nodded. "He said it wouldn't be right to sleep in his lordship's fine castle. He has insisted on remaining in the servants' quarters just off the stable. He seems to like the horses. Perhaps you have your stable boy after all."

Rourke shook his head and pressed the pad of his thumb to his lips.

"Why not?" inquired Selene.

"He's too young," he answered quietly. "A boy that age should be in school."

Selene rested her elbows on the table. "I don't disagree. I spent my earliest years amongst the scholars at the Library of Alexandria."

"That must have been amazing."

"It was. The Library has forever instilled in me a hunger for learning. A hunger for . . . ah, for books." Heat stained her cheeks. Only those closest to her knew of her uncommon predilection for the written word.

He smiled. "I have heard of your hunger for books, Selene."

She looked away. "All I intended to say was that you will not hear an argument from me about enabling the boy to have an education."

"Speaking of eating—did Nathan?"

"Ravenously." She nodded. "But he's worried about his sisters."

"Of course he is." He rested his hands flat against the tabletop. "I glimpsed inside his thoughts as I walked him to the carriage. He has witnessed and suffered terrible things at the hands of that man. And now his sisters . . ." His voice faded. She saw his mind working.

"You've already interfered too much, Rourke." She seated herself on one of the stools. "You know the rules."

He nodded stiffly before grasping a bottle of wine, coated in dust. With a square of linen, he rubbed the glass down and set about pulling the cork. Selene used a large wooden spoon to fill their plates. They sat across from each other at the table. Rourke poured her glass full and then his own.

Selene lifted her fork and sighed with delight. "*Not* root stew, oh, how I adore you."

She could not recall ever looking forward to a meal as much as this one. She shoveled in a few bites before realizing what an uncouth picture she must paint. She glanced at Rourke, to find him staring at her intently.

Selene asked, "What is it? Have I a potato mustache? Smashed peas on my teeth?"

He shook his head.

"Then what?"

"You're beautiful."

Her mouth fell open. "Ah . . . thank you."

His gaze lowered to her lips, and he gulped a swallow of wine. "God, that's all. I shouldn't have said it, considering . . . everything. Let's talk about something else."

"I rather prefer talking about how beautiful I am," she teased, her cheeks warming with pleasure at his compliment.

He smiled, but did not speak further.

"Oh, all right." She said, "Let's talk about this pile of rocks. Tell me about Swarthwick. You already told me that William bestowed it to you, but did you build the keep yourself, or did you conquer someone and take it from them? Come on, now, out with the bloody details."

He tipped his glass to his lips, then set it down. "There was nothing here then but the ruins of an old Roman fortification. I oversaw the keep's design and construction. She took three years to build."

"She is lovely. Did she ever take on an attack?"

"Yes." His gaze shifted, and he offered no additional details. For whatever reason, it was clear he didn't like that subject, or anything to do with his mortal past.

"When did you become immortal?"

"When I became a Raven."

"Not just a Raven. You have been the Ravenmaster from the start, have you not?"

"Yes."

Selene swirled the wine in her glass. "The decision to become an immortal . . . was it a difficult one for you?"

He peered up into the cavernous ceiling, one that must have once bustled with a score of servants. "I had nothing to hold me here."

"What about family. What about—"

He glanced down into his plate, and his jaw tightened.

She cut herself off. Too personal.

"A wife?" he finished for her.

She nodded.

"She died." He traced his finger around the base of his glass.

"I'm sorry."

He nodded and pursed his lips. She would not ask him about children. The mood between them grew too serious.

"Is there anything you wish to know about me?" She raised an eyebrow and lifted her glass to her lips. The wine, a rich red claret, warmed her blood and eased the flow of her words. "I'll tell you all about my husbands, if you like."

That lit a fire in his eyes. "How many have there been?"

"Well, there was the count."

"He was mortal?"

She circled the upper rim of her glass with her fingertip until the crystal sang. "Not for long."

He leaned forward on his stool and poured her glass full again. "What do you mean by that?"

"He was one of my assignments, well on his way to Transcending. Filthy creature, he took a fancy to me in Venice and inquired about a marriage contract." She shrugged. "At first I was disgusted—but rather entertained by the irony of it all. When I pondered the possibility further, marrying him seemed the most efficient way to bring things to a swift conclusion. I suffered through a brief courtship, survived a thousand repulsive kisses and Reclaimed him on our wedding night."

Rourke's brows went up. "How did you explain his mortal death to everyone?"

"He was a rather handsome but older fellow. I let them think he got . . . *overexcited*, if you know what I mean." She sipped her wine again, enjoying the warm languor that spread through her limbs. "Why are you laughing?"

"No other Shadow Guard I know would be able to manage that, being that they are all males. You might say that, as a beautiful woman, you were very much a Trojan horse in Reclaiming the Count Pavlenco."

Again, he had called her beautiful. "We all use our strengths to our best advantage, don't we?"

Rourke nodded. "I suppose we do. You called him a filthy creature, and yet you still go by his name."

"There was nothing wrong with the rest of his family. In fact, they were all very kind to me in my widowhood. They allowed me to keep everything given to me in the marriage contract. Two houses and a vineyard. Besides, I really do enjoy being the countess."

"Better than being a princess?"

She nodded.

"Better than a queen?"

"Yes . . ."

"You were married to the king of Nubia, were you not?"

She smiled. "History books. You don't believe everything you read in them, do you?"

"They say you were married to him, that you had his children?"

She exhaled through her teeth. "So you wish to know all my secrets?"

"Your secrets pass the time so much better than mine."

"He married my cousin, my aunt Arsinoe's daughter." She shrugged. "We had similar appearances, but she was . . . softer. Sweeter than I. They loved each other, and it didn't seem fair when Octavian chose me for that political marriage. Being that my mother had murdered hers, giving her my mortal life seemed a small gesture of apology. With my encouragement, some black kohl eyeliner and a headdress, off she went across the desert."

"And you chose this life."

She shook her head. "I did not choose to be an Amaranthine. By that time immortality already existed in my blood and in the blood of my twin brother. We were simply waiting to perfect."

"You say that you did not choose immortality."

"You know the story. Octavian's army defeated Mark Antony's and slowly closed in on the city of Alexandria. My mother knew it was the end. That was the first time I saw Archer, but he had not come to see me. He came as an emissary on behalf of the Primordials, with an opportunity for my mother and father to save themselves through immortality."

"I see."

"I still remember the flowers, the two perfect amaranth blooms. I thought they were so beautiful, but she wouldn't let me touch them. She waited for him—for my father, but he did not come. Not in the way she expected. When he finally did arrive, you see, it was on a pallet, and he was already dead. I still remember how she lay down beside him and wrapped herself around his body. She lay like that for hours before she finally moved again. Until then she had been the ultimate philopatris."

"Philopatris . . ." he repeated.

"One who loves her country. But in the end, he was more important to her than anything. More important than life. More important than Mark and me. In leaving us behind, she knew what would happen to us." Selene stared at the small circle of wine remaining in the bottom of her glass. "I'd never do that. If I were so fortunate as to ever have children, I would never abandon them. Even if I knew escape was hopeless, I would stand between my enemies and my children until they hacked me down with a sword."

The stem of the glass shattered in her hand.

Selene stared at the destroyed vessel, shocked.

Rourke lurched from his chair and claimed her hand. Amazingly, it didn't appear she had cut herself.

"I'm sorry," she whispered. "I just haven't talked about her to anyone in a very long time."

Not even Mark. They had lived their terrible memories together. There had been no need to ever speak of them again. Sharing such pain had seemed a weakness, when one had already turned to stone inside. At least, she thought she had turned to cold and unyielding stone. Something about Rourke's quiet strength and presence had brought the pain all pouring out.

And yet . . . he backed away from her. "I'd best go and see about Nathan."

Selene nodded, only then realizing her mistake.

Rourke turned the corner and entered the stable, only to be met with shadows and Nathan's lingering *trace*. There was no sign of violence or indication that the boy had been taken against his will. On the small table his empty plate had been left with his napkin laid across the top. The lamp had been extinguished and the bed neatly made, like a thoughtfully crafted message: *Thank you for the offer of safety, but no, thank you.*

He strode across the front courtyard, increasing his pace with each step. Bending his head down so deeply that his chin touched his chest, he curled his arms outward in two powerful arcs, awakening the muscles along his neck, shoulders and arms. Pain and heat streaked like forks of lightning through his back. In the next moment, his wings cast a long shadow on the earth and he took flight.

He found Nathan already three-quarters of the way to his home. He fought the instinct to swoop down and wrench the boy from what would certainly be a fatal path. In the brief moments he had rested his hand on Nathan's shoulder, he had glimpsed terrible memories of drunkenness and violence.

Rourke forced himself to turn back. But not toward

Swarthwick. Not yet. Instead he climbed higher, pushing himself into the blackness of the sky until the air thinned and chilled his skin, and his lungs filled with pain.

When he could bear it no more, he folded his wings against his back and torso and spiraled headlong toward the dark earth . . . only to repeat the climb and subsequent fall again and again, until his wings and his lungs and his body were exhausted.

Nearing Swarthwick, he evanesced into shadow and entered his room through a crack in the shutters.

Too close. To close to her.

An inexplicable anger rose up from deep inside his chest. Why couldn't he see her the way he saw other women, as faceless, meaningless and forgettable? She undermined his every resolve, his only hope at salvation. Salvation? Was that what he wanted? He supposed his mind had always backed off from such a hope. That he could punish and deprive himself so severely, so torturously, that perhaps one day . . . one day he might be forgiven for what he had done.

At the water basin, he wrenched his shirt over his shoulders and continued disrobing until he stood naked. He glimpsed his eyes in the mirror and quickly looked away, unnerved by the stark intensity of his own need.

Instead of exhausting him, the flight had only agitated, *heightened* his every sense. His blood coursed through his veins like mercury, silver and hot. He poured water from the pitcher into the basin and, taking up a cloth, dampened it. He scrubbed the sweat from his face, his neck and his chest. Every brush of the night air, every stroke of the cloth against his skin awakened him further. The thought of Selene lying in her bed, wrapped so lusciously in black silk . . .

Desire surged through him and made the hair on his neck stand on end. He bent over the basin and poured the rest of the pitcher of water over his head. He straightened, water sluicing down his back. Taking up a folded towel, he scrubbed the water from his hair.

A sound drew his attention, the pad of a bare foot on

wood. His head snapped up. He glimpsed Selene's face in the mirror—and then she was gone.

He tore the towel from his shoulders and bound the cloth around his hips, following her into the hallway.

She shut her door and turned the lock.

As if that could keep him out.

He darkened to shadow, swept through and materialized again behind her. Close behind her—so close that when she whirled her hair spun out to brush against his skin.

"Rourke." Her cheeks were flushed a dark pink. With her wide eyes and parted lips, she appeared altogether flustered, an especially alluring sight when he knew she wasn't the sort of woman, the sort of *warrior*, who flustered easily.

She didn't wear a black silk night rail.

Tonight the silk was green.

Chapter Twelve

Selene's gaze traveled down Rourke's naked chest and over his abdomen, to the place where he fisted the towel, low on his hip. Some nights she lit a fire on the hearth, but tonight there was only the light from one small lamp. Shadows and soft glow from the flame defined his taut muscles to perfection.

"I'm so sorry," she said in a gasp. "Well, no . . . I'm not *really* sorry. Just *look* at you."

He stared at her, his eyes dark and intense. He curled his fists and the muscles flexed along his arms.

"What woman would be sorry?" she babbled—or thought she babbled. She couldn't actually hear the words she spoke, for the blood pounding in her ears.

His hair, darkened by the water to almost black, spiked over his forehead, nearly covering one eye. With the two of them nose-to-nose, he stood at least two inches taller than she.

She sought to explain. "You didn't come back from checking on Nathan. I fell asleep waiting, because I still get very tired by this time of night. But . . . I woke up and went to your room. . . ."

She wouldn't mention her foolish dream from the night before, or how, after he had left her in the dark keep alone, the memory of it had closed in on her like a smothering Whitechapel fog.

"Get on the bed."

She blinked. "What?"

He couldn't have said what she thought he said.

His lips, sensual and hard, issued the order again. "Get . . . on . . . the bed."

Raising his arm, he pressed his fingertips to the center of her chest, just above the swell of her breasts . . . and pushed. She stepped back and he followed, exerting the same pressure against her skin. He maneuvered her thusly across the wooden floor until the backs of her knees touched the mattress.

His gaze burned with intensity, but behind the heat she glimpsed desperation.

"Rourke—"

He lifted the same hand higher and, with it, covered her lips.

The lamp extinguished.

Perhaps he realized how badly the dream had unnerved her and, in his impatience with her stammering explanation, simply wished for her to be quiet and sleep. He would stay here again with her, as he had the night before.

But he was wearing only the towel.

Huzzah!

In the darkness, she crawled across the mattress and lay down on her side, leaving more than half of the remaining space for him. Barely breathing, she awaited his next move. Behind her, the mattress sank beneath his weight. She bit into her lower lip. Goose bumps rose all down her back, his mere proximity awakening her body.

His hand rested on the bare skin of her shoulder.

Selene closed her eyes, almost not believing. She had craved his touch, and now—

His arm came around her, wrenching her body tight against his. Selene's lips parted in a gasp. His thigh hooked over her hip, effectively caging her. His face pressed into the curve of her neck, warming her skin with his breath and lips. The roughness of his beard abraded her skin, and his warm breath tickled her ear.

She could not stop herself from pressing her buttocks back against him. His erection grew, hard and apparent. Its heat burned through her gown, unencumbered by the towel that he must have discarded to the floor. His hand slid over the silk, up her rib cage and closed on her breast.

"Rourke," she whispered, lifting onto one elbow, reaching over her shoulder, wanting to touch his face, his jaw, his lips.

"Don't say my name," he whispered, kissing the center of her palm, winding his fingers through hers, but in the end planting—and abandoning—her hand on the sheet in front of them. "Don't look at me. Don't touch me."

He spoke so quietly she could barely hear his words. She remembered the desperation in his eyes, just beneath the surface of his desire. Willing to do anything to keep him in her bed, to continue this moment with him, she nodded her agreement.

His fingers thrust into her hair and he twisted its length around his fist, baring her neck. His mouth pressed against her nape in a firm, possessing kiss, sending such a strong tremor through her she thought she would die of pleasure. His breath, his teeth and his tongue tantalized. Her fingers curled into the linen. It was as if he knew exactly where to kiss a woman to unlock the full measure of her passion.

Releasing her hair to cascade down, he lowered hot kisses and teasing breaths down the slope of her naked back, stopping where her night rail formed a point just above her buttocks. He retraced the path, smoothing his thumbs up the indention of her spine.

Fever scalded her skin as his wandering hand came around to massage her breasts and skimmed lower, over her ribs and waist to clench her hip. His arm, clasped like a steel band between her breasts, held her captive. She felt trapped in sensation, imprisoned by pleasure. Restless and wanting more, she shifted . . . moved against his length until, with a curse, he caught the edge of her gown and, scoring his fingertips up the flesh of her thighs, removed the barrier between them.

His open palm pressed over her stomach, sliding lower, between her legs, to stroke and coax and tease. Her flesh throbbed. Ached for him. Seeking a deeper touch, she moved her hips. Yet he denied her that, so she clenched her thighs, increasing the friction offered by his hand.

Their bodies and limbs slid and twisted against silk and linen, a sensual battle, with Selene attempting to turn and face him and Rourke overpowering her, refusing to allow it. Where her weakness after the vaccine troubled her to no end, his strength over her only enhanced their love play. She did not fear his domination. Indeed, it thrilled her to be conquered, but only because the conqueror was Rourke.

There was also the satisfaction of knowing the only reason he was here was because *she had conquered him*.

At last he pinned her immobile, grasped himself and guided his swollen member to prod at the apex of her tightly clasped thighs. Biting her lip to keep from crying out, she lifted her hips in invitation. He slid, with a tight groan of satisfaction, not inside her—but between her legs. A cruel, exquisite tease.

Thrusting, he rubbed, slid and *dragged* his rigid erection against her swollen and aching flesh until her body relented, inviting him deeper, along her slickened channel. One hand slipping free, Selene reached behind, smoothing her palm over his abdomen, admiring the hard flex of his waist and hips as he moved.

He captured her wrist.

"Please," she pleaded, with a desperation even she found difficult to comprehend.

"Touch me again and I'll go," he threatened between clenched teeth.

"No, don't."

Binding her wrists together, he drew her hands high onto the mattress, above her head, rolling her from her hip to her stomach, her elbows propped on the pillow. He stretched himself over her, aligning his muscled body to hers. Still pinning her wrists with one hand, with the other he squeezed her buttocks, stroked and massaged her back and torso. He kissed her shoulder and forced his hand between the mattress and her body to cup her breast. Squeezing and stroking her nipple, his fingertips then traced the line between silk and flesh before tugging the fabric down. Her breast spilled out. With a slow, seductive grind of his hips, he moved between her damp thighs.

"*Rourke!*" He brought her so close, and yet she needed him inside her to escape this sensual purgatory. Why did he offer her only this?

"It's not enough, is it?" he demanded harshly. His heart pounded against her back, aligned with hers.

"No," she breathed. *It isn't enough*, some frantic part of her whispered. No wicked touch, no provoking words would ever be enough. "Rourke, I—"

His hand released her wrists—only to cover her mouth.

"Shhhhh," he urged.

He seized against her.

"*Nnhuh*," he gasped huskily. His arms came around her, binding her hips tightly against his. His member jerked, pulsed, and damp heat spread on the linen.

They lay a long time, entwined. At last, his grip on her eased and his breath slowed. With a hoarse exhalation of breath, he rolled from her onto his back and staved his fingers into his hair. Selene glanced at him over her shoulder and pushed her night rail down, covering herself.

He did not touch her. Not with a brush of his fingertips, or even a glance. She could *feel* the intensity of his thoughts, practically *hear* the regrets pouring from his mind.

He tilted onto his hip and pulled the blanket over her, binding it about her as if she were a small child being tucked into bed. Still, there were no kisses and he did not pull her close. He lay behind her, his only touch a hand against her hair.

She did not move, did not attempt to face him or speak, because she could not bear the idea of forcing some unwanted intimacy upon him. Whatever desire he had felt for her moments ago had clearly evaporated when he had spent himself.

They lay there for what seemed an eternity. Selene's stomach clenched; she knew things would forever be different between them. What had passed between them had been the singular most intense and thrilling sexual experience of her existence, and yet now she felt completely empty, she and Rourke lying side by side on her bed with a foot of space between them, his hand tangled in her hair. In her weakness, she had made a terrible mistake.

Eventually, he must have assumed she slept, because he quietly slipped from the bed. She heard the pad of his bare feet and the creak of the wood as he crossed to his room, then the scrape of a trunk lid and shuffling noises. He again entered the hall but did not return to her. He descended the stairs.

Tears stung her eyes. Why, she didn't know, because she had never been in the habit of crying over men. An eternity ago, she had learned to expect betrayal and abandonment, and to keep her softer emotions controlled, so much so that it seemed they no longer existed.

But Rourke . . . the way he had come to her . . . The way he had touched her, and kissed her so fiercely and yet refused to let her touch him or say his name . . .

What had in the moment thrilled her with its eroticism now left her twisted with unhappiness. He had used her, perhaps as she had used others in the past—to fill a momentary need, one that required only a warm and faceless human body of the opposite sex.

The sheets smelled of him. Shunning the bed she grabbed up a blanket, pulling it over her shoulders to mute the chill that had gathered in the room. Following the path he had taken down the dark stairs, she did not find him in the great room or his study.

Had he left her again? She hated being in this enormous keep all alone at night.

She didn't feel safe, not without her powers and lacking her usual strength. An uncomfortable thought when she, more than anyone, knew what kind of evil, natural and supernatural, existed in this world. Clasping the blanket tighter, she decided to return to her room.

In doing so she passed by the circular base of the keep's tower. The doorway to the stairs had always been locked, but now stood an inch ajar. Selene stepped inside and peered up the stone steps. The faintest glow of moonlight shone down from above.

Rourke's raven perched on a step, its glossy back to her and its beak pointed toward the sky.

The bird bounded two steps up before lifting into flight. Wings flapping, he rose higher and higher to disappear at the top. Selene climbed, her hands skimming over cool stone. Wind swirled down from above, casting a chill across her skin. When at last she reached the top, she found Rourke, his elbows braced upon the high edge of the wall, his hands spread over the back of his head. Though bare of foot, he wore trousers and a loose, unbuttoned linen shirt. A fierce wind dragged the cloth, revealing a swath of bare skin at his lower back.

Around the circumference of the wall perched seven stone ravens on square pedestals, their wings raised and half unfurled—no less forbidding than they must have appeared eight centuries before.

Rourke sensed her there, because he turned to confront her. His nostrils flared, and his eyes narrowed. "You should not have come here."

She responded sharply, "Don't you dare tell me to go back to my room."

A sturdy gust that smelled of the ocean sent her hair and the blanket billowing behind her.

He growled, "Don't *you* dare ask me to explain."

Just as before, he did not meet her gaze, a clear indication that he felt regret or even shame at what had just taken place between them. Certainly his regret did not exceed her own.

"I need no explanation," she said, moving nearer. "I understand completely what just happened between us. You came to my bed and made love to my body—but *not* me—and shoved my face into the pillow because you were thinking of someone else. Of H—"

He pointed a finger in her face. "Don't say her name, because it's not true, and I did not shove your face into the pillow."

"You might as well have," she cried. "If not Helen, Helen, *Helen*," she shouted, "then who?"

His green eyes flared in a sudden intensification of emotion. There was anger, yes, but a confession of rampant pain as well. In sudden realization she grasped his wrist. There was someone else. Instantly the fury in her breast dwindled, though she scrambled desperately to keep the flames stoked high. Anger, it seemed, was all she had to protect her heart from Rourke.

"It's this place, isn't it? *That* place." She pointed in the direction of the plateau. "Something from your past. Is it your wife, Rourke?"

He hissed and fisted his hands against his temples. Turning from her, he strode to the wall. She followed him across the cold stones, coming to stand just behind him.

"I know that as a man you must find it nearly impossible to confide. But I deserve to know who was in that bed with us tonight. What ghost of your memory or your past?"

Between clenched teeth he said, "Do you remember tonight, when you spoke of your mother, and the memories remained so fresh that you broke the glass?"

"Yes." She did not step closer to him. Did not presume that her nearness might offer him comfort.

He closed his eyes. "If I speak of these things, I'll break something—"

"Break whatever you like. Glasses. Chairs." Her breath hovered in her throat. She had known some hidden complexity lay beneath Rourke's surface. All immortals, it seemed, had lived long enough to claim countless tragedies in their past. "Sometimes breaking things makes me feel better too."

"I'll break you." The softly spoken words touched her. They indicated that despite the pain he had inflicted on her, he cared.

"If this immortal life has not broken me by now, Rourke, it cannot be done."

After a long silence, he shook his head. "I won't make my pain your own."

She waited for explanation, but he didn't offer one. Instead, he stared into the darkness.

In a sudden rush, the anger returned. She wouldn't do this to herself. She would not beg and plead to be privy to his heart. She was accustomed to being alone, and lived that existence well enough.

"Very well." She drew away in her mind, severing the bond between them, even if it was a bond that had existed only in her mind.

If he did not trust her enough to confide in her she would not press him to do so. But she couldn't be there for him, not to use as a faceless, anonymous female body on which to release his demons, though in her darkest heart of hearts, all she wanted was for him to touch her again. Perhaps she feared that he really *could* break her if she let him come too close. It was time to put her heart back in its locked metal box and forget where she hid the key.

"Don't come to me again, Rourke."

His jaw flexed and he nodded.

She refused to rush off down the stairs like a fleeing damsel. Doing so would be an acknowledgment of defeat—of his rejection—so she stayed. Needing to look at anything but him, she went to the nearest stone raven and peered over the wall. A band of fog encircled the keep. The low clusters of brush and jagged outcroppings of stone offered no shelter from the wind coming in off the ocean. Each gust tousled her hair and numbed her cheeks. She ran her fingertips over the raven's feathered wings. Time and the ocean's perpetual assault had left the stone pockmarked, and the carved ridges less distinct.

Rourke shifted and seemed to hone in on some distant point of interest.

She followed the line of his gaze. Orange spots of light burned like cinders on the other side of the river, where that afternoon there had been nothing but a blank field.

She hated that she could not magnify her vision and see through the darkness. She prayed her powers would soon return, so she would not have to rely on anyone but herself.

Too curious to remain silent, she asked, "What do you see?"

He leaned forward, resting his elbows on the stones. "Wagons."

"As in Gypsy wagons?"

"There are too many for a single band of Gypsies."

Selene's tension eased a bit. They spoke to each other as they had before, as two Shadow Guards sharing observations. Perhaps they could both forget about tonight and return to their prior state of companionship, minus the heated attraction of the days before.

"What do you suppose they are?"

"I'll find out in the morning."

He met her gaze and seemed to attempt a probe of her thoughts. Selene knew how to keep her mind blank and unreadable, and she did so now. She would share no more of herself with him.

"Good night, Rourke."

The next morning, Selene stood at her open window. Dark spots marred the distant field, evidence of the campfires from the night before, but the wagons had gone, their path toward the main road evidenced by deep ruts. Perhaps Rourke had ventured out early in the morning to investigate. She dressed with her usual care, today choosing a gown tailored from blue-and-yellow-striped taffeta, with a narrow, flounced waist. Opening her jewelry box, she selected a few pieces. Her gaze settled on two ivory scroll rods.

Three ancient scrolls had played an important part in providing knowledge to battle Jack the Ripper and his Dark Bride. At times she kept souvenirs from Reclamations. Nothing macabre, of course, such as a shrunken head or a string of teeth, but because the first of the three scrolls had been highly deteriorated, she had removed the two intricately carved rods from amidst the jumble of fragments and kept them.

Skilled in document preservation, she had painstakingly restored the papyri. Her brother had translated the ancient inscriptions so that they, along with Lord Black, could read the prophecies telling of Tantalus's intention to escape Tartarus, as well as attempt to anticipate the next stage of his attack on London and its citizens.

Not only had the rods struck her fancy because of their beauty—she liked to wear them as pins in her hair—but they also seemed to imbue her with mystical strength. This morning, they reminded her of who she had been before losing her powers—and who she *would* be again. She had to believe her Shadow Guard abilities would soon return. Without that hope, she would descend into despair.

She brushed out her hair and sectioned long strands up from her temples. Twisting the lengths around several times, she jabbed the rods through at her crown, leaving the remainder of her hair long, and falling down her back. Midway down the stairs she heard voices in the great room, Rourke's and someone else's.

He stood at the window, holding an envelope in one hand and an unfolded sheet of parchment in the other. His broad shoulders blocked much of the morning light. She denied the stab of longing that struck through her heart.

The visitor stood near the fireplace, removing his hat. Her eyes narrowed as she recognized him.

A dark patch covered one eye. The other widened at seeing Selene.

"*Leeson*," she hissed.

Rourke turned.

Leeson's bushy eyebrows ascended his forehead. "Just look at her face, Lord Avenage. The pure joy at recognizing a familiar old friend."

To Rourke she demanded, "Why is he here?"

She had expected Rourke to respond coolly toward her this morning; however, a smoky glint of mischief shone in his eyes. He shrugged. "You're the one who said we needed a Leeson."

"Did she say that?" Leeson smiled, looking back and forth between them. A thick leather case sat at his feet.

"Did you ask him to come?" she demanded of Rourke.

"No. Not specifically, but he is here," said Rourke, grinning. "*The* Leeson."

Leeson took two steps toward her, but no more. "Everyone in London is consumed with once and for all putting an end to Tantalus's threat against the city, but at the end of the day, Lord Black and Lady Elena . . . ah, I believe . . . would appreciate a bit of time to themselves, given their recent news. And Mark, well . . . he's off on a new adventure with his dear wife, Willomina. An adventure I don't really fit into."

"If you're not needed then why don't you take the opportunity to go on holiday?" Selene suggested darkly. "You like France, don't you? I've a house there, at Aix-les-Bains. You can go there. I believe the keys are in my jewelry box." She fisted her hands at her waist and bent toward him threateningly. "Let me fetch them now."

"Ah!" Leeson held up a staying hand. "But I have been assigned to Lord Avenage at Swarthwick."

"The Primordials sent you here?"

Rourke held up the envelope and paper. "Oh, yes. It's all rather official. Here are his orders."

She caviled, "There's nothing at all for you to do here. Avenage will start up the contraption and tell them your assistance is not needed at Swarthwick."

Leeson responded hopefully, "I could help his lordship with his daily correspondences, and help to put the place in order." He glanced around the room and up into the rafters.

"Swarthwick *is* in order. Enough, at least, for the few more days that we shall remain here. I'm certain we'll be returning to London shortly. You should get a head start on us, beginning *now*."

"Countess." Rourke lifted a finger. "Pardon me for intruding on your little tirade. But I do believe Mr. Leeson has been assigned to *me*."

"Indeed." Leeson reached for the documents presently in Rourke's possession, and the Raven handed them over. Squinting, Leeson lifted the paper to his eye and read the words. "'Lord Avenage.' I see 'Pavlenco' nowhere in my orders."

"Speaking of the aforementioned contraption," said Rourke, "I do believe that was the primary reason you were sent to Swarthwick. I'm afraid I'm not as adept with modern technology as Tres and Shrew. I require a bit of additional instruction."

Leeson bowed deferentially. "I am an expert in all things contraptionesque."

With a glare to Rourke, Selene said, "Don't expect me to be anywhere he is. I'm going to see about Nathan." She turned to leave them.

Rourke called after her, "Selene, wait. I forgot to tell you last night. He's gone."

Selene exclaimed, "Gone?"

Mr. Leeson interjected, "Nathan . . . a boy with sandy hair and blackened eyes?"

Rourke glanced to the little man. "You know of him?"

"Why yes." He nodded. "He was walking along the road to Swarthwick. He told me he and his sisters were coming here to work."

"Sisters?" Selene frowned. "And you left them there, on the road?"

"Well, of course not," he responded defensively. "I told them to hop into the wagon. When we arrived they made their way to the stables as if they knew where they were going. I just assumed they were expected."

Leaving the two men, Selene cut through the kitchen and crossed the rear courtyard. Passing through the stables, she entered the adjacent set of quarters.

Upon her entrance three faces turned toward her, Nathan's and those of two older girls. They all shared the same tawny coloring and freckled noses. All wore threadbare clothes and strained, hopeful expressions. A short distance behind them, two gray knapsacks had been dropped onto the wood table.

"Your ladyship," said Nathan. "These are my sisters, 'annah and Kate."

The girls curtsied.

"Hello, Hannah. Hello, Kate," said Selene.

Footsteps sounded behind her. Rourke, followed by Leeson.

Nathan stood a bit straighter and cleared his throat. "They was wondering—well, we was wondering—if per'aps your lordship and ladyship might be looking to 'ire any kitchen or 'ousehold 'elp."

"We're willin' to work very 'ard," Hannah offered earnestly.

"We know 'ow to sew and clean and cook," said Kate.

Rourke glanced at Selene before saying, "I'm certain we can find a place for everyone."

Nathan closed his eyes and whispered, "Thank you, sir."

Hannah reached for her sister's hand. Both girls blinked away tears.

"Mr. Leeson, would you make sure they have everything they need here? Clean linens. Blankets, soap and water."

"Of course, your lordship."

To the siblings, Rourke said, "Take the morning to settle in. Mr. Leeson will be the one to assign your duties here in the stable, Nathan, and girls, in the house."

They nodded eagerly.

After a few more moments of friendly small talk, Selene followed the two men outside the stables.

Rourke said to Leeson, "They can help here at Swarthwick until such time that Selene and I return to London."

Selene asked, "What if their stepfather comes after them? I suspect he's not the sort just to let this go."

Rourke met her eyes. Within them, she saw heated but controlled ferocity. "If he does . . . well, I'll take care of it. They won't be returning to that man's home."

"What do you intend for them?" Leeson inquired. "It's not as if the three of us can be their parents." He chuckled.

"Of course not," murmured Rourke, blinking and looking away. "But let us explore the possibilities for their futures. Their upkeep and education."

The one-eyed immortal nodded. "Very good, your lordship, I should be pleased to assist with those arrangements."

"They should be kept together as a family, of course," added Selene, thinking of her own brother, Mark, and how lost she would have been as a child if they had been torn apart after their parents' deaths.

"Yes, Countess. I'm certain that can be arranged."

Selene spent the rest of the day in her room, alternately reading and attempting to provoke her powers into existence. From time to time, she heard footsteps in the hallway outside her door, and Leeson instructing the girls in their new duties.

At around four o'clock a knock sounded on Selene's door.

"Yes?" she called.

The doorknob turned and Hannah peeked in, bearing a small stack of folded linens in her arms. "I thought y' might wish to be aware th't there is a gentleman and a lady downstairs speakin' to Mr. Leeson."

"A gentleman and a lady . . . Oh, blood and thunder. It is Mr. Silverwest and Mrs. Thrall. I completely forgot I had invited them for tea. I've nothing at all prepared."

Chapter Thirteen

"Countess." Mr. Silverwest stood from his chair when she entered the room.

His gaze held hers with rapt intensity as she drew nearer. Everything about him conveyed an awareness of her. An appreciation of her. Truth be told, he was even handsomer than Rourke, with his golden hair, beautiful male features and blue eyes that reminded her of Mediterranean seas. So why did she feel as if Rourke's presence hung over the room like a darkly possessive specter?

Mr. Silverwest's eyes held hers as he bent to kiss her hand. She *did* like him, very much, for an air of mischief emanated from him, and Selene so wished to have her mood lightened.

His beautiful sister stood across the room, smiling warmly. "The keep is absolutely lovely."

Only then did Selene notice the difference in the room. Sunlight streamed through the windows, revealing spotless glass and polished wood. The stone floors gleamed as if they'd been buffed with a thin layer of wax. Several rugs had been spread out. Though faded, they perfectly suited the rustic appearance of the keep. The furniture had been rearranged to better set off the large window, which offered a view of the rolling hills down to the river, but also to direct the eye toward the large hearth on which a hearty fire crackled and glowed.

A perfectly massive arrangement of wide-leafed greenery, punctuated with dark purple umbels and carthy red seedpods, graced the oversize table against the wall. Mrs. Thrall ran her fingertips along the glossy edge of one vivid leaf.

"Wherever did you find these?" she marveled.

I have no idea, Selene prepared to confess. How mortifying. She had not prepared tea or any silly little sandwiches or sweets. In London, one could simply call down to the hotel kitchen for such necessities.

"From the banks of the river," announced a quiet, cultured voice from behind. Leeson entered, bearing an enormous silver tray artfully cluttered with a gleaming silver service and all the necessary accoutrements. Though she fully expected him to throw her a taunting glare, he did no such thing. He simply lowered the tray to the low table that had been placed before the sofa. With a soft click of his heels, he bowed to Selene and said, "Please call, your ladyship, if you should require anything further."

She blinked at him. "Thank you, Leeson."

As Leeson departed the room, Rourke strode in, smartly dressed to receive visitors, in fawn trousers and a dark blue coat. Her heartbeat staggered, as she found herself caught up in his icy green stare. His long fingers smoothed over his tie, as if he had only just put it on.

"Silverwest." He nodded coolly. More warmly, and with a hint of a smile, he greeted the pale blonde who stood at the window. "Mrs. Thrall."

Selene could not help but notice the high flush that stained Mrs. Thrall's cheeks at his appearance. What irritated her more was that a similar warmth arose to her own.

Selene wasn't the domestic sort, but she knew full well how to serve tea.

"Please sit, everyone."

Rourke took the only available seat, that beside Mrs. Thrall on the sofa. Every time he looked at Selene, his eyes stung. God, he had never seen any woman more ravishing.

She sat in a high-backed chair at one side of the crackling hearth, and the bastard Silverwest sat in the other. They glanced at each other, looking like the goddamn perfectly matched king and queen of Thorn-on-the-Moor, he golden, and she all silky, catlike and dark.

Desire heated in his groin, stoked by the knowledge that he had effectively ended things between them the night before.

He had not slept one wink last night. Instead he had paced and cursed and ached to enter her room again to finish making love to her in a way he had only mimicked in coming between her thighs. The memory of her skin and her scent clouded his mind like a thick, unforgettable dream, and he felt eaten up by unsatisfied desire.

Glancing at him only fleetingly over the steaming teapot, she gracefully lifted a teacup and saucer from the tray and poured them full of amber liquid. After both visitors had been creamed and sugared and served, he grumpily accepted his from Selene. Every impulse goaded him to throw the porcelain against the stone wall just so it could splatter and shatter in a satisfying and dramatic display of his displeasure. Only then would his hands be free to claim the countess by the wrists, throw her over his shoulder and carry her to his room, something he wanted to do so badly—because now he knew he could not.

Every time Selene moved, her breasts, which he now knew to be no figment of his dreams, but authentically substantial, pressed against her bodice. Though respectably covered with shining, striped cloth, they seemed to size him up like two bold eyes and, after last night, find him completely lacking. God, he could only imagine the sorts of lacy, silken underthings she wore.

Perhaps he would not feel so damned possessive if Silverwest were not so attentive to her and clearly imagining the same sorts of things.

The small talk blurred into a meaningless hum in his ears until Selene's voice broke through.

"*Avenage.*"

He blinked. "Yes?"

"Mr. Silverwest asked you a question." She smiled at their visitors. "I apologize for my brother's lack of attentiveness. He has been endlessly distracted by matters in London."

"Business?" inquired Mrs. Thrall softly.

"Indeed," he answered.

Selene said, "Mr. Silverwest wanted to know if you were still interested in selling Swarthwick."

"My brother would certainly make an offer worth your while," Mrs. Thrall added, turning bright blue eyes to him. She wore a small green hat draped in black netting and flowers. Her blond hair shone like polished sunlight. For a moment, its color distracted him. Then he remembered the question he had been about to answer.

"I'm sorry," he said. "But after spending the last two weeks here, I have changed my mind."

He would sell the place to Nathan for a shilling over Mr. Silverwest's offer of anything. It was a petulant and ridiculous reaction, he knew, but he couldn't help it.

"No apologies are necessary," Silverwest responded good-naturedly, grinning his damned boyish smile at Selene. "Sometimes it takes coming to the brink of losing something to understand just how dear it is to you."

The man looked at him directly, and in that glance, perhaps even unconsciously, he conveyed an unspoken intention, one that only another man would understand. In any room of mixed company, there was always one dominant male. Silverwest wished to be it.

Not so, growled Rourke's inner competitor.

"We shall simply have to visit often to admire the place," said Mrs. Thrall. "How wonderful that we have you as neighbors."

Silverwest retrieved a gold watch from his trouser pocket. Glancing down, he said, "I've an appointment to look at some livestock at five. Have I told you? I've extended my lease on the Astley place, and if I'm going to do this country-gentleman thing right that I must clutter up the place with some cows and goats and bulls."

Mrs. Thrall said, "Before I forget, were you able to gather any items for the church bazaar? Don't forget that it's tomorrow. You will attend, will you not? The sale is even more important now that money must be raised to pay for a new steeple." She smiled at Rourke. "I've embroidered some handkerchiefs and donated them for the cause. What gentleman ever has enough handkerchiefs?"

She glanced at Selene, her delicate brows raised. "I know the parson would appreciate anything. Anything at all."

Selene nodded. "Of course. I'm certain I have something. If you could wait here for just a moment?"

She arose from her chair. Simultaneously, Rourke and Silverwest stood in polite acknowledgment of her exit. Their eyes met. Silverwest smiled engagingly. While Selene was gone, Mrs. Thrall prattled on about the Astley estate and the villagers she had met. *Blah blah, blah blah blah.* Rourke nodded at polite intervals and said, "I see," when it seemed appropriate, eventually resting his chin on his curled fist. Silverwest moved about the room, looking at every stone and tapestry and gewgaw, his hands clasped behind his back.

At last, Selene returned, holding a basket by its handle.

"I'm afraid I am not very talented with a needle and thread. Or yarn. Or paint . . ." She smiled self-deprecatingly and waved a hand. "Or food or . . . Well, you understand, so in the alternative I have gathered a few belongings I no longer need."

Mrs. Thrall insisted softly, "But certainly you have many talents."

Defeating evil souls. Cutting off heads. Stabbing swords through wicked black hearts. Driving men sexually insane. Rourke seethed.

Selene shrugged. "I enjoy riding and archery."

"Ah, a sportswoman," said Silverwest admiringly. Rourke observed his heated gaze travel over Selene's corseted waist and the lush profusion of her bustle.

Rourke growled.

Silverwest glanced at him. "Pardon?"

"There's a bit of smoke from the fireplace." He raised a finger, pointing at nothing in particular. "Just clearing my throat."

Selene handed the basket to Mrs. Thrall, who nearly dropped it. "Oh, my. It's heavier than I expected." She reached inside and pulled out two books tied together with an orange satin ribbon. She turned the scarlet, gilt-lettered volumes to the side and read their titles. "*A Pictorial History of the Thames*. And *Voyages Extraordinaires* by a . . . Mr. Verne. I have never heard of that author, but they are lovely. From your own collection?"

"Yes, but it seems my tastes have changed of late. You are welcome to sell them at whatever price you see fit."

"What is this?" Mrs. Thrall pulled out a bright turquoise velveteen bag tied with a thick red tassel. Setting down the basket, she tugged at the cord.

The young woman gasped.

Rourke choked. Silverwest's eyes widened.

From Mrs. Thrall's upturned palm spilled thick gold chains, a large ruby pendant, and several jeweled rings.

"Are these real?"

"I assume so," answered Selene. She gathered teacups and saucers and returned them to the silver tray, clearly oblivious to everyone's shock. "I've never had them appraised."

"Those jewels are worth twenty new steeples," declared Silverwest.

"Well, then, perhaps they can afford new stairs as well. I saw them from the road. If they are not replaced, one day soon someone will fall straight through."

Mr. Leeson appeared with Mrs. Thrall's shawl and Mr. Silverwest's overcoat.

Mrs. Thrall extended the basket to Rourke. "Could you hold this for me, please, Lord Avenage?" She pulled her shawl about her shoulders and worked to tie it artfully over her breast. "The rest of my day will be spent collecting items from the remainder of the gentry in the area, and pricing them for tomorrow's sale." Her prattle interfered with his ability to overhear whatever Mr. Silverwest was saying to Selene. That wouldn't normally occur, but his present state of agitation likely thwarted his abilities—which was exactly why he needed to forget his obsession with the countess and return himself to the single-minded warrior he had been for the past eight centuries.

Once the visiting pair had gone, he strode off in the direction of his study.

"Where are you going?" asked Selene quietly.

"To see if Leeson has returned the contraption to working order. Perhaps there will be instructions to return to London, and I can be spared the misery of any further afternoon tea with neighbors."

Selene watched him go, knowing he wished, more than anything, to get away from her. It wasn't in her nature to persist, to attempt to seduce a man who had no interest in her. So she again withdrew to her room. There, she found Kate dusting and Hannah refilling the water pitcher.

"Good afternoon," she said.

"Good afternoon, my lady," Kate responded cheerfully. Hannah nodded and curtsied shyly.

Days before, Selene had hung a number of her dresses on the far wall so that the creases from their being packed into the trunks might ease.

Kate, clearly the more outgoing of the two, said, "Your gowns are lovely. Do you have them made in London or Paris?"

"Wherever I happen to be at the moment."

Selene could not help but notice again the faded and threadbare state of their clothing. They were ill fitting and overly large, and she could only assume the plain shirts and long skirts had once belonged to their mother. Even as a child, Selene had always been splendidly adorned. Her mother considered her and her brother, Mark, trophies of her love affair with Mark Antony, just as their elder brother, Caesarian, had represented her relationship with Caesar. Even after Cleopatra and Antony were dead, Selene had made a glamorous prisoner. Octavian had paraded her and Mark through the streets, his war prizes shackled in gold chains.

She was actually very fond of children—she just did not have much experience with them.

Seeing how the girls' eyes repeatedly returned to the silks and satins and taffetas on the wall, she unlatched the second of her trunks and peered inside.

"I have been meaning to unpack this trunk. Could both of you assist me?"

Two pairs of cheeks flushed, and in the passing of a second, the girls stood on either side of her. She lifted a rose-colored gown. The color reminded her of Mrs. Thrall on the afternoon of their introduction. Though the woman had done nothing to offend her, remembering how the petite blonde had sat beside Rourke on the sofa during their call and gazed up at him so worshipfully . . . well, Selene didn't think she would ever wear that shade of pink again.

"I don't know why this gown was sent up from London." She sighed. "The garment is too small for me to wear, you see. The modiste cut the fabric to the wrong measurements, but I was abroad at the time, and when I returned it was too late to send it back."

Kate bit her bottom lip.

"That's a 'orrible shame," declared Hannah, appearing truly traumatized.

"Do either of you like pink?"

Their eyes widened, so big and excited she feared their blue-irised eyeballs would pop right out of their heads. "And here's another."

Green. Mrs. Thrall had worn pale green this afternoon. Apparently green was also the color of Selene's damnable envy. Selene selected four in all, the most modestly styled and trimmed of the lot. Her poor modiste in Paris took the blame for each "imperfect" garment. Given how much money she had earned from Selene over the past several seasons, Selene didn't think the woman would at all mind.

Selene threw open the wooden cabinet. "I've got a sewing kit."

Elena, always a practical girl, had included the silly thing in one of the trunks. Selene didn't exactly *know* what to do with the contents of the sewing kit, but she gave it to the girls with the hope that they could work the alterations out themselves. Hannah and Kate beamed at her over the heaps of voluminous fabric in their arms. After planting new petticoats atop each pile, she sent them out the door with orders to "rest" for the remainder of the afternoon, as they would all be traveling into town for the church bazaar the next day.

Again, Tedium-on-the-Moor proved an apt moniker for the village. Anyone else, on observing the reactions of joy on the girls' faces, would have thought they'd been invited to one of Lady Kerrigan's famous Curzon Street fetes.

Selene closed the door and lay back on her bed. That bit of generosity had felt *good*, just as it had felt good to know her donated items would help with the purchase of the new church steeple.

"Dear Lord." She giggled, staring at the high, beamed ceiling. "Thank goodness no one saw that."

The barest hint of fragrance drew her attention to her bedside table. There amid the clutter of her books and her brush and perfume was a single black lotus bloom, a purple ribbon tied onto its thick green stem.

Taking it in hand, she swept from her room. The kitchen was empty, save for the marvelous scent of whatever simmered over the fire. She caught up to the girls as they crossed the back courtyard, their arms still loaded with their inherited finery. "Kate! Hannah! I've a question for you!"

"Yes," answered Hannah.

"Did the two of you leave this flower in my room?"

"Yes," said Kate. "It's very pretty. Mr. Leeson said he brought it with him all the way from London."

Leeson. Her chest tightened with realization.

"Do you know where Mr. Leeson is at present?" she inquired.

"Last we saw, on the hillside beating carpets with Nathan."

"Thank you, girls." Selene left them and, still carrying the bloom, rounded the side of the keep and took the incline. Sure enough, she found Leeson and Nathan beating carpets that hung over a rope that had been drawn between two tall posts. Both held paddles formed of wood and crisscrossed metal bands.

"That's the way." Leeson chortled. "Smash it again! We'll make a winning cricket player out of you yet!"

Nathan laughed, swinging at the carpet. A puff of dust sprang out. He sputtered.

"Mr. Leeson." Selene announced her presence imperiously.

He turned, his one eye watering. He coughed and rubbed it free of dust.

"Keep at it, boy; I'll return in a moment." Wary of expression, he walked toward Selene, his gaze descending to the bloom she held in her hand.

"Yes, my lady?"

"*You.*"

"Me, what?"

She softened. Melted. "You have been leaving me the lotus blooms. The ones in London, and now today."

He shrugged. "The girls . . ."

"No, *you.*"

"Yes, me," he admitted, flushing a deep red.

"How am I supposed to despise you now?"

"You could always just . . . give up on that," he offered hopefully. "I must say also that something about the country . . . or Transcension . . . seems to agree with you." He laughed softly. "I am, of course, jesting about the Transcension part. I truly believe Lady Black's serum cured you of that. Don't you?"

"I do," she answered quietly. "You must report your opinion on that subject to the Primordials next time you're on the contraption. I so desperately wish to return to London."

"I will." He nodded, peering up at her. "I most certainly will."

She grasped his face in her hands. His bristly handle-bar mustache tickled her palms. His eyes widened as she bent over him and planted a kiss at the center of his balding forehead. "I suspect I have always adored you. I just didn't know it."

A smile of unadulterated joy spread across his aged features, crinkling the skin beside his brown eye. "There's the difference. I've always known I adored you. You just weren't a true match for Lord Black, and he wasn't a true match for you."

"Maybe *you* are the man for me," she suggested slyly, but the image of Rourke's stern face flashed through her mind.

"Oh, my, Countess." He squeezed her hands where they still rested on his cheeks, and flushed even more deeply scarlet. "If only that were true."

The next few days passed in a uneventful cycle of activity. With Leeson in the house, as well as Nathan, Kate and Hannah, it became easier to avoid Rourke, and likewise for him to avoid her. She passed time with the girls, taking walks and answering every question they had about the world and Parisian fashion and books. Rourke, for his part, kept company with Nathan and Leeson. They were always fixing something about the keep. Hammering, tinkering and sawing. During the days, she felt rather confident she could maneuver through her remaining time at Swarthwick and avoid the loss of her heart. Only the nights were difficult as she lay in her bed. The effects of the vaccine seemed to have worn off in that she no longer suffered a need to sleep so heavily, or for extended periods of time. Instead, she suffered the extended periods of wakefulness she had experienced since childhood. In London, Rourke retreated to his room only late at night, likely when he thought she already slept. She would hear him through the open space in the wall. He did not speak aloud; it was just the sound of his bed creaking or his sheets rustling as he turned. Very rarely he snored, and for some reason that made her smile. The sound made her lonely too.

And yet on this morning, after she dressed, she made a point to find him. Customarily he began each day in his study, reviewing the night's reports from London, both from the Primordials and the Ravens, and in turn preparing his orders to the Ravens. And indeed, when she entered his study he sat at his desk. A bronze headpiece circled Leeson's head, one that featured an earpiece. He muttered unintelligibly, at least to her. Unlike Leeson, she wasn't an Ancient—one of thirty-nine surviving beings who had begun their lives at the start of time as Amaranthines—and as such, she could not comprehend what he was saying. The language simply wasn't teachable to others. It was born into them.

Rourke met her eyes. "Good morning, Selene."

She could not help but perceive the way his attention lingered on her lips and descended to drink in the rest of her. Though her body awakened in response, she rejected his interest.

He had no business looking at her like that. She almost told him so but in the end decided it was better to simply pretend she hadn't noticed.

With a tilt of her head, she inquired, "Is there any word?"

He wouldn't give her specifics; she knew that. Not until he had clearance from the Primordials to do so. However, he had since their arrival provided enough generalities to satisfy her curiosity about the state of things in London.

He leaned forward in his chair. "Archer sends word that nearly all of the Eye of Pharos has been recovered from the Thames."

The Eye of Pharos was a powerful mirror once used in the legendary Lighthouse of Alexandria, Egypt, during the third century B.C. to shine a brilliant light out over the ocean to provide guidance to incoming ships. Its intense reflective light and heat could also be used as a weapon against attacking fleets or armies. Tantalus's *brotoi*, the Dark Bride, had sought to use the Eye as a weapon in the dominion of London. Weeks before, as the Shadow Guards had fought against her, the mirror had been lost in the river Thames.

"Why do you say 'nearly all'?"

"Apparently the mirror shattered as it descended into the river. The Primordials had to ask for assistance from the Nereids to search for and recover all the pieces."

"They do like small, sparkly things," said Selene. "Still, the Thames is filthy. I can only imagine how difficult it was to find every shard."

"Other than that news, they suspect there is another *brotoi* on the loose. Your Reclaimers caught hold of a powerful thread of *trace*, only for him—"

"Or her," said Selene. In her experience, the female *brotoi* could be just as bloodthirsty as the males.

"Correct." Rourke tipped the point of his ink pen to her. "Only for him or *her* to disappear into Whitechapel."

Selene nodded. No doubt Whitechapel would remain the hunting grounds of Tantalus's *brotoi*. The dense concentration of misery in that poverty-stricken district, inhabited by the most desperate and forgotten poor of London, assured them a hiding place. A Reclaimer's hunting skills relied, to some extent, upon the emotions and thoughts—or the utter absence thereof—that emanated from Transcending souls. When such deteriorated souls were immersed so thickly in the hatred, envy and despair of that district, the Reclaimers' ability to distinguish them from the rest of the population became much more challenging.

Here in the country, it would be rather easy to pick up a *brotoi*'s trace.

"I assume they are scouring the morgues?" she asked.

"Yes, but so far they have found no victims they can link to a *brotoi*."

Such deaths would be easy to single out from the others in the city. So far all the *brotoi* the Reclaimers had encountered seemed to favor knives. They stabbed, cut, mutilated and dismembered their victims with bloody glee. There was also the lingering question of missing body parts, both internal and external.

Heads, for example . . . someone was hoarding heads.

"Sounds a bit too quiet in London to me," said Selene.

He steepled his fingers, tilted his chair back and stared up at the ceiling. "Which probably means something big is about to happen."

She gnawed at her thumbnail. "My thoughts exactly."

Leeson removed the bronze headpiece and turned from the contraption. With a nod to Rourke, he announced, "Your reports have been submitted to the Primordials and your orders conveyed to the Ravens in the Tower of London. Will there be anything else this morning, your lordship?"

"No, there is nothing more," said Rourke.

Selene sighed. "I suppose that as we've been excluded from the biggest, most important battle against evil since you-know-who got cast out of you-know-where, we might as well do the next-best thing and go on with our plan to attend to the church bazaar."

Chapter Fourteen

A half hour later they arrived at Thorn-on-the-Moor, under the watchful escort of Rourke's raven, who flew escort in the sky high above.

Nathan, Rourke and Leeson rode up top on the driver's bench, while Selene and the girls traveled inside. As they entered the village, they pushed open the windows and leaned out to observe the ongoing festivities. The churchyard was already crowded with people, all dressed in their finest.

Selene searched the multitude for the children's stepfather, knowing that Rourke and Leeson did the same. Unlike her, the two male immortals had the added benefit of their Amaranthine senses. However, Leeson had never had a personal encounter with the man, so he would be unfamiliar with the mortal's *trace*. Additionally, although the children's father was clearly a lost soul, he was not Transcended and would not give off the same stench as one of those highly deteriorated souls.

Would Rourke recognize the man's *trace*? Remembering how out of his mind with rage he had been at witnessing Nathan's beating, Selene suspected not. His thoughts likely would have been too clouded at the time to commit such a memory to mind, which was why they would all have to be vigilant and keep not only their minds but their eyes open at all times. Still, Selene fully intended to have a wonderful afternoon. She had always loved dinner parties, balls and elaborate costume productions—the clothes, the crush of people, the pageantry and the wine. She supposed that until life got back to normal, events such as the church bazaar would have to do.

It was in her nature to draw attention, to seek admiration through her appearance and even, yes, her independent and sometimes outrageous behavior. Even though she had difficulty admitting it to herself, perhaps it was because she didn't think Selene . . . just *Selene* . . . would garner anyone's loyalty or love. But she was just Selene today, and already she was having the most marvelous time with Kate and Hannah. She had curled and pinned their hair, and they glowed with pride wearing their altered gowns.

Still, some habits were difficult to break. She had chosen to wear a chartreuse gown, slightly more green than yellow. With her Mediterranean coloring, she could wear the color with confidence and know she would catch the attention of every eye.

Rourke drew the town coach into a field beside rows of wagons and curricles. Everyone climbed down onto the grass.

"Nathan. Kate. Hannah." Rourke produced a leather pouch from his trouser pocket.

He addressed the three. "Mr. Leeson tells me how hard you've all worked over the past few days, getting my filthy, previously feline-infested house in order." He pressed several coins into each of their hands. The siblings grinned at one another. "This is not part of your weekly pay, but in addition to it. One word of caution— don't spend your coins all on sweets."

Selene experienced the overwhelming urge to kiss Rourke hard on the mouth. But, of course, that wasn't possible. Instead she thrust her wide-brimmed straw hat onto her head and averted her face so that he would not observe any trace of her admiration.

While the men declared their intention to play horseshoes, she and the girls set off in the direction of the secondhand sale. On their way, Selene smiled and greeted all the village ladies who turned to gawk at her chartreuse gown, and politely ignored all the men who did the same.

Amidst a gaggle of women, Selene recognized the two elderly matrons who had days before sold her the eggs in the grocer's shop. She stopped to offer her greetings and to marvel at the size, taste and quality of the eggs. In doing so, she made several new acquaintances. Looking up, she saw that Hannah and Kate had moved on to wander among the tables of goods set out for sale.

"Countess," called a female voice. Sunlight glimmered off blond hair. Mrs. Thrall waved from the steps of the church.

Selene crossed the grassy lot. Mrs. Thrall, dressed in green—a distinctly Avenage shade of green—reached for her hand. "I want you to know, my dear new friend, that nearly all of your jewels have been sold—likely for astoundingly low prices—but we have already earned twice the amount needed to replace the church steeple. The parson is absolutely beside himself with happiness."

"I am so glad to hear that, Mrs. Thrall."

"Please, we are not in a London parlor, but in Thorn-on-the-Moor. You must call me Dora."

"And you must call me Selene."

It seemed only right to offer the familiarity in return.

Dora drew her in the direction of a cluster of chairs that had been set out on the lawn. There a number of ladies sat with circular hoops on their laps, poking needles into stretched squares of linen.

Dora gushed, "You must come and admire the lovely handiwork of the village ladies."

Oh, dear. Needlework. Anything but that.

Selene glanced over her shoulder, desperately searching for Hannah and Kate. Seeing them nowhere, she answered, "Perhaps for a short while."

After an hour of playing horseshoes and a number of other country games, Rourke had left Nathan and

Leeson at one of the crowded tables, feasting on meat pasties. He had gone in search of Selene and the girls, just to be sure they were safe and well. Though the occasion for the gathering centered about the church and the replacement of its lightning-felled steeple, he had observed a bit of drunkenness at the edges of the crowd, and in the back of his mind, he wondered if Nathan's stepfather would make an appearance and cause trouble. He had picked up on that fear as it ran through the minds of all three of the children.

At present, he stood in the shadows beneath a large tree and watched Selene. It appeared that the last of her baubles had just been purchased by a hunchbacked old farmer for his hunchbacked old wife. Having apparently been impressed into service, the countess had packaged the necklace up herself, and sent the beaming couple on their way before taking a seat among the other village women.

The afternoon light had softened, and she had removed her hat. It currently hung off her knee, suspended there by its wide velvet ribbon. At the moment, she appeared to be a vivacious, mischievous girl in the midst of a cluster of older married women. He rather liked her chartreuse gown, and apparently, from the thoughts being bantered around the churchyard, so did all the other men of the village.

God, how he wanted her, and he did not know how much longer he could hold himself distant. He had decided to put in a request to the Primordials in the morning for either a replacement Shadow Guard to be sent to continue the duty of watching over her, or perhaps she could be left in Leeson's more than competent hands. As a better alternative still, he would press the Council to allow them all to return to London. Selene had shown no sign of Transcending, and though her powers had not returned, who could say they ever would? They could not remain in Swarthwick forever. Who knew how long this thing with Tantalus would extend? Decades? Centuries, perhaps? Something had to change.

If things went on as they had, he would be begging

her to allow him back in her bed by week's end. He couldn't allow that to happen.

It wasn't about the sex. He thoroughly sated his desires on other women, never holding back on completing the act as he had with Selene. But those women had been faceless and, by his choice, pale haired. In his mind, they merged with the mistress of his nightmares in such a way that he never derived true pleasure or intimacy by committing the act of . . . lovemaking?

No, never.

The difference with Selene . . . bloody hell, his gut felt twisted with it.

He *saw* her. Felt her. Ached inside from just knowing she existed on the earth, so close to him—and that he could not touch her. Not in the way he so desperately wished.

Eight centuries before, as he had felt the fire and pain of immortality consuming his mortal blood, he had made a vow to remain eternally alone in penance for his sin, understanding that the only way to ever leave immortality would be death—and certain deliverance into the waiting fires of hell.

One didn't just walk away from a vow like that. But part of him argued that as many times as he had made love to her in his dreams and in his fantasies, he might as well follow through. Certainly the consequences couldn't be any worse than his present state of torture.

Suddenly, in a chartreuse blur, Selene leapt up, leaving her hat and her chair overturned behind her. She streaked across the churchyard.

His gaze snapped to the source of her concern. A hulking monolith of a man dragged Hannah and Kate toward a wagon—quite literally, with his hands fisted in their hair. It was Nathan's stepfather. In the haze of his prior fury, Rourke supposed he just didn't remember how large the man was, but he dwarfed the girls as they stumbled and tried to keep up with his long-legged pace.

Rourke could not shift into shadow and be there in an instant, not in front of this crowd. Instead he raced toward them on foot.

"You, there," Selene bellowed. "Stop."

Hannah sobbed. Selene leapt onto his back. Instantly he released the girls, but reached over his shoulders to grab Selene. He whirled, wrenching her off. She landed sprawling on the gravel. The girls crawled toward her. Suddenly, his arm went up and metal flashed—a knife. Voices shouted. Screamed. The emotions of shock and fear clouded the air.

The girls' stepfather lunged toward the girls, plunging the knife down, but Selene threw herself across them.

Rourke reached them.

An arm swung, knocking the bastard flat onto his back. Not *his* arm.

Silverwest, his face a grimace of anger, yanked the dazed man to his feet and escorted him to the edge of the yard. There, he released him to a horde of men who had quickly gathered, and who hustled him into his wagon. Someone slapped the haunch of his scrawny horse and off they all went, escorting the half-unconscious brute toward the edge of the village.

Rourke retrieved the knife and knelt beside Selene and the girls. "Did he hurt you?"

Silverwest reached down and offered her his hand. Selene accepted, and he pulled her up. "Lady Pavlenco. Girls. Are you hurt?" He rested a gentle hand on each of the girls' shoulders.

Hannah and Kate gazed at Silverwest through red, tearstained eyes, but with such obvious worship Rourke wanted to poke his own eyes out. Selene, though more reserved, did the same.

He exhaled. It was ridiculous for him to be angry in any way when Silverwest had done exactly what he himself had intended to do. The man ought to be commended.

Swallowing his pride, Rourke extended his hand. "Well-done, Silverwest. Thank you."

Silverwest thrust his hand into Rourke's. "I saw him and how he had the girls by the hair and . . . I just lost my mind. I only wish I'd gotten here sooner. How could anyone be so violent toward children or women?"

Rourke nodded. "Tomorrow morning I will travel to York to speak with the authorities. He can't be allowed to hurt the children or anyone else again." Also foremost in his mind was Nathan's revelation that his stepfather had been responsible for his mother's death. He had wanted to give the boy and his sisters a bit more time before putting them in the position of testifying against their stepfather, but this afternoon's incident added urgency to the matter.

"Agreed. I shall ride with you if you wish." Silverwest looked at Selene. "But as for this moment, the countess is to be commended for her bravery and her selflessness. I shudder to think how near she came to death, throwing herself in front of the girls that way." He grasped her elbow. "Did you see how dangerously close the knife blade came to your breast? To your heart, Countess?"

For a moment, Selene looked perplexed. The rigidness of her shoulders softened. "I'm just relieved they are safe."

The crowd around them slowly dispersed. Mrs. Thrall rushed up, her face pale. "Is anyone hurt?"

"Truly, you are all right?" Silverwest inquired of the girls and Selene, touching each of the girls atop their heads. Everyone nodded. Mrs. Thrall ran her hands over the girls' sandy hair, smoothing the snarls their stepfather had made.

To Selene, Silverwest said, "You are something exceptional, do you know that?" His eyes glowed with admiration.

Leeson and Nathan trotted up.

"We heard a commotion," Said Leeson.

" 'at was him, wasn't it?" Nathan stared, stricken, toward the road down which the wagon had disappeared.

Rourke, too, peered toward the edge of town. "I don't think he'll be coming back."

Silverwest arched his arms around the shoulders of the three siblings. "What do you all say to some punch? My treat."

He herded them in the direction of the grocer's table, where Mr. Harbottle and his wife had been selling drinks and prepared foods to the villagers.

Leeson looked up at Rourke. "He seems to be a nice fellow."

Rourke closed his eyes and nodded.

An hour later, Rourke approached the happy group. Hannah and Kate had spent their coins on ribbons for their hair, and Nathan peered at everyone and everything through his newly acquired telescope. Selene sat between Mr. Silverwest and Mrs. Thrall on a large red-and-white-checked blanket.

The last time he had seen Leeson, the old man had been flirting outrageously with the youngest of the two gray-haired egg ladies.

Peering up at the fading sky, Rourke crouched beside Selene. "We'd better return to Swarthwick. It will be dark soon."

Softly, so only he could hear, she responded, "Can't we stay a bit longer? You can see in the dark. Leeson too."

He answered, "Are we pretending to be mortals or no?" He tilted his head toward the street. "Do you see? Everyone's making their way to their wagons."

"I suppose you're right." Turning to the others, she said, "Everyone, it's getting late. Time for us to return to Swarthwick."

Together they stood, and Selene and Mrs. Thrall—or Dora, as she had insisted on everyone calling her—folded the blanket. When everyone had gathered their hats and other belongings, they walked toward the carriage.

Rourke stilled. He was taller than anyone else in the crowd, and above the laughter and voices, he heard something. A jangling of sorts.

Selene felt Rourke's hand close on her arm, and his body moved close behind hers. She didn't move a muscle, wanting to savor his nearness for as long as possible. He stared toward the east end of the village. Everyone else walked on, oblivious.

"What is it?" she asked.

"Something is coming."

In the purpling twilight, the announcement came off as a bit ominous.

True to his word, five men marched out from around the corner of the stables, each bearing a blazing torch. The muted *boom*, *boom*, *boom* of drums followed them.

Smiling broadly, they spread out across the road. The villagers, whose faces reflected a mixture of mistrust and enraptured interest, fell back, giving them a wide berth.

Four young women dressed in scarlet harem costumes and veils that revealed only their thickly painted eyes spun out from between the torchbearers, shaking tambourines and drawing gasps of admiration—and likely shock—from the crowd. By modern standards, the young women were scandalously underdressed, although the "bare" skin of their arms and stomachs was, upon closer examination, demurely covered by flesh-colored fabric.

A small band formed of twelve performers strode out behind. Trumpets sounded and cymbals crashed. Fully emerged onto the street, they rattled off a raucous tune. A horse clip-clopped past, a girl in a green spangled dress balancing in a pirouette atop its back, her arms out to her sides. Clowns with painted faces and wide white collars passed out printed notices.

They shouted, "Acrobats! Pantomimes! Dancing bear!"

Along the edge of the procession walked a tall, thin man with a narrow mustache, wearing a scarlet coat and a very high top hat.

"It's a *circus*!" shouted Nathan. Beside him, his sisters went up on their toes in excitement.

"Look!" Hannah grasped Selene's sleeve, her eyes wide. "That's a kangaroo."

The animal bounded past, accompanied by a keeper who held its leash.

Selene read from the bill. "It says they'll be putting on shows for the next five nights."

"Where?" Dora inquired, her lips tilted in amusement.

Selene held up the bill so everyone could see. "It says in the field on the edge of town. I suppose that is where they always set up, is it not?"

The circus band halted in the street outside the churchyard and struck up another lively tune. The clowns paired up and comically danced with one another, while the harem girls plucked farmers and youths from the crowd and drew them into the steps.

Soon, other couples took to the street, joining arms and spinning around in a traditional country dance. Nathan, Kate and Hannah ran to watch. Someone touched her arm. Glancing up, she saw that Mr. Silverwest had come to stand beside her. His eyes glinted with mischief. "Countess, I cannot pass up this opportunity. Would you do me the honor of dancing with me?"

Selene loved to dance. She nodded her assent. He claimed her hand and pulled her into the growing crowd. From the first turn, she knew he was a skillful dancer. Like a matador brimming with competence, he twirled her and guided her through the crowd with nary a pause. The night grew darker, and the scene a bit surreal. They danced through one, two, three more songs. She glimpsed Nathan and the girls in fragmented snatches as they moved past. The torches flashed. The drums boomed.

"I'm so dizzy," she murmured in Mr. Silverwest's ear.

Laughing, he guided her out of the crowd and beneath the grocer's shop awning. It was darker there.

His eyes suddenly smoky, he bent over her.

Transfixed, she watched his handsome mouth descend. Her mind produced one thought: *Rourke*.

"*Selene*," called Rourke sharply, striding toward them.

In the distance, Leeson steered the carriage from the field onto the dirt road. Through the open windows, she could see Nathan and his sisters' faces. "We've gathered everyone else. It's time to go."

Silverwest smiled and watched her go.

Rourke forced himself not to glare at Silverwest. His displeasure far exceeded that of a protective brother.

Instead he guided Selene by the elbow along the edge of the crowd toward the waiting carriage.

He tried to keep the words inside, but they burned up from this throat to burst from his lips. "He was going to kiss you."

She shrugged. "Maybe he was."

"Would you have let him?" he demanded.

She did not respond.

"Would you have let him?"

"I don't know," she muttered in a low voice.

With a tug of her arm, he turned her toward him. "Did you want him to?"

A wide-mouthed clown circled them, legs bent at the knees and arms swinging out to his sides like a gorilla. A group of children followed in a long line, laughing and mimicking his comical stride.

Confusion flickered across Selene's face. "I don't know that either."

Her softly spoken admission stung, even though he'd forced it from her under duress.

"You go from kissing me to—"

She pulled her elbow free. "I have never kissed you. I have only kissed you *back*. Once."

"You have kissed me," he blurted, his words somehow freer because of the surreal scene going on about them. "But you wouldn't remember."

She halted in the street and whispered, "What do you mean?"

"In the carriage, on the way from York. You kissed me and you told me you dreamed about mc all the time."

She frowned and glanced toward the carriage, then back to him. "Why would you say that now, after everything that's happened between us these past few days?"

He could not answer. He did want her, but he couldn't have her. How could he explain that to her without spilling out the blackest secrets of his soul?

Her gaze did not waver from his. "I do dream about you."

She stepped closer, too close for propriety on a public

street, but then, he supposed to everyone else they just appeared to be a quarrelsome brother and sister.

She continued, "If you must know, I think I even dreamed about you while I slept in the Tower. Sometimes we talked, but mostly, Rourke—"

"We made love," he finished.

Her lips parted and she exhaled.

"I had dreams too. Possibly the same dreams. All the time you were in the Tower, and afterward."

"I suspected." She nodded slowly. "That night, when I had the dream about that filthy worm and you came into my room, I saw the tattoo of the raven's wings on your back . . . I already knew they would be there."

Rourke swallowed.

"What does this mean?" she whispered.

"I don't know. But the dreams have made it damn difficult for me to be around you. Come on. People are starting to stare."

Again, Rourke took her elbow and led her toward the carriage. She climbed inside with Nathan and the girls. He climbed onto the driver's perch. As twilight darkened into night, he took the reins from Leeson and they departed the village. Though Leeson scoured the road for any irregularities, for the sake of the horses' safety Rourke kept the pace moderate. For that reason, half an hour later, they were still only halfway to Swarthwick.

The sound of a horse's hooves thudding against earth carried on the air. A rider appeared out of the darkness. He overshot the carriage, but circled back around.

Rourke said, "Good evening, sir."

The man's face shone pale in the night. He gasped for each breath. "Your lordship. There's something terrible up there. You won't want the children to see."

"What is it?" Rourke demanded in a quiet voice, gesturing for the man to sidle his animal closer.

"It's a dead girl," he hissed. "Off on the side of the road. She's been slashed to bits."

Chapter Fifteen

The man continued, "My companions are going to re-main with her until I return with the law."

"Go, then." Rourke nodded.

"Damn," cursed Leeson. "There is violence and mur-der everywhere in this mortal world. Even here."

The rider clattered off.

Rourke twisted in the chair and looked down. Selene leaned out the window.

"Did you hear that?" he asked quietly.

She nodded. "I told the children that someone is hurt. Rourke, they asked if it was their stepfather. We are rid-ing alongside his property, you know."

Indeed they were.

There was no alternate route to Swarthwick. With a flick of his wrists, he continued onward until the light of a lantern held aloft became a visible bright spot in the night, illuminating a circle of high grass and the faces of two men. He told Leeson, "Stay here. I'm going to go have a look."

He climbed down and approached the men.

"I am Lord Avenage," he announced. "My property, Swarthwick, is just up the road from here. I understand there has been a death."

With their wide eyes and blanched faces, they ap-peared scared half out of their minds. All at once, he felt someone beside him. Selene grasped his arm. "I want to see as well. Leeson is staying behind with the children."

"Oh, sir," called one of the men, striding toward them. "You won't wish for the lady to see this."

She quietly announced, "I must see if it's anyone I know."

"I think perhaps his lordship should look first," he said, stepping back.

"Very well," agreed Selene.

They could not know—nor could he tell them—that throughout her existence she had seen many corpses, and so many of them terribly destroyed.

"Go on," she whispered to him.

Rourke approached. The girl lay faceup in a circle of tall, bloodstained grass, her blue eyes wide open. She had red hair and clasped one of the circus bills in her hand. Whoever had killed her had indeed slashed her to bits.

"How did you find her?"

The taller of the two men answered, "Both of her shoes and the contents of her valise were strewn across the road, with bits of her clothes." He pointed, and Rourke followed the path he indicated. Indeed, it appeared the girl had been chased across the road. Spools of thread, a number of handkerchiefs and a set of metal measuring cups were scattered about. Blood stained the dirt. Selene closed her eyes. The young girl's last moments had clearly been ones of terror.

"Is it Hannah the tinker?" asked Selene.

"It would be difficult to tell," answered one of the men softly, "if not for her hair. That's Hannah, all right."

Rourke looked into the darkness at the side of the road. Though the depth of the night was such that the mortals beside him would not be able to see the same distance, he perceived a small hovel of a cottage. Outside, an old horse wandered beside a wagon. It was the same wagon in which the children's stepfather had come to town.

At that moment, the cottage erupted into flames.

* * *

Four days later, the parish constable who had led the investigation into Hannah's murder rapped on Swarthwick's door and, after being invited inside, shared the results of his investigation. Selene ensured that Nathan, Hannah and Kate were occupied with Leeson in the back courtyard with their daily cricket lessons before rejoining them.

"Yes, your lordship." The constable nodded. "After the mishap with her wagon, our poor Hannah apparently spent a few days traveling and encamping with the circus folk. From what I've been told, she eventually set off on her own, ahead of the rest, with the intention to return to her home at Thorn-on-the-Moor. At some point she must have crossed paths with her killer. We found him in the burned-out cottage, the knife at his feet. There were other items found that people recall seeing in Hannah's wagon. He may have kept her prisoner there, in his house, for days before she attempted escape. We do believe that after killing the girl, he killed himself, either with the blade or by committing himself to the fire. Clearly the fellow was out of his mind."

Selene moved to stand beside Rourke. She didn't know what to say. While on one hand she felt relief that he would never hurt the children again, the gruesome deaths hung like a dark cloud over the valley.

After breaking the news of their stepfather's death to Nathan, Kate and Hannah, she and Rourke had moved them from the stables into the house. While the children didn't appear to be saddened over his passing, they were nonetheless affected. Nathan now slept with Leeson in what had once been the servants' quarters off the kitchen. While Rourke worked to convert one of the storerooms into a bedroom for the girls, they slept on pallets on Selene's floor.

"Thank you, sir." Rourke led the constable out. Turning to Selene, he said, "I suppose that's it. I'll send a report to the Primordials, letting them know the constable's conclusions."

The morning after the murder, she had been present as Rourke had disclosed the occurrence of the murder to the Council, and Selene's proximity to the crime. He and Leeson had both offered personal testimony as to her whereabouts when the murder would have been committed. Rourke had also emphasized his belief that the Transcension in her mind had been completely reversed. Although she had not seen a return of her powers, he requested permission for them all to return to London. As for the children, no firm decisions had yet been made as to their future home and education.

The past four days had been spent pleasantly enough, with neither she nor Rourke revisiting the extraordinary possibility of their shared dreams. Every afternoon, however, she had observed him leaving the keep and making the trek toward the plateau. She had not attempted to follow him again.

Selene returned with Rourke to the great room. "The children have been asking to go to the circus. Tonight is the final show before they travel on. After the terrible news about their stepfather, I think clowns and acrobats would certainly boost their spirits."

He nodded. "All right. Then let's take them."

When the time for the show neared, Selene again climbed inside the carriage with the children. As they traveled past their stepfather's burned-out cottage, the last place they had known as home with their mother, Selene attempted to distract them, but solemnly, they observed the scene.

Soon enough they saw the large blue-and-red circus tent and a number of smaller ones dappling the field on the edge of the village. Rourke pressed a coin into the hand of a young boy who would watch over the horses and carriage. Already the day darkened into night, but the sky was lit by an enormous moon and a thousand twinkling stars. They would have no difficulty seeing their way home tonight. Rourke paid for their admission and they proceeded to the entrance, which was lit with torches on either side. Inside, the benches were already crowded with villagers and country people and those who had come from the surrounding parishes to enjoy an entertainment that most certainly was rare for the area.

The children spied friends from the village and, after asking permission, rushed off to join them. Leeson stayed Rourke and Selene with a wave of his hand. "I'll make sure they don't get into any trouble. I've got money for candied apples and games and all the rest."

Selene looked up at Rourke. "It's just us then."

The interior of the main tent was not so very large and, mimicking the larger productions one might see in London or Paris, featured three small rings at its center. Crude wooden chandeliers had been fashioned around each structural support post. At least a hundred burning candles jutted out from each.

The tall, thin man she had seen in the village at the time of the circus parade strode to the center of the ring, his arms spread wide. His deep voice echoed across the crowd, commanding silence.

"Tinsel and tawdry! Say not so
Of these, the trappings of the show!
Splendors, instead of Eastern kings.
Glitter around the triple rings. . . ."

With a sharp wave of his arm, a leather whip unfurled and cracked, echoing throughout the tent.

Suddenly, four tiny figures flew through the air, three males and one female, their arms spread like wings and their toes pointed behind.

"Acrobats!" exclaimed the woman next to her.

The troupe wore sparkling white costumes and, with the use of a trapeze bar, dipped and flipped through the air with startling speed. Another troupe in red took turns balancing on a high tightrope while juggling bowling pins and riding a unicycle. A solitary player balanced atop an enormous blue ball covered in yellow stars, deftly taking the sphere up and down planks that had been propped into various severe angles against sawhorses.

The audience around them tittered and *tsk*ed about the shocking nakedness of the athletes. Though the performers were covered from neck to ankle in white cloth, the closely fitted costumes left nothing to the imagination. At last, when their act was finished, the four in white slid down ropes to the dirt floor and ran toward the section of the tent where Selene and Rourke were seated. Their small, pale faces seemed strangely wide-eyed and innocent.

"They're only children," said Selene.

"No, they're not," he murmured in response.

Indeed, as soon as she had spoken the words, she realized she was wrong. As they drew nearer, she saw that the acrobats weren't children. They were adults, diminutive in size. They wore wigs and had old, solemn faces. The only smiles on their faces were formed of red greasepaint.

From behind a dark canvas screen came the pounding of a drum, and then the blare of trumpets. A horse trotted in, wearing a feathered headdress. On its back, the girl from the parade balanced, turning in a perfect pirouette.

Selene and Rourke remained for the entirety of the show, through the presentation of the dancing bear and the clowns and the full-cast reenactment of the "epic battle" of Troy, and, though not quite as amazed by all the feats of physical skill as the mortals around them, they were entertained nonetheless.

At last, when the show ended, they sidled out of their bench and exited the tent. In the distance, Leeson followed the children toward the gaming tables.

"You'll lose all your money," shouted Rourke.

"Happily!" Leeson shouted back.

Selene surveyed the smaller tents that dappled the field. Bonfires had been lit around the edges of the encampment. Villagers moved from attraction to attraction.

Rourke gestured across the narrow clearing. "There's Silverwest and Mrs. Thrall."

A small shimmer of disappointment moved through Selene. While she liked Mr. Silverwest and Mrs. Thrall, she did not crave their intrusion. She had hoped to spend the next hour seeing the circus attractions with Rourke.

"Greetings," called Mr. Silverwest, as attractive as ever. His gaze settled warmly on her.

Mrs. Thrall smiled, clearly pleased to see them. But as she leaned forward to lightly embrace Selene, her expression tempered into one of consolation. "Such terrible news about your neighbor and that poor girl, Hannah."

"Yes, it is," Selene answered.

Mr. Silverwest held his hat in his hand. "Along that same troubling vein, I'm hoping you might have seen my housemaid, Miss Taylor."

"No, we haven't," said Rourke. "Why would you ask?"

"Perhaps the recent unfortunate events have made us overly fearful, but we worry she too has gone missing. In the brief time we've employed her she's been a dependable, hardworking girl, but also very quiet and shy. I have to say I didn't notice her absence until my sister mentioned it. Mr. Harbottle told that you were looking to add a few more servants to your staff, and so my sister and I were hoping you'd simply hired her away from us."

"How long has it been since you saw her?" asked Selene.

"The night before last. She lives on the property, in the servants' quarters. I could be wrong, but I don't believe she was unhappy in her position."

"Does she have family living nearby?"

Mrs. Thrall provided, "She confided in one of the other servants about sending an aged aunt money each week, but certainly if she intended to go for a prolonged visit, she would have told someone."

"Perhaps you should seek out the parish constable and inform him. I do believe he comes to the village to hear complaints and to take reports every Tuesday."

Mr. Silverwest nodded solemnly. "If she does not reappear before then, we shall certainly do that."

Mrs. Thrall looked about at the tents. "We actually came here tonight on the bizarre chance that she had run off with the circus." She lowered her voice and her brows furrowed prettily, as if what she was about to share troubled her deeply. "Did you hear that Mr. Harbottle's wife has apparently taken up with one of the clowns?"

Selene's eyes widened in surprise. "No, I hadn't heard that. How unfortunate."

Mrs. Thrall pressed her lips together. "That on top of the murder and suicide . . . it's as if, over the past few days, the world, or at least our dear Thorn-on-the-Moor, has gone mad."

"Whatever the case, it's very kind of you to be so concerned for the girl's welfare. Perhaps she has simply gone to visit relatives."

"I hope that is true," said Mrs. Thrall.

The children raced past, followed by Mr. Leeson.

Selene smiled at Rourke. "It doesn't look as if they are ready to leave just yet. We might as well walk the grounds and see whatever curiosities there are to see."

The four of them meandered among the smaller attractions. Rourke paused outside the first tent, the mysteries within touted by a garishly painted sign as ABERRATIONS OF NATURE. A long line of men and male youths waited to enter.

Rourke bent to read the smaller writing on the sign.

"They claim to have a giantess and a living skeleton. Also a fish boy with gills. Do you want to go inside?" he asked Selene.

As a Shadow Guard she had seen enough true aberrations of nature to last a lifetime, and had no interest in seeking out false imitations.

"Not at all." She turned from him and continued on past the next several tents and booths until she found one that raised her curiosity.

"Rourke, look at this one—"

Selene turned back and found him gone. Her eyes searched the shadows. She found him easily enough, his broad shoulders outlined by his white shirt. He stood with Dora, watching a group of pale-faced pantomimes. The petite Mrs. Thrall looked up and, laughing gaily, touched his arm. He looked down and nodded.

It wasn't as if Rourke had kissed Dora or laughed at her flirtation. He hadn't even smiled, but somehow that one attentive glance wounded Selene just as deeply.

"Countess." Mr. Silverwest joined her.

He gestured toward the tent. "You were about to go inside this tent, were you not? Come, let us see what we may."

The small canvas structure that had moments before drawn her attention was constructed in the shape of a pagoda. A sign propped outside the door proclaimed in red lettering, on a vivid turquoise background: THE DEVIL'S MENAGERIE.

She glanced once more at Rourke. Was it her imagination or did he and Dora stand an inch closer together than before? Suddenly all she wanted was to leave the circus. She didn't want to see any more girls balancing on horseback or freakish clowns or dancing bears.

Selene forced her attention back to Mr. Silverwest at the pagoda. He stood sideways, peering inward over the shoulders of others who watched the same spectacle, which was a relief, as she didn't want him to see her pining for the man who, for everything he knew, was her brother.

She joined him. "What is it?"

"They are astounding. Here, come closer. You must see them with your own eyes to believe them."

He guided her by the elbow, drawing her deeper inside the tent.

A knock sounded on Selene's door. She straightened from scrubbing her face at the basin. They'd returned from the circus only a half hour ago. Earlier in the afternoon the girls had moved their things into their new room downstairs. While Selene had enjoyed their company, she was glad for a return to her privacy. It was late and everyone prepared for bed. She had already undressed and put on her robe.

Drying her face with a towel, she crossed the room and opened the door.

"What in the hell is this?" demanded Rourke. He stood bare of chest, wearing only a pair of loose flannel trousers. He raised her snake and wiggled it beside his head. He wasn't referring to Mrs. Hazelgreaves, who at last check remained nested in the wall outside, but rather the automaton serpent that Mr. Silverwest had purchased in the pagoda tent and in turn gifted to her.

"It's a toy," Selene answered coolly, snatching it out of his hand. "I told Nathan he could play with it, but I said nothing about you."

She tried to shut the door, but he elbowed inside.

"It's not a toy," he growled. "It's a bloody self-mechanized automaton, and it would be very expensive to purchase."

She shrugged. "I wouldn't know."

She placed the snake on the end of the bed.

"You shouldn't have accepted such an extravagant gift," he said.

Her shoulders stiffened and she turned back to him. "And why not? Mr. Silverwest is attentive and polite and—"

When she stood close to him like this, singing the praises of another man, Rourke couldn't think straight. He wanted to touch her, to remind her of the hot attraction between them. Instead, he caught her wrist, a bit too roughly.

"You should not have accepted the gift," he murmured harshly. "That's all I'm trying to say. What do you think Mr. Silverwest expects in return? Men don't just buy expensive things for women, for no reason at all."

When she had disappeared inside the tiny circus tent with their handsome neighbor, his jealousy—and the memory of their prior, only half-satisfied intimacy—had driven him almost insane.

She stared down at where he held her arm. "He had already purchased the snake—I had no idea he intended to give the thing to me. It would have been rude of me to decline." The spark of anger he had incited in her eyes moments before now turned into a full-blown flame. "Besides, call me a fool, but in that moment, his attentions pleased me."

The last thin vestiges of his self-control disintegrated.

"Damn snake, it gives me the willies." He lunged past her and seized the metal serpent from the bed. She reached for it, attempting to get it back, but he held it high over her head.

He chuckled evilly. "I shall throw it into the ocean, where it will sink and rust into tiny bits."

He whirled toward his own room, and grasping the wooden frame of the doorway, lunged across the threshold. Unexpectedly, her body slammed against his back. She wrapped her arms around his neck and her bare legs around his waist. He grinned, her physical reaction to his thievery of the snake even better than he expected. He growled in pleasure at the feel of her full breasts against his back.

Avoiding her outspread arms and grasping hands, he tossed the snake onto his bed. Releasing him, she dropped to the floor and ran toward the snake.

With a sideways kick of his foot, he tripped her.

He stepped over her, only to have her hands seize his ankle. Caught off balance, he staggered. Reaching, his hand struck the snake. The metallic serpent flew off the mattress to slide across the floor. With a laugh of delight, she crawled past him. *Enough.*

Snaring her ankle with his hand, he easily dragged her back. He grasped her wrists and, with his knees between hers, spread her against the carpet.

She kicked, struggled. In the process her dressing gown parted, revealing one long, deliciously shaped leg and, higher still, a glossy thatch of dark, curling hair.

He froze, staring down. She squirmed, which only revealed more.

"Rourke," she whispered, her voice thick and distant.

"Don't move."

She ceased all movement. With a firm press of his leg, he widened hers until he saw the narrow pink slit of her entrance.

"Rourke," she repeated. "Stop."

His gaze lifted to hers. His eyes conveyed determined mischief. His cheeks were flushed ruddy and dark. "Do you mean 'Stop,' or do you mean, 'We shouldn't, but let's do it anyway'?"

Selene swallowed. Her eyes widened. "Let's do it anyway."

Desire blurred his mind—had blurred his mind for days. He had suffered enough of this torture, of this self-deprivation. At last he surrendered, knowing he would pay hell for it.

Still poised above her, muscles corded and taut, he hooked his thumb into the waist of his linen trousers and dragged them down. His sex fell, heavy and long, against her thigh, but he rolled, pulling her on top of him. Crouched above him on all fours, she bent to press a fervent kiss to his mouth, and at the same time stroked her hand along his whiskered jaw. Her hair fell like heavy silk against his chest. His palms moved over her face, skimming down her neck to squeeze her breasts, still tantalizingly concealed by her robe. His abdomen flexed as he wrenched upward to suckle her nipple through the satin. Damp and ready, she rubbed her sex against him.

He lay back, holding her at the waist.

"Take me inside of you, Selene," he whispered.

She nodded. He watched, enraptured by the erotic sight of her grasping his penis midstaff. With a sharp exhalation of breath, she squeezed and stroked his length and the taut sac beneath before planting the crown against her entrance.

"Rourke . . ." she groaned, deep in her throat.

Bracing above him, her thighs smooth and flexed, she lowered herself inch by delicious inch onto his turgid sex, taking him inside her slick, tight heat until impatiently he hooked his hips upward, pushing in the last few inches.

She moaned, her muscles clenching against him. She flattened her hands on his chest, bowed her head and shuddered. Her body pulsed its satisfaction. He let out a tight, husky chuckle. Now that he was here, he intended to make her come again, and again, and again. Reaching up, he twined his hand in her long hair and pulled her down for an openmouthed kiss.

Lifting away, she stared down, her eyes glazed, her cheeks flushed and delicious-looking.

"Why now?" she whispered, rocking, circling her hips against him.

He let out a husky groan, delighting in the way her body massaged, pulled and pleasured him.

"It's all I think of. It is all I've thought of since the first time I saw you. In Cravant, Selene, as you slew a score of men with your sword."

"What?" She gasped, her dark-lashed eyes wide with shock.

With a jerk, he loosened the tie of her robe and parted the satin to reveal her breasts. He stroked his hands up over her rib cage, to cup and squeeze them. "And then in Venice—"

"Venice . . ." Her head dropped back, and her eyes rolled slightly before focusing on him again. "You were the man in the mask."

He chuckled, thrusting. "There were many men in masks."

She shook her head. "I remember your eyes. You touched me as you went past on the bridge. I wanted to see your face, and I would have too, but I was on the way to a feast with the Count Pavlenco."

Gripping her legs against him, he rolled her onto her back and pulled out. His member was thick, veined and covered with evidence of her pleasure.

"Mmmm, Rourke . . ." She licked her bottom lip.

She reached between them and gracefully guided him back inside her pink, swollen lips. But instead of releasing him, she stroked and squeezed, with her thumb banded around the base of his cock. He pushed inside her, only to withdraw again, wickedly torturing them both with the slow, sensual repetition. Bending, he took her nipple in his mouth. She arched, stroking her hands over his cropped hair.

"We've done this before," she breathed, wrapping her legs around his hips. "I've been with you like this."

"In dreams, but this is different. It's real. You are in my arms. Tonight, Selene, you are mine."

She embraced him with her arms, her legs, her body. In his ear, she whispered, "Trust me, Rourke."

Suddenly, he could control his desire no more. Pumping into her, he groaned, all reality exploding into a spectacular sensual demise. She lifted her hips off the floor, frantically bucking against him until he throbbed the full, hot measure of his passion deep inside her.

Her body shuddered, and he inhaled her throaty scream into his mouth.

Selene awoke in Rourke's bed, but he wasn't there. He stood at the window looking outward. Morning's wan light revealed his face to her. Turning, he met her gaze. Though his eyes conveyed a new ease and warmth toward her, his lips did not smile. He crawled onto the mattress and stretched out beside her, resting his chin on his crossed arms.

He kissed her nose. "It's very early. Go back to sleep."

Content just to be with him, she drifted off again. A short time later, when she awoke he sat in the chair beside the bed, already dressed.

She pushed up onto one elbow. "What is it?"

"When you're ready, I want you to get dressed and come with me."

She crawled off the bed, holding the blanket to her naked body. Sliding her dressing gown onto her arms, she held it closed long enough to cross the hallway and enter her room. A leather tome lay at the center of her bed.

Rourke's footsteps signaled his descent down the stairs.

He had left her this, the gift of his past. Almost too afraid to look, she perched on the edge of the mattress. The name Avenage had been painted in gold on the cover in staid lettering but had faded with time. The pages of the book had been sewn by hand down the spine, and the entries written by a number of different hands, likely by Avenage's steward. A few pages were loose and so delicate she feared they would disintegrate with her touch.

Indeed, just as he had told her, Rourke was Norman, and as a young warrior had aligned himself with William. He had stood alongside his lord at a number of battles, including Hastings. The ferocity and skill with which he fought apparently gained him much favor with his king, and he was granted a title and a generous portion of land. What followed on the pages was a history of his life, and of the estate of Swarthwick.

Her fingers trailed along the outer margin until one word caught her eye. Marriage. He had married a young woman by the name of Rowena—Rowena of Abigorn. Selene frowned. Even though the woman had been dead for centuries, she couldn't help but be envious. Married to Rourke. To have stood beside him and taken the vows. Something about the name snagged in her memory, and she flipped back to the previous page.

Indeed, Abigorn had been the name of one of the local Saxon noble families who had been forced to surrender their lands to the invading Normans. Such history was oftentimes the basis of the romantic stories she liked to read . . . and eat. But in reality, such conflict often ended in turmoil, violence and even death. She read on. A year into their marriage Rourke fell ill. Very ill. Ill unto death. Was this the moment in Rourke's history when he became immortal? His physician alleged poisoning, and an investigation was undertaken.

The poisoner was discovered to be Rowena.

Selene closed her eyes. Even now, with centuries passed . . . she could only imagine how Rourke had felt after such a betrayal. Had he loved Rowena of Abigorn?

After being interrogated, the young woman confessed and implicated her father and brothers in the same plot. The last page in the tome was an entry memorializing the young woman's death.

Selene closed the cover.

Knowing there was more to the story, Selene washed and dressed quickly, leaving her hair long down her back.

Rourke waited for her downstairs, his expression revealing nothing. Under a sky thick and dark with storm clouds, she followed him down the path she had seen him take so many times. When they passed the place where she had taken her tumble he threw her a reserved smile. They came to the steps, centuries old by the look of them, cut into the stone. He climbed first and she followed. As she reached the top, he reached down and helped her up the last few. Not that she needed his help, but she did appreciate the care he showed her.

Here on the flat plateau of earth, the wind plastered her skirts against her legs. He walked to the outcropping, and looked out over the ocean. She heard, but did not see the waves crash against the stones below. White spray exploded, creating a shimmering arc about him.

The mist bathed her skin and dampened her bodice. A white marker stood in the center of the plateau. She walked toward it and knelt to read the words. Time had worn the edges away, and she had to rub her fingertips over them to make them out.

Moments later, she stood behind him, but did not dare touch him. No matter how much he looked like he needed to be comforted, and no matter how badly she wanted to, she knew better than to try.

"The stone marker says 'child.'"

He nodded, meeting her eyes only fleetingly, looking out again over the water.

"Your child."

"Yes," he whispered, so softly she barely heard the confession.

"And you buried him here?"

"No, I didn't."

"But there's a headstone."

He shook his head, drawing his thumb across his lower lip. "It's just a marker."

"Where is he then, Rourke?"

"Out there, somewhere."

"In the ocean?" The blood inside her head thundered even louder than the ocean crashing against the stone. "How did your child get into the ocean? What happened here?"

Dark eyelashes speared damply around icy green irises, until he closed them against her. With a low groan, he ran his hand through his cropped hair, leaving a path of dark spikes in the wake of his palm.

"This is where I killed his mother."

Chapter Sixteen

"Rourke, no, you didn't. You wouldn't have—"

"I did." He nodded and, turning, strode past her toward the slab. "I killed her that day with my words, with my anger, and in doing so killed my own child."

She followed close behind. "I read your history. She betrayed you. Those were different times, when betrayal almost certainly brought the consequence of death."

He shook his head and stared upward, into the clouds.

"It's not just the child you grieve. You loved her too," Selene surmised softly.

"Beyond reason."

"And she loved you too, didn't she? But her loyalty to her family exceeded that love, did it not? She did what they asked?"

He nodded. "We were married up here, just the two of us, the priest and a few of my men as witnesses. She married me against the wishes of her family. Things went well for a time. I thought I was enough for her, but I wasn't. When I learned the truth about how she had poisoned me, she escaped here and I followed her. I was so furious, Selene, so furious I swear my vision, my thoughts went black. She had forced my hand—I would have to punish her and her father and brothers dearly to maintain the respect of my men. Of my king. I was young then. Hotheaded and arrogant. I shouted at her and said terrible, unforgivable things."

"No matter how much you loved her, she tried to poison her husband, to murder you, the lord of these lands," exclaimed Selene incredulously. "What man would have reacted differently?"

He pounded a fist to the center of his chest, his expression fierce. "I should have."

The words seethed out of him in a hiss. "If it had been today, everything would have been different. You know how these mortals are, Selene, with their ideas of privilege and status—as a noblewoman, she'd have been committed to a comfortable asylum in the countryside, where she would have given birth to our child, and afterward would have remained sequestered there for a few more years until she returned to live with her family. The child would have been given over to me. We'd have divorced, of course. The scandal would have been written about in the papers. None of that would matter, though, because she and my child would be alive."

"What happened, Rourke? What happened here? How did she die?"

"She told me she was carrying my child. I had not known until that moment, you see. She did not have any of the sickness, or other telling signs." He closed his eyes and exhaled heavily through his nose. "She told me that she couldn't bear to look me in the eye ever again, but that she wouldn't leave our baby behind to be hated for what his mother had done. And she went to the ledge—"

"Oh, no, Rourke . . ." Seeing him so tortured by the memory was almost unbearable. Tears glazed her eyes, and she reached for him.

He shook his head, drawing away. "I tried to stop her, but she jumped off the ledge. By the time I climbed down the rocks, the tide had pulled her body out to sea."

"She did not give you a chance to show her mercy."

"Somehow none of that matters, even now. In the ferocity of my anger, in the blindness of my pride, I brought about the death of my own child. I had never wanted anything more than them, my own family. I was a bastard, Selene. A castoff that no one wanted until I proved how good a killer I was. But I was going to be a different sort of father. I never saw my child's face. Never held him. And so for him, I took a vow. . . ."

"A vow to what?" she gasped through her emotion. "To live alone? To never love again?"

"Yes, all of that," he answered in a rush.

"Your life as an immortal was intended to be spent in solitude, as a memorial to the child whose death you believe you caused."

"I kept my vow, Selene, until you."

Selene moved closer, but did not attempt to touch him again. "I understand your grief and that you think you can somehow absolve your guilt by punishing yourself for an eternity. But let it go, Rourke. You have punished yourself enough. It's time to let your vow go."

He flinched, as if unable to imagine doing so. "You misunderstand, Selene. I don't want to be absolved."

"What are you telling me, Rourke?"

"I became immortal for the sole purpose of ensuring my . . ." He cleared his throat and looked away.

The realization of what he did not say thundered in her ears.

"Your eternal punishment."

He nodded. "Even in death Rowena bound herself to me. Every night, Selene, I dreamed of her. *Until you.* Every night I dreamed of her hair in my hands. Of her lips on my skin and her words of hate and accusation in my ears. *Until you.*" He gritted the words out through clenched teeth. "I tried to forget you. Even with other women who looked like her, to keep you out of my head, out of my heart, but damn you . . ." His words faded on the wind.

At last she touched him, and he did not flinch away. Her fingers curled into his shirtsleeve.

"What now, then?" she queried softly.

"I don't know, Selene."

They remained on the ledge for a long time afterward, side by side, looking out over the ocean. An hour later, when they returned to Swarthwick, they found Leeson on a ladder between the high archways that led from the great hall to Rourke's study. The mosaic floor around the base of the ladder was littered with narrow boards that he had pried from the ceiling.

"I hope you don't mind," he called down. "I discovered there was stained glass underneath all these boards, and the preservationist in me wanted to be certain all the solder was holding before we shut down the keep and returned to London."

Selene stared upward at the colored glass. "Did you design the serpent to do that on purpose?"

"Do what?"

Looking to Selene again, Rourke saw her point her finger upward and make a zigzag motion. "Place the serpent at the base of that tree so that if the sun moved directly above, its eye would glow?"

Rourke put his hands on his hips and looked up. Sure enough, the sun hung directly above them, a golden orb in the morning sky, visible through the colored glass above. Yet when one was standing beneath, perfectly positioned, its light illuminated the dark green jewel that was the serpent's eye.

He answered, "I wish I could say I'd thought of it, but truly, I think it's just coincidence."

"Leeson, when you referred to shutting down the keep and returning to London, did you mean we had received instructions?"

Leeson's voice echoed down. "On your desk."

After reading the letter, Rourke lowered himself into the chair. What a culmination of events. He felt raw and drained from sharing his soul's deepest secret with Selene, and now this. . . .

He did not know how to feel. He did not know what words to say, or what actions to take.

"That's it, isn't it?" she whispered. "My banishment has ended."

Rourke folded the parchment. "The Council asks that I return to London as expediently as possible to fully resume my duties as Ravenmaster."

Selene nodded. Her lips thinned as she pressed them together. She tapped her fingertip against the surface of his desk. "The letter . . . doesn't say anything about me returning to London posthaste, does it?"

"The Primordials say you may do as you wish."

"How maddeningly noncommittal of them." She blinked rapidly, and her hand trembled. She tilted her head and demanded softly, "Have I been relieved of my duties as a Shadow Guard?"

He came around the desk to stand before her. He wanted to grasp her by the arms and pull her against him. A voice inside his head told him not to make things more difficult than they already were.

"There was nothing about that in the letter."

He could see her mind working. "Maybe they are waiting until I return to London to end things."

"There's no reason why they wouldn't be able to give you more time. And from everything we've heard, Lady Black has continued to adjust her vaccine."

"No." Selene shook her head. "No more vaccines."

Rourke announced to everyone at Swarthwick that they would leave in two days. Everyone but the children, that was. His and Leeson's inquiries had revealed that McGregor, of the queen's royal foot guard, had retired. He had a well-educated daughter and a schoolteacher son-in-law who had regrettably remained childless over the years. Rourke had invited the three of them to take residence at Swarthwick as caretakers of both the property and the children, and his invitation had been enthusiastically accepted. They would all live in the keep until construction of a new caretaker's cottage was completed.

At present, Rourke and Leeson purchased nails, wood and other necessities for the final repairs the keep would require before the new residents moved in. As he left Mr. Harbottle's, which, oddly, was now staffed by one of the harem girls from the circus, a voice called from across the road.

When he saw Mr. Silverwest crossing toward him, ice

water spewed through Rourke's veins. Even he, a man, had to concede that Silverwest was too handsome for words. The man's teeth were white and straight, and his clothes were always perfect. Rourke doubted his shirt and trousers had ever known a wrinkle. Rourke stared down at his own mud-encased boots. He closed his eyes and exhaled through his nose, praying that he could contain his instincts to do violence to the ever-pleasant Mr. Silverwest.

"Lord Avenage. I was hoping to see you."

"Mmm-hmm." It was all the acknowledgment he could muster.

"My sister and I were entirely unprepared for the announcement that you and the countess would be departing for London."

Rourke nodded. "It is past time for us to return. We never expected to stay as long as this."

"I wanted to speak to you on a matter of a more personal nature."

The hair upon his neck arose in Rourke's suspicion of anything Silverwest might term personal. Somehow he already knew "personal" meant Selene.

"And what would that be?"

Silverwest removed his hat and smiled. "This is awkward."

"No, please." Rourke tortured himself, already sensing at least the nature of the words that would come. He deserved to be tortured for not claiming Selene outright as his own. "Speak freely."

"I hope I do not overestimate myself when I say that I believe your sister has grown fond of me."

"I think we can all agree on that. She enjoys the company of Mrs. Thrall as well."

A relieved smile warmed his face. "I understand a man cannot be parted from his business for long. But as for the countess, my sister and I wish to invite her to stay on as our guest at the Astley estate for another few weeks. In all honesty, your lordship, I think there's a certain spark between your sister and myself, and I'd like us to get to know each other better. Mrs. Thrall, of course, would be there to provide the appropriate chaperonage. Would you be agreeable to such an arrangement?"

"My sister"—how he had grown to hate that word—"is her own woman. It's really up to her to decide."

And clearly Selene wanted him. Rourke. The past two nights in his bed proved that. So why couldn't he say what needed to be said? Why couldn't he offer her a commitment that was more than physical? A true and lasting one?

A smile broke across Mr. Silverwest's face. "Perfect. You've made me very happy."

Yes, perfect. Rourke glowered as he watched Silverwest go.

That afternoon, when he and Leeson returned from the village, a man stood on the front steps of the keep, a saddled horse waiting on the drive. Selene stood a few steps higher, within the shadow of the archway, reading from a square white card. They drove the wagon around to the stables and unloaded the supplies. Entering the house through the kitchen entrance, Rourke found Selene in the great room.

"I received a note from Mrs. Thrall saying she would like to wish us a safe and happy trip to London. She's invited us to supper at the Silverwest estate. For tonight. How nice. I'm writing back to accept for both of us."

Rourke almost stopped her. Spending another hour with Silverwest and Mrs. Thrall sounded almost as entertaining as an hour spent in Bedlam. But in some twisted way, he wanted to be there when Selene turned down Silverwest's offer to explore their "spark."

As evening approached, Rourke assisted Selene up into the carriage. Leeson sat in the driver's seat. The children waved from the window as they departed.

Selene had chosen a vivid red gown. The satin sparkled with tiny black beads. Though their intimacy had continued in his bed in the hours after dark, he knew she held back when they were not alone behind closed doors. Even now, as they traveled to join the company of others, she did not sit beside him on the carriage seat.

She offered him no meaningful glances. She waited for him, he knew, to say things had changed. That he didn't wish to continue his path to eternal damnation, at least not alone. But he hadn't decided. Every time he was around her, she eclipsed all thought and numbed his still raw feelings about his dead wife and child. And yet when she wasn't, he could not stop chastising himself for choosing passion and sensual need over what was right.

Besides, every time he tried to think of how he and Selene could share a future, his thoughts went into a tangle. His entire immortal existence was tied up in his role as the Ravenmaster and hers, in turn, as a Reclaimer. It wasn't as if they could just set up house together.

Once they returned to London and she regained her powers—which he could only expect she would—he feared that they would find themselves two completely different people again, with very different priorities that would not include each other.

For the third time he untied the awkward knot at his throat, which bulged in all the wrong directions. "Would it be possible for you to arrange my necktie?"

Selene leaned forward and took in hand the dangling ends. Staring at his throat, she whispered, "Don't wear the necktie."

"No?"

"No."

"I'm relieved to hear you say that."

"You should relax and stop frowning."

"I hadn't realized I was." His emotions about the evening were mixed. He had desired to return to London so badly, and yet now that the eve of their departure had come, he wished for just a few more days at Swarthwick with Selene. It irritated him that their last night would be spent in the company of people who jabbed at his every nerve. As soon as they arrived, he knew Silverwest would be at Selene's side, and he would be relegated to the sugary sweet, wide-eyed Mrs. Thrall.

"Mrs. Thrall has gone through all this trouble to give

us a going-away dinner. You must suffer through, and be polite."

"Will there be other guests?" he asked.

"I have no idea."

He grumbled and, resting his curled fist against his lips, turned his head to stare out the window.

"Just be thankful it's a dinner, and not a ball. We should be finished and back in the carriage by ten thirty."

"You know how I feel about him," he muttered, hating the admission, but compelled to say it anyway. "About the way he looks at you."

"How does he look at me, Rourke?"

"Like he wants to eat you up."

She shrugged. "Maybe I should let him."

Rourke's eyes narrowed. "Don't use him against me."

"I'm not trying to use him against you or provoke you." She leaned forward in her chair and in a hushed voice said, "But I don't know who I am anymore. Our impending return to London forces my thoughts to a host of unpleasant questions. What if I cannot return to my role as a Reclaimer in the Shadow Guard? What if I find myself . . ."

Her voice broke huskily.

"What?"

"Mortal . . . I've wondered if that's what is happening to me. I feel so empty of my prior self."

"Don't say that."

"If I were mortal, things between us would be even more impossible than they are now."

He reached for her hand, but she moved back, out of his reach. That she rejected that small touch of comfort grieved him more deeply than he would have expected.

Her eyes gleamed with tears. "Whatever happens, Rourke, I want you to know that—"

The door beside them flew open. Rourke blinked. He hadn't even noticed the vehicle stopping. Selene brushed her gloved finger against her eyelashes and gathered her bag and shawl. Without looking at him again, she accepted the hand of Silverwest's footman and descended the stairs. Rourke followed her.

Inside, a number of people from the village and the local gentry were circulating about the manse, which in size and decor was far grander than the keep. As Rourke had predicted, Silverwest appeared in a blast of charm and warmth and whisked Selene away on his arm. Mrs. Thrall, in turn, claimed Rourke's arm and pulled him from person to person, formally introducing him to anyone he had not already met. Everyone responded to her enthusiastically, and it was clear she was well liked. Her shining hair teased a glance from him time and time again, but for whatever reason she had the opposite effect on him than she did on everyone else.

Mrs. Thrall was like a mouthful of sugar. Too sweet. Too excessive. When she smiled at him, even his teeth hurt. No question about it: He had lost his taste for faceless blondes.

Because he loved Selene.

A quiet, firm voice deep inside his head made the shocking announcement. Rourke closed his eyes and exhaled, barking back a silent denial.

He allowed himself to be seated in a chair of honor beside the piano, where, after Mr. Silverwest stood and prattled on about enduring friendship and offered a few quotes from dead poets, Mrs. Thrall seated herself on the upholstered piano bench and, with a crescendo of the keys, began to warble.

Love. To this point, he had managed to keep even a breath of that dangerous emotion from his existence. He had even convinced himself that if things went any further with Selene, their relationship would simply be termed "intense, but temporary" in his mind. His mind reviewed the memories of recent weeks. Her every smile. Their every kiss.

Someone said his name.

He blinked, and his vision focused on Selene. How much time had passed?

From her place beside Silverwest, she smiled encouragingly. "I said, doesn't Mrs. Thrall have the loveliest voice?"

The song, it seemed, had come to an end.

"Indeed." He forced his glance to Mrs. Thrall. "Lovely. Thank you for sharing with us your gift of song."

He ground his back teeth together. *Thank you for sharing with us your gift of song*? Who said such things? But Selene's smile grew wider, and her eyes warmed with pleasure. Apparently his ridiculous response pleased, or at least amused her.

From her place on the bench, Mrs. Thrall considered him intently. He had looked at her before, of course, at her hair and her nose and forehead, but never really looked at *her*.

Peculiarly, she did not radiate the slightest mental or emotional vibration. She was a beautiful, yet blank slate. Brilliant blue eyes dazzled, but beyond the highly pigmented irises there seemed to be nothing but an empty void.

"Everyone," Silverwest called, standing from his chair beside Selene. "I have a special announcement. As all of you can certainly tell by now, I have developed a strong affection for my lovely neighbor, the Countess Pavlenco. Perhaps it is impetuous of me, but acting on instinct, as men must so often do, I have asked her a very . . . important question. . . ."

A slow grin turned his lips. The excited murmuring of the gathered party rippled around the room. Rourke's heartbeat staggered to a stop.

Silverwest nodded and lifted his hand toward Selene. "I have asked the countess—and to my pleasure, she has *agreed* . . ." Again, he paused teasingly.

Their excitement heightening, the gathered party exchanged stunned glances and hopeful laughter.

Rourke stared at Selene's serenely smiling lips. Lips that had felt so perfect against his mouth and his body. The thought that they might never touch him again knocked him half out of his mind. His hands clenched the armrests of his chair.

That damn country squire had asked Selene to marry him.

But that wasn't the worst of it, Rourke realized. Something told him that in her present state of self-examination, she just might have said yes.

Silverwest's eyes fell directly on him and their gazes clashed.

The other man's lips quirked into a broader smile.

"To accompany me to the circus," he exclaimed.

With a broad sweep of his arm, flashes of light burst outside the expansive window, revealing a trapeze on the lawn. The acrobats they'd observed in the tent just the night before sprang from their perches and soared through the air. Clowns juggled, and the dancing bear danced. A boy ran from post to post, lighting torches.

The room erupted into excited exclamations and everyone leapt from their seats to migrate to the door. Glowering, and clearly forgotten, Rourke followed Selene and Silverwest. Feeling a touch on his arm, he glanced down to find Mrs. Thrall, her hand resting on his sleeve. Numbly, he escorted her out of the house and onto an expansive lawn.

Beneath a silken pavilion, a buffet had been set out and clowns liberally poured bottles of pink champagne. The circus band, seated in chairs underneath the trees, played a polka. Silverwest led Selene onto the paved terrace and into a dance, joining several other couples.

Rourke found the whole charming scene impossible to watch. Returning to the house, he meandered aimlessly through the parlor, and then to the library. As soon as he entered, though, he realized he wasn't alone. The balding, bespectacled Mr. Harbottle and the young harem girl Rourke had seen at his store wrestled with each other on the couch, smacking loud kisses and grasping at each other's clothes.

He backed out and shut the double doors behind him.

Hadn't Mrs. Thrall said *Mrs.* Harbottle had taken up with one of the clowns?

Something moved beside his foot and he jerked,

nearly stepping on . . . a slithering snake. His eyes widened with interest. Not a real snake, but a herky-jerky automaton like the one Mr. Silverwest had given Selene. The narrow, self-powered machine gave off a metallic *whir-whir-whir* as it zigzagged down the hall. He followed the snake until it disappeared into a shadowed room.

He gripped the doorframe, his muscles flexed to respond in any way necessary. . . .

A smell met his nostrils, unlike anything he had ever smelled. So good. So alluring.

Mrs. Thrall whirled from the window overlooking the lawn. Just over her shoulder, Roman candles shot bright streams of color into the sky. Blue. Red. Gold.

"Lord Avenage," she murmured, her eyes widening. "What a pleasant *surprise*."

The pointed tail of the snake wiggled and disappeared beneath the hem of her skirt.

She had removed her fitted jacket and now wore only a sleeveless bodice that sparkled with tiny crystals. Behind her, a cone of incense burned. Red-tinted smoke wafted up, scenting the air with the most sensual, delicious fragrance he could ever recall invading his nostrils.

Mrs. Thrall really was extraordinarily beautiful. The memory of Selene dancing in Mr. Silverwest's arms made her even more so.

He blinked. Where in the hell had those thoughts come from? He was not attracted to Mrs. Thrall in the least.

Oh, but he was.

"It seems that you, like me, have had quite enough of the circus," she said, yanking the curtains closed over the window. "I don't know why my brother is so enamored of such spectacle. I believe a quieter, more *intimate* setting can produce results no less spectacular."

"I agree," he said, staring at her breasts, which were smaller than Selene's but altogether lovely.

She pulled a jeweled pin from her hair and shook out the pale tresses until they streamed in gleaming splendor over her shoulders and back.

Selene . . . who was Selene again?

He blinked and shook his head clear. Selene was the woman he loved.

Rourke's instincts told him something very interesting was going on at the Astley estate. He intended to find out just exactly what.

Chapter Seventeen

"Perhaps you could pour us both a drink?" suggested Mrs. Thrall. Her teeth were perfectly straight and as white as pearls. She lifted a slender hand. "There is whiskey on the cabinet."

"Certainly." He turned from her and stared at the decanter. The light from the lamp made the cut crystal sparkle too brightly. The twist and turn of the light fragments dazzled . . . dizzied him like stars too close to his eyes.

From behind him a low growl sounded, as sly as a jackal's.

His muscles tensed.

A body slammed against his back—so hard the air vacated his lungs. He gripped the edge of the cabinet.

Thank God. He grinned. *Some excitement in the country at last.*

Skirts flashed around his shoulders as her knees crushed his ribs and her arm snared his neck. With extraordinary strength, she yanked his head back against her shoulder. Incisors tested the flesh of his ear.

"Mrs. Thrall . . ." He twisted, reaching to grasp the back of her bodice. He tugged, but neither her thighs nor her teeth released.

How to get her off his back when she seemed to be stuck there like a leech?

"I suspect that perhaps there has been some sort of misunderstanding between us—"

Lips clamped on his neck and sucked. "Mmmmm. So delicious."

The smoke from the burning incense wafted up his nose, swirled through his lungs and twisted up into his brain, interrupting and rearranging his thoughts. The scent was difficult to place, but . . . better than flowers. Better than spice. Better than sex, even.

He didn't want the smell to ever dissipate.

Mrs. Thrall dropped off his back and shoved him onto the sofa. Leaping astride his hips, she ripped open her bodice to reveal a sheer black corset.

"Do you like what you see?" she purred. Grasping his head, she forcibly planted his face between her breasts.

His mind flashed with pictures of Silverwest smiling at Selene. Silverwest kissing Selene, openmouthed and with his tongue. Silverwest undressing Selene. The urge to betray her first flamed high.

God, no. Those weren't his thoughts.

While admittedly an enthusiastic woman was usually an alluring woman, something troubled him about Mrs. Thrall. Closing his eyes, he narrowed his avian senses and honed in on the bothersome detail. . . .

She whirred.

Tiny, almost imperceptible pings and rattles came from inside her breast, to vibrate against his lips.

Women did not whir or ping. Not natural women.

"Mrs. Thrall, tell me your name . . ." he murmured, kissing her neck.

"Dora," she breathed, grinding her pelvis against him. "You know that, silly boy."

To his dismay, his body reacted.

Angered, he wound his hand in her hair and roughly pulled back her head. Kissing her on her neck, and then her beautiful, cold lips, he whispered, "No . . . your *real* name."

Silence.

"Come, now, you can tell me," he coaxed with his voice and his lips.

"I really shouldn't...." She sighed. Mouth still pressed to hers, he opened his eyes. Her bright blue eyes glimmered back.

"Might it be Pandora?" he asked.

"Why, *yes*." She grinned.

With a growl, he twisted her arm behind her back—and ripped it from her torso.

She shrieked in his face.

Copper wires and metal pegs glinted from the stub where he had torn off her limb. The flesh hung in shreds, and *blood*, which he had not expected, trickled down to stain her bodice. He shoved her from his lap.

Now that he *knew* Mrs. Thrall's true identity, the scent—the spell—she had been weaving around his mind evaporated as if it had never existed. His thoughts cleared and the incense clouding the room took on a rancid edge. She leapt up, skirts hissing. Her beautiful face contorted into a snarl as she clawed and slashed at him with her remaining hand. With a retaliatory swing, he clubbed her with her own arm. With that blow her head slanted sideways and her blond hair flew out in all directions, some falling in chunks to the carpet.

"You'll die, Ravenmaster!" she screeched, then rolled and flipped backward, her skirts a stiff fan, and disappeared out the door.

Rourke pursued her, but eleven, twelve, thirteen doorways lined the long hall, some of them open and some of them closed. Her overpowering scent, now rank to his nostrils, flooded the place. She smelled of metal, stagnant blood and decayed flesh.

Hell on fire, Mrs. Thrall was Pandora.

Ancient mythology preserved her tale. Created in ancient times, she was the world's first artificial being—an automaton, just like the snake that Silverwest had given to Selene.

Alluring, beautiful and deadly, she had been the death of countless suitors throughout history. He raced through the first three rooms, and in the fourth spied a snarl of blond hair peeking out from under the carpet. He lifted its edge and found a square panel with a rope handle. Raising the panel just an inch, he peered inside.

Selene walked through the garden, through green lanes boasting the largest red flowers she had ever seen. She lifted a heavy bloom—almost the size of her head—and inhaled. The fragrance . . . she felt drunk on it. Silverwest's kiss still lingered on her lips, and his touch on her skin. He had tried to be naughty with his hands, but she had put a stop to that. His eyes stormy with desire, he had told her to wait here, in the garden, while he went to get her present.

A present, he said, that would be contained in a small velvet box.

She broke the stem of the flower, thrust it into her hair and peered up into the sky. The brass garden lanterns framed her view. They sizzled as they burned, and from within them wafted a luxurious red haze.

Though the haze and a thin layer of clouds above, starlight twinkled through. Why would she ever want to leave this place?

"Selene," a voice called, rather furtively.

"Yes?" she answered.

"Quiet."

Splendid. It was Rourke. She was angry with Rourke. Everything always had to be *his* way. The flower fell from her hair. Silverwest had told her Rourke had gone off with Mrs. Thrall into the house. And Silverwest had *winked* afterward.

She understood well enough what that wink had meant. She snatched the fallen bloom up from the ground.

Rourke rounded the corner of the sculpted evergreen. "There you are."

He was so handsome that she hated him. She threw the flower at his face. The bloom, weighty enough for good loft, smacked him in the nose.

"Why did you do that?" he demanded.

"Because I don't like you anymore."

Picking up the flower, he thrust the center to his nose

and inhaled. Scowling, he threw it to the ground. "Don't smell the flowers."

"That's one reason why I no longer like you. You hate flowers."

"No," he answered testily. "Just these flowers." He grasped her wrist. "We've got to go."

She jerked free. "I don't want to leave."

"Don't argue with me," he ordered.

Again he reached for her arm. She pivoted on her heel. He grasped her around the waist. When she opened her mouth to scream, he slapped his hand over her face. She kicked and swung her arms, but he lifted her up, clasped her tight against his chest and *ran*.

Her teeth had nearly rattled loose by the time he tossed her into the carriage.

"Go," he shouted to Leeson.

"What are you doing?" she demanded, wedged into the far corner. "Take me back."

Mr. Silverwest was probably standing in the garden right now with the velvet box, wondering where she had gone.

The carriage jerked and scrabbled down the drive. She grabbed hold of the door handle, but he pried her loose.

"Stupid Rourke," she wailed.

He slid onto the bench beside her, and with his big hands squeezed her shoulders. "Listen to stupid Rourke. Mr. Silverwest and Mrs. Thrall are not what they seem."

"You're just mean," she argued. Why had she never seen how mean he was until Mr. Silverwest brought it to her attention?

He shook her, gritting his teeth. "Come on, Selene. Think past it. The scent has you confused. It's in the house, in the yard, and in the garden."

"I hate you," she shouted.

"Listen." He grasped her face and leaned over her.

"No." She shoved against his chest.

"I ... *love* ... you," he bellowed. "I love you."

His mouth pressed to hers, a deeply urgent kiss. Her palms and her fingers curled into his shoulders, and with a moan she pushed at him with all her might. But then . . . her tangled thoughts reversed. Clarified. Rourke's scent replaced the other. She inhaled the smell of fresh-cut wood and rain and warm, delicious man.

She remembered . . . that sweet, peculiar smell. She had grown dizzy. Mr. Silverwest had whispered all sorts of untrue things in her mind and for some reason her brain had accepted them as true.

Mr. Silverwest and Mrs. Thrall are not what they seem.

That damned smell had let him manipulate her.

She did not like to be manipulated. Her temper sparked, and at the same time an exhilarating thrill spiraled through her chest and upward through the top of her head.

I love you.

Heat flared in her blood, and deeper, in her marrow, a searing sensation of pain and pleasure. Grasping the lapels of Rourke's coat, she twisted and pushed him back. She straddled him on the seat.

"I'm no longer stupid Rourke?"

She shook her head, smiling, her eyes wide and full of emotion. "Darling Rourke. My Rourke. You said you love me."

His hand touched her face. His gaze did not waver. "That, I do."

The heat and pain intensified. "Rourke!"

Her palms tingled . . . burned. She gasped at the intensity of the sensation, throwing her head back. Light flashed, and when she next looked, she held within her fists two Amaranthine silver daggers. Rourke's voice . . . Rourke's *love*, had somehow returned her to immortality.

Looking into Rourke's wide eyes, she shouted, "*Huzzah!*"

The carriage arrived at Swarthwick. Rourke hastily fastened his trousers, but there was simply nothing he could do about his buttonless shirt. Selene peered out the window, jerking her skirt and bodice back into place.

In the passing of a second, her face transformed from sultry to sharp.

Rourke exited first. Leeson jumped down from the bench.

He said, "What in the hell was going on back there? Several times I thought the vehicle was going to overturn."

"Why are the windows dark?" Selene demanded as she strode past. With a swipe of her arm and a slash of silver, she growled, "If they have hurt the children . . ."

"*Selene*," marveled Leeson. "You've *returned*."

He looked at Rourke's still flushed cheeks and his gaping shirt. His eyes widened, and his lips formed an O.

They followed Selene inside. She lit a lamp and carried it from room to room, calling, "Nathan. Hannah. Kate."

Voices shrieked and the tower door flew open. Each of them soon had a child in their arms.

Nathan said, "We hid in the tower."

Rourke met Selene's gaze. "I told them to go there if anything ever happened. The walls are five feet thick, and the door braces from inside."

"What did you see?" asked Selene.

"Lightning," answered Nathan.

Kate cried, "A terrible wind."

"It broke the glass." Hannah pointed.

Together they walked beneath the archways. Their shoes crunched over the shattered fragments of the stained-glass window. Leeson ran out from the study, speaking in silence, clearly so as not to further alarm the children.

The contraption has also been destroyed.

We're cut off then, surmised Rourke. *There's no way to inform the Primordials of what we've seen tonight.*

We've got to go back, said Selene. *Leeson, you must stay with the children.*

Leeson nodded, but his gray eyebrows gathered and his mustache drooped, indicating a scowl. Though he was not a Shadow Guard, the old immortal liked a good fight as much as any of them.

Together Rourke and Selene left the keep, but left the carriage parked in the drive. She stopped only to stoop down and collect Mrs. Hazelgreaves, who had slithered out to greet her. The serpent wound around her arm. Side by side, she and Rourke shifted into shadow and entered the night.

They hurtled over gravel, river and grass until they again arrived at the Silverwest estate. The circus actors still entertained, but the crowd had decreased. Rourke and Selene passed, unseen, through the rooms and hallways of the manse. Red mist clouded the air. Two men shoved and grasped at each other, slamming their fists into each other's faces.

"She's mine," one shouted.

"Not now, because you're dead. Do you hear me? Dead!" bellowed the other.

Countless others lay sprawled, their limbs entwined on couches and settees, in various stages of undress.

Through the parlor window they observed Mr. Harbottle running nude across the back lawn. Neither Mr. Silverwest nor Pandora was anywhere to be seen.

"Come with me," said Rourke.

He led Selene to the bedroom with the trapdoor and, after lifting the panel, descended first. Cut from clay and stone, the stairs slanted at irregular angles and crumbled in places.

Half crouched and peering into the darkness, he waited as Selene descended the last few steps. His elegant hands curled into fists at his sides. She knew that if provoked, he would extend his claws in a beautiful yet terrifying display, and because she wished to see it and because her reawakened instincts craved the satisfaction of a fierce, punishing fight, she prayed they would soon root out and corner Pandora and Mr. Silverwest in their hiding places.

Rourke strode over a packed-dirt floor, his gaze shifting from cool green to red. "This is as far as I got before."

Selene pointed the tip of her dagger along a dark, narrow tunnel. "You go that way and see what's there."

She glanced in the opposite direction, where another tunnel speared into darkness, like a wormhole that had been bored through the earth.

"Are you ordering me about?" he asked.

"I am." She lowered her blade. "Do you like it?"

"Possibly." His lips curved into a slow smile, but only fleetingly, as he turned from her to disappear into the darkness.

With the tip of her blade, she pushed the nearest door open. At the center of the room stood a wooden desk. Its surface and the floor all about were littered with newspapers and hundreds of black sticks. Upon closer examination, she saw that the sticks were grease pencils, many of them snapped in half, or sharpened down to inch-long nubs.

Selene lifted a newspaper from the desk and saw a number of black circles drawn and headlines underlined. Anything concerning a murder or a suicide or a death. Leaving that room, she moved on to the next. The door hung open, revealing a bed strewn with tangled linens and frayed lengths of rope tied to the bedposts. A torn chemise lay on the earthen floor. A pair of women's shoes lay, separated, at opposite corners of the room. Her skin crawled with the knowledge of what must have occurred there.

"Foul," growled Rourke beside her.

"Yes," she whispered.

"Perhaps just as foul as what I've discovered. Come see."

She followed him out of the corridor and through the cellar to the other side of the basement.

He pushed the door in. It appeared they weren't the only ones who had been in possession of a contraption. Copper tubing snaked between round glass beakers, each filled with liquid in varying shades of red. The tubing hissed and hummed, and scarlet liquid drip-drip-dripped into a copper vat. Selene sniffed. "It's that smell from the incense."

"Very interesting, don't you think?"

"Indeed."

"There's more."

"Tell me."

He didn't answer. He merely waited for her to see ... something.

Then she did. Her heart stopped. Behind the laboratory contraption, something gleamed. A series of large glass jars occupied a deep wooden shelf. As she moved farther into the room, the acrid scent of spirits became apparent.

"It smells like a morgue."

"Indeed it does," he softly agreed.

Selene approached the jars and sighed heavily. Staring out from the greenish yellow liquid were two wide, unseeing eyes, and the masklike face of a woman. Scrawled on the lid in black grease pencil were the words "Miss Taylor." Sadness weighted Selene's chest.

"Poor girl. At least she's not missing anymore."

"Look at the others."

Selene didn't want to look at the others, but she did. There were twelve jars in all, each containing the remains of a different woman.

Rourke lifted up one of the smaller jars. "This is Catherine, one of Jack the Ripper's unfortunate girls."

Selene read softly. "And here is Elizabeth's missing head."

"Elizabeth ... murdered by the Dark Bride."

Selene lifted the lid from a shallow metal tray and grimaced. "It's got to be Pandora. Look."

He joined her and peered down. "She's taking their hair and dyeing it to use as her own. I'd say she's also patching herself with their skin."

Leather books lined a nearby shelf. Selene pulled down and opened one. There were words, but she didn't recognize them. The characters were complex—patterns of slash marks and exotic whorls—and ordered into both vertical and horizontal patterns. She selected another of the books and found it to be filled with the same.

Rourke shook one of the metal beakers and grimaced. "She's using at least some of the victims' remains to create this substance. There are ... er, *parts* in here."

Selene stared into the book. "I think she's trying to make herself into a woman. A real woman. I can't read the words, but look at the pictures." She held the book open for him. "They record experiments where she's attempted to replace her own mechanical parts with those of her victims." Selene frowned. "By the way she's dug her pen into the paper and scribbled all over everything, I'd say her experiments haven't worked."

She gathered the books into her arms.

"We can't take them all, not yet," said Rourke. "Just take one. The last one, there, because the leather appears newest. We'll come back for the others and send them to London for translation."

"We know Mrs. Thrall is Pandora," Selene mused. "The question remains . . . who is Mr. Silverwest?"

A scream sounded from above, and a moment later was joined by others.

Rourke scowled. "I smell smoke. The fire kind, not the blood-incense kind."

"No, we need more time."

The house groaned, and heavy thuds sounded from above, the sound of collapsing plaster and falling chandeliers.

Rourke led the way out. When they emerged from the trapdoor, fire licked the curtains of the bedroom and rolled in waves across the ceiling. Passing the parlor, also in flames, Selene looked out the window. "The trapeze and all the circus actors are gone."

One of the Greek columns slanted and fell. Selene deflected it with a fierce shove.

Once outside, she cursed. "I dropped the book inside. I'll be back."

He did not argue with her or attempt to escort or protect her. Now she was like him again—she was a Shadow Guard.

She disappeared inside the house for only a moment. When she emerged, she strode across the lawn toward him, the book clasped in her hand. Her hair had fallen free and her skirts had caught fire. Despite the tension of the moment, a smile curled on Rourke's lips, for he had never seen anything as beautiful as Selene with her skirts on fire. With an irritated glance down, she paused and ripped the burning layer free and threw it to the ground.

Dazed villagers wandered the lawn, some sobbing at the sight of the burning house. Others' faces had been painted like clowns. Mr. Harbottle ran in delirious circles, still naked.

Mortals did not boast as hearty a constitution as his and Selene's. It would take some time for the effects of the red smoke to wear off.

"There are going to be a lot of very embarrassed villagers in the morning," said Selene, her eyebrows raised.

"At least they are alive," answered Rourke.

She grabbed the nearest person, who turned out to be one of the ladies who had sold her eggs. "Could you tell me, please, which way the circus went?"

The woman nodded morosely and pointed toward the river. Sighing, she whispered, "They left us all behind."

Rourke and Selene returned to shadow. They coursed over the field and down the rolling hillside to the place where the pasture met the river. Colorfully painted wagons and carts littered the banks. A few horses wandered, appearing as confused as the villagers.

"They've all disappeared," Selene murmured. "How?"

Side by side they walked to the river. The water moved rapidly, crashing and whirling against jutting rocks. Pointed shoes, sequins, harem pants and one very tall top hat littered the stone riverbank.

"Jack the Ripper . . . the Dark Bride . . . they all stayed close to the Thames." Rourke crouched beside the water. "I think they've gone into the river."

Chapter Eighteen

"For you, Callianassa," whispered Selene. She pulled the pearl ring from her finger and dropped it into the circular gazing pool. Scales flashed, and a pale hand captured the jewel. With a ripple of dark hair, the Nereid disappeared into the shadows again.

"Did you make a wish?"

She turned to see her twin, Mark, crossing the lawn toward her. "I did."

With his golden appearance and gregarious manner, he was in so many ways the opposite of her. When he had come closer, he whispered, "Was it about Avenage?"

She shrugged.

Two weeks had passed since their return to London from Swarthwick. She had not seen Rourke since. She had immediately rejoined the Reclaimers, and he the Ravens.

She had also compulsively and in secret eaten nearly a library full of pages since then, and done her best to conceal their empty covers from anyone who might take notice.

"Soon you won't have any jewels . . . er, or books left. I found your stash of empty bookbindings in the rubbish bin."

Selene sniffed. "Don't accuse me. Clearly you've a book vandal amongst your staff."

"Mmm-hmm."

He tilted his head toward the manse behind him. "That Raven, Tres, just called for you again. Left his card. Tried to be charming. I told him you were out. He's been very persistent."

Selene smiled. "Which is very flattering, but no."

Mark, upon his return from Egypt, had quickly skimmed over Pandora's journal and concluded that Mr. Silverwest was, in all likelihood, Tantalus. The revelation had shocked everyone. While the Reclaimers had scoured London for any evidence of his arrival there, he had made his first appearance in the Outer Realm at Tedious-on-the-Moor, likely in hopes that Transcension still lay sleeping in Selene's mind, and that she could be recruited as one of his own.

Selene had argued that there had to be more to his choice. After all, Pandora had made inquiries about Swarthwick prior to Selene's being sent there under Rourke's guardianship.

As the Reclaimers attempted to predict where Tantalus would appear next, the Ravens strengthened their numbers in monitoring the city and any points beyond. Given his disappearance into the river and his prior interest in the Thames, Callianassa's sisters, the Nereids, who had been so critical in the recovery of the shattered Eye of Pharos, patrolled the murky waters below.

"Come inside. Mina's putting on tea."

Her return to the ranks of the Reclaimers had kept her very busy, but upon Mark and Mina's return from Egypt, she had moved out of the Hotel Metropole and into one of their upstairs bedrooms. They had insisted, and Selene had realized that the only reason her brother would be lost to her through marriage was if she pushed him away. Though she didn't have much time for anything but her duties and sleep, they had worked in their reunion in bits and pieces. They joined Mina in the blue sitting room.

"Tell me more of your work on behalf of the Atheatos."

He grinned. "I was hoping you'd ask."

Her brother's raven-haired bride, Willomina, arrived with a tray bearing tea service. "We can't tell you, Selene, how relieved we were to hear of your return to health. It troubled Mark so deeply to leave you in the Tower of London in the care of the Ravens whilst we traveled to Egypt."

Mina had tested the waters of "sisterhood" with Selene very gently, and Selene could not blame her for moving with such caution. She had not been so very nice to Mina when learning of her marriage to Mark. Selene could confess now that she'd simply been afraid of losing her twin, the only person who understood her personality and darker moods. But since her stay at Swarthwick, she felt more human than before. Less selfish and, as a result, hopeful of forming a friendship with her new sister-in-law.

Selene said, "The Atheatos is a wonderful opportunity for you both. I do not begrudge either of you for accepting the post, and offering your talents toward the defeat of Tantalus."

Mina covered Selene's hand and squeezed.

Mark said, "Let me tell you about our discoveries to date."

"Please do," encouraged Selene.

"So far we've identified at least six ancient artifacts that could be stolen from collections around the world or unearthed from their as-yet-secret hiding places and used by Tantalus or his followers for untoward purposes. One of the more dangerous artifacts we would prefer to locate rather quickly is the Pupil of the Eye of Pharos."

Selene scowled. "You must be jesting. The *Pupil* of the Eye of Pharos? That's a ridiculous name for an artifact."

Willomina rolled her eyes and conveyed to Selene a cup and saucer. "Mark, I told you she wouldn't believe you. Cream, Selene?"

"Yes, thank you." Selene nodded, but eyed her twin.

Mark snorted, clearly pleased by his own humor. "Yes, I'm jesting. But really, there is a pupil of sorts. It's a large, faceted stone that, when placed at the center of the mirror we know as the Eye of Pharos, actually intensifies its power."

"Well, how fortunate that the Eye has been recovered, because the *pu* . . . ah . . . *stone*—"

Straight of face, Mark whispered, "You almost called it the pupil, didn't you?"

"Mark," chastised Mina.

Selene continued, "Without the Eye, the faceted stone is useless."

"That is correct. And the most interesting thing to learn is that all of these items were implanted into the world about us, if you will, centuries ago. Many in plain sight, so that they might be preserved and utilized when the necessary dangers arose. Some of them must be used in specific combinations with others—as we so recently learned with the obelisk, Cleopatra's Needle."

"Whoever put this plan into place, why did they make things so complicated?"

"I suspect the system, and the mystery thereof, was created to keep these objects from being used for the wrong purpose, of course. At the same time, the mystery poses a problem in that no one seems to hold possession of the master key identifying and explaining them all. So it's very important that we locate them."

"Who implanted the artifacts? Who created the key?"

"Ancient mortals or immortals." He shrugged. "We don't yet know."

"Archer and Leeson are Ancients. Can they tell us nothing?"

"The first immortals numbered in the thousands, and populated all corners of the earth. It's possible that those who held the secrets of these powerful relics did not survive the centuries to the present day."

"Speaking of relics . . ." Selene touched the long ivory sticks that held her hair in place. "Should I relinquish the scroll rods?"

Mark stood and examined them. "Hmmm, that's not necessary. I'm veritably certain they've served their purpose. Besides," he added drolly, "you've likely destroyed their power by sharpening the ends into points. Vain temptress, keep them for the time being if they please you, but I beg you don't gift them to Callianassa. I may change my mind, and you know what a snarling sea harpy she transforms into if you try to take one of her sparkly baubles."

"When will you finish translating Pandora's journal?"

"I've already translated a sampling of entries throughout."

She leaned forward on the sofa. "Tell me more."

"Most of the journal records Pandora's ravings about Tantalus and how he doesn't love her enough because she's not a natural immortal. And as you saw, she had also sketched out a number of experiments."

"Was I right, Mark?"

He nodded. "She's been trying for centuries, apparently, to find a way to transform herself into a real woman. She uses their skin and hair and even infuses herself with their blood to enhance the naturalness of her appearance."

"She's harvested other parts from her victims as well."

"It's those more complex experiments that don't seem to have worked for her. The ones involving internal organs and . . . the female reproductive—"

"Oh, Mark. That's horrible." Mina shook her head and looked away.

"And then there are her chemical experiments. She's perfected a way to extract the essence of mortals—a very specific chemical compound that conveys warmth and attractiveness and sensuality. She's converted that essence into incenses, ointments and the like to make her more human and irresistible."

"I think she and Tantalus both have made use of that awful discovery."

"You might be correct about that. That essence may be why neither you nor Rourke realized a Transcended soul was seated right beside you, sipping tea."

"But Pandora and Tantalus are lovers, you believe?"

Mark nodded. "He has kept her hanging on for centuries, but he has a preference for the real thing, not automatons. But the journals also make repeated reference to her belief that he owes her for something. I believe she helped him improve his appearance somehow, for his emergence into the Outer Realm."

Mark's butler entered. "Your lordship."

"Yes?"

"There's a visitor for the countess." The man's eyes were wide and his eyebrows raised, as if he were impressed by the guest. Selene's heart leapt. *Rourke*.

"Who is it?"

Selene moved past.

". . . declined to provide a card or name."

No one stood in the foyer. She crossed into the east parlor. A woman stood looking out the window, into the garden, but she turned at Selene's entrance. Her highly ruffled and trimmed blue silk day gown displayed her tiny waist to perfection, and a small velvet cap perched like a crown atop her flawlessly styled blond hair. A reticule and parasol lay discarded on the nearby sofa.

"Hello, Selene," she said, flashing a dazzling smile.

Selene halted midstep, yet her skirts continued moving. Her hem hissed against the marble floor. "Helen."

"Well, don't look at me like that." Helen sauntered closer, making her bustle sway with practiced allure. She spoke in low, silky tones, and her blue eyes assessed Selene from head to toe. "We're old friends, after all, are we not? It's been so very long since we've talked."

"Don't call us friends," Selene responded. "We were never friends."

Helen gave a brittle laugh. "You're just like your mother. Jealous and hateful."

"You tried to take Antony from her. What did you expect?"

Selene steeled herself for Helen's response.

Helen. Rourke. Helen and Rourke. Was Helen here to flaunt Rourke's return to her bed?

She fought the urge to cover her ears with her hands. Helen liked to brag about the important and powerful men who fell under her enchantment. If she had come to taunt her about Rourke . . .

Helen shrugged. "A little friendly competition amongst historical temptresses? Certainly not a knife to my throat."

"Why are you here?"

Helen straightened. Resting one delicate hand on her waist, she lifted her chin. "I think you know."

Selene felt like retching.

Instead she responded, "You know one Amaranthine cannot read the mind of another."

Helen's eyes narrowed. "Don't throw it in my face, Selene. It's clear what's happened." She paced, crossing her slender arms over her breasts. "Helen gets to learn a little lesson. Helen gets to take a dose of her own medicine. He went off . . . with you . . . on 'official business' for the Primordials. And since he's returned to London, he hasn't been back to me."

Selene listened.

Helen prattled on, "I'm not a fool, little girl. This was your chance to try to hurt me. To pay me back. Well, you've won. There, I've said it." To Selene's dismay, Helen's eyes filled with tears. "Now give him back."

"Avenage is not mine to give back."

Helen blinked, her eyes widening. *"What?"*

"But if he were, I'd keep him. Forever."

Lips parted and eyes gleaming, Helen snatched up her reticule and parasol and flounced toward the door, clearly displeased at having humiliated herself when there had been no need.

There was a startled exchange in the foyer between Selene's caller and the footman, she demanding her shawl and he scrambling to comply, and then the door opened and closed.

Selene stood for a long time in silence, not knowing whether she ought to rejoice or cry.

Rourke wasn't seeing Helen anymore.

But neither had his immortal shadow darkened her doorstep.

Selene pulled on her long black cloak and kissed Mark's and Mina's cheeks. "Good night. I'll see you tomorrow at breakfast."

A footman held the door for her and she swept out into the deepening night. Low wisps of fog clung to her hem as she took the narrow walkway to the street. Tonight, Shrew drove the carriage. She wiggled her gloved finger at him, and he chuckled in response. Climbing up the stairs . . .

She found herself face-to-face with a pair of pale green eyes.

Avenage extended his gloved hand. "Countess."

Robbed of her breath, she placed her hand in his and moved past him to sit on the leather bench beside Tres. Rourke seated himself opposite her. The situation offered no opportunity for conversation. As the carriage started its travel, Leeson laid down a map across their knees. By the time they arrived in Whitechapel, they'd each been assigned their territory for the night.

The vehicle slowed and they exited, slipping off in different directions down alleyways, into boardinghouses or into pubs.

For the next three hours, Selene mingled and meandered among the prostitutes and drunks, keeping her mind open for any abnormal trace that would lead her to Tantalus or one of his followers. As the night advanced, so did the fog from the Thames. It hovered everywhere. Every so often, the wings of a raven darkened the cobblestones upon which she walked.

At last, when she turned from Commercial onto Wentworth, he stood on the walkway before her, a broad-shouldered shadow. The tails of his dark coat whipped in the wind.

"Selene."

"You are encroaching onto my territory. This is my street."

"I'll stay only a moment. How have you been?"

She walked closer. "My brother has returned from Egypt. I've been fully reinstated as a Reclaimer. The search for Tantalus has kept me occupied."

"The Ravens have kept me occupied as well."

"I'm not good at small talk, Rourke. Not with you. You'd better go back to your side of Commercial."

"I miss you," he whispered.

With his words, everything inside her faltered. The sharp words that sprang to her tongue evaporated. "I miss you too."

"I just . . ." His gloved hands flexed, and he stepped forward to touch her cheek. "I can't figure it all out."

"Neither can I." She tilted her face against his hand, craving his touch, even here, even now. "Why are you wrinkling your nose like that?"

"I smell something," he responded, dropping his hand and circling about. "Don't you?"

"Yes." She brushed past him. "It smells like death."

They discovered the girl's body, or what remained of it, on Pinchin Street, beneath one of the archways of the Great Eastern Railway. Soon, Leeson, Lord Black and all the other Shadow Guards who patrolled the district that night joined them. It was clear to them all that the murdered victim had been placed there to get their attention. She had been dead for days prior to her body being placed on the street. The parts of her body had been arranged, almost ceremonially, into a careful heap, just *feet* away from three drunken men who even now slept in a nearby archway. Just like Jack the Ripper and the Dark Bride, this killer had a vicious sense of humor.

Selene lifted a scrap of paper from the body. "It's one of the circus playbills."

In shadow, Leeson wrote into a paper book, documenting the exact position of the body, what parts were missing, and its deteriorated state.

Rourke said to Tres, "You'll make sure the authorities discover her."

"Yes, my lord." Tres withdrew into the shadows, headed toward a nearby alehouse.

Selene stared down at the circus playbill. "This was left on purpose."

Rourke stood close to her and spoke in a low tone. "Just like the girl at the side of the road."

"Yes . . ."

"What else are you thinking?" His gaze fell to her mouth.

"What if it's an invitation?"

"To go where? That's the same exact advertisement the circus used at Thorn-on-the-Moor. There are no specifics."

"'In the field at the edge of town,'" she read.

"There are many fields at the edge of this town."

She met his gaze. "Which ones are near water?"

"I don't think they'd be out in a field by a river, set up just as they were in Swarthwick; otherwise we'd have already found them. Also, likely they would not be traveling as a circus any longer. They abandoned all their wagons, costumes and tents on the side of the river."

"Perhaps we should be looking underground?"

"Let's mention it to Leeson. He can see what sewers and aqueducts might be out of use. For the rest of the night I think we should maintain our patrol." Glancing to the girl's body, he said, "Obviously they are here, among us."

Returning to her patrol, Selene searched methodically for any further sign that Tantalus or his minions intended to kill again. She approached Castle Alley, the place where she had been discovered lacking any memory of how she had come to be standing over another one of his victims.

She paused, catching not the trace, but the scent of something sweet and familiar. It was Pandora's scent, the same one that had been so cloyingly evident at the Astley estate. Her pulse increased, and with a twist of her hand she issued forth her Amaranthine silver daggers. The shadows were deeper at the end of the lane. She blinked, altering her eyes to pierce through the darkness. There, two figures struggled. She evanesced to the end of the alley and grabbed the attacker's arm as it swung up, blade in hand, over a cowering woman in dark clothing and a simple hat—likely one of Whitechapel's many prostitutes. Though a pale braid streaked down her back, she wore a man's coat and trousers.

"Pandora. Stop," Selene commanded.

Pandora yanked her arm free. Her face shone as pale and perfect as a porcelain doll's, beautiful and macabre at the same time.

"Hello, friend," she growled.

"You call me friend?" Selene feigned a cordial voice. "And yet you haven't taken the time to pay me a single call in London? I'm hurt. After all, we were such dear friends in the country."

"You were so easy to fool," taunted Pandora, circling her. "You thought I was so sweet."

"I did indeed. I can't believe I fell for it."

Pandora slashed at her with her blade. "I've had an awful lot of time to perfect my act."

Selene fended off the blow and lunged forward, but Pandora twisted away and disappeared down the alley. Her laughter echoed off the walls of the warehouses.

Selene pursued her, but cautiously, not wishing to be led into a trap. She also sent out a silent shout into the night, hoping Rourke or any of the other Shadow Guards would receive the message.

Pandora's here.

But at the end of the alleyway, there was no sign of Pandora. Instead, a carriage awaited, one she recognized from just a few months earlier, from her hunt for the Dark Bride. Grayish vapor clung to the roof, doors and wheels of the enormous town coach, one that would have been seen on London's streets a hundred years before. The same haze rolled off the backs of the monstrous team horses, harnessed and stamping at the forefront. The driver turned his pale face to her and, with jaunty flair, lifted his tattered stovepipe top hat. The towering gas lamp across the road offered enough light to glimpse his eyes. They rolled and whirled in their sockets.

"Greetings, Countess."

"Hello, *you*," she answered.

He had been one of the Dark Bride's toadies, the empty souls who had done her bidding. No doubt he had a new master now.

He leapt down. Clouds of vapor sprang from his boots at their impact on the cobblestones. The sash he wore across his moldering suit of clothes had once been embroidered in red thread with the initials DB. A crude white patch had been stitched over those initials, one emblazoned with what appeared to be black grease pencil, with the letter T.

He opened the door to the carriage, and three other toadies tumbled out, pushing and stomping on one another. His usual companions. Toad, Toad and Toadie. They hooted and guffawed until they nearly ran straight into her.

The three fiends bowed low, their eyes whirling just as frantically as the driver's.

"Oh, Countess!" exclaimed one.

The second crouched and bobbed. "It's you."

"Our master—"

"You *know* him."

"You do!"

"—extends an invitation."

"To 'is party."

"Please come!"

The driver held the door. The other three lifted their hands toward the vehicle in unified invitation.

She smiled. "You know I can't turn down a party."

Toadies were harmless without a *brotoi* around to incite them to violence.

She climbed inside the vehicle. The musty scent of rotted upholstery clouded the air, and she pushed out a window.

The driver's face appeared in the opening.

"Your costume be there on the bench."

"Splendid."

Several loud thunks came from the roof as the toadies leapt onto the back perch. As the carriage left Whitechapel, she dressed in the costume—a Cleopatra costume, complete with a golden headdress shaped like an asp. Had Rourke or any of the others heard her call, or would she be alone in this? Though she expected to be taken somewhere secluded, to her surprise the vehicle rolled to a stop in front of a grand Mayfair town house. Light streamed from every window, and music filtered into the street.

One of the toadies leapt down to open the door. The moment her foot met the walk, the driver *heeyaw*ed and snapped the reins. The carriage clattered into the night. Selene climbed the front stairs, which were crowded with revelers dressed in the most extravagant of costumes, and entered the open doorway. On either side of a large downward staircase, enormous candelabra blazed with light and dripped with wax.

"The Countess Pavlenco," bellowed the majordomo.

Through a crush of masked guests, Selene descended into a grand ballroom. Trays of half-emptied champagne glasses showed that the party had been going on for some time before her arrival. She skimmed along the edge of the main floor, which was thick with dancing couples.

The crowd parted, and from within their midst appeared a tall, broad-shouldered figure wearing a floor-length cape and the mask of a raven.

Mesmerized, she watched as he came toward her. He extended his gloved hand and, taking hers, swept her into the colorful, twirling throng. He held her scandalously close, and with every turn she felt the flex of his muscles beneath the costume. The ballroom, with its soaring ceiling painted with clouds and angels, spun as he led her in the dance. When the music came to an end, he lowered her backward, over his arm, in a dramatic finale. With his other hand, the raven pulled off his mask.

Blue eyes peered down at her and unsmiling lips hovered so close over hers she anticipated a kiss. But with his gaze fixed intently on hers, her dancing partner lifted her up . . . righted them both—and released her. Slowly, he stepped backward.

"I am not who you expected?" he demanded.

For a half second his attractiveness stunned her, but all she had to do was remember that this was not Mr. Silverwest, the country gentleman. This was Tantalus, the underworld creature who, in his plot to possess the

world, had unleashed violent, bloodthirsty killers like
Jack the Ripper and the Dark Bride on the mortal
population.

"No," Selene whispered. She had to gain his trust
and get him alone. She could not engage him in battle
here, in the middle of a room filled with mortals. "You
are much better than whom I expected. Better than the
Raven."

But, of course, he wasn't. Where was Rourke? Had he
received her message? Did he know she was here?

His gaze, which had been cool, sparked with fire.
He grasped her wrist and forcefully pulled her into the
crowd. The orchestra leapt into the next piece. Faces
moved past in a blur, and laughter and conversation
blended into a loud roar until suddenly they came to a
hallway and a large paneled door pushed inward by two
wigged servants.

Just inside the door, he spun away and others crowded
about to grasp her arms. They had faces she recognized
from the circus at Thorn-on-the-Moor.

"Relinquish your weapons." Tantalus spun on his heel
and lifted his hands in a dramatic display. "If I can trust
you, you should have no difficulty in agreeing."

Though her mind echoed with curses, she surrendered her daggers, giving it over to a diminutive acrobat
who awaited the Amaranthine silver weapon by wearing thick chain-mail-covered gloves that would protect
his hands from the searing heat.

Tantalus smiled and drew her through another pair
of doors. Exquisite furnishings filled the sitting room,
fashioned of dark woods and scarlet and dark blue silk
upholstery. He closed the door behind them.

He bit perfect white teeth into his bottom lip and
drank in the sight of her, and the fitted gold column gown
she wore. "Beautiful. I chose the costume especially for
you. Not because I want you to be your mother, darling, but because I think you'd make a ravishing queen
in your own right."

"What are you saying?"

"I told that Raven that I thought you and I had a special spark. We do, don't we?"

She lowered her chin, but did not look away. "You left me there that night, waiting in the garden. You told me you'd bring me a gift."

He shook his head. "You left with that Raven."

"He forced me to go. When I returned you were gone. It has taken me this long to find you again."

"Why did you want to find me?"

"Don't you know?"

"Tell me."

"I've come for my velvet box."

"Velvet box?" shouted a voice.

Tantalus drew Selene against his side.

Pandora had entered the room behind them and strode toward them, shaking her curled fist. "The box is mine."

"Not anymore," he countered.

"I can be everything you need," she exclaimed. She cast a sharp glare at Selene. "If only you would give her over to me. Her immortal body could provide everything I need to bear your sons—"

"Why would I want that?" he shouted viciously. "Why would I want one of your unnatural experiments to bring about the birth of my child? I am a *real* man. I have *always* told you I want a real woman."

"But I can be a real woman," she cried.

He lunged forward and grasped her arm. With a growl, he dragged her to the door and shoved her into the arms of the guards.

He swiftly closed the door behind his back. "That felt *good*. I've been trying to be free of that creaky piece of rubbish for centuries. You . . ." he said, his eyes burning with sensual heat. "Come with me."

He shoved on a wall panel and led her into the darkness. First down a staircase, and then into a series of tunnels. They went on forever, it seemed, providing the perfect labyrinthian domain for an underworld villain. As they descended deeper beneath the manse, and indeed, farther into the earth, the air grew colder. At last they came to the smooth stone wall of an old Roman aqueduct. The sound of rushing water filled the tunnel, fed by one of London's subterranean rivers.

"Just a bit farther," he promised, watching her face for her reaction.

Chapter Nineteen

The tunnel widened. Selene bit down on a gasp at her first glimpse of Tantalus's underground palace. Clearly the structure had been created over time, perhaps even over hundreds of years. The walls glittered like obsidian, but drawing closer she suspected the surface was coated in volcanic sand, and had been constructed from below . . . from Tartarus. There were no windows, just two large doors guarded by three snarling mastiffs. The dogs shrank back when Tantalus passed.

Inside, the rooms were cavernous, the walls covered with murals and tapestries depicting the seven deadly sins and scenes from mythology. Selene recognized more of the actors from the circus, but here there were scores more, interspersed with just as many whirly-eyed toadies. Filling countless rooms, they played games, wrestled and lounged on dark furniture. The pale red haze of Pandora's incense hung in the air.

Though a smile turned his lips, wariness still hovered behind Tantalus's eyes. He offered her his hand, and she accepted it. He led her past a thick screen. An enormous chandelier illuminated a massive bed on a raised dais. He led her, however, to a large table covered in cloth. From a standing golden chest, he retrieved a large red velvet box worked in gilt and tiny jewels.

"Pandora's box?" inquired Selene, her eyebrows raised.

"No. Selene's box." He grinned expectantly. "Open it."

Selene unfastened the golden latch and opened the lid. Inside, on a bed of black satin, lay a perfectly round green jewel.

"What is it?" she whispered.

He pulled the cloth aside, revealing what lay on the table. Twelve jagged shards of a broken mirror.

"That's the Eye of Pharos."

"Yes."

"I . . . had heard that the Shadow Guards recovered the Eye from the Thames."

"No. My followers recovered the Eye. The Shadow Guards, however, recovered an old mirror I bought at a wharfside rubbish store." He grinned. "Don't you think it eased their minds? Believing that they recovered the Eye before it fell into the *wrong* hands?"

He chuckled, and his lips drew back to reveal pointed incisors.

The skin at the back of Selene's neck crawled. She now had a good idea of the importance of the jewel in the box: Tantalus had the damn pupil.

"Where did you find the center stone?" she asked lightly, forcing a gleam of ravenous interest to her eyes.

"In the stained-glass window at Swarthwick. As you well know, Countess, there are many Reclaimed souls in Tartarus. Dangerous souls who have walked this earth, and observed useful bits and pieces of history. Down below, in our dark, cold Hell, there's not much else to do but talk and share stories. One of William the Conqueror's scribes—a very curious man whose tendency to pry into his lord's most private papers got him imprisoned was all too pleased to tell me that the king gave the window to that Raven as a gift those many years ago, with the stone hidden inside the eye of the serpent. Avenage, the oblivious bastard, had no idea he was to be its caretaker. William, as frail mortals have a tendency to do, died before sharing that particular secret. It is why

I went to that godforsaken speck of dust on the map in the first place. It's been there ever since, waiting to be discovered. I was simply waiting for the right time to join the two together. You were just a wonderful surprise. Clearly the time is right."

Before her eyes he lifted the jewel from the case.

"Wait—" she warned.

"No, I'm ready to do this now. I'm ready to start our lives together. The Eye has the power to destroy and to conquer. No one can stop us. The world will be ours."

He lowered the green stone to the center of the shards. For a moment the glass shifted on the table and drew together as if it would re-form itself around the stone, but . . . nothing occurred.

Tantalus scowled. He lifted the stone and lowered it again . . . and again . . . to the same result.

"I don't understand," he growled. "This stone doesn't work, and if it does not work that means . . . that means . . . that means the true stone was taken by someone in that keep." He glared at her, his nostrils flaring and his breath a hiss from his throat.

She backed away from him, eyes widening. "Not I. If I had the stone, I would give it to you without hesitation. I want what you want."

He stood up and strode a few steps away, spearing his fingers through his hair.

"How can I know that I can trust you?" he seethed.

"What do you ask of me?" she said.

He glanced to the bed. "I think you know."

He reached down and took her by the hand. Without a word, he led her toward the dais and the bed. Intently, he unfastened her gown. He pushed the garment from her shoulders and it slid to the floor. She stood in only her petticoat, corset cover and corset. His gaze moved admiringly over her.

Revulsion rippled through Selene. Wanting to move things on so she could get straight to ending his filthy existence, she summoned all the strength within her. Grasping him by the collar, she kissed him with feigned ardor. She tasted his stench on her lips.

"Please, I have waited so long, and am impatient for your touch," she lied, pushing him toward the only place where she knew he might become vulnerable enough for her to take him off guard. The scroll rods were still pinned in her hair. There had been six rods in all, and four of them had been used in the defeat of the Dark Bride. She had to believe the two in her possession might be useful in the end. Without her Amaranthine silver blades, she had nothing else.

She led him to the bed and, smiling, urged him to lie down. Pushing him back onto the pillows, she boldly straddled him. His hands worked at her buttons and fastenings.

She kissed him again, as thoroughly as she could bear, and, smiling above him, touched her hair. "Do you want my hair up or down?"

"Down, Selene, let your beautiful hair down."

Her heart thundered. Either the scroll rods would work, or she would be dead in the next instant. She lifted her hands to the rods and pulled them free. The desire to kill him arose fierce in her chest. His eyes widened, and too late she realized she had allowed her hatred to reveal itself in her face.

As she plunged the rods toward his heart, he slammed his fist across her face. She flew off the bed and down the stairs. One of the rods rolled across the marble floor.

He leapt from the bed and crouched above her, the second rod spearing out from the center of his chest. "You play me for such a fool?"

He yanked her by the hair. She clawed his face. His skin, his *nose*, came off in her hand. For a moment he twisted away, shielding his face with his hand, but then he turned flat, milky eyes toward her. His handsome face was no more. He dragged the remnants of the mask away, and in doing so released the full power of his deteriorated stench upon her. She groaned, nearly dizzied by it. She remembered the horrible smell with sickening clarity. It was the same as from her nightmare that night at Swarthwick, when she'd dreamed the enormous worm was in her bed. Only now, she realized her nightmare had been no dream.

Whatever face Tantalus once had no longer existed. His cheekbones were swollen knots and his skin sagged like melted white plastic. The scroll rod still jutted from his chest, and he yanked it free.

"What's wrong, Countess? Don't you like what you see?" He lurched toward her. "How do you think you would look if you had been banished to damp, cold darkness without the light of the sun since the beginning of time? I've adapted, and so have the others."

At that moment the doors burst inward. Shouts came from without. Pandora's face appeared at the door, and in both hands she hoisted a sword—Rourke's Amaranthine silver sword. Because she was inhuman, it appeared she could hold the silver without being burned. Tantalus roared.

"Darling," she cried at seeing him. Her pale hair streamed over her shoulders. "What has she done to you? I'll fix everything."

"The stone!" he raged. "One of the Shadow Guards has the real stone, and without it, the Eye is useless."

"No, listen! I have the stone," cried Pandora, grinning in triumph. She whirled toward the door and motioned to a guard. "Present my prisoners."

Rourke and Leeson were jostled forward, their wrists and ankles shackled in heavy chains.

Pandora narrowed her gaze on Selene. "The countess has been shouting out in that silent language of theirs, and they followed her here."

Rourke stared at Selene. "We'll trade the stone for Selene. Do it now. It won't be long before the other Shadow Guards arrive, and they won't allow the exchange."

"Do you hear that?" gloated Pandora. "They'd rather see you dead, Shadow bitch, than give up the stone to save you."

What ruse was this? Selene knew nothing of any stone being discovered.

"Ah! But there will be no trade," shouted Pandora.

"The stone is ours! The old man's got it in his pocket. Take it from him."

Five pairs of hands, each belonging to a twirling-eyed toadie, searched Leeson, thrusting into his pockets and patting his shirt and trousers down.

He laughed and jerked and nearly toppled over because of his shackles. "Stop that. Stop that. You're tickling me."

"I won't give you up." Tantalus grabbed Selene's arm and dragged her to her feet. "But you won't be my queen. You'll be my slave!"

Pandora laughed and waved the sword. "Our slave."

"Don't touch her." Rourke broke free of those who dragged at his arms and legs, and lunged forward, but the chains held.

"I said *stop that*," bellowed Leeson. The power of his voice jolted through the room and everyone froze. To Tantalus, he shouted, "Old Dora told you I had the stone, and indeed I do."

He raised his chained hand to his eye patch and flipped it upward.

A searing green beam of light shot out of the socket— not empty, but filled with the green stone.

Tantalus screamed as the beam tore through his flesh.

"No!" Pandora screamed.

Suddenly Rourke was there, his eyes gleaming and his dark wings spread. He wrenched the sword from Pandora's hands, and with a pass of the blade his chains fell as if they were made of paper. He moved like lightning, leveling the sword against Pandora's neck—

But just as quickly, she ducked and rolled away.

Leeson stepped closer, staggering beneath the weight of his own power. Tantalus crumpled to the ground beneath the continued pulse of the green light, but crawled on his elbows and knees toward them.

Leeson shouted to Rourke, "You must still use the Amaranthine silver. Do it, Ravenmaster."

Rourke raised his sword. Tantalus twisted, lunged up.

"Yes," Selene shouted. "Do it!"

Rourke plunged the silver into his chest. With a roar, Tantalus tried to stand. He grasped at the sword and tried to pull it free. Rourke bellowed and planted a boot against his chest, struggling to keep him down.

Selene, acting on her original instincts, took up the discarded scroll rods and plunged them into his chest.

While their efforts with the emerald, the sword and the scroll rods had not been enough to defeat Tantalus when employed singularly, their combined power proved strong enough. Tantalus howled, and his eyes and mouth exploded in fire. Rourke, scrambling backward, dragged Selene away. Leeson lowered his eye patch and raced to join them.

Pandora threw herself on top of Tantalus. As his body blackened, hers burst into flames, and they writhed for a moment before collapsing inward on themselves. All around the room, Tantalus's followers dissolved into the same volcanic sand as their master.

In the aftermath, the three Amaranthines stared down into the blackened crater. Within moments, more Shadow Guards, both Reclaimers and Ravens, joined them, wearing hopeful expressions of amazement . . . and disappointment that they'd been left out of the final battle with Tantalus. Among them stood Mark. He rushed forward and enveloped Selene in his arms. Over her brother's shoulder, her eyes met Rourke's.

Archer glanced down at Leeson. "Where did you get the stone?"

Rourke answered, "When he was checking the solder on the stained-glass window at Swarthwick. The eye of the serpent—a perfectly round emerald—was loose. Realizing its value, he substituted one of Nathan's marbles, for altogether aesthetic purposes, until a proper repair could be made. When Tantalus shattered the window, he took the marble."

Leeson nodded. "I actually forgot I had the emerald until it fell out of my pocket this evening. Your brother saw it and started babbling something outrageous about a pupil."

Mark chuckled. "So imagine my shock when he decides to play the comedian and put the pupil in his apparently very powerful empty eye socket."

Selene gasped. "What happened?"

Rourke murmured, "He burned down half a wall in your brother's house, that's what."

Leeson secured his eye patch. "I'll have that wall repaired within the week." He smiled. "You know how your brother has translated the ancient texts about Tantalus's wish to rule this earth, and how the scrolls and tablets prophesied that certain artifacts and even people will turn out to be important in the end? I'm an Ancient. I've been here on this earth since the beginning of time. I was born without an eye, and as you can imagine, more than once I cursed my poor luck. Now I know there was a purpose. My curse is instead a blessing. I'm amazed . . . astounded to find that I, little old Leeson, was always intended to be important in the grand scheme of things."

Selene kissed his forehead and whispered softly, "I'm not astounded at all."

"Come, let us begin," called the queen, leading Selene into her privy chamber, where Archer and Elena, Mark and Mina waited with Leeson, and a score of others, both mortal and Amaranthine.

Selene wore a royal blue gown fashioned of thick satin, and elbow-length white gloves. A tiara, given to her by Marie Antoinette, glimmered atop her gleaming coiffure. She shoved the small volume of poems into the velvet bag dangling from her wrist, and quickly swallowed the first stanza on page thirty-two. For days, she'd been so nervous about this night that she'd taken to eating several volumes a day.

She glanced down the long hallway. "Your Highness, we should wait. Avenage has not arrived."

Beneath her lace cap, the queen snorted. "He never attends these events. Indeed, over the decades I've saved a box full of ribbons and medals and sashes belonging to him. He's simply never shown an interest in being recognized for bravery or military skill or whatnot."

Disappointment feathered through Selene. Since Tantalus and his followers had been destroyed, Rourke had again retreated to the Tower. Had all the emotions they had shared faded away for him? Painfully, they had not for her.

"Ahem," interrupted a voice just behind them.

Selene paused, afraid to turn, afraid to be disappointed.

"Avenage," exclaimed the queen. "I can't believe you're here."

In a blur, he came to stand beside her.

"Your Highness," he said by way of greeting. "Selene."

Together the three of them joined the rest of the party. Selene took her place between Leeson and Rourke, feeling almost dizzied by his silent presence.

Moments later, the queen lifted a medal dangling from a gleaming gold ribbon, and fastened it to Leeson's puffed-out chest. "In recognition for your bravery, Mr. Leeson. You have our sincerest thanks."

"Thank you, Your Majesty."

Victoria did the same with Selene, murmuring a few personal words as she pinned a medal to the shoulder of her gown.

"Dear Avenage—" began the queen.

"Please don't think me impertinent or rude, but I am not in attendance this night in order to claim a medal."

"Oh?" Victoria's eyebrows rose. "Why, then, are you here?"

Selene kept her eyes fixed on the sparkling green butterfly pin in Elena's blond hair.

"Selene . . ." Rourke said quietly. She saw, in her peripheral vision, that his face turned toward her.

A tremor moved through her body. Something in his voice . . .

"I came for Selene."

Murmurs moved through the room. Archer's eyes widened. Elena clasped a hand over her mouth. Mina grasped Mark's arm.

Slowly, Selene turned her face toward Rourke. Their gazes met.

Firmly, he repeated, "I . . . came . . . for you."

For a long moment, there was nothing but absolute silence. Then the queen announced, "Let us all go into the dining room for our meal. Unfortunately, I do believe we are two place settings short." She chuckled. There were many winks and smiles and over-the-shoulder glances as the party left the room, but at last the two of them were alone.

"Why now?"

He turned to her, closing the space between them. "Because I can't imagine this eternity without you."

"What has changed?"

His hand came up to bracket her chin. She closed her eyes.

"Nothing," he answered, his voice tight with emotion. "And everything. I've gone centuries waiting for absolution through my self-imposed damnation."

"To what end?"

"I must forgive myself."

"Oh, Rourke," she whispered, her heart swelling inside her breast.

"I forgive myself."

Selene embraced him, wrapping her arms around his neck and fervently kissing his lips, his cheek and his jaw. Love poured out of her in a great, pent-up rush.

He pressed his mouth against her temple and pulled her hard against him. "I can imagine no greater reward. No newer beginning."

"I thought women weren't allowed to live in the Tower," said the young Raven, as Rourke carried Selene past.

"That's not *a* woman," Tres answered sharply. "That's Selene. And you'll call her Lady Avenage until she allows you to do otherwise. Do you understand?"

"Is that your new recruit?" Selene murmured to Rourke.

"That is him."

The long train of her wedding gown trailed over his arm. He kicked the door inward with the heel of his boot. Inside Rourke's small room, Selene's things cluttered every spare space. There were trunks and gowns and baskets. They would eventually look for a house of their own, but they hadn't wanted to wait even another day to wed. Within moments, they had stripped each other naked and stood before the fire.

At the barest brush of her fingertips against his skin, he sucked in his breath. Firelight bathed his skin, revealing his masculine perfection to her ravenous eyes. The muscles of his abdomen constricted, forming cut indentations in his belly. Desire bloomed in Selene's blood, swirling up from the arches of her feet to weaken her legs, swell her breasts and lighten her head. She closed her eyes and exhaled.

Delirium.

Husband.

She pushed free and, with her hands planted against his chest, pushed him toward the bed. Mischief flared in her eyes as she shoved him over the footboard.

"Lie back," she ordered.

He complied, crawling away from her to rest on the pillows. Desire sparked anew in his green eyes. She crawled over him, straddled his hips and pulled his wrists above his head.

"I've been fantasizing about this for months," she confessed.

"What?" He flexed up to kiss her mouth.

Something corded tightly about his wrists and his ankles, binding him to the four posts of the bed.

"That," exclaimed Selene, laughing.

A glance revealed her wicked plot—eight tightly coiled snakes, two on each limb, held him prisoner.

"Selene," he growled, but her mouth distracted him, placing a trail of warm, urgent kisses down his chest.

"There's no escape for you. Now that I've finally got you, I'll never let you go."

AUTHOR'S NOTE

While writing *Darker Than Night*, I researched a number of subjects, including traveling circuses. One particular book, *The Ways of the Circus: Being the Memories and Adventures of George Conklin, Tamer of Lions* by Harvey W. Root, published in 1921, began with a verse written by Don C. Seitz. The verse instantly transported me to another time and place, before television, three-dimensional animation and video games, where sparkling sequins, human drama and spectacle provided excitement and thrills to eager, paying audiences. I hope you, the reader, enjoyed Mr. Seitz's verse as well—in chapter 15, the circus ringmaster recites the following excerpt:

"Tinsel and tawdry! Say not so
Of these, the trappings of the show!
Splendors, instead of Eastern kings.
Glitter around the triple rings...."

K. Lenox

Read on for a special preview of
another novel of the Shadow Guard

NIGHT FALLS DARKLY

Available from Signet Eclipse

Spitalfields slums
London
April 1887

"Come out, Mr. Winslow." Archer stepped out from the stairwell onto the dark tenement roof. "It's your time to die."

Wind, biting and ruthless, sent the tails of his great-coat snapping behind him. He wove between crumbling chimneys and piles of rubbish, avoiding the sagging tar paper and rotted beams that might collapse and send a more careless being into the black oblivion of the abandoned building below. He pulled the leather gloves from his hands and tucked them into his hip pocket. Another gust twisted his long hair about his shoulders. Inhaling deeply, he savored the scent of fear on the air.

"How rude of you to run and hide, when I've traveled all this way *just . . . to see . . . you.*"

This was his favorite part of the hunt, the exquisite, slow torture of his prey right before Final Reclamation. He could choose to darken into shadow and make quick business of things, but no—a deviant like Winslow deserved to be terrorized on a much grander scale.

Archer closed his eyes and summoned the quickening. Heat seared his skin and fluxed through his veins.

When he opened his eyes again, he knew they were no longer gray, but wholly black. He spread his palms at his sides. Eight claw daggers hissed out, nearly to his knees, their blades formed of equal parts fire and primeval silver.

A crumbling stack of bricks stood at the south end of the roof. Though the fog was dense and the sky held no stars, he required no light to discern even the minutest detail. The air fairly quivered around the bricks. With a growl, he leapt the distance and leveled them with one blow.

Winslow reeled into the open. Though he was Herculean in stature, his scream rang as high-pitched as a child's. Unexpectedly, he dragged with him a tempest of woolen skirts, slender limbs and pale hair. Archer bit out a curse, his pleasure in the hunt instantly soured. He had sensed no other presence but Winslow's. How could this be? Never before had he made such a grievous mistake. With a scowl, he advanced.

"Wot the 'ell are you?" Winslow gaped, his eyes fixed in terror, first on Archer's claws and then his eyes. Scarlet furrows scored one cheek, evidence of his captive's mettle. "A demon, or the devil 'imself?"

Winslow dragged the girl toward the far ledge.

"Let . . . me . . . *go*!" She cuffed his jaw. Her lower lip was bruised and swollen. One of her sleeves gaped open, torn and flapping in the wind.

Archer hissed. How was he to Reclaim his target without sacrificing the life of the girl?

Winslow's heel pierced a weak spot in the roof. Both went tumbling. Recovering quickly, he clamped one arm around her chest, the other in a high choke hold against her neck, and hauled her backward onto the ledge. Behind them the slum lay blanketed in sooty darkness. Heedless of the danger, the girl flailed her arms and kicked at the beast's shins with her bare feet.

"Stop fightin' me, bitch!" Winslow ground out between yellowed and broken teeth. He struggled for balance atop the narrow ridge of crumbling mortar.

Archer halted. Any fall would be fatal for both. He cared not about Winslow—nothing could save the bastard now—but he would not be held accountable to the Primordials for the death of an innocent.

"I hope he kills you," the girl shouted, clawing at the meaty hands, trying to pry them away. "Kills you for what you did to me. For what you did to the others."

"Shut your mouth." A jealous animal guarding his claim, he wrenched her hard against his body. The ledge shifted. Bits of brick and mortar splintered out. "I'll jump before I let 'im cut me wi' them wicked blades, an' I'll take you wi' me."

"Then do it now, coward!" challenged the girl, her voice a defiant sob. "Jump!"

Archer searched the darkness of his mind and found her name there.

Elena, he commanded in silence. *Stop.*

She froze. Her arms and legs eased in their tension until the tips of her toes almost touched the muddied cuff of Winslow's boots. She rasped, fighting for breath, and with visible effort, tilted her face to stare wide-eyed and disbelieving at Archer.

What odd eyes she had. Brave eyes, one blue and one brown. Time, which usually rushed past him with the speed of a tumultuous, engorged river, almost stopped. His pulse—or hers?—beat in his ears, a dark cannonade. Beyond her tears he saw dignity and strength, and a reflection of himself as she saw him.

Cruel. Violent.

Beautiful.

His mind reeled to another existence, to a time when he had lived and loved. Dreams or memories? He couldn't be certain anymore.

"Do what you will," she whispered to Archer.

Winslow spewed blasphemies, his face a mere blot against the background of the night.

Archer stared at Elena, puzzled that he could not break the connection he had put into place between them. How could it be that with only a glance and a few words, a woman—a mortal woman at that—could penetrate him so completely? He felt all tangled up with her, something his mind rejected, but his soul craved.

Unnerved, Archer looked away, and into the eyes of something he understood better. "It's time we brought this dance of ours to an end."

"Go ahead," Winslow warned, wrenching the girl's head higher against his shoulder. "But she'll die too."

"You think it all ends with that?" Archer whispered. "With death? I'm afraid not. You can't escape, so let the girl go."

"She stays with me!" bellowed Winslow. His beefy fingers pressed into the pale flesh of Elena's throat.

Throughout time, Archer had always hunted with the dispassionate precision of a wolf, but now rage welled within him, so black and intense he felt he would disintegrate from the inside out. He cursed the limitations of his power, wishing he could slay by mere glance. Instead, left with no other choice, he darkened into shadow. With a frantic gaze, Winslow shouted and searched the rooftop. He sidled along the ledge as if to escape.

Mortar crunched, then slid and crumbled. The girl screamed.

Archer retracted his claws and lunged for her, but too late. A flash of petticoat, and she disappeared with Winslow over the edge.

Frantic to save her, he fell against the bricks and thrust out his arm, his only reward a brush of fingertips and her terrified stare locked onto his as she spiraled out of reach.

September 29, 1888

Elena grasped the girl's wrists. With the weight of her body and every bit of her strength, she pinned the young prostitute to the table.

"Bastards!" Lizzy shrieked, and heaved herself up with such force she nearly threw Elena off.

"Shhhh, shhhh," Elena soothed. "He'll make sure it goes fast."

With a *pop,* the bone slid into place.

"Success," announced Dr. Harcourt.

"You see?" Relief coursed through Elena, along with an electrifying charge of pride. "That wasn't so bad, was it? I told you he was good."

She eased off Lizzy, but carefully. In her brief time on the ward she'd learned one could never be certain of a patient's response. Some reacted with gratitude, others with a strike to the jaw. Glancing down, she saw twin rivers of tears streaming over Lizzy's temples and into her bright red hair. The girl's pallor nearly matched the white enamel of the table beneath her. Smelling salts might be in order.

"Lizzy?" Elena smoothed an unruly curl off a freckled forehead. The girl was very young and clearly alone in the world. "Are you all right?"

Suddenly slender arms seized Elena in an embrace so fierce her feet rose inches off the floor.

Lizzy sobbed, "Oh, thank y', miss. Thank y' for stayin' wi' me. I ain't never been so scared in all me born days."

Her patient smelled of tobacco and gin rather than soap and flowers as a young girl should, yet Elena felt sympathy for her and admittedly, a sort of kinship. Who could say she wouldn't be living on the street and doing *anything* to survive if fate hadn't handed her a different set of circumstances?

"You've been so brave through all of this, Lizzy." Elena gave her a squeeze. Stepping back, she slipped a hand into her apron pocket and pulled out a handkerchief. "Two days ago I watched a grown man fall to pieces when faced with the same procedure."

"Truly?" Lizzy gave a sheepish smile and gratefully accepted the folded square of linen. She dabbed at her eyes.

In the corner of the tiny room Dr. Harcourt gave instructions to the young medical student who had assisted with the procedure. Elena listened as well, hungry for any bit of knowledge, be it simple or complex. They would employ a wood splint and sturdy bandaging to ensure the girl's knee remained safely aligned for the next several days. His instructions given, the doctor strode toward the door.

"Wait, Doc," Lizzy called out, raising herself onto an elbow. Her threadbare waistcoat stretched across narrow shoulders.

Dr. Harcourt paused, a shock of blond hair tumbling over one eye until he brushed it aside. "Yes, Miss Harper?"

He wore a physician's smock and trousers, an understated uniform for the highborn second son of one of England's wealthiest and most influential families. He was tall and athletic of build, and the top of his head nearly met the upper frame of the door.

Lizzy blurted, "I'm ever so sorry to 'ave called you a bastard." She glanced toward the student. "You too, sir. So very sorry."

Harcourt flashed a warm smile, the one Elena saw him employ often with his patients. Unlike many of the older physicians on staff, he had a way of putting his subjects at ease. His gaze lifted to Elena for a brief moment before returning to the girl. "Don't think of it again. I'm pleased to have been of assistance."

With that, he disappeared into the hall.

Lizzy's grin revealed a row of crooked teeth. "Lor', if the doctor ain't the most 'andsome man I ever seen. 'Ow can you even stand workin' with 'at one?"

Elena laughed softly but offered no response. Harcourt *was* a handsome man, but he had been her personal physician in the months following her accident. Now he was her mentor. Though over time they'd become something like friends, she didn't think of him in terms of attractiveness.

Oh, *bosh*. That was a filthy lie if she'd ever told one.

But she did take her position at the hospital very seriously. Only out of desperation had Harcourt dropped his insistence that she devote herself to "pursuits more appropriate to her station" and granted her a probationary role among the nurses. The proximity of the vicious Whitechapel killings to the hospital infirmary had inspired a wave of panic amongst its female employees. A number of nurses had resigned their posts, leaving the London sorely understaffed. It had been a full three weeks since the last murder, but in that time the authorities had made no firm arrests, and a thick pall of fear hung heavy across the district.

Elena wasn't afraid of the killer—not here on the actual premises of the hospital—and she'd do anything to stay.

She helped Lizzy into a seated position and arranged the girl's woolen skirts discreetly at her knees. "All that remains is for this good gentleman to bandage and splint your leg. I'll go to the dispensary and see about getting you a pair of crutches. Have you anyone to see you home?"

"Oh, I won't be goin' 'ome again. . . ." Her voice faded into melancholy silence.

"No?" Elena hadn't pressured the girl to explain the circumstances of her injury. The ladies who came here for charity services rarely admitted to being the victim of a brutish "old man" or customer. She kept her voice light. "Where will you go, then?"

"Me good mate Catherine'll be waitin' for me in the ward—Catherine Eddowes. She's like me ma, you see." Lizzy nodded, and smiled bravely. "She stays at a nice place, real regular, on Shoe Lane. Maybe I can stay wi' her. . . ."

"I'll fetch her, then."

"She's wearin' a black straw 'at and a coat with some fur on the collar."

Two slats of wood in hand, the student scooted his stool closer to Lizzy's injured leg. He and Lizzy eyed each other warily.

"You're certain this one knows wot he's doin'?"

"He's had the very best teacher," Elena assured her as she left the room.

Nurse James, the head nurse, swept past, balancing a

tray of rolled bandages. "Dr. Harcourt asks that you see him in the chemist's laboratory."

"Thank you, ma'am."

Elena did not miss the sharpness of Nurse James's tone. For the most part, the nurses on staff were much older than she, and of modest backgrounds and means. They resided in the on-premises dormitory and lived little of their lives outside the hospital walls. Though she'd made her share of friends, a good number of the women had not taken kindly to her intrusion into their ranks— she with her fine Mayfair address, private carriage and driver, but she'd held her own. Not wishing to appear to hold herself above the rest, Elena had recently taken to spending two to three nights a week in the dormitory as well.

She smoothed her apron and hurried a few doors down. There she found the doctor scribbling out an order at the chemist's desk, his spectacles low on his nose. Ointment pots, glass carboys and stoneware jars dotted the shelves behind him. The air held the distinct tincture of camphor.

"You require my assistance, Dr. Harcourt?"

"Miss Whitney. Thank you for coming. I wish to speak with you about an application that arrived on my desk this afternoon."

Suddenly, the room seemed much smaller, its walls and ceiling, closer.

Elena straightened her shoulders. "Yes, sir."

He wore a professional, but pleasant, expression. She could read nothing in him that would lead her to believe he would grant or deny her request.

"You have managed to surprise me yet again, Miss Whitney."

"How, so, sir?"

"Most young women of your privileged means wouldn't deign to drive down the street in front of this hospital, let alone work in its charity ward. And now I hear you have engendered the admiration of our resident human oddity."

"I wasn't seeking anyone's admiration, Dr. Harcourt.

Truth be told, my first visit with Mr. Merrick was completely accidental. It seemed only polite that I should stay and chat for a moment."

Just days before, one of the other nurses had thought to chase Elena off the job by having her carry a tray of beef tea into the room of a "private patient," only for Elena to discover the man was Joseph Merrick, a former sideshow attraction vilified in the papers as the Elephant Man. It would be a lie to say his appearance hadn't startled her, but after introductions were made, they had spent the better part of a half hour conversing on all manner of subjects.

"He wishes you to know he enjoyed the books very much."

To be certain Mr. Merrick knew she had not been repelled by his deformation, and that she had truly enjoyed their visit, Elena had made a point to return the next day, bringing him several of her favorite selections from the library at Black House.

"I am glad."

The doctor considered her for a long, silent moment. Elena resisted the urge to clasp her hands, or adjust her apron.

"With regard to your application—"

"Yes, sir."

"The path you seek is one fraught with difficulty, and unfortunately, much prejudice against your sex."

She attempted an easy smile. "I have put much thought into my decision, even before my time here at the hospital began."

"I know you have." He nodded, removed his spectacles and slipped them into the pocket of his smock. "But what about marriage? Children? As you know, Lord Black left instructions that if you should wish to marry, he would bestow a generous settlement."

Her lip twitched. "Yes, Lord Black has been quite generous."

Indeed, her mysterious guardian—a man she could not recall ever having met—had left her mistress of his Mayfair residence, an opulent, expansive manse worthy of the queen herself. She also had at her disposal a ridiculously large allowance, and accounts at all the finer establishments.

Why was it so hard to understand that she needed more? She needed identity. Purpose. Somehow, this felt *right* and true to the person she must have been before. Elena glanced at her apron, at a smudge in the shape of a child's handprint. Her fingertips brushed over the precious bit of filth.

"Nonetheless, Dr. Harcourt, my interests lie outside the home."

"And you wish for me to write a letter of reference?"

"Only if you believe I would make a competent physician."

Slowly, the corner of his lips took on the curve of a smile. "Of that, I have absolutely no doubt."

"Thank you, Doctor." Elena exhaled, stunned and flattered by the uncharacteristic warmth of his words.

"I will write the letter—"

"I shall be forever grateful."

"—on one condition."

"Yes, sir. Anything. I shall scour bedpans or—"

"Not bedpans, Elena."

Elena flushed at hearing him speak her given name. He had never employed such a familiarity before.

"Mother's birthday fete is tonight."

Anxiety speared through her stomach. "I received the invitation. Regretfully—"

"I know it is difficult for you to move amongst society, and to suffer the inevitable questions about your past."

An understatement, to be sure.

"It's not only that, Dr. Harcourt. I now work under your supervision."

"And so your attendance would be inappropriate? Nonsense. We are neighbors, and Lady Kerrigan adores you. She was quite disappointed to receive your note declining."

Dr. Harcourt's mother had made several visits to Black House during Elena's recovery. Likely, the countess had simply been curious to get a good look at the reclusive Lord Black's amnesiac ward, but all in all, the lady's blatant nosiness aside, they had gotten along exceedingly well.

Harcourt pushed back his stool and stood.

"With the adjournment of Parliament, most everyone has left for the country, so the event should be a rather small affair."

How could she refuse him? He had already done so much for her, and now that the esteemed physician had agreed to write her letter of recommendation, she was assured of acceptance into the London School of Medicine for Women.

"You have convinced me," Elena capitulated, and smiled despite her dread of the impending evening. "Please tell Lady Kerrigan I would be pleased to attend."

"Excellent." His voice warmed with pleasure. "Then you must return to Black House at once, as I doubt you've a suitable gown amongst your things in the dormitory. And a few hours of rest, doctor's orders. You've been on your feet since dawn. Lady Kerrigan would be highly offended if you came to her party only to nod off in a corner chair."

"Thank you, Doctor. I'll just finish up with Lizzy. Do you think one of the cart drivers could see her and her companion to their place of lodging? One of the casual wards on Shoe Lane, I believe."

"Yes, certainly. We shall look forward to seeing you tonight, then." He smiled as she pulled the door to, behind her.

With a quick glance at the timepiece pinned at her waist, she scurried down the corridor and into the crowded reception rooms. She didn't bother a glance toward the left, for that space would be filled only with men—sailors, factory workers and other male laborers. Instead, she steered right.

"Mrs. Eddowes?" she called. "I'm looking for a Mrs. Eddowes."

Coughs and moans punctuated the lively murmur

of the large, ill-lit room. A few faces turned in her direction, but quickly looked away. Women and children milled about or sat on wooden benches. Some slept on the floor or in corners. The air smelled like sickness and human filth. The unfortunate ladies who surrounded her were bundled up tight, most wearing every piece of clothing and miscellany they owned. Each face told a different story through its scars or wrinkles, its expressions or missing teeth. She could not explain, even to herself, why she felt more at ease in this gloomy ward than at afternoon tea in the sumptuous drawing rooms of Mayfair. Likely the answer lay hidden in her past.

Elena circled round toward the back of the room. "Mrs. Eddowes?"

Two young boys, fists swinging, tumbled into her path.

"I'm the Knife, boy! I'm going to cut your guts out an' leave you for the dogs ta' eat."

"Help! Police!" bellowed the other, falling to the floor at Elena's feet.

"You two stop that," Elena ordered in her best imitation of the hospital matron's authoritative voice. She helped the boy up by his arm. "No horseplay or out you'll go. Whom are you here with? All right, then. Take your seats by your mum, there against the wall."

She gave one last call, "Mrs. Eddowes?"

No one raised a hand or stood. Elena prayed Lizzy had not been abandoned, not when she so desperately needed the constancy of a friend. She retraced her steps to the center of the two reception rooms where the day porter sat behind his desk.

"Mr. Morgan, I know chances are slim, but I'm desperate to find a woman wearing a black hat and a coat with a fur-trimmed collar. Might you have seen her?"

The porter nodded wearily. "Oh aye, I remember *'at one.* Got 'erself into a bit of a row with the big-mouthed tart on the front bench." He hooked his thumb in the direction of the doors. "She took off about a quarter hour ago."

"Damn," muttered Elena, curling her hands into fists.

He gave a phlegmy laugh. "Lor', but aren't you startin' to sound like a Whitechapel gel!"

Elena shot him a rueful smile as she pushed through the large paneled doors, to stand upon the covered portico that ran the length of the hospital. Vaulted archways provided a dim view of Whitechapel Road. Though the afternoon hadn't fully surrendered to night, the shadows were long, and a wispy, gray fog hovered all around. An old man in a dented hat and patched coat sat on the top step, smoking a cheroot. Beyond him, a hansom clattered past, its side lamps illuminated by orange flame.

"Sir," she called. "Was there a woman here, waiting?"

He nodded, and pointed rightward, in the direction of Raven Row.

"Thank you, sir."

The air carried an uncomfortable chill and a faint chorus of voices from one of the nearby dramshops.

"Ta-ra-da-boom-di-ay, ta-ra-da-boom-di-ay . . ."

Elena crossed her arms for warmth and traversed the length of the walkway. A low wind caught at her skirts and twisted them about her legs. Reaching the end of the portico, she circled the final column but saw nothing besides fog and shadows. She frowned. It seemed there was nothing to do but tell Lizzy that Mrs. Eddowes had left without her. Besides, she didn't want to remain out here any longer. She wasn't one to claim odd feelings or premonitions, but there was something discomfiting about the moment, something that teased the vulnerable, exposed skin on the back of her neck and made her want to hurry back inside.

Just then she heard a woman's laughter, low and flirtatious. The sound was close, yet difficult to place as far as direction. Though she could easily see a stone's throw all around, fog muddied anything beyond.

"Hello?" She descended the steps and continued along the sidewalk until she came to stand beneath a towering lamppost. She peered up toward the source of its comforting glow, only for the gaslight to waver as bright as a guttering candle and be extinguished.

A chill scratched up her spine.

Though the hospital's façade loomed above, stalwart and filled to its chimneys with all manner of science and humanity, she suddenly had the feeling of being utterly cut off.

A sound echoed about her, a breath or a gasp. She twisted, searching the gossamer wall around her. The hair on her arms and neck rose up.

Someone watched her. No one she could see, but she *felt* the presence—its intensity and malice—as certainly as if the person's rancid breath dampened her skin.

Footsteps met her ears, heavy and purposeful. A man's boots.

"Who is there?"

Fragments of newspaper accounts surfaced in her mind.

. . . throat cut from ear to ear . . .

. . . the abdomen had been ripped up . . .

. . . murder in its most horrible form . . .

Elena dashed toward the stairs. The toe of her shoe snagged in her hem, and with a hard strike to her knees, she fell. The steps came closer.

Just a person, walking along Whitechapel.

No, a *killer.*

The boots picked up pace, and from the corner of her eye she saw a dark shape lunging toward her. She parted her lips to scream—

Only to realize the person who wore the man's boots also wore skirts. Blue with red flouncing, to be precise.

A woman said, "Oh, *luhhv.* Did you fall? The fog's a terrible sort tonight, isn't it?"

A firm hand helped her up by the elbow. "*Soooo* good to see you breathing. At first . . . well, you know what I thought. Thought the Knife had gotten you." The lady chuckled a bit nervously. She wore a straw hat upon her russet curls, and a fur-trimmed collar framed her narrow face.

"Mrs. Eddowes?" Elena gasped.

"Aye. Oh, dear. Did you come out here looking for me? *Sooooo* sorry. Had to step out for a bit." Though her words were tellingly slurred, Mrs. Eddowes's careful speech revealed the faded polish of an educated woman. She considered Elena with shrewd, glassy eyes. A small green bottle peeked from her hip pocket. "Lizzy all right?"

Together they climbed the steps, and Elena led her toward the infirmary doors. She glanced, just once, over her shoulder, to be certain no one followed.

"The doctor was able to repair her knee. Thankfully she suffered a simple misalignment, nothing broken." Elena spoke carefully, still working to calm the panic in her veins. How foolish of her to have frightened herself to such a degree.

"I can take her home, then?"

"Lizzy told me she can't return home. Can I trust you to find her suitable lodging for the next few nights?"

Mrs. Eddowes's laugh held a defensive edge. "What do you mean, can you *trust* me?"

Elena glanced pointedly toward the bottle.

The woman sighed heavily and rolled her eyes. "I've only had a touch, to take the edge off my aching head. I didn't expect to sit in this charity ward all damn day."

They crossed through the wooden doors into the noisiness of the waiting room. The warmth and bustle eased Elena's tension immeasurably.

"I'm certain Lizzy appreciates your concern."

Mrs. Eddowes's expression softened. "She reminds me of my own dear daughter. I was planning to go to Bermondsley to see my Annie this afternoon, you see. I stopped by to see if Lizzy wanted to go as well, but I found the poor girl like that. Her bugger of an old man had thrown her down the stairs, he had."

Elena bit down on her lower lip and frowned. No one deserved such violence, especially a gentle soul like Lizzy.

"No." Mrs. Eddowes shook her head resolutely. "I won't be taking her home. She can stay with me, only I've got to come up with eight pence for our bed, else we'll both be eating skilly at the poorhouse tomorrow morning."

"Mrs. Eddowes—"

The woman waved her off. "I'll come up with the money. I always do."

Elena knew what that meant. It meant venturing into a dark alley with a stranger, at the risk of disease or death, all for a paltry coin or two. Such an endeavor was dangerous enough without the added peril of the Knife stalking women like Lizzy and Catherine on these very streets. They left the reception rooms and entered the quiet of the central corridor.

"Wait." Elena placed a hand on Mrs. Eddowes's arm and brought her to a stop. She looked about to be certain no one would see. The seamstress had sewn a small pocket inside the band of her apron. She withdrew a few coins and pressed them into Mrs. Eddowes's thin hand. "Take these, for you and Lizzy."

Elena prayed she wasn't making a mistake. She'd been warned by the other nurses against offering personal charity. They told her she'd only be disappointed with the outcome. But for some reason Lizzy had touched a deep chord within her, and Mrs. Eddowes truly seemed to care.

"Such an unexpected kindness." She stared, disbelieving, at the coins in her hand. "Lizzy will be so grateful."

"Don't tell her they came from me. Let the kindness be your own."

For the first time, their gazes truly met. Suddenly, the woman's expression changed into one of realization. "Heavens, dear, I know you from somewhere, don't I?"

"I've been working at the hospital for three weeks now. Perhaps you've seen me here?"

Mrs. Eddowes frowned. "I've come here a time or two for my Bright's, but no. It was that common house on Berner. I'm certain of it. Remember? Filthy place, and overrun by rats. I'm glad to see you've gotten out of there, and found respectable work for yourself."

Elena smiled and shook her head. "I'm afraid not. I grew up elsewhere and only arrived in London—well, not so very long ago. Since then, I've resided at only one address, outside of Whitechapel."

A simple explanation for a complicated span of months.

"Odd. I could swear you were the girl, one and the same." Mrs. Eddowes scrutinized her face. "I remember those eyes. One brown and one blue. So different. I'd never seen anything like them before."

Elena's smile faded. She'd never met anyone else with eyes like hers either.

But Mrs. Eddowes had to be mistaken. Elena had grown up on the Ivory Coast with her widower father, a missionary physician. She had traveled to London only after his death to live under Lord Black's guardianship.

Not that she remembered any of that firsthand, of course—not since the carriage accident that had cruelly stolen her memories. She simply knew them to be true because . . .

Lord Black had told her so in his letter.

Archer crossed the narrow gangplank. Water, black and fetid, slapped against the embankment below, a reflection of his dark mood. Behind him, a dense wall of storm, tangled up with the night, bore down upon the Thames, moments from engulfing the city.

Impatience left him ill-tempered. Another Reclaimer's incompetence had forced his premature return to England, when he ought to be on the far side of the earth bringing his own assignment to a successful end.

His dark-skinned captain stood beside the customhouse officer, the *Corinthian*'s leather-bound logbook in his hand. "I shall await word at Tilbury, my lord."

"Two to three days, Charon. A week at the most."

He stepped down, onto the dock. A discarded newspaper rolled toward him and wedged against the narrow toe of his boot. Its headline read, THE WHITECHAPEL MURDERS. The first few drops struck the cobblestones and dampened the shoulders of his greatcoat. Archer closed his eyes and breathed in the amalgam of scents from the city. Too dirty. Too complex. Rain would cleanse the air and quicken the hunt.

The other members of his party waited off to the side, amidst twining strands of fog: his secretary, Mr. Leeson, and Selene, with her raven's-wing hair rippling over her shoulders. Their umbrellas spread above them like large, black toadstools.

His town coach rolled into view, its silver, artisan-hewn harnesses boasting four black, perfectly matched Hanoverian geldings. Powerful muscles bunched beneath their gleaming coats. A footman leapt down to open the door. Leeson marched forward, his eye patch a dark spot against his skin. His arm extended toward the vehicle, an invitation for Archer to proceed.

Lord Black, he bellowed in silence, in a tongue so ancient that even if overheard, no one but Archer would understand. *Welcome home to England.*

KIM LENOX

Night Falls Darkly

A Novel of the Shadow Guard

Ever since an accident took away her memory,
Miss Elena Whitney is unable to recall the secrets
of her own past. All she knows is that with her
mysterious benefactor Archer, Lord Black,
returning to London she should seize the
chance to get some answers.

A member of the immortal Shadow Guard,
Archer has been summoned to London to
eliminate the soul of an evil demon—Jack the
Ripper. Archer feels not only bound to protect
the women of the night, but also his beautiful
young ward, Elena, whom he spared from death
two years before. But with a wave of panic
spreading across London, Archer fears that Elena
is his weakness—a distraction he can't afford,
especially since she's likely to become the
Ripper's next target.

"Lush, dangerous, and darkly sensuous."
—*New York Times* bestselling author Kerrelyn Sparks

Available wherever books are sold or at
penguin.com

KIM LENOX

So Still the Night

A Novel of the Shadow Guard

Marcus Helios was a member of the Shadow
Guard until one reckless act changed it all,
bringing him to the edge of madness. His hope
for salvation lies in the cryptic message in an
ancient scroll, which is now in the possession of
an enigmatic beauty named Mina.

But someone else has designs on the mystery of
the scrolls, and on Mark. She is Jack the Ripper's
jilted bride whose malevolent embrace will trap
everyone within reach—and whose own dark
secrets will challenge the powers of all she is
destined to destroy.

**"Kim Lenox is a blindingly bright star
in the paranormal world of romance."**

—National bestselling author Cindy Miles

Available wherever books are sold or at
penguin.com

Drawn into Darkness

Annette McCleave

Between angels and demons...
Between the living and the dead...
There is the Soul Gatherer.

Serving a five-hundred-year sentence as a
Soul Gatherer—one who battles demons for
the souls of the dead—Lachlan MacGregor
keeps his distance from humans. That is, until
the lovely Rachel Lewis knocks on his door,
begging for help.

As they struggle to rescue her daughter from
the clutches of a powerful demon, Lachlan
finds himself increasingly drawn to the artistic
single mother. But when Death assigns him an
unbearable task, he's left wondering who will
provide for his own soul.

Available wherever books are sold or at
penguin.com

Penguin Group (USA) Online

What will you be reading tomorrow?

Tom Clancy, Patricia Cornwell, W.E.B. Griffin,
Nora Roberts, William Gibson, Robin Cook,
Brian Jacques, Catherine Coulter, Stephen King,
Dean Koontz, Ken Follett, Clive Cussler,
Eric Jerome Dickey, John Sandford,
Terry McMillan, Sue Monk Kidd, Amy Tan,
J. R. Ward, Laurell K. Hamilton,
Charlaine Harris, Christine Feehan...

You'll find them all at
penguin.com

*Read excerpts and newsletters,
find tour schedules and reading group guides,
and enter contests.*

Subscribe to Penguin Group (USA) newsletters
and get an exclusive inside look
at exciting new titles and the authors you love
long before everyone else does.

PENGUIN GROUP (USA)
us.penguingroup.com